BLAZE OF NOON is a novel that is so
completely realized that William S. Phillips
can visualize almost every mile of
the route flown by the air mail pilots.

The detail from the above painting that appears
on the cover of this edition is used by
courtesy of The Greenwich Workshop.

P9-DTU-515

Ernest K. Gann writes books about piloting that the professionals admire. His book *The High and the Mighty* is part of every airman's library.

*Blaze of Noon* is about the early days of air mail.

"Mr. Gann is at his best in transporting you through a cumulonimbus cloud, or landing you at a fogged-in airport."

—D. Dempsey, *The New York Times*

# THE BANTAM AIR & SPACE SERIES

To Fly Like the Eagles . . .

It took some 1800 years for mankind to win mastery of a challenging and life-threatening environment—the sea. In just under 70 years we have won mastery of an even more hostile environment—the air. In doing so, we have realized a dream as old as man—to be able to fly.

The Bantam Air & Space series consists of books that focus on the skills of piloting—from the days when the Wright brothers made history at Kitty Hawk to the era of barnstorming daredevils of the sky, through the explosion of technology, design, and flyers that occurred in World War II, and finally to the cool daring of men who first broke the sound barrier, walked the Moon, and have lived and worked in space stations—always at high risk, always proving the continued need for their presence and skill.

The Air & Space series will be published once a month as mass market books with special illustrations, and with varying lengths and prices. Aviation enthusiasts would be wise to buy each book as it comes out if they are to collect the complete Library.

# BLAZE OF
# NOON

**Ernest K. Gann**

BANTAM BOOKS
NEW YORK · TORONTO · LONDON · SYDNEY · AUCKLAND

This edition contains the complete text
of the original hardcover edition.
NOT ONE WORD HAS BEEN OMITTED.

BLAZE OF NOON

A Bantam Falcon Book / published by arrangement with
Henry Holt and Company, Inc.

PRINTING HISTORY
Henry Holt edition published 1946
Bantam edition / June 1991

ISBN 0-553-29037-1

Published simultaneously in the United States and Canada

PRINTED IN THE UNITED STATES OF AMERICA

OPM    0  9  8  7  6  5  4  3  2  1

TO THE EARLY AIR-MAIL PILOTS WHO
FLEW FROM THE BEGINNING UNTIL 1930
THIS BOOK IS HUMBLY DEDICATED
BY ONE WHO WAS FORTUNATE ENOUGH
TO FOLLOW IN THEIR PROP WASH

# SEPTEMBER
# 1925

The cumulus cloud had ladled a sprinkle of rain on the fairgrounds a little while before and the grass smelled sweet and strong and full of clover. The four brothers lay stretched out under the wing, their legs and arms almost touching. First came Roland, nearest the landing wheel, and then Tad and Colin, and finally Keith—in the order of their creation. They lay under the wing because it shaded them from the hot sun and because they had lain under it all over America, in the grasses and on the dirt, in the sands and even in the mud.

It was a good place to relax and think about things, and study the pattern of the wooden wing ribs as the sunlight glowed through the translucent fabric. And whenever they wished, they could reach up and snap their fingers against the taut cloth, making a sound like a drum. Or they could pick up little bunches of grass and clods of earth and toss them lazily at each other's faces.

They could hear the twenty-piece band over in the grandstand, playing background music for a troupe of trained dogs, some Japanese tumblers, a family of high-wire performers, the American Legion crack drill platoon, a blonde girl riding a horse off a high platform into a tank of water, and an autopolo game played by young men in stripped model-T Fords.

Even to an audience that had not spent the morning apathetically viewing prize heifers, jellies, apple pudding, models of farm machinery, manual-training exhibits, new-type creosote shingles, and pulsing windmills, it would have been a good show, but it held little interest for the brothers.

3

They listened as the band played *Marche Orientale,* for the third time by Roland's count, and now in each of them there was a little movement of anticipation. Roland turned over on his stomach and peered through a latticework of grass at the crowd beyond the race track.

"Here we go again," he said.

He pushed himself slowly to his knees. The others did not answer, but stirred heavily as if awakening from a deep sleep—as if it were necessary to pry themselves from the grass. When at last they stood up and stretched and looked carefully at the sky, they moved as one. They turned their backs to the crowd and began to tend their ships and themselves in efficient, familiar little ways.

Now as the sun eased its hot compression and the band stopped playing, the crowd became curiously subdued. Here and there hoarse hawkers begged the crowd to buy the last of their candy floss. Their voices, echoing against the covered portion of the grandstand, melted suddenly in the oppressive quiet. Only in the distance, somewhere behind the grandstand, was there any recognizable sound—the bleat of a calliope, the ringing of a gong, the rumble of a wagon.

Then a man in a respectable gray suit and a straw hat stepped to the wooden platform in front of the band. He grasped the silver microphone placed before him by a policeman.

"Ladies and gentlemen! In cooperation with the Pringle Great Outdoor Shows, your state fair management has provided this afternoon one of the most daring exhibitions of the world." He paused and mopped his brow with a clean white handkerchief. After a hopeful glance at the sky, he examined a sheet of paper that had been handed him.

"Will Doctor Lester R. Seeley please report to ticket booth number four immediately? And now, ladies and gentlemen, if you will look to your right, just over the Hall of Agriculture, you will see two airplanes. The young men at the controls of these machines, and those who will perform for you, are—all four of them—brothers. The MacDonald brothers! Ladies and gentlemen, I give you the Flying Scots!"

A green flare shot up from behind the band. The two dots

*Hisso-Standard*

that had been hovering in the sky wheeled together and sank toward the grandstand as if sliding down an invisible wire. Their dual wings became visible and the sound of their engines grew from a gentle drumming of the atmosphere to a heavy throbbing.

In the rear cockpit of his Hisso-Standard biplane, Colin MacDonald watched the crowd turn their faces upward . . . yet he was hardly conscious of their existence. He was too deeply absorbed in the position of Roland's Travelaire, in keeping his wing tip in exact alignment with his brother's wing tip. As the two planes slipped through the rising and falling air currents in the long dive toward the grandstand, that exact distance became increasingly difficult to maintain. If the space between the wing tips became more than three or four feet, Roland would laugh at him when they returned to earth, and call him an old lady.

It was not a pleasant experience to be laughed at by Roland MacDonald. Colin recalled only too easily the days when Roland was teaching them to fly, and spent most of his time laughing at all of them—at Keith and himself, and even at

Tad. "You're all fatheads—ham-handed lamebrains!" he'd yell above the wind in the wings. That was when Roland came back from the war—not a hero, but a simply a man whom his government had taught to fly an airplane.

In the cockpit a few inches ahead of him, Colin could see the back of Tad's helmeted head. Now and then it lolled crazily from one side to the other, as if Tad were in a restless sleep, but Colin knew it was only his brother's way of showing elaborate unconcern.

Beyond the exhaust manifold and the blur of his propeller, Colin saw the crowd change from a speckled mass to individual bodies. He could tell almost exactly how fast he was flying by the tone of the wind in the flying wires. It was said of a Standard that if a bird were placed between the wings and contrived to escape, there was a flying wire missing somewhere. Colin always listened and hoped that the song of their strength would not prove false when it came time to pull out of the dive.

Just above the grandstand, close enough to make the crowd quail in their seats, Colin pulled back on the control stick between his legs—gently at first, then with increasing pressure—in exact harmony with Roland. The two ships flattened and zoomed upward together. The crowd fell away underneath them.

Colin felt his cheeks sag and his rump sink heavily into the seat as gravity fought to hold him. The Standard's nose passed up along the ramparts of a cumulus cloud, then there was only blue sky ahead. The flying wires sighed to a low vibrato as Colin, still pulling on the stick, brought the Standard over on its back. Now the crowd was above him and the blue sky beneath. The cumulus cloud reversed its position and stood on its dome. Colin felt the rush of blood to his head as he hung on his safety belt. Watching Roland's wing tip, still but a few feet from his own, he cut back his engine with his left hand. In the momentary quiet that followed he heard a sound that would have been fantastically out of place, if it were not so familiar.

"Oh, YE-E-E-E-S, we have no BA-N-A-A-A-N-A-A-S!" It was Tad in the front cockpit, singing at the top of his lungs.

The Standard quivered heavily. Colin pulled the stick back again slightly. The crowd chased the sky around again. The cumulus cloud slid back into place. The flying wires resumed their high whine. The Hisso engine sputtered anxiously as Colin pushed the throttle forward. Both ships, still wing to wing, were fifteen hundred feet above the grandstand.

Once more they dove together and when they were exactly over the center of the crowd, Colin and Roland moved their hands and feet in unison. Colin pulled back on his stick and at the same time pushed hard on the rudder bar with his left foot. The Standard swung up and over on its back again, in a snap-roll to the left. The Travelaire, with a somewhat less lumbering effort, swung up and over to the right. In the space of a few seconds the two ships maneuvered around their invisible axis until they were both right-side-up again. When they were a mile apart, they circled lazily, like hawks awaiting prey.

Colin looked down at the crowd. He knew they would be waiting now, a little uncomfortable inside, but impatient. He hated this crowd, as he did all crowds. He hated their reason for being where they were. From now on, if anything went wrong, Tad or Keith would be killed—painlessly of course, except for the interminable fall—but they would very certainly be killed. Colin knew that the crowd would not be displeased if this should happen.

They were watching now in fascination, watching for something to go wrong. It would give them something to talk about besides the butter and cheese exhibits. Colin had seen it happen before. In the multitude there would not be a single tear or a thought of pain. A few women would be sick perhaps, the men would clench their fists and open their mouths; but the sight of Tad or Keith twisting and clutching at nothing as he turned over and over would not spoil anyone's dinner. Not even when he thumped wetly into the earth. Colin hated the crowd as much as he did the part of their show that was to come.

Tad climbed out of the front cockpit and stood on the footwalk that covered the fabric where the lower wing joined the fuselage. The slip stream tore at his white coveralls. He braced his long legs and turned his back contemptuously to the wind. He leaned back, with one hand holding on to the cowling just in front of Colin. With his other hand he pushed up his goggles, and Colin saw that his black eyes were laughing. He leaned closer and yelled above the wind.

"Do you see that dame in the box down there, Colin?" As Colin looked down instinctively, Tad caught him a resounding swack across the helmet with the palm of his hand. Tad never hit gently. When Colin looked up, he was a little dizzy and angry. But Tad was laughing.

"Ho! let that be a lesson to you, Colin, my boy. Keep your eyes on your business from now on. Save day-dreamin' and your women till we get on the ground!"

Without waiting for an answer he pulled himself forward along the fuselage until he reached the center-section struts. He grasped a bar they had set into the leading edge of the upper wing and swung himself up and over to the top wing. Working slowly against the power of the wind, he pulled back two strips of adhesive tape that held a belt and four thin wires in place. He strapped the belt around himself, so that the wires stretched taut from the wing, and then worked his feet into two leather stirrups set on blocks of wood. Then he stood up. He bent his knees slightly and waved his arms.

It was his signal to Colin that he was ready. Colin pushed on the stick and the Standard dove in front of the crowd. When they were barely five hundred feet above the racetrack, Colin pulled back sharply on the stick. He disliked going so low before he began the loop, but Tad always insisted on it.

The Standard swept up and over on its back. Tad's feet were first heavy, then light, in the stirrups—but he had no sense of motion save tremendous pressure. The wind tore at his stomach and rippled the flesh between his fingers. The racetrack and grandstand moved as if they were turning slowly on a gigantic pinwheel. He waved to every flash of colored dress as Colin brought the Standard down again in the last part of the loop.

When they were in level flight again, he unfastened the straps, climbed down from the wing, and worked his way down until he could sit comfortably on the spreader bar they had built between the landing wheels. He took a pinch of resin from a little tobacco pouch that hung round his neck and rubbed it between his hands. Then he watched the Travelaire slip in just below him. Keith was standing on the upper wing, his arms jauntily akimbo, his grin apparent even from a distance.

The two ships banked against the sun and came back toward the grandstand again. Tad swung himself down between the landing wheels and hung by his knees. The ships flew together now, in exact line. Roland brought the Travelaire up until it was very close to the Standard, but just a trifle behind.

Tad swung his hands down and flexed his fists. Roland brought the Travelaire ahead and up, very slowly. Keith stretched his arms upward. Their hands were but a foot apart one moment, then six feet away the next. Contact—that was the ticklish part; it demanded patience, which was hard for both Tad and Keith. They must be absolutely certain not to grasp each other's wrists until their hold could be firm; there must be no chance of their being torn apart. During these few moments Tad was very careful, for if he held anything in tenderness it was his youngest brother Keith.

*Travel Air 2000*

The ships crept slowly together, then fell apart again. Then together—but it was too late. They had passed the grandstand. Tad waved away Roland and the Travelaire. The ships banked around toward the sun for another attempt. Tad swung himself back up on the spreader bar to clear the blood from his head and rest his legs. Although missing the first pass made a better show for the crowd, the brothers would have preferred a contact the first time. Every minute they were in the air used up gasoline they could ill afford to waste.

Now they were in line again and very close together. As Tad and Keith stretched out their arms, their fingertips almost touched. They swept past the bleacher section. Inch by inch the ships crept together. Now—almost. Another moment. If the air would hold smooth for a few seconds. . . . Then Tad sensed the time. He closed his strong hands tightly on Keith's wrists. Keith freed his feet from the wing straps. Abruptly he swung free against the slip stream. The Travelaire fell away into the depths.

Keith looked up at his brother's face and smiled. "Hi!"

"Hi!" Tad grunted. "You get heavier every time!"

"Growing boy!"

"Gettin' fat! Lay off the home brew!" They had passed the grandstand. Colin banked the Standard back for another run. He could not see his brothers beneath his wing, and in a way he was glad of it.

Tad took a tighter grip on the spreader bar with his knees. "Ready, Keith?"

"Yeah!" Tad contracted the muscles in his stomach and pulled up with his arms and knees. Keith freed his left arm. He reached out and fastened a snap hook that hung from the spreader bar to his parachute harness. With his free hand, Tad passed him another hook. Keith clipped it to his right-side harness. He shot a final glance at the lines, and then at the duffle bag fastened beneath the lower wing. He himself had packed the parachute in the bag that morning, laying pieces of newspaper between the shroud lines as he folded them over and over so they would not tangle.

He swung by one hand until they were opposite the grandstand again. Then he kicked, and began to swing wildly, as if he were in trouble.

"This is what gets 'em!"

"So long, boy!" Tad increased his pressure on Keith's wrist for a moment, then let go completely.

Keith dropped almost straight, with sickening speed. Tad could fairly feel the crowd gasp, and he held his breath as he always did. But in a moment there was a muffled report. Keith's parachute snapped open in the sunlight, like a suddenly blooming flower, and he swung slowly down beneath the Standard.

Tad smiled with satisfaction and climbed back to the spreader bar. He wanted a cigarette. Their day's work was done.

## 2

The sunlight cut past the cretonne curtains and slanted through the fortune teller's show wagon to the coffeepot bubbling on the stove. It was ten o'clock in the morning. Madame Moselle took the pot off the stove and set it on a tray with four cups. She moved about her tiny kitchen with an air of ritual, like a high priestess who must not make a single mistake. Madame Moselle was a very small woman, rather beautiful in a faded sort of way. There was a softness about her, felt rather than seen. And since the boarders had come to share her red wagon, this softness had increased day by day.

So this morning, as on every morning, she carried the coffee tray with important little movements. As she placed the telegram against the pot, her hand shook with excitement. She maneuvered the tray down the narrow hallway that separated the two ends of the wagon and finally edged into the bunkroom. The furnishings were temporary and simple—a box, a chair, a washbasin hanging on the wall, several battered suitcases, a phonograph with a stack of records beside it, and four bunks set in double tiers. They were all occupied. Here slept the MacDonald brothers.

Madame Moselle set the tray down on the box and stepped over to Roland, who was snoring mightily. She studied his big face, heavy and lined even in repose, like a dozing mastiff with bushy eyebrows. She felt an almost irrepressible urge to smooth his tumbling blond hair back from his forehead. She watched his full, curling mustache twitch slightly with his breathing, and she thought it a thing of beauty. She moved back softly, on tiptoe, poured a cup of coffee, and placed it carefully on the floor beside Roland's bunk. There was no haste in her movements, for this was her own time— her moment in every day when she could give in to her maternal instincts, which had never had any release before.

Peering into the bunk above Roland's, she was just able to see Keith, sleeping in childlike peace as he always did, his strong young fists doubled up under his chin. Like Roland's, his hair was blond, almost red, but it was cut very close to his head. There was a small scar under his right eye. Madame Moselle didn't know how it came to be there and she didn't want to know; she preferred to watch the deep dimple just below the scar. It made Keith look even younger than he was. When he smiled, it matched his eyes in mischief. It made him look as if he always had a good taste in his mouth.

She crossed to Tad and stood on tiptoe once again, her mouth apart a little in wonder, for Tad looked so unlike the others that he hardly seemed their brother. They were all good-looking, but Tad was handsome in a dark, almost swarthy, way. Roland once said he had Highland-clan skin like their mother. Tad lay flat on his back with his arms stretched straight down his sides. The sheet but half covered his chest. His arms, though relaxed, looked tawny brown and tense with power. But it was Tad's face that interested Madame Moselle. He seemed to scowl, as if even in sleep he found combat. She was somewhat afraid of Tad, although he had never given her reason to be, and she was a little ashamed that she felt this way.

She bent to Colin, who lay stretched in the bunk below Tad. He was the one who seemed to bridge the gap between Tad and the others. His hair was straight, but neither dark nor light. Even as he slept there was a quiet dignity about his face—a quality that Madame Moselle knew would become more evident when he awoke. He lay on his side now with his face toward her. A shaft of sunlight tipped his straight nose and glanced across his mouth, shadowing the cleft in his chin so that it looked deeper than it was. Madame Moselle gazed at Colin a long time, reflecting what it would be like to have a son like this one.

Reluctantly she went back to the tray and poured him a cup

of coffee. Then she stood motionless a moment. She hated to break the spell, to interrupt her dreaming; there was no other time during the day when she felt so content. But the coffee was cooling and Roland would not like that.

She reviewed again the performance that Roland demanded of her each morning. At first the words had choked in her throat and she had fumed in embarrassment. But in time she had come to enjoy her little act.

She turned on the phonograph and set the needle on "Don't Bring Lulu!"—Roland's current favorite. Then she stood in the middle of the room, exactly as Roland had directed, and yelled above the music: "Wake up, you bums! Are you going to lie in bed all day?" Roland snorted fiercely and stirred in his bunk. Keith groaned and raised his fists in the air. Colin and Tad slowly opened their eyes.

"Wake up! Wake up! Let's get the show on the road!"

Roland eased back the covers, revealing his flaming red pajamas. He opened an eye and groped for his coffee. Each movement was obviously torture. His grunts sounded like a wounded stag.

"Good morning, my little kumquat," he croaked finally. "My, what a lovely voice you have!"

Good mornings rumbled from the other bunks. Madame Moselle was elaborately busy handing up cups of coffee to Tad and Keith. Then she pulled the cretonne curtains and let the sunshine spill into the room. She came back and handed the telegram to Roland.

"A messenger boy from the telephone office brought it a little while ago," she said.

Roland stared at it suspiciously. "Was it paid for?"

"Yes."

"That's bad. Can't be anybody I know very well." He tossed the telegram to the floor.

"Aren't you going to open it?"

"No. The hell with it. Somebody wants to borrow money."

But telegrams didn't come to Madame Moselle's wagon every day—in fact, this was the first she had ever handled, barring the imaginary messages so prominent in her card readings. She picked it up and handed it gingerly to Colin.

"You read it, Colin. Please."

"It's addressed to Roland. Maybe it's something personal."

"Go ahead, read it. I've got nothing to lose but my reputation." Roland roared with laughter and sang "Don't Bring Lulu" along with the record.

Colin opened the envelope. "Did you ever know an M. L. Gafferty?"

Roland stopped singing and caressed his mustache. "Gafferty? Mike Gafferty?"

"Maybe. The initial is M."

"Yeah, if it's the same guy I'm thinking of. We learned to fly together at Kelly. He came along in '18. A complete pain in the neck." Roland took a loud sip of coffee. "How much money does he want?"

"He's offering you some."

"Go away . . ."

Colin smiled quietly. He was not taken in by Roland's apparent indifference. "Do you want to know what's in this wire or not?"

"A complete pain in the neck," Roland grumbled into his cup. "Go ahead."

MERCURY AIRLINES EXPECTS MAIL CONTRACT OCTOBER STOP
CAN USE YOU ALSO SEVEN OTHER QUALIFIED PILOTS STARTING
EARLY SPRING SALARY SIX HUNDRED MONTHLY STOP IF INTER-
ESTED WIRE AND REPORT FIRST WEEK JANUARY AT NEWARK
MUNICIPAL AIRPORT

Except for the closing strains of "Don't Bring Lulu," there was silence in the room.

"Is that all?"

"That's all. Signed M. L. Gafferty."

"Well, I'll be damned."

There was silence again.

"That's a lot of money," Keith said to the ceiling.

"Ho! Not enough," said Tad.

"Correct," said Roland. "Because you can't spend it in hell. Some friends of mine in the Army, they flew the air mail for a while. They're all dead. Four years is the average life of a mail pilot. Dangerous. Besides, Gafferty is a pain in the neck, like I said, and anyway, this air-mail business won't last very long anyway. People are bound to get wise to it. Most times it takes longer than the train."

"I dunno," said Colin. He swung his feet down to the floor. Though he was wearing nothing but shorts, he betrayed absolutely no embarrassment in Madame Moselle's presence. "We're not getting anywhere here, except paying off on the planes. Maybe we ought to consider the idea. . . ."

"I won't work for the government. I had enough of that during the war." Roland threw himself back in his bunk. His head ached from the four quarts of home brew he had consumed the night before. "I will not work for the damned government," he insisted. "It's bad for your digestion. They'll make a monkey out of you sooner or later."

"Sure, look what happened to William Jennings Bryan," said Tad.

"Trouble was, he didn't drink. Why, they'll make you fly like a bunch of blind ducks. No, it's no good. Let's forget it right now." Even though it was agony, Roland shook his head emphatically.

"I think I'll try for a job," Colin said quietly.

Roland snapped straight up in his bunk.

"You mean leave us?"

"You can get somebody else. . . ."

"Who, for Christ's sake? . . . Beg your pardon, Madame Moselle," he added hastily, for the one refinement Roland strove to maintain was a polite tongue in the presence of women, especially those over thirty.

"Maybe you could get one of the Murray boys. . . ."

Even Colin was not prepared for the histrionics that followed. Roland sat up deliberately and planted his feet carefully on the floor. He lit a cigarette as if it were the last smoke of a condemned man, then rose to his full, heavy six feet with an air of deeply wounded dignity. For a moment he stood there stiffly, scratching the mat of reddish hair on his chest. He seemed at a loss for words. A stranger might have thought him torn between rage and tears. He walked to the phonograph and turned it off, allowing the record to groan down to a stop.

"Murray," he said finally, with a pitiful tremor in his voice. "Murray! Now, who the hell is Murray, when we have the nucleus of the world's greatest flying circus right here in this humble room? The man is an amateur, a charlatan. And what happens to me, who have given my time and skill, risked my neck, in fact, teaching you to fly, giving you the benefit of my hard-won experience? What happens? Do I get thanks? Loyalty? No! I've thrown pearls to swine. Stabbed in the back by my own brother. Abandoned. Deserted. Forsaken, at the height of the season. It's fratricide. It's worse than incredible. You wouldn't do it. You couldn't. It's impossible!" He sat down on his bunk and raised his eyes to the ceiling with the look of one betrayed.

"Are you finished?" asked Colin.

"I don't care to discuss the subject any further." Roland climbed back in his bunk and turned his face to the wall. Colin exchanged a knowing smile with Tad, then when a sufficient period of silence had passed—sufficient to indicate that he was stunned by Roland's address—he called across the room.

"Roland."

"Yes."

"Your coffee's getting cold."

"Humph." But Roland turned in his bunk and retrieved the cup from the floor. He glanced up at his brothers from beneath his bushy eyebrows with an air of patient resignation, then once again became the stoned martyr. It was a pose the others were accustomed to—a mood of many moods employed by their eldest brother to get what he wanted. Madame Moselle was almost in tears, but the brothers eyed him coldly.

In the years since Roland came back from the war, they had seen all the moods. After he was demobilized he had nothing to look forward to except earning a living somehow, and that prospect filled him with open disgust. He threw his entire mustering-out pay into a dice game in San Antonio, Texas, and came out with eleven hundred dollars. He promptly rented a hotel room, furnished it with a large table covered with food, and a thirty-dollar phonograph to play "Smiles" and "I'm Always Chasing Rainbows." For two hundred and fifty dollars a bootlegger obliged him with two cases of fine whisky, allegedly brought over the Mexican border only the

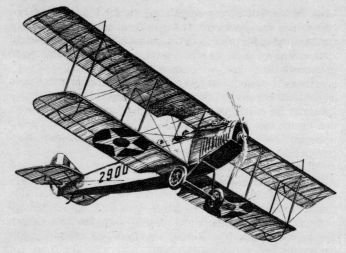

*Curtiss JN-4 "Jenny"*

night before. Two young ladies agreed to grace Roland's quarters for the surprisingly reasonable fee of fifty dollars each. The party lasted for three days, after which, in cooperation with the hotel management and the police, Roland left the city.

With his remaining five hundred dollars, he bought a war-surplus airplane from the government. It was a Curtiss JN-4 powered with an OX-5 engine—the kind of ship in which Roland himself had learned to fly. With the help of a baffled garage mechanic, he unpacked it from its crate and eventually flew it home to Wisconsin, where he taught Colin, Tad, and Keith to fly.

He gave them lessons in stalls and power stalls, one-eighties, three-sixties, and seven-twenties, Chandelles and slips, and showed them how to tell the look of firm ground from swamp ground. He taught them how to back and spin a prop, to patch a hole in fabric, to sand and dope and rig.

Out of this instruction came "The Flying Scots"—the name given them by Mr. Pringle of Pringle's Great Outdoor Shows. For a half-hour's stunt flying a day, they were paid two hundred dollars a week, the brothers furnishing two airplanes, the gasoline, and the nerve. A clause in the contract stated that Pringle's Great Outdoor Shows disclaimed all responsibility in the unhappy event of death or of damage to the machines.

To save money, the MacDonalds shared the red wagon with Madame Moselle, and thus managed to keep up the installment payments on the two new airplanes they were using—a Standard powered by a Hispano-Suiza engine, and a Travelaire powered, after a fashion, by a melancholy OX-5 engine.

It was during those early days that they had come to know Roland so well. At first they used to hang on every word and feel humiliated when he made fun of them. Then gradually, one by one, they discovered that his shouts and growls and protestations of despair were simply his carefully chosen way. He could not abide the thought that someone, some time, might discover his soft heart.

And so they waited for him to finish his coffee and come back to the subject of Gafferty's telegram. At last Madame Moselle could contain herself no longer. Here was disaster threatening her wonderful world, and she would fight it.

"I'll get the cards," she said. "It will all be in the cards. The truth will be in the cards!" She pattered off down the narrow hallway.

"She actually believes that," said Tad. He swung his long legs out from his bunk and let himself down to the floor. He went directly to the mirror and began to comb his thick black hair. "I've got half a notion to go with you, Colin," he said to the mirror. "Anything new would be a relief."

"I am afflicted with two insane brothers," grunted Roland. "As well that Mother's in her grave to miss this dereliction of her issue. A brilliant future in your grasp—and you want to become messenger boys." He snarled and rocked his big head from side to side. "Back and forth, back and forth, the same old route, the same old way, back and forth—until you go crazy. Back and forth until you run into a mountain some night. Even your iron heads aren't hard enough to tangle with a mountain."

But Roland received no answer. Tad began to shave methodically, and Colin pulled on his flying breeches. Keith was absorbed in a copy of *Judge* magazine.

Then Madame Moselle came back, her face glowing with excitement. She shuffled the cards quickly and spread them out on the box, murmuring softly to herself. Suddenly she fell silent. When she spoke again, she did so in a monotonous, professional litany.

"It would be better if you stayed with us," she said. She pointed to the four jacks aligned across the top of the cards. "See, here is Colin and Keith and Tad, and here is Roland." She ran her thin fingers down the lines of cards beneath the jacks. "Come see. Keith, you will be the first to go. After the snow flies. Then Tad. . . ."

"I must meet a beautiful blonde somewhere in there."

"You do. But you cannot escape the other if you choose this new life."

"See, I told you so!" Roland shouted triumphantly. "You're a couple of dead pigeons right now. The cards never lie, do they, Madame Moselle?"

"I wouldn't let them lie to my boys."

Colin suppressed a grin. He knew only too well that Madame Moselle guided her own life by her cards. She always explained that it was merely unfortunate the cards hadn't done better by her.

"How about me?" Colin asked. "Do I make a million dollars, or live to a ripe old age, or both?"

"The cards are mixed and vague, but black is predominant. They forecast—"

"Sawed off in the prime of his life!" Roland shook his head sadly.

"Only Roland will survive," Madame Moselle intoned.

"Because I'm by God going to stay right here, where I'm well off!"

"Are you two in cahoots?" Tad demanded.

Roland began to sing the ode to an OX-5 engine:

"Take the carburetor out of my stomach,
    Take the pistons out of my head;
    Send my arms back home to Mo-o-other-r-r,
    Tell her I . . . am finally dead."

Colin finished pulling on his boots. He stood up and slipped on his leather jacket, then stooped and kissed Madame Moselle very gently on the top of her head.

"What you need, Madame," he said briskly, "is a new set of cards. Those are bad for business. I'll see that you get some today." He kissed her again on the cheek and patted her bottom. "Keith, get your nose out of that magazine and listen. I'm going down to the telegraph office and send this fellow Gafferty a wire. I'm going to sign Tad's and my own name to it. Shall I sign yours too, or do you want to spend the rest of your life swinging from a trapeze?"

"Well golly . . . I . . ."

"Okay. I'll sign your name too." He looked quickly at Roland, who avoided his eyes—he was doing his best to look forlorn. "What about you?"

Roland put his head in his hands. "Herod. Judas. Somebody's got to take care of you. Put my name down too."

Smoke from the surrounding factories joined with the dank January mist and formed a sullen canopy over the Newark airport. Hangar doors were shut as if frozen in the cold. Between the road past the airport and the swamps to the south there was no life or movement of any kind. There was only bleakness—an almost forsaken squalor that depressed the brothers mightily. Even the big, newly built hangar seemed forlorn. The four men walked slowly toward it, their shoulders hunched and their hands deep in their pockets. They walked questioningly, as sailors might approach a strange dock.

They did not speak to each other as they crossed the field, avoiding the little patches of half-frozen water with elaborate care. They looked behind them furtively, as if they thought someone was following them. Here, supposedly, was America's busiest airport, a Mecca to those men who flew because it was their life—yet now it seemed deserted.

The brothers felt strangely unwelcome. Each wondered why they had come and thought about the warmth and sunshine that must be playing on the wings of their own ships. They had sold them when they reached Tennessee, and with that sale went a little part of each one of them—a little part that daily grew larger as they realized that the old life was finished forever. There was something hard and desperately commercial about this new existence. They could sense it in the pounded cinders beneath their feet, in the way the bus driver had looked at them when they asked to be let off at the airport. They guessed it had something to do with their landlady's demand for rent in advance when they mentioned their profession. Here there was no music from a neighboring circus wagon, no calliope in the distance, no Madame Moselle—and there would be no more lying on the cool grass in the shade of their wings, waiting for their turn before the crowd. There would be none of those agreeable things.

Still, they were together and their old accustomed unity lost no strength or flavor in their new surroundings. Each knew that the pattern of their lives was about to change, and each was secretly determined that the change would bring no division among them.

Over the small door at the corner of the hangar there was a sign that read MERCURY AIRLINES. Roland led them through the door and they stood inside a moment, looking about. There was the good smell of engine oil and the ever so delicate odor of "dope" on tight-stretched fabric. They felt a little better until they studied the several airplanes huddled together at the far side of the hangar. There were two De Havillands powered with Liberty engines. There were also a Jennie, like Roland's first ship, a Fokker, and an OX-powered Waco. A home-built machine with a damaged wing tip and a blown tire stood meekly in the corner.

"That monstrosity must be powered with a rubber band," said Roland quietly. He surveyed the collection with obvious disgust. Then the vapor of his breath shot forward angrily. "Junk!" he said. "Now, when we get up there, don't say anything more than you can help. Let me do the talking. This Gafferty's sour as a lime. He had a wife once and she sawed his heart in half when she ran off with some Canadian. Nobody's ever seen the guy really smile since."

They climbed the stairs that ran up the side wall of the hangar and let themselves in through a door marked OFFICE. A girl with black shingled hair said, "Good-morning-what-can-I-do-for-you?'' She plainly had little desire to do anything.

"We want to see Mike Gafferty."

"Who's calling?"

Roland looked around at his brothers. His lips tightened and his eyes narrowed.

"How about that? Who's calling? You'd think it was an audience with the Pope. Tell him the MacDonald brothers, young lady."

She rose reluctantly from her chair. A totally inadequate skirt that stopped two inches above her knees swung jauntily as she turned back toward a glass-paneled door.

"Pleasant little baggage, isn't she?" said Roland.

They sat down on a bench that ran along the wall. As if at some secret signal, they reached almost simultaneously into their pockets and brought out whatever supply of small change they had. Tad flipped a nickel several paces ahead of them. It spun in the air, bounced against the wallboard, and rolled just in front of the glass-paneled door. Without breaking their silence, they began to pitch pennies, solemnly rising to pick up their winnings at the end of each round. The game absorbed them. Even the return of the secretary failed to distract them until she announced for the second time that Mr. Gafferty would see them now. Still they did not hurry.

They jingled the change in their hands, and each looked long and hungrily at the secretary as she sauntered past. Tad was the last to pick up his coins. He did so, just at the girl's feet, then stood up quickly and looked down upon her. He put his face very close to hers and half-smiled evilly.

"Boo!" he said, then followed the others into the office.

Mike Gafferty was a dun-colored man with thin, pale lips. The skin of his face and hands seemed almost a part of his tan shirt. His eyes were deep brown but, instead of being soft as brown eyes usually are, they were cold and expressionless as they peered out from below a brush of dead-black eyebrows. His nose was sharp and chiseled like a bowsprit. His ears held close to the sides of his head. Though freshly shaven, his beard was heavy and it shadowed the outlines of his firmly set jaw.

Gafferty was smoking a cigar—his third of the morning.

His movements were slow and rather graceful as he touched off the ashes and slipped it back between his teeth.

His office was a Spartan cubicle. A plain oak desk was set across the corner of the room at an angle so that his back was toward the windows looking out on the airport. On his desk were a metal model of a Travelaire, a radium-faced clock that looked as if it had been taken from the cockpit of an airplane, an ashtray made out of an engine piston, and a few papers. There was no carpet on the floor. A parachute and a pair of fleece-lined flying boots cluttered up the corner near the door. A leather flying jacket hung on the coat rack beside his hat and coat. A map of the United States was thumbtacked to one wall, and below it stood a line of plain oak chairs.

When the brothers filed into the office, Gafferty got up quickly from his chair and extended his hand, but there was little warmth in his voice.

"Hello, Roland. These are your brothers, I take it."

"This is Keith, Colin, and that handsome bastard is Tad."

"Glad to know you. Have a seat."

They scraped the chairs across the bare floor and sat down. They opened their coats in silence and looked uncomfortably out the windows at the mist.

It seemed a long time before any of them spoke, and Gafferty wanted it that way. Hiring pilots was a delicate operation, and although Gafferty considered himself an expert at it, he was aware that each man he hired might, alone, either shatter or realize his dreams for him. There were no niceties in hiring pilots, no effusions or exchanges of personalities such as might have occurred were Gafferty hiring salesmen or businessmen. Gafferty was not at all concerned with their outward personalities, or their dress, or their philosophies. He was looking for something he would have been hard put to describe: a quality rather than a quantity—a spirit, strangely eloquent to those who knew how to listen.

It was hard to sit in an office, warm and quiet, and divine what a man might do alone at night in the cockpit of a ship, his hands and feet numb with cold and his brain perhaps half-frozen with fear. It was hard to guess what the loneliness might do to his courage and his judgment and even his skill.

It was hard to decide whether a roaring engine might tear his nerves and so affect his reactions, or whether worry about the faithlessness of a wife might distract him and so eventually kill him. There were many little and unrelated things that Gafferty had to know.

"Hell of a day, isn't it?" he said finally. He looked at each brother searchingly, but they only nodded and looked back at him. Gafferty appreciated this. A man didn't tell in words how well he could fly an airplane. Words were words and had nothing to do with the feel of a stick or the exact angle of a glide. A virtuoso didn't say how well he could play a violin—he played it. Gafferty turned to Roland.

"Had much fun since we left Kelly?"

"Here and there."

"How are your girls?"

"I'm getting old."

Gafferty shifted his cigar to the other side of his mouth. "How old are you now?"

"Thirty, last month."

"Humph. How about you, Tad?"

"Twenty-six."

"You and Roland are the two oldest, aren't you?"

"That's right."

Gafferty looked at Keith. There was something about Keith's quiet smile that made Gafferty like him instantly. "What's your age, young fellow?"

"Twenty-one."

"Did Roland teach you to fly?"

"He tried to."

There was the proper answer, thought Gafferty. One didn't say he *could* fly, or would; a good pilot's ability was consciously depreciated, but only by himself. The proof of an active pilot's talent lay in the fact that he was still in one piece.

Gafferty looked at Tad. His eyes caught the swagger, the power in Tad's frame even as he sat in the chair. Here would be a handful of man.

"Getting tired of swinging by your ears from a landing gear . . . Let's see, you're Tad, aren't you?"

"I'm Tad. No, I'm not tired of it." Tad's look was challenging, as direct and hard as Gafferty's own.

"Then what are you doing here?"

"It seemed a good idea to stick together."

"I see." Gafferty shot a glance out the window, then turned back to Tad. "We don't go in much for heroics around here." Maybe that would get under his skin.

But Tad only crossed his long legs and stared back at him. "We're no heroes," he stated flatly.

Gafferty felt faintly annoyed. He wasn't finding out what he wanted. "Maybe I should talk to you boys one at a time," he said. "I'm not so sure I can handle all of you at once . . . either now, or later on."

"We'll stick together, Mike." Roland got up and walked to the window. "You might as well know the truth, Mike. None of us think much of this except Colin. We came because he wanted to come. Seems to think there's some kind of future to this air-mail business. . . ."

"Colin's right. Why, a couple of years from now we'll have all kinds of ships flying and fill 'em with passengers to boot. This country's way behind on air transport. You ought to see what they're doing in Europe. This thing is just in its infancy. It stands to reason that a lot of people would want to fly clear through to Cleveland or Chicago, if someone gave them a chance."

Roland's back made a slight movement, but he did not turn around. "That's poppycock, and I'm surprised you'd try to pull that on me after all these years. It's been tried and it won't work. People have got sense. When they want to go somewhere, they climb on a nice comfortable train . . . and I don't blame them."

"Do you want to go to work or not?"

"Who else is going to be mixed up in this clambake?"

"Shorty Baker, for one. Then there's Whispering Johnny Dycer, Clem Graves, and Inkie Williams, and Porkie Scott is over in the hotel right now, trying to make up his mind."

"Where is that last tub of lard?"

"Room five-eleven at the Gladstone. Porkie said he was going to sleep till we got our ships. That will be in April, so you'll have to do some waiting around, too."

"That's going to be hard on my constitution. I know all the others, but who's this Shorty Baker?"

"Little guy about six inches tall. Used to be with Gate's circus." Gafferty paused a moment, then looked at the end of his cigar and frowned. "Now there's a few questions I'd like to ask—that is, if you don't mind, Roland?" He glanced out of the corner of his eye as Roland wheeled slowly to look at him from underneath his thick eyebrows.

"Like, for instance?"

"How much flying time have you got now?"

"About two thousand hours. The boys there have around a thousand apiece."

"How much of that is padded?"

"Not more than a hundred hours or so."

"You're frank about it, anyway."

Roland smiled and turned back to the window. 'It's good, honest padding."

"How much night time?"

"Two hundred for me. The boys have around a hundred, with Keith running maybe a little less."

"Are you pulling those figures out of your hat? Can't your brothers speak for themselves?"

"I told them to keep their mouths shut when we came up here."

"Oh. Send over your logbooks. They should make interesting reading—interesting if not factual." But Gafferty was pleased at the way the interview was going now. Logbooks were only cold figures that meant very little. He was more interested in Roland's antagonism. That almost defiant independence was exactly what Gafferty wanted in a pilot. Such a man would be best able to take care of himself when there was no one around but God to help him. Gafferty was satisfied that Roland had not changed through the years.

"Ever fly on instruments, Colin?"

"No."

"Think there's any future in it?"

"A good way to break your neck," mumbled Roland from the window.

"I'd like to try," said Colin.

"Stick around. You'll have a chance. This is a lot bigger

thing than it might appear now. So you're the one who wanted to try air-mail flying?'' Gafferty was already satisfied with Colin, but he wanted a diversion while he studied Tad. He seemed unable to stare the man down.

''Are you married, Colin?''

Colin smiled and shook his head.

''Ever think of it?''

''Once in a while.''

''How about you, Tad?'' Gafferty shot the question at him.

''Never gave it a thought.''

''What kind of ship do you like to fly best?''

''A Waco.''

''If you had your way, how would you change its design?''

Tad looked at the floor a moment, then out the window toward where the sky should be. ''I'd strengthen the center section and widen the landing gear.''

''Why?'' Gafferty appeared not to listen, but he was asking questions that told him many things. Tad's answer would show him how the man thought and what real experience he had had.

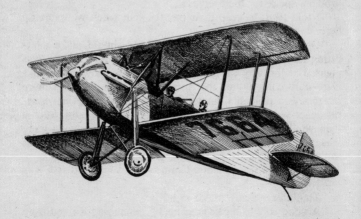

*OX Powered Waco*

"The center section is too weak for real acrobatics. I never saw one buckle myself, but I know they have. Besides, it's a mental hazard. It wouldn't take much to strengthen it. If it had a little wider landing gear, the ship wouldn't have such a tendency to ground-loop."

Gafferty withheld his agreement. He was content that the answer was a very good one. He turned to Keith and had to catch himself to keep from smiling back at the boy.

"Young fellow, can't you find any better company to keep than Roland MacDonald?"

Keith grinned his embarrassment and leaned far forward in his chair. He began to rub a blister on his hand. From time to time his blue eyes glanced up at Gafferty with a friendly, puppylike expression. It made Gafferty want to go over to him and put his hand on his shoulder and say, "Oh for Christ's sake, son, you can be on my side any time. . . ." But Gafferty thought he was a hard man and he wanted others to be convinced of it.

"Keith," he began slowly, "supposing you were lost above an overcast somewhere along the East Coast here. You have about an hour's gas left, and for everything you know, the stuff goes right down to the ground. In a case like that, I suppose you'd just jump out and say the hell with it?"

"No, I don't think so, Mr. Gafferty."

"Why not? You've done plenty of jumps."

"It'd be sorta hard on the airplane for one thing, and besides, I'm not a very good swimmer. If I'm lost, I might be bailing out over the ocean."

Gafferty allowed a trace of a smile to creep across his thin lips. "What would you do then? Let down and run into something? Or maybe fly on out to sea and try to creep back in over the wave tops?"

"No, a solid overcast might be right down on the water, and if I got out there and couldn't get contact, I would be up the creek right then."

"So—?"

"I may be wrong, Mr. Gafferty, but I think I'd head west toward where the mountains ought to begin. Mountains some-times break up an overcast, at least enough to chance for a hole. Maybe there'd be a hole big enough to spiral down through and plunk the ship down in a pasture. Anyway, there'd be more chance than over flat land like around here.''

"Suppose there just wasn't any hole?''

"I'd be about out of gas by then. I'd have to jump, but at least I'd have had a try.''

"Good boy!'' Gafferty said it in spite of himself.

## 3

Colin tried hard not to stare, but he found he had little control over himself. He kept rubbing his hands together and setting one foot on top of the other, oblivious to the fact that he was ruining a brand-new shoeshine. He listened as carefully as he could. The girl in white was asking him very personal questions and making little check marks and notations on a form. But it was not the questions so much as the girl that bothered him.

"Were you ever subject to epileptic fits?" she asked.

"No—no, I don't think so."

"Well, make up your mind."

"No! Oh, no, never!" he managed to reply. He had already told her that he was twenty-five, that he was born in Chippewa Falls, Wisconsin, and that, as far as he knew, there was no insanity in his family.

The girl was coldly impersonal. She had only once looked up from the form, and it had almost made him forget why he was there. He was no fool and he had seen pretty girls before—the fat, the short, the thin and the tall—and he was no virgin. But there was a beauty about this girl in her crisp white dress that enchanted him. Maybe it was the white dress that made her skin look so golden and warm. Maybe the plainness of the dress made her lips seem a little too full and her eyes so much bigger and more exciting than any eyes he had ever seen before. But she wasn't a beauty. Colin thought that was the damnedest thing about her. For one thing, she had a snub nose sprinkled with freckles, and her hair was just hair, neatly combed, about the color of wet brown earth. And she was tall—very tall for a girl.

"Childhood diseases?" she asked.

"How do you mean?"

"Chicken pox, measles—that sort of thing."

"Oh, yes, yes, of course. Lots of them."

"Lots?"

"Well, you see there were four of us—brothers—you know." Colin tugged at his tie.

"Yes, I know. They were in here this morning." She said it out of the corner of her mouth and there was a trace of bitterness in her voice. That was another thing: Colin couldn't make up his mind about her voice. It had a plaintive, metallic tone, but still it was soft and full of shading. There was something about her voice that reminded Colin of a tinkling bell.

"Broken bones?"

"What?"

"I said, any broken bones?"

"Oh, yes. Let's see. Broken collarbone, broken arm, wrist, couple of ribs—"

"That's enough. It must have been wonderful to be your mother. Ever have pneumonia, diphtheria, trachoma, continuous headaches, syphilis, gonorrhea, tuberculosis?"

"No. No!"

"Wet the bed nights?"

"What!" Colin shook his head and blushed.

"That will be all of *that*," she said, without pausing. She put down her fountain pen and took a thin black book out of the desk drawer. She placed the bottom of the book on the desk blotter and opened it toward Colin. The top of the book reached just to her chin.

"This is the Ishihara test. On some pages you'll see numbers. Call them off to me as I turn the pages, please."

Colin looked at the first page. It was mottled with hundreds of varicolored dots. At first he saw only the dots, then gradually he made out a large number formed by some of the dots.

"Fifteen."

She turned a page.

"Twenty-nine."

She turned another, but Colin's attention had wandered.

"Look at the book if you please, Mr. MacDonald."

Colin looked down from her eyes to the book again. "Sixty-four."

She turned another page. Colin was silent.

"Well?"

"I don't see any number this time."

"You're right. There isn't any." She snapped the book shut, and almost before he realized what had happened, she slipped a thermometer into his mouth and stepped to the door.

"Hold that for five minutes, then the doctor will see you. Maybe it will keep you quieter than your brothers." She was gone through the door before he could mumble a protest.

The thermometer kept Colin as quiet and bored as only a thermometer can do. He sat in enforced silence, mouthing the thing. He felt stupid and unwanted. He wondered momentarily if perhaps the whole venture might have been a mistake. There were a lot of things, it seemed, they hadn't thought about.

There was this business of licenses. The brothers thought that if a man could fly a plane without killing himself, that should be the end of it. But the newly formed Bureau of Air Commerce had other ideas. They demanded licenses and periodic physical examinations of all pilots. Gafferty's first order to the brothers was to get themselves straight legally; otherwise they could go back to the sticks, as he put it. That first physical examination, which Roland insisted was ten dollars thrown in a toilet, was a trying experience for flying men all over America. They came, one by one, from the little airports hidden in the mountains, from the converted pastures of Ohio and Iowa, from the dusty fields in Texas, and the seedy, comfortless fields that somehow managed to meet their taxes in the big cities. They came a little humbly, nervous with fear, and were pounded and felt and looked at like slaves before an auction block.

It seemed a long time before the door opened and the girl came back. She removed the thermometer from Colin's mouth, glanced at it, and then at him.

"The doctor will see you now."

Colin followed her into the other room. The doctor was a potbellied little man with eyebrows that angled so sharply upward at the ends that they seemed about to take flight from his face. A sprinkling of dandruff covered the shoulders of his blue coat.

"Sit down, young man." The doctor pointed a stumpy finger at a stool near the wall. "Miss Stewart, will you do the usual?" So that was her name. Colin heard it and hung on to it almost desperately. Stewart. Let's see, did he know anyone named Stewart—someone he could ask her about? There was that fellow who ran the penny arcade in Pringle's Outdoor Shows. But his name was Hubert. Not close enough. Colin couldn't think of anyone named Stewart.

"Cover up one ear and repeat the numbers you hear, after me."

She was standing almost in darkness at the far corner of the room. Colin covered up his right ear and wished he could see her better.

"Fifteen," she whispered.

"Fifteen," said Colin.

"Eighty-eight."

"Eighty-eight."

"Nine and two."

"Nine and two." Colin like the way she whispered.

"Now try the other ear."

"Anyway, I'm not deaf, I guess," he said when they had finished.

"No, you're not deaf."

There was a quality in her voice that suggested he might be a few other things—all of them unpleasant. Colin thought he knew why. He had a sudden uncomfortable picture of Roland and Tad taking the examination. That was it—that must be it. He could almost hear their remarks, and Roland's in particular.

She switched on a light over an eye chart on the wall and then moved around behind Colin. To his astonishment, she placed one hand on his brow and covered his left eye with a paper card. Her hand felt soft and warm.

"Read the smallest line of letters you can."

"D, E, F, P, O, T, C."

"Is that the best you can do?"

"What's the matter with it? The chart's a long way off."

"I just thought you might do better."

So? Why should she give a damn one way or the other?

Well! Colin smiled inwardly. He wanted to ask her why she thought he might do better, but her hand was still warm against his brow and why's kept exploding in his head like popcorn. So he started to read the smallest line he could see.

"L . . . E . . . . . F . . P . . O . . . R . . . S—" and he halted. He wanted to do well, but the letters were so small.

"Go ahead. Now get the last few letters. Take your time."

Colin blinked his eyelids. He felt his face grow hot and moist with effort. He took a deep breath.

"T . . E . . . . . . R . . . . . . . V . . . Z!"

"You have good eyes," she said.

"So have you." Since she stood behind him Colin could not see her face, and it was as well he didn't. But he did feel the slight pressure of her hand against his brow. She changed the card to cover his other eye and they repeated the test.

"You read twenty-fifteen with both eyes," she said without enthusiasm. "Better than your brothers." She took her hand away. "Now see how you do with this."

She placed in his hands the ends of two long strings that led to a black box on the table below the eye chart. They passed through two holes in the box and controlled the forward and backward movements of two upright black sticks. Colin could see them through a small window cut in the box like the proscenium of a miniature stage. She pulled one of the strings and a stick moved forward.

"The idea is to get them exactly together. You'll have six tries. I'll separate them each time, and you pull them together again. Take your time and be careful."

She pulled the sticks wide apart and Colin, holding the strings like reins, slid them together again. She stepped to the box and made a notation each time he did it. When he had finished, she took the strings from him and threw them over the end of the box.

"That's fun," said Colin. "What did it prove?"

"Depth perception."

"You mean that's got something to do with my terrible landings?" He smiled, but he didn't mean what he said, and he knew from the look on her face that she did not believe him. Since there could be no sweeter thing than the graceful flare of a good landing—the first gentle brush as the wheels kissed the earth and the steady, even rumble of completion—Colin wanted to show this girl a good landing.

"It hasn't so much to do with your landings," she said. "You ought to be able to land by this time. But it might keep you from clipping a telephone wire or a tree some night. That is, if you couldn't pass."

"Did I?"

"Yes."

She stood in front of Colin and pressed the end of a ruler-like stick against the bridge of his nose. There was a small upright card on the stick that slid back and forth. The card was covered with very fine black and brown printing.

"I'll move this card back and forth. Read it when you can."

Colin tried to concentrate on the printing, but she was very close to him, bending over just a little. He could count the freckles on her nose and he could follow the subtle, flowing line of her breasts at the opening of her collar.

"Watch the card, please," she said icily.

Colin read off the names of some rivers and cities and told her that they made no sense.

"The point is, it tests your angle of convergence—your near vision," she said.

Then recklessly, before he had considered his words, Colin looked directly at her. "I'm certainly glad there's nothing wrong with my vision," he said very slowly.

"Watch that!" the doctor grunted, but he winked at Colin and rose from behind his desk. "Maybe I'd better carry on from here, Miss Stewart."

Colin couldn't tell whether she was furious or pleased when she went out the door.

The doctor flashed a small light into Colin's eyes. He looked at the blood vessels in the retinas and examined the optic nerves. He told Colin to look straight ahead, then he held his fat little hands wide apart and brought them slowly together vertically and then horizontally. He asked Colin to tell him when he first saw the tips of his fingers. Then he checked Colin's degree of diplopia on a phorometer, asking him to speak up when the red illuminated line crossed through the little ball.

"Two degrees vertical, right eye," he observed. He flipped the lenses in the frame on the phorometer. As he moved about the machine he hummed tunelessly to himself. "Tum-te-de-dum-de-dee-dum-dum-dum."

Colin thought the doctor was not unlike a very small goblin. "Tum-te-dee-dum-tee-dee-dum. Now take your clothes off, please."

"All my clothes?"

"All of them."

So Colin stripped and felt foolish and helpless—the way every man feels when he stands naked and alone before another man. Then as the doctor directed, he stood on one foot with his eyes closed for what seemed an eternity, and then on the other foot for a second eternity. He wiggled his hands when the doctor told him to, then he wiggled his feet and he bent his knees. He was embarrassed when the doctor placed his finger just behind each testicle and asked him to cough, and even more embarrassed when he had to bend over and spread his buttocks apart. He submitted silently when the doctor bound the rubber wrapping around his arm and watched the mercury rise and fall in the glass as he pumped the band tight to measure his blood pressure. He perspired a little when the doctor held his wrist with his chubby fingers and seemed lost in the contemplation of his watch. Then he obediently stepped up and down off a chair until the doctor told him to stop so he could take his pulse again. He was mightily relieved when the doctor stopped humming, and told him he could put on his clothes again, and handed him a small bottle.

"Fill this up," he said pointing to a door. "The lavatory's in there."

Colin took the bottle and went into the lavatory, where he stared vacantly at the wall and stood for a long time, lost in thought.

# 4

The cheapest and most powerful wine and the best spaghetti in Newark were served at Romeo's—a fact that had been discovered by Roland almost the first day in the city, despite the ritual of admittance maintained by Romeo for the edification of his customers. On the street door there were two Yale locks, a chain lock, and a sliding peephole at which Romeo himself occasionally enjoyed doing service. It was of no matter that the locks were obviously stronger than the door itself, or that Romeo would never lock the door against anyone. The elaborate pseudo-barricade, the cozy furnishings, and Romeo's quiet air of dignity were all calculated to give the customers a sense of belonging to a very exclusive club.

It was in this mellowing atmosphere that Colin acted upon the decision he had made before leaving the doctor's office. That very evening, after a dish of spaghetti à la Romeo and a final fortification with Romeo's wine, he told Lucille Stewart that he wanted her to become his wife.

She did not answer him for a long time. Then she took a long drink of wine. She felt a little dizzy.

When she finally spoke again, she tried to keep her voice even and steady, but it was difficult. She could not recall ever in her life being so surprised and shocked by a few words.

"You said something . . . I think . . . ah . . . that is, you did, didn't you?"

"I said—I'll repeat it just so you won't think it was a slip of the tongue. I said, I think it would be a fine idea if you and I got married."

"Well. . . ." A little sigh of exasperation escaped her. "I *thought* you said something like that."

"The more I think about it, the more I like it."

Lucille contemplated excusing herself from the table and just not coming back. Maybe that was the way to handle a madman. If Colin had been lounging in his chair with a dreamy look in his eyes, or pressing close to her in some attitude of desire, she would know how to handle him. She could mark him off her list as a reckless ladies' man or an incurable romanticist in his cups. But the way he sat—straight, almost rigidly upright—told her that he could not be classified as either. She was positively frightened by his intensity.

"How long have you been thinking about this?" she ventured, to gain time.

Colin made a ceremony of looking at his watch. "Seven hours and forty minutes—about."

"You . . . you wouldn't consider that hasty?"

"Maybe—but you can talk yourself out of anything if you think about it long enough."

Like all madmen, he made some sense, she thought. She studied his face. Certainly there was nothing unusual or terrifying about it. Deep, clear blue eyes—the skin at the corners creased a little from looking at the sun. A good hard mouth that still had no hint of cruelty about it. Even in Romeo's soft candlelight there was absolute determination in his cleft chin.

"I suppose you're used to getting whatever you want," she said.

He looked at her in honest surprise and some of her fear melted. "No. I'm not." Then a new softness came into his voice. "I never wanted much before. It seemed like we had everything, and I guess we did."

"We? That's you and your brothers?"

"Yes. We'd get up in the morning and begin living when we were ready to live that day, and not before. For some reason we never had much ambition for anything else. I guess we were too busy with flying and with little things like who stole whose socks. It was a good life, but we weren't getting anywhere."

"You wanted to get somewhere?"

"No . . . not exactly." He made a fanlike design with four

matches on the tablecloth. "You see, we four were together like this. We gave each other strength because in the beginning we were joined together. We went our separate ways, but we always started at the same place and came back to it—and that place lacked foundation." He took a fifth match and laid it across the base of the design. "Now . . . that match sort of ties the other four together. Makes them solid . . . see? That fifth match is you."

"Me?"

"Yes. Looks reasonable, doesn't it?"

She looked at the matches and at Colin, and shook her head slightly as if to clear her thinking. Now I am a match, she thought. Fanciful. Then she realized with a sinking feeling that she wanted him to go on talking.

"Ah. . . ." was all she could manage to say.

"I think you could handle the job. I've thought so from the first. It might take you a while to get the swing of things, but that would be all the more interesting . . . sort of a challenge and—" He looked at her with the slow smile that had won her consent to have dinner with him in the first place. "And, well . . . I think you're the kind of a girl who likes a challenge."

"Just who would I be marrying, you or your brothers?" She couldn't help that—he had left himself open to it.

"Me, of course. But they would probably be around pretty much. In time you'd even get to like the setup."

The way he said it made her laugh. Her freckled nose wrinkled up and Colin thought that might be another reason he wanted her so much. Then, quickly, she sobered.

"Look here. You can get in lots of trouble going around saying things like that. I could already sue you for breach of promise. Just supposing I said yes?" That would scare him. Now he would haul down his flag and run. But although she knew his height and weight and content of albumen, his pulse standing and sitting and after exercise, she did not know Colin MacDonald.

"That would be wonderful. Let's see, this is Saturday, so tomorrow will be Sunday . . ."

"Are you quite sure of that? We've got to be logical." This was the way out—join his madness without making fun of it.

"Perfectly logical. You can't get a license on Sunday. So we'll have to wait until Monday morning."

"So long? Supposing in the meantime you discovered the truth about my parole from Dannemora and my two-headed sisters. Couldn't we make it sooner?"

"We could drive down to Maryland tonight. They take care of you right away there."

"You seem to know a lot about it. Have you been married many times lately?"

"Five or six times in the past month. I can't honestly remember. Roland says it's this waiting around to fly. Fraternizing with the groundlings, he calls it. Well . . . what do you say?"

She laughed very faintly and her voice sounded hollow in her throat. She wondered at her own embarrassment.

"I say no!" Then she found herself wanting to straighten his tie, and this impulse, which was suddenly accompanied by other even more urgent feelings, frightened her very much. "Now please take me home," she said weakly. "I don't think this wine agrees with either one of us."

Romeo's was filled with smoke that night, and crowded with people. It is curious that only two of them understood the true potency of Romeo's wine.

When they stepped out into the street it was snowing, in soft, gentle flakes that sifted down in slow, dreamlike repetition of themselves and covered the streets with silence.

In Newark that night there must have been hundreds of young people standing in doorways, colder than they were willing to admit. There were some who planned, and some who dreamed, and some who hoped the moment would never end. There were some who loved with words, and some who loved desperately with their bodies, and some who fought, or excited themselves in other ways equally lacking in satisfaction. Such things always happen in doorways, with their hint of inevitable separation.

Then there were those like Colin and Lucille, who stood a little apart, thinking quickly but talking slowly—standing apart because they were afraid to move closer together.

"Have you made up your mind?" asked Colin. The street light reflected on the snow and plainly lit her face. The light touched the droplets that had melted on her cheeks and made them glisten. "Have you made up your mind?" Colin asked again.

"About what?" She knew very well what he was talking about.

"About marrying me?"

"Really, Colin, of course I can't marry you. Come around next year. If you feel the same way then, maybe we could talk it over."

"What difference does it make how *I* feel? I'll be the same guy six months from now. It's how *you* feel that counts. If you'll be interested six months from now, you ought to be interested right this minute. That's logical. Either you like me now, or you never will. People are like that."

"It isn't a question of liking you. I like you very much." She wished she hadn't said that. "I mean . . . well, you should be in love with a person before you marry them. It's sort of customary."

"I love you."

"Don't say that!" She stamped her foot and little flakes of snow scattered from her hair.

"Why not? Damn it, that's the way I feel!"

"You don't know what you're talking about. You *are* crazy . . . just like your brothers! I'm going to change your physical report as soon as I get back to the office."

Colin stepped back and leaned against the stone doorframe. When she looked at him she could not deny, even to herself, that Colin was most certainly a man to be considered. His casual air did not deceive her—he was a reasonable man, stubbornly embarked, for some reason or other, upon an unreasonable design—and this made him doubly difficult to handle. She was already aware that Colin would never become simply a memory.

"Wouldn't it be nicer if you gave me some time to think things over?"

"Certainly. I guess I have rushed you a bit."

"A bit. Yes, just a trifle here and there."

"Then sleep on it. We can't do much till Monday anyway. I'll be around in the morning. Ten o'clock sharp. We'll go to a church. It will start us off kind of right."

He took her hands, and she thought he was going to try to kiss her, but instead he smiled and squeezed her hands until they hurt. Then he was gone down the steps in a swirl of snow. When he reached the sidewalk he turned to look up at her, and clasped his hands over his head like a boxer entering the ring.

"That ought to give you plenty of time," he called.

Lucille thought she saw him laugh. She wished now he had tried to kiss her.

"Oh, yes . . . plenty of time!" she said, and then he was gone.

The day the brothers had moved into the upper floor of Mrs. Antofogasta's house, Roland had promptly shortened her name to "Mrs. A," a label that at first left her a little dazed but somehow pleased.

"Without a question of a doubt," she said, "Antofogasta is too long a name for convenience. I don't know why someone didn't shorten it before—except, of course, it was the only last name poor Nicholas ever had. You are right, without a question of a doubt." Mrs. A constantly sprinkled her conversation with references to "poor Nicholas"— her dead husband—and "without a question of a doubt."

She was a full-blown woman of indeterminate age, whose house was as ample as her bosom. Physically she looked like an elaborate white birthday cake gone a trifle stale. She wore too much makeup and her black hair was too obviously dyed, but she had not surrendered to her years and had no intention of doing so.

Mrs. A was en route to the icebox for her customary bedtime bottle of her own home-brew when Colin met her on the stairs. Even on the wide, carpeted stairs there was no detouring Mrs. A.

"Well, young man, what have you been up to?" She asked the question with a mischievous little-girl smile. Colin leaned against the balustrade and pushed his hat back on his head. He knew he had to talk to someone—it made little difference whom, since at the moment he felt in love with everyone.

"What would you say, Mrs. A, if I told you I was about to get married?"

Mrs. A patted her throat and cleared it. She fluffed up her hair behind and wriggled a little in her corset. "My boy," she demanded dramatically, "who has been trifling with your affections?"

"The most wonderful girl in the world."

"Without a question of a doubt. But who is she? For the length of time you've been in Newark, I'd say she worked very fast."

"It wasn't her idea. It was mine."

Mrs. A patted her throat again and rolled her eyes. "My dear boy, that is what *you* think." And so saying, she swept grandly past him down the stairs. But near the bottom she paused as if she had just thought of something. She turned back to him and smiled, displaying her unconvincingly perfect set of teeth. "I shall hate to lose you, Colin. Maybe you could bring your bride here. Maybe . . . think it over."

"Maybe," said Colin, and started up the stairs again.

Roland was sitting up in bed smoking a cigarette and reading the Sunday morning funny papers. A half-empty bottle of whisky stood on the table beside his bed. There was no glass: Roland seldom bothered with one. He barely glanced up from the paper when Colin entered and hung up his coat in the little hallway that separated their room from the one shared by Keith and Tad.

Colin wasn't anxious to talk to Roland. As he undressed slowly he tried to think of some way to break his news—some line of presentation that would make sense, if not to Roland, at least to himself. He was a long time taking off his shoes and he hung up his pants very carefully. Roland did not once emerge from behind his funny paper. Yet finally it was he who broke the silence.

"You've got something on that so-called mind of yours. Spill it."

Colin sat down on his bed and stared thoughtfully at the ceiling. "Well . . . it's a long story."

"I'll bet. Didn't you pass your physical?"

"Yes . . . as a matter of fact, I did."

"What do you mean, as a matter of fact you did?"

"Well . . ."

"Well?"

"There are other things to consider."

"Stop talking like a damn fool. What's more important than passing your physical? Without that you don't fly, and don't ever forget you got us into this!"

"You're not likely to let me forget it. You see, Roland, there are other things in life besides flying. . . ."

Roland slowly lowered his funny paper and forced a blast of smoke through his nostrils. "Now. Is that so?" he inquired in a tone of astonishment.

"I might as well tell you now. Many things have happened. Can you stand a shock?"

Roland closed one eye and leered at him with the other. "No."

Colin handed him the whisky bottle and grinned. Roland took a deep swallow, snorted, and shook his head.

"I'm going to get married, Roland."

Roland took another swig of the whisky. Then he looked at his toes beneath the sheet and began to mutter angrily. "Oh, Jesus, Jesus . . ."

"It's one of those things, I guess," said Colin dreamily.

"Oh, why the hell couldn't you be more careful!" Then Roland's eyes opened wide. He tossed the funny paper on the floor. "By God, she *can't* blame it on you! We've only been here three weeks! Won't stand up in a court of law!"

"No, wait a second. You've got the wrong idea. I just met her today."

Roland peered at him suspiciously from beneath his bushy eyebrows. "What the hell have you been drinking?"

"It's that girl in the doctor's office."

"You asked her to marry you?" Roland was incredulous.

"Yes."

"Jesus, Jesus. And she said yes?"

"Well, sort of . . . I think she will."

"Sure, she will! Of course! They always do!" Roland looked about him desperately. "Now, you listen to me. There's a hundred bucks or so in my wallet. It's all I've got till we start flying, but we'll make out somehow. You take it. Go down to the station and get a train. Never mind where it's going. Just get on it. Ride to the end of the line and send us a wire when you get there. I'll fix things up with Gafferty until this thing blows over. If the girl calls I'll say you're off on a special flight. You spun in and broke your damn-fool neck. She can go see you in the morgue if she wants. . . . No, that won't do, women are crazy and she might go for the idea— give her a chance to cry. I'll say your remains are unidentifiable. I'll make Tad and Keith wear black ties if I have to.'' Roland put out his big hand and patted Colin's knee. ''Don't worry, old boy. Don't worry about a thing. We'll get you out of this!''

## 5

In Lucille's small room there was a window that looked down on the street. It was set in a medieval turret projecting from the face of the house, and everything seen through the curved pane was wildly distorted. People on the street below looked either two or ten feet tall. Ordinarily, this trickery was a source of mild amusement for Lucille, but on this Sunday morning the twistings of the window were far too much like a continuation of her dreams.

She had slept very poorly. Even now, with the cold daylight creating order, she felt lightheaded and confused. She had gone without breakfast, and the long, warm bath she had taken to calm her nerves had done nothing of the sort. She glanced through the paper and tried to interest herself in the report that the Prince of Wales had fallen off his horse again and the news that a certain Countess Cathcart had been refused entry to the United States on the charge of moral turpitude. In the book section she read a review of *Gentlemen Prefer Blondes* and went to the mirror to check on her own dun-colored hair, wondering absently whether there was anything to that theory. She even flipped through the sports section and learned that Suzanne Lenglen had beaten Helen Wills in a tennis match. She liked the picture of Helen Wills; maybe her hair was not her glory either, and she probably had as many freckles as Lucille did.

Finally she dressed very carefully in her best black silk dress, the one with the touch of embroidery at the neck and wrists.

She tried not to watch the time, telling herself that the

whole project was ridiculous, that Colin had probably sneaked some drinks before he met her and was really drunk when he proposed. Besides, the one thing she had vowed to herself since she began working for Dr. Timothy was not to marry a flier. But twenty minutes before Colin was due, she was standing at the curved window fully dressed and ready, with her best black hat already pressing too tightly against her ears. She knew she was weakening and had even begun to accept that fact with a little smile—until it occurred to her that Colin might not come at all. Then she stopped smiling. She swept the whole newspaper to the floor beneath the window seat.

While the minutes passed alarmingly, and only a few nuns presented themselves for distortion in the window, she sought some escape for her pride. If he didn't come, she might go to New York and have dinner and see a movie. Perhaps *Blossom Time*, with Ben Lyon in the lead. . . . But no, that wouldn't do—she had heard there were airplanes in it. The movie with Dorothy MacKaill would be easier to handle. Then she saw Colin.

There was no mistaking his easy, swinging walk, even though both his height and his width varied through the crazy window. There was no mistaking, either, the identity of the three men who swung along in step beside him. There was Roland, and there was Tad, and there was the youngest, whose name she couldn't remember. Apparently they disdained the sidewalk, for they were walking abreast down the middle of the street, kicking the light snow with their feet. She could hear them laughing loudly against the still Sunday morning air.

Lucille put down a sudden desire to crawl back into bed and cover her face and pretend she was sick. Instead, she made a feeble effort to compose herself by sitting down on the window seat and waiting for the bell to ring.

She could hear them talking as they turned in at the stoop. It seemed a very long time before the bell rang. She heard Mr. Turtle, the landlord, let them in—he was probably in his slippers and suspenders. There was some hearty, indistinguishable male talk; then she heard them clumping up the stairs. At the knock, she took a deep breath and started to open the door without saying anything. Then she changed her mind and called "Yes?"—trying to sound surprised.

"It's me. Colin. Open up!"

"Oh"—as if she were uninterested.

She took a turn around the room, as though to convince herself as well as Colin that his coming was of no consequence. She heard grumbling talk in the hall. Somehow she summoned the nerve to turn the knob and say "Good morning" as casually as she could.

They filed solemnly into the room and stood looking at her with their hats in their hands. As she shut the door behind them, their eyes followed every movement. When she faced them she felt as if her nose were shining, her hair a dust mop, her stockings twisted shreds, and she herself naked—naked in front of four men on a Sunday morning.

"Well," she began. She wanted to say, "Well, this *is* a surprise," or something a little gayer, but her voice failed her. "Well," she said again, and looked about her frantically for a place to hide. In the awful silence, she sought sympathy in the eyes of Colin, but for once his face was inscrutable.

She made vague motions with her hands to indicate that they might sit down somewhere, anywhere—on the bed, on the window seat. Keith and Colin retreated to the bed together and Roland backed warily to the window seat. Tad leaned against the wall near the door and smiled a little. But none of them took their eyes from her. Lucille was never able to remember how long they stared. She knew that she had time to walk to the dresser and begin smoothing on her black gloves. In the mirror she saw Tad leisurely lighting a cigarette. Then Roland spoke from the window.

"Not a bad dish at that," he said.

"I brought my brothers along," said Colin. "They wanted to meet you."

"They met me yesterday at the office," she said, a little fiercely. If Colin wanted to take her to church, all right. If he wanted to marry her—well, she saw no reason not to consider it, but he didn't have to bring a delegation along with him.

"I think she looks much better in black than she does in white," said Tad. He blew a cloud of smoke toward the

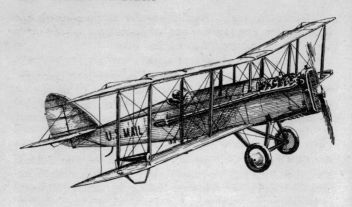

*De Havilland DH-4*

ceiling and his dark eyes wandered up and down her figure. "Damn healthy-looking female!"

"Thank you." On the dresser there was a heavy jewel box that her mother had willed her. Perhaps Tad would like that tossed at his confident head.

"Maybe her wedding dress could be sorta black," said Keith, with a mischievous grin. "Black would cut down her hips some."

"I'm not planning on getting married," she said, her back to them.

"We hear different," said Roland.

"Well, you heard wrong!" Lucille, turning, stamped her foot and threw a look at Colin that dissolved the smile on his face.

"Now, don't get in a sweat, young lady," said Roland. "We're just kinda lookin' after Colin's interests. We're the only family he's got." He paused a moment until he was certain of her attention. "Pays to be careful these days, with all kinds of women litterin' up the countryside. Of course, in your case it's different."

"What's different?" Lucille was thoroughly aroused. She stood with her feet together and her arms thrust straight down her sides, ending in tightly clenched fists.

"A man can't be too careful, as much for the woman's sake as for his own. Now, you take Porkie Scott, for example."

"I don't know Mr. Porkie Scott!" She almost choked on the name.

"You will. Now, there he was, married to as sweet a little girl as you could ever imagine—down in Atlanta one winter after the season went dead. Sweet as a nut she was, and him with a brand new OX-5 Travelaire half paid for, and a contract to dust crops all spring at a hundred bucks a day and insurance. What happens?" Roland spread his hands wide as if she must surely know what happened.

Lucille suddenly found that a search of her upper drawer was necessary—she wanted a pin or something. She had to keep her hands busy.

But Roland was under way. "What happens? The wedding breakfast is no more'n over than she's after him to quit flying so he won't kill himself and leave her a rich widow. She talks Porkie into selling the Travelaire and opening a garage down at the bottom of Texas somewhere. Porkie piddles around with this garage and half starves to death to keep the little woman happy. The only thing he gets to eat is his heart out.

"Then one day a pal drops by in a beat-up old De Havilland and explains to Porkie that there's lots of money in the transport of whisky from Mexico if a man is properly qualified. So Porkie starts flying back and forth across the border at night. But the little woman gets suspicious at all the money floating around and his being away so much at night. She tips off the customs men—who know all about the deal anyhow, and are willing to live and let live so long as Porkie gives them their cut. Fine. Then what happens?"

"I'm not the slightest bit interested," Lucille murmured furiously into the back part of her dresser drawer.

"You should be. Comes a night Porkie gets greedy and puts one case too many in the front of the De Havilland— with the result that the Liberty has more than its share of work to do for a character in its condition. The Liberty overheats and bursts a piece of plumbing trying to keep Porkie in the air. He has to set the DH down right where he is, in the night—which turns out to be smack dab on top of the customs shed. The DH burns like all DH's when they crack up, and so does the shed and most of the evidence; but since his wife has blabbed all about it, the customs men have no choice but to slap Porkie in the tank for six months, superficial burns and all. Porkie now pays that little girl—who is still sweet as a nut, mind you—a considerable chunk of alimony. And all because she didn't want him flying. . . ." Roland sighed heavily and looked out the window. "It is precisely to avoid mistakes of such nature that we are here. Understand?" As if overcome by his own bitter recollections, Roland blew his nose with great force.

"I understand perfectly," said Lucille. She turned to Colin, carrying her nose high. Her underlip stuck out and the corners of her mouth crept down. "I thought we had a date to go to church. Are we going, or do you always do things en masse?"

But Colin only grinned and looked at the beads of melted snow on his shoes. "It's something you'll sort of get used to," he said finally.

Lucille searched vainly for signs of apology in his voice.

"We came along to look you over," said Tad evenly. "Anything wrong with that?"

"Supposing I don't like being looked over?" She felt the anger rising through the cords of her neck. The jewel box. She would throw it yet—about the time they pinned a red and gold ribbon on her for first or second or third of class.

"Four minds are better than one," said Roland. "We must assume the duties of our dear mother. As she would have said, don't you think it would be nice to sit down for a spell so we can get better acquainted?" He folded his hands over his stomach in a gesture so successfully maternal that he seemed about to offer a recipe for blueberry jam.

But no woman as angry as Lucille could appreciate Roland's mental rocking chair. "Get out of here. Get out—all of you, before I lose my temper!" And her hand did close over the jewel box.

Roland raised a warning finger. "There—you see, Colin? By self-admission, she does have a temper."

"Get out, or I'll have the landlord throw you out!" She fought to keep her voice down.

"See, Colin? A tendency to shift responsibility—a thing that could lead to difficult situations in later life."

Lucille gasped for air. There were things to be said, but they would not come out.

"If you won't leave, I will!" she countered lamely. She stalked to the door. "And I hope the walls fall in on you!"

"There again, Colin—vengeful, vindictive. Typical. Desirous of satisfying imagined hurts by bringing disaster to others."

Lucille turned at the door. It was not in her sex to be robbed of the last word. "I'm not imagining *anything* when I say you are all extremely rude and have one hell of a nerve!" And so, before the tears blurred her vision, she did go, slamming the door behind her.

Roland sat motionless for a moment and then his great body seemed to relax completely. He lit a cigarette and waved out the match with a gentle, thoughtful motion. He reached with grunting difficulty for the newspaper at his feet. He unfolded the pages with an air of preoccupation. Then he looked up at his brothers.

"Colin, there's something about that girl." He stopped and gazed at the end of his cigarette for a moment. When he raised his eyes, they were a little moist. "Leave now, Colin. She won't go very far. Pursue her if you must. I think we can smile upon this union."

Somewhat out of breath, Lucille arrived at the church during the singing of "Holy, Holy, Holy." She slipped past the usher, who frowned discreetly at her tardiness, and found a place in one of the half-empty pews in the back. By the time she had followed the minister in the Sentences of Praise and heard the Invocation, she had calmed down considerably. During silent prayer she even forgot about Colin, and prayed, as she always did, for her mother and Dr. Timothy and for the grace to be worthy of her many blessings.

The congregation repeated the Lord's Prayer in unison, and the murmur of solemn voices about her brought her a deep serenity. Then she sat back to listen to the scripture lesson which the Reverend Dr. Pelly was reading from Romans XII. Dr. Pelly was a very small man with large, pointed ears. His elflike head barely rose above the slant-topped pulpit, and those in the front rows could not see him at all. Yet there was nothing small about his voice, which filled the church from the pulpit to the rose windows at the rear, resounding with practised venom when he spoke of evil and rippling melodiously up and down the aisles when he mentioned love.

Let love be without dissimulation. Abhor that which is evil; cleave to that which is good.

Be kindly affectioned one to another with brotherly love; in honour preferring one another;

Not slothful in business, fervent in spirit; serving the Lord;

Rejoicing in hope; patient in tribulation; continuing instant in prayer;

Distributing to the necessity of saints; given to hospitality.

Bless them which persecute you: bless, and curse not.

Rejoice with them that do rejoice, and weep with them that weep.

Be of the same mind one toward another. Mind not high things, but condescend to men of low estate. Be not wise in your own conceits.

Recompense to no man evil for evil. Provide things honest in the sight of all men.

If it be possible, as much as lieth in you, live peaceably with all men.

Dearly beloved, avenge not yourselves, but rather give place unto wrath: for it is written, Vengeance is mine; I will repay, saith the Lord.

Therefore if thine enemy hunger, feed him; if he thirst, give him drink; for in so doing thou shalt heap coals of fire on his head.

Be not overcome of evil, but overcome evil with good.

Dr. Pelly closed his Bible with a soft smack of decision and sat down, thus becoming invisible to the entire congregation.

As the soloist rose to sing "Consider and Hear Me," a low, husky voice in Lucille's ear startled her. "Did you hear what the preacher said?"

Lucille half-turned in her seat and met Colin's smiling face. If her handbag had not been the best leather, she might have torn it in two.

"Go ahead. Heap coals on my head, but curse me not. I just want to marry you. . . . Let love be without dissimulation."

"Leave this church, or I'll call an usher!" she whispered hoarsely over her shoulder.

"I certainly will not. I have a perfect right to come to church. Now, are you going to marry me, or shall I kill myself?"

"Go ahead and kill yourself! Just leave me alone!"

Their voices were rising, but fortunately so was that of the singer. Only a few heads turned.

"You'll be sorry with my blood on your hands . . . you'll be s-o-o-o-o-r-r-e-e. . . ."

Lucille ignored him, or tried to. She sat primly erect, gripping the handbag in her lap. She would not turn around again, no matter what he said. The very next morning she would ask Dr. Timothy for a week's vacation and get away from this madman.

When the soloist finished, Dr. Pelly made the weekly announcements and then asked his flock to join him in the singing of the hymn "Send Down Thy Truth."

Lucille was so choked with anger that she could only move her lips, but she could hear Colin's baritone rising loud and clear behind her. Then they sat down again.

"You are not in very good voice this morning," murmured Colin.

She concentrated on Dr. Pelly as he removed his spectacles and approached the pulpit.

"But you look so lovely in the light from that window, no one cares whether you can sing or not."

Dr. Pelly began to speak, and Lucille did her to best to listen to him and him alone.

"The window give you sort of a golden look. . . ."

That was quite a thing to say, she thought, and she blushed a little.

There was a long period during which the minister held forth on the subject of brotherly love. Just as Lucille began to wonder if Colin had given up, he spoke in her ear again. "I like this guy. Talks a lot of sense. We'll go see him right after church and get him to do the marrying."

"We will not!" To her embarrassment, Lucille found herself speaking out loud. Blushing to her toes, she kept her eyes straight ahead.

Dr. Pelly paused, emerged momentarily from behind his pulpit, squinted nearsightedly in her direction, then disappeared again. Only his sonorous voice gave proof to those in the front pews that he had not disappeared down a trap door.

From that time until the benediction and the organ postlude, Colin spoke in a mere whisper, but it was loud enough for Lucille to hear and she melted a little at his earnestness.

"I'm really sorry," he said once. "I'm not used to proposing and I don't quite know how to go about it. I guess I've made an awful botch of this one. The least you can do is wish me better luck next time. . . ."

She found herself wondering about a next time and hoping, to her surprise, that there would not be a next time—at least, for anyone else.

"You see, I fell in love with you. Sure, it was in a hurry, but you can't regulate things like that. It wouldn't have made any difference where I saw you the first time. The result would have been the same. I certainly didn't plan it, and maybe because it's all so unplanned . . . maybe that's why I've made so many mistakes. I know you didn't like having Roland and Tad and Keith come to see you like that. I know it now, but I didn't know it then. They aren't so bad as you think . . . and they haven't had much experience at this sort of thing either. . . ."

Then he was quiet for a while. Lucille's shoulders eased their tension. Basically, she told herself, he was a fine man speaking from his heart. If only he weren't so impulsive! But it was possible that she had been a trifle—just a trifle—hasty in discouraging him.

"I'm glad I saw you in a church," he said softly, after a

time. "I'll never get over the way those colored windows make you look. It will be a nice way to remember you . . . all golden and beautiful."

In spite of herself, Lucille turned around and smiled at him. Their eyes locked.

After the benediction, Dr. Pelly walked down the aisle with his head bowed in meditation and waited to bid farewell to his flock. The very first to receive the fatherly smile and the cordial handshake were Lucille, who could not bring herself to look into his face, and Colin, who thanked him warmly for a very, very beautiful and effective sermon.

# 6

At noon, Porkie Scott had just got out of bed, not because it was Sunday nor even because it was a particularly gloomy Sunday. It was February, and Porkie held the firm conviction that the animals were right. Each year since anyone could remember, he had contrived to imitate their hibernation. Wherever he might be, he retired to his room in late November and did not emerge again until late March, except for occasions of extreme emergency—such as the funeral of a comrade who had been so foolish as to fly in the wintertime.

Porkie did not retire in the manner of a sick man. Rather, like a squirrel, he accumulated certain stores before he disappeared from public view. He stacked his room with books on every conceivable subject; he never got around to reading many of them, but he liked to think they were handy if he wanted them. He subscribed to the local newspaper, whatever it might be. Although he drank comparatively little himself, he made arrangements with the local bootlegger to replenish his supply of gin and home-brew at stated intervals.

Porkie made few contacts with the outside world. He deliberately chose a room with a window looking toward a wall or an alleyway—the temptation to observe his fellow men in the pursuit of their daily tasks was, he admitted, too great—and he wanted nothing to disturb the serenity of his mind. Consequently, he never knew whether it was raining or snowing or blowing, and he didn't care.

Porkie somehow resembled a potato dumpling. It was not that he was overfat, but his flesh hung sleekly on him like the skin of a well-fed seal. He had a considerable belly, but it seemed not to hinder his movements. His hands were pudgy and expressive and were usually engaged in deftly flicking ashes from his cigarette to the floor. His head was cushioned comfortably on a pair of enormous jowls and looked very much like an egg standing on its large end. His keen but peaceful blue eyes stood out like jewels in an otherwise phlegmatic face. And he had an astoundingly deep voice.

During his periods of hibernation, Porkie followed a loose schedule. Awaking just before noon, he removed whatever home-brew bottles had accumulated in the tub and took a leisurely bath. Then he 'phoned his bookie and, according to how much money he had, placed a few judicious bets. Afterward he would sit and think a while. Since his disastrous marriage in Georgia, he had found it easy to forswear the company of women, hence his thoughts were remarkably pleasant and untroubled. At about two or three in the afternoon he would order his one meal of the day, which he ate with solemn gusto. Then, if there was no other pressing business at hand, he would take a nap for an hour or so. Awake again, he would tidy up his room, read, put some brew on ice against expected visitors, shave, roll up his almost nonexistent laundry, or send for the barber to give him a haircut if he needed one. Thus Porkie's "day," as he pleased to call it, was a surprisingly busy one. He went back to bed around eight in the evening. Owing to the tranquillity of his mind, he had no trouble whatsoever in sleeping.

Such a day, Porkie maintained, was extremely satisfying to his soul and his body, and since no man could reasonably be expected to live out his life year after year without making serious mistakes, it followed that a certain portion of each year should be devoted to the contemplation of those mistakes.

"A duck who has been shot at one pond does not return to the same pond the next year—not the same duck, anyway. He goes down South and thinks it over with the sense God gave him, and next year he stays the hell away from the place." So Porkie was fond of saying, and among his fellow pilots he was considered a very wise man.

The only major variation in Porkie's daily schedule was the arrival of visitors, and since Porkie was a good listener to other people's troubles, and avoided argument on any subject, he had a great many visitors. If they were pilots, he sat up all night while they drank and talked about themselves, their ships, and their women. He was equally agreeable with mechanics who talked about themselves, their engines, and their women. On occasion, he would entertain his bootlegger, who talked about himself, his liquor, and his women.

Porkie was in his bath when Roland and Tad and Keith MacDonald arrived for consultation. Roland took one look at the tub and turned to Keith.

"Go call the police," he said. "A walrus has escaped from the zoo."

Porkie blinked his blue eyes and ignored Roland. "Sit down, Tad." He indicated the toilet. Then he splashed a little and lay back. His breasts, pink and devoid of hair, curved like a woman's just beneath the water.

"We need a drink," said Roland.

"No doubt. There's brew in the cooler over the can and gin in the closet. None of it's any good, but take your choice."

Roland removed the tile cover from the watercloset tank and fished up a cool bottle of home-brew. He found some glasses in the medicine chest.

"Have the ships arrived?" asked Porkie.

"No."

"Are we all fired?"

"Not yet."

"Then what are you so worried about?"

"A pretty terrible thing has happened."

"Who got bumped off?" asked Porkie, with immediate interest.

"Colin is going to get married," said Tad.

There was silence in the room, broken only by Porkie's uneasy stirring in the tub.

"Oh—oh. . . ." he said finally.

"We don't have to tell you how we feel," said Roland.

"No."

"But we want to make the best of things. Be sporting. We decided that together."

"Of course."

"If these things are going to happen, they're going to happen. . . ."

"Of course."

"The girl is not too bad," said Tad.

"Naturally." But Porkie wore a mask of tragedy. His jowls sagged with sympathy.

"We are planning certain festivities," continued Roland. "Mrs. A has offered the use of her living room, dining room, and kitchen. We'll invite Gafferty and hope he doesn't come. Johnny Dycer's mother just sent him a smoked ham—we'll have that. And Shorty Baker said he would dig up some dynamite."

"Dynamite?"

"Yes. This girl is from Pennsylvania. She will expect dynamite at her wedding. It's customary there."

"Of course."

"Will you come, Porkie?" asked Keith.

Porkie considered the question a moment. He splashed water beneath his chins. He chased the soap down between his legs. Finally, he looked up decisively.

"Son, I shall be there."

"Now, Tad and Keith and me, we've decided we want to give them something—not just candlesticks or silverware. We want something unique—something they'll always remember. Unfortunately, as you know, the MacDonald brothers have not flown for some time." Roland leaned intently forward as he spoke.

"Ah. . . ." It was difficult to tell whether Porkie was registering understanding or swallowing water.

"We want to really fix them up right—give them a start in life, you might say. Something in the neighborhood of two or three hundred fish." Roland took a long swig of the home-brew and eyed his curling mustache importantly in the mirror.

"Of course. That would be a fine thing to do."

"We felt sure you would agree. Now, unfortunately—hrrm—we have not got two or three hundred fish."

"That's too bad." Porkie took a sudden absorbed interest in his navel. Another long silence fell upon the room.

"We doubt if Gafferty would advance us that much," Tad said.

"No. I don't think he would."

Roland wet his lips with the brew again and rocked back and forth on his heels. He worked his mouth thoughtfully.

"Frankly, Porkie, we thought you would be more cooperative in this matter."

Porkie raised himself to a standing position with a mighty cascade of water. He reached blindly for a towel and Keith quickly handed him one. He began to rub his face and neck vigorously. When he emerged from the towel he asked for a cigarette. Roland moved instantly to serve him and Tad held the match for him. Then he began to dry his chest and belly.

"As I understand it," said Porkie in a voice that rumbled against the tile walls, "you are trying to put the bite on me for two or three hundred dollars."

"That is a rather crass way of putting it, but substantially correct," said Roland.

"What were you going to buy?"

"Two tickets to Atlantic City, a hotel room for a week, and a set of matched luggage."

Porkie sawed the towel gravely back and forth across his ample hindquarters. Then he stepped gingerly out of the tub and helped himself to a glass of brew.

"Nothing doing. It would be a waste of money. I thought you wanted to give them something they would always remember. Let me tell you that there are certain things about a honeymoon nobody wants to remember. If the bride is inexperienced—as I trust she is in this case—going off with a strange man to a hotel room is not exactly a pleasant experience, even though she may consider herself wildly in love with the guy—a condition which is unlikely since she can't possibly know much about him. Furthermore, the events leading up to a wedding have a tendency to give the poor girl what is known as 'bride's bellyache'—a nervous condition which prevents both of them from honestly enjoying wassail for some time afterward. She may say she's the happiest girl in the word, but actually she is scared and miserable. I invite you to examine the fixed but courageous smile on any bride's honeymoon picture."

Porkie paused and searched for his bottle of mouth wash.

When he found it he gargled decorously. Then he screwed the cap back on the bottle and put it carefully away.

"As for the groom, he is in a hell of a fix. He is faced with the messy task of deflowering a girl whom he considers inviolate—or he would not have married her in the first place. If it *isn't* messy, he gets to wondering. Unless he is a millionaire, he is spending five times as much every day as he ever can again for years—just at a time when he comes to the realization that two cannot live as cheaply as one."

Porkie sat down heavily on the edge of the tub and sighed.

"Then there is the business of loneliness. Living together has brought them a lot of new problems and they don't know each other well enough yet to sit down and talk them over sensibly. They get lonely. Ever notice how people on a honeymoon fall all over an old friend if they happen to meet one? They gotta talk sense to someone. The man is busy proving he is a man and that she has hitched her wagon to a star—he's trying to convince himself as much as her. And the girl is busy trying to convince him and herself that she will stick by him, come what may—just like it said in the ceremony. Finally, custom demands that they can't leave each other's sight for more than five minutes, and that just ain't natural. No. I wouldn't loan you ten cents for a honeymoon."

Porkie rose and paddled out to the other room. Tad shrugged his shoulders and they followed after Porkie.

As he clothed himself leisurely in pajamas and dressing gown, the brothers assumed strategic positions about the room. From time to time they looked up from their study of the carpet designs and threw a quick glance in Porkie's direction. No one said anything. The brothers were each aware that this was a matter for the most delicate timing. Even Porkie, who had deliberately armed himself against persuasion, found that he was uncomfortable. He thumped down on the bed and flicked some ashes from his cigarette to the floor.

"I talked to Gafferty on the 'phone yesterday," he said brightly. Certainly the brothers would be interested in such intelligence. Porkie allowed a look to play across his face indicating he possessed considerable important information.

But the brothers refused the bait. Then suddenly they

ignored him altogether. They may have exchanged some mute signal—Porkie could not be sure. But he felt as if he had been dropped out of the window. When Roland spoke at last, it was to talk right through him.

"I'm glad we three are together," he said, mellowing under the influence of the home-brew. "I guess we have nobody else. There *was* a time when one pilot could depend on another pilot—a fellow had old friends who would trust him, come what may. But those times are gone. Nowadays pilots think only of themselves and their money. Flying has become big business. They get a little money and they hang on to it as if it was a third leg. Old pals, who perhaps gave them a lift up, maybe loaned them a little gas now and then when they weren't doing so well—old pals who were even ready to fight when some guy said So-and-so had become a tight-fisted bastard—old pals like that are forgotten. . . ."

"Let that be a lesson to us when the check arrives," said Tad.

Porkie heard the word "check" and Keith heard it, and they were both surprised, but Roland took it in his stride.

"We will take the principal and put it in government bonds," said Roland. "No fancy stock deals for us. Of course, we might hold out a thousand or so for a good bang-up party. But afterwards we must return to the same simple life we have always known."

"And we'll keep the same old friends," said Tad.

"Just what the hell are you talking about?" asked Porkie.

They looked at him with curiosity, as if he were a stranger they had never seen before.

"Our uncle in Ecudaor . . . our adopted uncle," said Tad simply.

Porkie's eyes became mere slits of suspicion. "I s'pose he died and left you a fortune?"

"Not exactly a fortune. Just a modest sum. He was a fine man. General Pedro Gonzalez Jesus Matanomez. He led a revolution in '22 and I went down to help him. Needed pilots bad. Must say he didn't forget me. I didn't think you'd heard about it, Porkie."

"You never flew south of Juarez in your life."

"Too bad the check won't be here before Colin's wedding.

That boy is going to be real hurt,'' mused Roland. ''Real hurt,'' he repeated, with the rustic honesty of a rail splitter.

''All right, goddammit . . . I'll let you have some money,'' sighed Porkie. ''But it's got to be on my terms and spent the way I say. And don't get the idea I believe you were ever within five thousand miles of Ecuador!''

''What are your terms?'' asked Roland in a tone that indicated he was doing Porkie a favor.

''Not on account of any of you, but because Colin is a swell guy who's in trouble, I'll loan you seventy-five bucks until you get your first pay check. Not a dime more, and I'll go with you when you spend it—just in case. You're going to buy them something they can use—something they can regard with love and affection for whatever period they may spend together. It will not only be ornamental; it will be a bridge of understanding between them, and a barrier against disaffection. It will bring them together when they most need to be brought together. They can cry or they can laugh, and the final result will always be the same. Tomorrow afternoon I'll meet you at Newberger's furniture store on the corner. You're going to buy them a large double bed.''

## 7

The office was still and comfortless and Gafferty wished he had not come there. If he had taken enough to drink, he might have stayed at the wedding party—though he had suspected he was not wanted. He could have done that, or he could have gone to Romeo's for more drinks, or he could have called up Edna, the airport whore. But instead he had come to his office and lit a cigar and sat down at his desk with his head in his hands.

After a little while it seemed a good idea that the office was so quiet. A heavy spring fog clung dreamily to the windows; everything was grounded. No itinerants would come slipping down out of the night to disturb his thoughts.

He reached in his desk drawer and brought out the map again—for the hundredth time. He spread it across the desk and anchored one end with the ashtray made out of a piston. Although he knew the map almost by heart, he examined it now with renewed interest, for at last in the hangar below there was some tangible evidence of his labors. It had arrived that very afternoon before the fog closed in. He could almost feel its presence.

Gafferty did not delude himself that he was an empire builder. He was an operations manager—the link between a group of businessmen who didn't know a stabilizer from an aileron and a crew of pilots and mechanics who most certainly didn't know a watered stock from a debenture. It made Gafferty's task no easier to realize that neither group had any desire to enlighten themselves.

It seemed as if everyone in America were making money—

fast. The businessmen expected a prompt and ample return on their investments. They hired Gafferty to arrange this detail for them. Despite his warnings, they remained oblivious to the vicissitudes of attempting to fly the mail regularly day and night. They believed what they read in the featured articles, and besides, wasn't Henry Ford going in for this sort of thing?

But Dow Jones averages did not interest the men who flew. They knew nothing of averages, or trends—or money.

The businessmen had called Gafferty over to New York for lunch that day—a lunch that seemed as standard as their pressed suits of quiet gray, the two quick drinks of excellent Scotch in the locker room at the club, then the oysters on the half shell, and the rare roast beef au jus. There was the usual figuring on the tablecloth with gold and silver automatic pencils, and automatic laughs at anatomical jokes. There was some talk about how much Mussolini had done for Italy in his seven years of office, and then someone told the latest Silent Cal story. One of the businessmen invited Gafferty to join a party at *The Desert Song* that evening, but he declined; he had some work to do, he said. He didn't tell them that he was going to the wedding feast of one of their pilots, because they wouldn't have cared. It was not their job to care about those things. It was Gafferty's.

Finally, when the tablecloth was strewn with figures and cigar ashes, they laughed and put their pencils back in their vest pockets, and shook hands all around. Gafferty suggested they visit the airport and they laughed some more and said they would do just that as soon as they had time. But Gafferty couldn't see them in the same room with, say, Keith MacDonald.

If his own marriage had not broken up after two years, he would have wanted a son like Keith. Though he had seen the boy only twice—the day he had hired him and this evening at Colin's wedding—Gafferty was struck by his own feeling for the youngest MacDonald. How much of this was due to Keith's quiet, impish smile and his merry eyes, how much to his own secret yearning for a son, Gafferty could not say. But he thought of him when he looked at the map—of Keith, not of the businessmen.

The route was marked in red pencil. It extended from

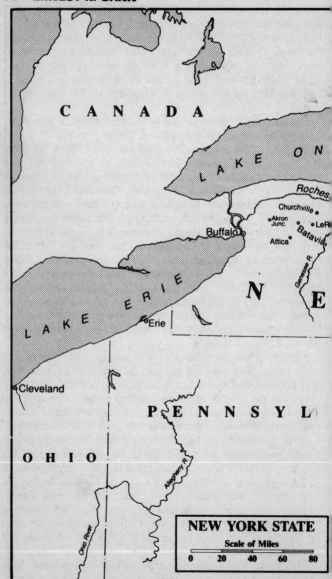

CANADA

LAKE ON

Roches

Churchville •
Akron •    • LeR
Junc.    • Batavia
Attica •

Buffalo

N    E

LAKE ERIE

• Erie

• Cleveland

P E N N S Y L

O H I O

Allegheny R.

Ohio River

**NEW YORK STATE**

Scale of Miles

0    20    40    60    80

Newark to Albany, from Albany to Syracuse, from Syracuse to Rochester and Buffalo and Erie and Cleveland. Not very much of America—not when you could visualize its whole extent, as Gafferty could because he had flown its length and breadth. But it was a beginning. A little beginning. Somehow inept and unofficial. It was hard to say what would come of it.

The lines were straight, because what Gafferty and the businessmen proposed recognized no earthly barriers. But a pencil line, no matter how finely drawn, did not make a route for the transport of goods and chattels or for carrying the mails. Neither could dollars make a route, nor conferences at lunch, nor figuring on tablecloths, nor sitting alone in an office in the middle of the night staring at a map. It had always been the Keith MacDonalds who made a route by sea or land.

This route did not now exist. It was an air space only, an invisible, ownerless gas, changing in its three dimensions each moment of time. Gafferty's red pencil lines signified only the piercing of the gas that happened to be there at the time. So the route existed only in men's minds—young, unfearing men like Keith MacDonald and Tad and Colin, and Porkie Scott and all the rest.

Up the Hudson to Albany wound the railroad tracks of the New York Central. That was a *real* route, thought Gafferty. You could walk along it if you wanted to, in the sunshine and in the rain, and it would be the same each time; you could reach down and touch it if you wanted to. At first, Gafferty admitted, there must have been difficulties. There were probably washouts, and mountains to be removed or cut through. And probably after the railroad started westward from Albany they had trouble with the Indians. Gafferty tried hard to remember his American history. Even if they did have trouble it was a natural route, since the valley of the Mohawk was the only natural break in the Appalachians. Even before the railroads felt their strength, the trade from the hinterlands of New York and Ohio came that way—down the Hudson to the Atlantic.

Now it was to be done all over again, and there were no such understandable reasons why Gafferty's route had been chosen. Someone in the Post Office Department had simply drawn some lines and connected them with other lines that stretched across the face of America. Fly those lines, gentlemen. But the Catskills were full of thunderstorms in summer, and Canada spat blizzards at northern New York in winter, and there were sandstorms in El Paso and fog in Oregon. Didn't they think of that when they drew the lines so easily, or didn't they know, or didn't they care? And there were a lot of other odd things—ice in the clouds and deep snows on the fields, powerful winds that swept across the prairies and devoured an airplane's gas supply.

Gafferty remembered only too well the first attempts to translate those lines into actuality: Chicago to New York in December 1918. It didn't work. Not a plane made it. It was the middle of 1919 before the route began to function, and then it cost twenty-four cents to send a letter over the route. No one but the pilots who nursed their De Havillands over the Alleghenies cared very much. Then in 1921 Nutter and Eaton and Murray and Frank Yeager and finally Jack Knight passed the wand from one to another, like runners in a relay race, flying the mail straight through from San Francisco to New York. They flew both day and night—an achievement so remarkable that Congress had a change of heart and appropriated a little more money. But that same year, twelve pilots met their deaths along those pencil lines. Gafferty remembered that, too.

By 1922 and 1923 there were some beacon lights along the airways, and now and then a new emergency field opened up, but these were seldom underneath a pilot's wings when he really prayed for them. The surplus war equipment, the DH's designed for wartime reconnaissance and haphazardly converted, were not qualified for the job. They were too heavy; their gliding angle was too steep; they labored dangerously out of small fields. Too often they were maintained by the relatives of politicians. The Post Office Department did what it could, but when the Kelley Bill was passed in 1925, giving the whole headache to private contractors, no one in Washington who had anything to do with the air mail objected.

That was when the businessmen came in, and Gafferty, and—through him and his kind—the Rolands and the Keiths,

the Colins, the Shorty Bakers, and the Johnny Dycers. Gafferty
and his Mercury Airlines were not alone in their enterprise.
There were Southern Air Transport, Robertson in St. Louis,
N.A.T., Western Air Express, and the Varney Speed Lines;
each, in its own domain, complete with maps and offices,
and even planes. Only their ability to fly those planes day in
and day out had yet to be proven. There, standing out like a
tear in a wing's fabric, was the catch—there indeed, thought
Gafferty.

The airport beacon light moved a solid yellow finger through
the fog. It swung round and round, shortening and blazing
suddenly when it hit a mass of cloud that hung brooding just
above the Jersey swamps. Tad and Keith stood watching it,
their faces wet and shining with dampness.

Because Keith had drunk his fill of beer and Tad none at
all, they had left the others when the wedding party reached
its climax. That was part of the agreement and Mrs. A had
sternly enforced it. Her house belonged to Colin and Lucille
this night. All the others could make their own arrangements.
She had cried a little and messed her mascara when she said
it. So Roland had gone off with Porkie and Johnny Dycer and
Shorty Baker, to finish their drinking. In a way Tad and
Keith envied them. For numerous reasons it was a good time
to get drunk. It wasn't every day you lost a brother, and it
was in that light that they considered Colin's marriage. Maybe
it would work out and maybe it wouldn't. Maybe Lucille
could move in and become one of them, maybe not. As far as
Tad and Keith were concerned they would maintain a sort of
armed truce until they started to fly. Then they would see.
The advent of Lucille into their tight circle had already done
one thing to their clannishness: Colin was understandably
preoccupied. And since Roland as their normal chieftain had
always stood a little apart, Tad and Keith were brought even
closer together despite the difference in their ages.

As they walked slowly through the fog toward the airport,
the street lights behind them projected their bobbing shadows
far ahead into the fog itself and showed up the strong contrast
in their figures. Tad's shadow swung along on tremendously
long legs and his broad shoulders almost vanished in the
gloom, with all the man's jauntiness and the loose, easy-

swinging freedom. Keith's shadow seemed to flow along beside Tad's, but it was square and stocky all over, as if a longer man had been foreshortened. They walked in step with their elbows sometimes touching, thinking and watching the shadows preceding them, very much together.

"You should grow some, Keith," said Tad.

"Yeah? I can remember when you complained because I was too heavy."

"No. I mean grow lengthwise for a change."

Keith looked up at him and they laughed together, thinking of those sunlit afternoons when their lives depended on each other. Tad rubbed his hands together thoughtfully and flexed his arms.

"I'm getting soft already," he said. "Wonder if I could still swing you. . . ."

"Maybe you could practice on the mail sacks."

"It's going to be hard to get used to."

"Yeah," said Keith, and they fell silent again, because they both knew they were thinking of Colin and Lucille and not of the mail sacks.

They walked to the airport because they didn't know of any other place to go, except back to the hotel room they had rented for the night, and they had no desire to return there. They were drawn to the airport because it seemed friendly, even in the fog. They would not have admitted it, even to each other, but they both felt depressed. Something they believed would go on forever had ended without their willing it. It was very hard to imagine how the four of them could ever be together again.

When they reached the airport, they stood staring at the beacon for so long that they both began to feel a little foolish. They looked away finally and moved toward the blackness where the docks nestled against the airport boundary. They heard a steamer whistle hoarsely somewhere out in the Narrows, perhaps beyond Staten Island. Then they came to the hangar, where the road turned into the airport.

"Gafferty's light is on," said Keith.

It was a moment before Tad answered. The light burned brightly even through the fog, shafting down an invitation.

"Want to go see him?"

"I'm not sleepy yet, are you?"

"No."

They went in the front way and climbed the stairs to Gafferty's office. They knocked on the door and Gafferty told them to come in. When they entered he looked up, surprised and pathetically pleased.

"Hello," he said. "Party over so soon?"

"Yes. Colin deserves some sort of a honeymoon."

"Wish I could have stayed longer." They didn't believe me when I said that, thought Gafferty. They'll never believe me because I'm on the other side—because they'll never know what a damned lonesome job this is. He looked down at the map a moment and then at them, standing limply near the door. There are my map makers, he thought. But he said, "I had a little homework to do," and he imagined he had said it very lamely.

"When do we go to work?" asked Tad.

Gafferty saw there was no hardness in the man now; somehow he had wilted. And even Keith, his blue eyes squinting against the glare of light, was not smiling.

"Want to sit down and chew the fat for a while? Or maybe you'd like to go down in the hangar and have a look at something that might interest you." Gafferty wished they would sit down and talk to him—about little things, or maybe he had forgotten how big they could be: things like air speed and altitude, and downdrafts and fishtailing into small fields, and rigging for speed, and how So-and-so was planning to fly around the world just as soon as he could get the money.

"Sure. . . ."

They didn't seem to care what they did.

"I didn't want to say anything about it at the party this afternoon. Didn't want to mix business with love." He smiled a little.

"What's up?"

"Go have a look for yourself. The sooner you get acquainted the better. The light is on your left at the top of the stairs. There's another switch on the floor when you go out."

They left, mumbling good nights, and Gafferty envied them the next few moments. He wished he could have gone down with them; but now it was too late—the particular little moment had gone.

They stood at the top of the stairs a moment and looked down into the hangar. It was a stark place. The girdered ceiling seemed heavy and brooding. The vast space between the concrete floor and the curving roof was out of all proportion. And the planes, nestled and intermingled with one another, seemed to be not resting but dead. The lights festooned across the girders, designed so that mechanics might work upon the engines, were too bright, like the lights in a morgue. Tad and Keith looked solemnly down at the planes and came to identify each one as a friend, or an acquaintance, presently asleep. Save one. And it stood out brilliantly among the others, strange and bright and poised with life. They knew instantly that this was what Gafferty had sent them to see.

They bent low beneath the wing of a De Havilland and came upon it quietly. For a long time they stood together, almost motionless, their faces still damp and pale in the garish light. They could not explain their feelings to each other, yet they were aware that their emotion was very much the same. They both understood the significance of this meeting between themselves and the new machine. For in this machine—and it would be a little time yet before they would come to regard it as anything else—they would be cold and achingly lonely; their courage, though conditioned to the element in which they functioned, might be drained in one shrill moment, or it might ooze out little by little over a period of several intolerable hours, until there remained in control not a heart fit for combat, but merely a collection of bones and blood in a sack of skin. Arrayed only in leather, they could in this machine achieve regal splendor, command an empire of unlimited space. But they must rule according to certain pre-established laws, cunningly contrived to keep them the rulers. The penalty for violation of these laws would be immediate and final. These things they silently understood.

Tad stepped toward it first. He passed his hand tentatively along the fuselage, caressing it as he might the bare shoulder

*Pitcairn Mailwing*

of a willing woman. But half-aware of his desire, he pressed his body against its side, softly at first and then with increasing pressure. Then, still holding the palm of his hand against the fuselage, he moved slowly back toward the tail until his passage was interrupted by the stabilizer. He noted the way the rudder fin curved up from the fuselage—not merely an appendage, a mechanical afterthought that seemed tacked on, as did so many fins. It seemed to grow out of the fuselage itself. Then he read the name on the rudder—Pitcairn Mailwing.

He walked around behind the tail and stood looking forward. His eyes searched for imperfections in line and balance, again as he might regard a woman who had come to share his bed: did the curve of her breasts flow smoothly and match in grace the curve of her hips and legs pressed together? —was there too short a sweep of cowling there, an awkward heaviness perhaps where the wings made union with the fuselage? Did her hair flow pleasingly about her neck and shoulders?—was the lilt in the lower wings, the dihedral, easy and promising? Tad concluded that all he had seen thus far was beautiful.

By contrast with the ponderous, dowdy De Havilland beside it, its sleek beauty was as a maiden to a hag, fresh and clean-looking. He sauntered around the wing tip and thumped it lightly as he passed. He paused and studied the way the aileron was set into the wing. He reached up and shook the drag wire that ran from the top wing to the landing-gear strut. He stood close to the fuselage again, just behind the engine, and breathed deeply, enjoying the faint odor of oil and metal.

The engine, a Wright J-5 Whirlwind, was the finest and most powerful that Tad or Keith had ever seen. It swung a two-bladed propeller of a type that was new to them. The propellers that they had known were wooden, fashioned with infinite care, and sometimes they had balanced their own. This was of metal, and it was painted black on the back to protect their eyes against the glare when it sabered through the sunlight.

They stood together for a time, looking up at the engine, following the gentle, symmetrical twist of the blades. They studied the rocker boxes and the way the exhaust manifolds joined with the ring and flowed back beneath the fuselage. Then, still wordless, they walked back together to the cockpit, past the painting on the side that announced its assignment: U.S. Air Mail.

Keith climbed into the cockpit and adjusted himself carefully in the seat. He put his feet on the rudder pedals and moved them slowly back and forth. He looked over his shoulder and watched the rudder move dreamily from side to side. He grasped the control stick, moving it backward and forward, watching the elevator flippers rise and fall. He moved it from side to side and caught the balance of the ailerons. Tad watched him in silence; they were listening and feeling, sensing the character of this machine that would soon become a part of them, in conquest or defeat.

They began to study the instruments; there were more than they had ever seen in one plane before. The compass, of course, to guide them directionally in space. Below it a turn-and-bank instrument which they did not thoroughly understand and hence mistrusted. They knew only that it was intended to supplement their faulty human senses—senses confused by lack of normal vision when the earth's horizon disappeared in the storms or night. It presumed to show them when they were turning to the left or right, or when they banked the wings. And the indicator beside it would show them whether they were climbing or descending when they could not see. With such instruments they should be able to fly the machine without relation to the earth below—but they rejected the possibility. It was safer, far safer, to rely on the feeling in the seat of one's pants.

There were, besides, an air-speed gauge, an altimeter, a tachometer, an oil pressure and a fuel gauge. These were trustworthy though unaccustomed luxuries. And so they examined everything with wonder and tried to imagine what it would be like to have a ship like this at their command, and what designs they might paint upon it, if, as Gafferty had implied, they were each to have one to call their own.

Finally Keith climbed out of the cockpit. His foot sought unfamiliarly for the metal step, and he lowered himself to the floor. They turned away from the ship reluctantly. Then they switched off the lights at the hangar door and let themselves out into the night.

The fog had turned to a soft mist and it had begun to rain. They looked up at Gafferty's window; it was black and empty. So without pausing they started down the road to the edge of the airport.

The beacon was brighter now, pointing through the rain. It flashed against the dripping buildings, first white, then green, cutting the shadows of the road ruts in sharp relief. They kept their heads bent to avoid being blinded and because they were lost in review of what they had seen. When they reached the main road, Tad turned around and looked back toward the hangar. It looked transparent, insubstantial—a vision in the gloom.

"What are you thinking about?" asked Keith. "Why so silent?" He asked, though he had reason to believe he knew.

It was some time before Tad answered, and when he did, his voice sounded muffled and far away, even uncertain. He put his hand on Keith's shoulder and squeezed it gently because he could express his need and affection in no other way.

"It's funny. I guess it started in there. I was thinking about how the four of us used to get some beer and girls and sing 'Just a wee doch-an-dorris' and how we used to be pretty good at it. Then I was thinking about how we used to wake up together in the mornings and Roland would have a hangover and sometimes you would, too . . . and I was thinking about Madame Moselle. . . .''

"Yeah," said Keith. "Those are good times to think about."

●**8**

Lucille told herself she had married Colin because she was stunned—ambushed by the swiftness of his purpose. She was outtalked and greatly outnumbered. But these were causes, not reasons. Sometimes she admitted—but only to herself—that she would have married him without half the campaign. The season, or the year, or the stars, or the way he parted his hair—they were right, and that was all. As she explained to the uncomprehending Dr. Timothy—she just woke up one morning and found herself married to four men. It didn't sound sensible to say that she had been carried off like a Sabine woman, that her demands for time fell upon deaf ears, that her acceptance was taken for granted not only by Colin but by his brothers and all his friends. People would only ask why she hadn't called the police, and there was no answer to that.

Lucille was treated tenderly, rather like a Moslem bride, she thought. There was no asking what her wishes were, and this both annoyed and pleased her. It was taken for granted that she would live at Mrs. A's. Grumbling thickly through his mustache, Roland moved in with Keith and Tad. They were very crowded, but no one even suggested larger quarters. It was plainly expected that she would become one of them—instanter, with no fiddling around about it. No one, not even Colin, bothered to show her how.

She was sitting up in bed reading *Gentlemen Prefer Blondes*. Roland had brought it to her during the first week of her marriage and presented it with the blunt suggestion that she do something about her own hair: dye it—either black or yellow, he advised—but do something. At the time she wondered if she could find some orange dye somewhere—that would fix him. But she did nothing.

This was the first time she had been alone long enough to look at a book. It was a problem that seemed to bother no one but Lucille. When she wanted privacy, she went to the bathroom between the two rooms and locked the door. This procedure invariably conflicted with the desires of one brother or another. They called to her through the door pleasantly enough, but they were all firm. Lucille could not remember how many times she had heard them walk away growling about women taking too damn much time in the bathroom. And once, during that first fantastic week, she forgot to lock the door. She was indulging in a long, hot bath with plenty of suds, the way she liked, when Tad came in and sat down on the edge of the tub. She was too astonished to protest. Certainly Tad saw nothing out of the way in it.

He crossed his long legs, lit a cigarette, and leaned his head against the wall. He shot a quick glance of appraisal at her face only, and then looked up at the ceiling.

"Look here," he began easily, "you've been around a week or so now . . . done a pretty good job as far as I can see . . . lots better than I expected. There's just one thing worrying me."

"Couldn't we worry about it later, after I've finished my bath?"

"No. It's something I want to get settled right now. Keith and I were talking about it. I hate loose ends in my mind."

Lucille could believe that; Tad always reminded her of a saber, neat and lean and polished to perfection. She had suspected that his graceful, almost careless, way of lounging in a chair gave no indication of his mind. No, a better guide to his intenseness was the way he always climbed the stairs—two at a time.

"Are you getting around to saying that I'm a loose end?"

"You might be. Supposing we don't go for this air-mail business."

"Well?"

"We'd go back to barnstorming then. What would we do with you?"

She wanted to ask him why he didn't let Colin worry about that; then she thought of the way he said "we"—and she knew that this attitude was exactly what she had been hoping for. Here was a sign, however slight, that she was being accepted. She looked up at him and smiled.

"I guess I'd just go along . . . if I was invited."

"Ho—you couldn't do that!"

"Why not?"

"Living in tents? Eating when you get around to it . . . sleeping on the ground sometimes. . . ." He looked down at her and his dark eyes flashed with mischief. "Never getting a hot bath . . . well, hardly ever. Ho—you couldn't stand that!"

She snapped back instantly, almost rising above the suds in her quick anger. "Ho yourself! I could too! And I will if I have to. Now get out of here with your loose ends!"

He rose slowly, taking his time as he sauntered to the door. "You mean that? You'd go?"

"Of course I mean it. I married Colin, didn't I? As long as he wants me I'll tag along wherever he goes."

He paused at the door and scratched his chin reflectively. A reluctant smile crept across his mouth.

"You know," he said, as if reviewing the whole matter, "maybe there *are* some good women after all. You're beginning to sound like a real MacDonald." Then he winked at her in a way that seemed to seal their understanding, and left her alone.

When she told Colin about the interview, he only laughed. That, thought Lucille at the time, is *my* husband.

No one asked Lucille whether she liked double beds. The first she knew about theirs was on the afternoon of the wedding, when it arrived and was promptly set up under the puffing supervision of Porkie Scott and Roland. They had a drink on the matter when it was done. Lucille preferred not to remember her wedding evening, with the spasmodic dynamite explosions lasting until the police came. But that was past. Now she looked about the room, feeling for the first time as if she were something more than an overnight guest.

Her efforts at homemaking were another thing: she just couldn't make an impression. Her brush and comb and a few bottles of perfume were on the dresser. Her dresses and a new gray suit were hanging with Colin's clothes in the closet. A precious ivy plant, barely tolerated by the brothers, was on the window sill. Those were the only changes she had succeeded in making. Roland had moved his phonograph out of the room, but most of the records were still stacked in the corner. When he wanted to play some particular one, he would come in and search through the stack for it, regardless of what was going on. A set of dumbbells, manipulated on very rare occasions by Tad, lay beside the records. On the clothes tree were a leather flying jacket, which she thought belonged to Keith, a helmet, and a pair of goggles with one cracked lens.

In ten minutes, perhaps fifteen if she took her time, she could be packed and gone forever and no stranger would know that she had ever been in the room. It made her feel useless and unimportant when she thought of it—but she did not want to leave. She snuggled down a bit in the double bed and felt certain of that.

It was their first night apart. The flying had begun. The brothers had been busy at the field for days, and had come home each time a little more thoughtful and absorbed, less inclined to slap her smartly on the bottom by way of greeting. She made no attempt to pry into their thoughts, believing that they would speak them when the time came. She saw that they were not afraid or brooding, but only thinking about things they could not yet share with her.

Then one by one they went off—not in haste, not neglecting to kiss her, each in his own fashion, but this was different from the way they had always left before.

First Roland, then Tad. They were in Albany or Buffalo or somewhere in their mystifying heights between, and they would be back tonight or tomorrow night—she didn't know which. Then Colin: he had said he would be back—soon. Now only Keith was left, and tomorrow he would go too. Lucille was discovering various ways to say good-bye.

"Take it easy," Colin said.

"I will." Lucille remembered she had managed to smile.

"Don't run away."

"Why not?"

"I find I need a wife. Good thing to have around. It gives me something to worry about."

"I need a husband. Come back. Fast."

He smiled at that and kissed her lengthily, even pushing her back toward the bed until she said something about the time.

"Sure it will keep?" he asked.

"It'll keep. Colin, what a thing to say!"

As she covered her mouth he laughed at her. Then he gathered up his jacket, his helmet, goggles, and gloves. She blew him a kiss that hurt when he jogged down the steps. Then she prayed a little.

She took up her book again. She stared at it without reading. The book only made her think of Roland and the way he had given it to her, in challenge. The surly bear. Roland was untouchable, like a high priest. Yet if Colin were not around, if something happened to him this night or any other night, Lucille felt that she would go to Roland. And Keith? She found herself studying the clock on the dresser. Where was he? It was not late, but where was he? She had not heard him rushing up the stairs as he always did, or whistling "Show Me the Way to Go Home" as he always did when he made ready for bed. She looked at the clock again. One—almost five after. A boy like Keith should be in bed. Tomorrow he was flying. A boy. She was surprised that she felt the way she did about him.

And here, so close to her in this room, was Colin. His things: his hat, bent and beaten, his spare shoes piled grotesquely on the closet floor. She could shine those shoes tomorrow. There was some paste on the shelf, but she would have to go out and buy a brush. His ties were hanging like wrinkled, tangling vines on the closet door. She would press those tomorrow. Mrs. A would lend her the iron again. Valet? —well, maybe, but doing it for Colin was fun. And she would straighten out his drawer in the dresser. It was a mess of his small possessions. Colin was not the kind of man to acquire many. There were photos of the Flying Scots, keys to things he had long forgotten, a tie clip, a worn wallet, a broken cigarette lighter, badges of admission to various state fairs, a fountain pen that leaked, some old letters, a pipe she had never seen him smoke, a hunting knife, some clean handkerchiefs, and, she remembered suddenly, a photograph of a very pretty girl. She wondered briefly why Colin had not put it away when they were married, and then she decided not to care. No, she would not touch the drawer. Those were entirely Colin's things. They weren't like his ties and shirts and shoes—half hers, reminders of him when he was away. There was a difference, she reasoned, narrow but important.

She had no idea when she fell asleep. When she awoke, the light was still on and the book still lay open at her side. Someone was knocking on the door. Keith was calling her name over and over, his voice sounding thick and miserable. She looked quickly at the clock. It was three.

"Yes—what's the matter?"

"I dunno. Could you come here? I—"

Before he had finished she was out of bed. She slipped on her robe and opened the door.

Keith was leaning weakly against the wall by the bathroom, holding his hands over his eyes. His collar was torn open and his face was wet and white. There were nasty-looking smears of food on his shirt front. The smell sickened her. She pulled at his hands.

"Keith! What's the matter?"

"I dunno . . . I dunno!" He kept repeating the words almost hysterically. Then he tore himself away from her and lurched into the bathroom, vomiting wildly as he went. She followed him and held his head. When it was over, she bathed his face and neck with a cold towel. He kept shaking his head and reaching clumsily for her. Then he began to vomit again, but little came of it, and then he subsided into a steady, hollow retching that made him fight for breath. When finally he could speak again, he only repeated her name, whimpering like a small, beaten dog. Then she realized he was not really drunk.

She led him to his bed and made him lie down. When he had quieted and his breathing was easier, she asked him what had happened.

"I ran into Poppy. She's here with a show," he said, as if

that explained everything. He reached for her hand and squeezed it roughly. Then he rocked his head on the pillow and began to whimper again.

Lucille brushed back his hair. She wanted to call Dr. Timothy, but she was afraid to leave Keith for even a few minutes. She began to undress him.

"Who is Poppy?" she asked, when he relaxed again.

"Poppy Samonetta . . . she played lots of the same fairs we did. High diver. Sings, too. Nice gal. I took her to the movies. Felt all right then. Went back to her room after. She had a bottle. Wanted us to have a drink for old times' sake. Wanted to know all about Tad, and especially Colin. Never liked Roland. Wanted to know all about you, too. She used to be sort of crazy about Colin. . . ."

"Sounds like a nice gal," Lucille said, hating her. Then the way Keith held his hands to his eyes banished every other thought. "Did you drink with her?"

"Some."

"How much?"

"Just a couple."

"What was it?"

"Gin . . . sorta."

"Then what?" She asked the question softly and calmly, against the dread that was growing within her.

"I left. Started home. Don't know what happened. I felt awful sick . . . all of a sudden. . . ." He began to rock his head again.

"What time did you leave her?"

"About midnight. I got sick on the street and then—" His whole body stiffened; he took his hands from his eyes and looked at her. "Lucille . . . ?"

"Yes, Keith."

"Have you got all the lights on?"

"No, dear—just the one by the bed."

He turned his head and blinked toward the light. "I . . . I can't see it very well, Lucille. Do you think . . . ?" His voice broke and he began to sob. Then he began to retch again.

Lucille whipped back the covers and led him quickly to the bathroom. She knew what she had to do now: get rid of as much of the poison in him as possible and then call Dr. Timothy. It didn't take very much bad alcohol—everybody in America knew that. Thank God, he hadn't had very much. She wondered about the girl Poppy; maybe she hadn't known the liquor was bad.

She stuck her fingers deep in his throat and with the other hand pressed hard on his stomach. When the spasm was over, even though she was afraid he was going to faint, she made him a physic and insisted on his forcing it down. Finally she led him back to bed. He was talking both to himself and to her, incoherent and bewildered.

"If I can't see! If I can't see!" He said it over and over again. Then he began asking for Tad and Roland.

"They're away."

"No—don't go away. Please!" He reached for her desperately.

"Don't worry, dear. I'll stay right here." She cushioned his head, very hot now, against her bosom.

"If I can't see . . . I'll never fly again. I won't fly, Lucille. . . . They just won't let me fly."

"Try to rest now, Keith. You'll see—in a little while."

"Are you sure?"

"I'm sure." She was guessing. Maybe. It depended.

"If I can't fly again . . ."

He was mumbling the secret fear of all pilots, a fear that lies like a small, sharp stone deep within each one of them. Fear of something, some time: a heart that skips now and then, a kidney giving trouble, a sliver of steel in the eye caught as one walks down the street—these were things mentioned seldom and then only in quiet awe, as the ancients spoke of witchcraft. It was not like death, for death was spoken of freely, with grudging respect; it was familiar and definable. But a sickness—something that might strike them on the ground—was an unknown evil spirit capable of transforming them into groundlings. It was a thing of terror, and Keith had mentioned it in spite of himself. The words were hot and melting in his mind.

"If I can't fly again . . ."

It was dawn before he slept. During the night he vomited many times. Lucille was glad he did, though she had to lead him from the bed and almost carry him back. And once, in his delirium, he had a bowel movement. She cleaned him and changed the sheets, not daring to leave him even long enough to telephone or to rouse Mrs. A. But at least his young body was throwing off the poison, and that was the important thing.

At last, exhausted, she lay down on the bed beside him, half-awake, listening to his labored breathing. Then she fell into a troubled sleep. When she awoke, his head was still in her arms and the noises in the street were beginning.

Dr. Timothy came soon after she called him. He hummed tum-te-dee-dum several times and was very serious. There wasn't much they could do, he said, except wait. He decided against a stomach pump when Lucille told him about the night. It was much too late anyway, he thought.

By that time Keith was totally blind. He lay very still, his hand clutching Lucille's tightly. He said nothing except sometimes to ask for water. Lucille could only guess what he was thinking. She prayed that Colin or Tad or Roland would come home soon so they could talk to him. She called Gafferty and told him Keith would not be able to fly for a few days; he had eaten something that had disagreed with him. And that was all she said.

In the yellow light of evening, Madame Moselle sat on the steps of her red wagon and watched the town lights come on one by one. Seeing the houses light up gave her a rare sense of living with settled people, and she liked to imagine it was herself who switched them on.

She dealt and redealt the cards, peering at them with difficulty in the dusk.

When at last she slipped the cards back together with her practiced fingers, she had lost the feeling of being a part of anything, even the houses. The indications were obvious to her, and she accepted them with quiet resignation, as she had always done.

Madame Moselle had not rerented the bunkroom. She had left it exactly as it was the morning the MacDonald brothers kissed her on the forehead and went away. For a long time she had hoped they would come back to her and make her days and nights happy and lively again.

But now they were never coming back. And there was nothing, nothing, nothing she could do about it.

Thus, as night came, she surrendered to her now old and certain feelings. It was time to rent the bunkroom. They would never be back, not Keith, nor Colin, nor Tad, nor blessed Roland—either alone or together.

## 9

They sat in the model-T Ford roadster the brothers had bought with money they had wheedled out of Gafferty. This project had required endless figuring on paper, and hurried, heated conferences on those few occasions when the brothers had been together. Since they flew away or arrived back at Newark at different times, the original scheme had been to shuttle the car back and forth. Whoever drove the car to the airport would leave the key hidden under the seat. The next arriving brother would then pick up the car and drive it to Mrs. A's when he landed. Only the plan didn't work. The car was invariably in the wrong place at the right time, owing to petty complications for some reason or other inseparable from the life of pilots. There were accusations and explanations, and more drawing of lines on paper, with A being here and B being there, shortly after the arrival of C, who would turn the car over to D. It made absorbing nonsense.

It was finally Lucille who solved the stubborn quadrangle by offering to drive them to the airport or pick them up—at least, when Colin was out of town. She said she did it to keep the peace, but that was only part of her reason; what she did not say was that she had trouble sleeping when Colin was gone. And there was another reason that she had trouble explaining even to herself. Like this very early morning with Keith beside her.

First of all, he was well now. He was able to lean his head against the back of the car seat and smile up at the stars. She was proud of this, and prouder yet of the feeling of closeness she had found with Keith. She felt it in the way he came to

*Model T Ford Roadster*

her with little things when, after the first three days of darkness, he began to see again. There was a bond somewhere, but it was still ill-defined. She only knew that it had not weakened after his recovery. It might have been the way Keith had accepted her so completely, making her feel one of them. Or it might have been that she was a woman who had helped something helpless and so had come to love it.

This was to be Keith's first flight with the mail. She was strangely proud of that, too, although she was uneasy about his leaving.

"Terrible hour to get you up," he yawned.

"I'll sleep better when I get back to the house." She looked up at the stars with him. "Maybe I'll just wait here till you leave," she said.

"No, don't. Go back to bed. The mail won't be here till almost four. Anyhow, if you stuck around much longer, I'd have to talk to you and I'd get sentimental."

"About what?"

"About what you've done for me since that night."

"Forget it."

"No. I never will. I think you're pretty swell."

"Good."

"Tad and Roland think so too."

"You'd never know it."

"Don't mind them. They're . . . well, give them time."

"I will."

They sat quietly for a while then. Finally Lucille asked the question that had been so long on her mind.

"That girl . . . Poppy. What happened to her?"

"I dunno. Tad went to see her. She was sick and had a headache—that was all."

"That was all?"

"She said she was sorry. I think she moved to New York."

She wanted to ask him about Colin and Poppy—how well they used to know each other; but she decided it was none of her business.

"Aren't you afraid, Keith?"

"Humph! What of?"

"Roland said you haven't flown much at night. I think he was a little worried about you."

"Tell that guy the next time you see him that he's a regular old lady. I can take care of myself. Besides, nobody's flown very much at night, Roland or anybody else."

"All right. I was just asking." But from his quick speech she knew that he must be a little afraid.

"Nothing to it . . . like shooting fish in a rain barrel." He pinched her cheek lightly.

Then he slipped out of the car, tucking his toilet kit and clean shirt under his arm. He crushed his helmet jauntily over one ear and made a slow gesture with his hand across his face. He winked heavily, screwing up his mouth in a saucy way she could never forget.

"Take it easy. . . ."

"If you see Colin, tell him to hurry home!" she called after him.

He swung around and walked backward toward the hangar lights. "I'll tell him his old lady is waitin' for him!"

"Keith!"

"Take it easy, Lucille."

"I will," she said to herself. She stepped immediately on the starter because she had to do something to choke down a silly woman's premonition.

Keith let himself in through the hangar doors. He stood a moment looking at the older ships and breathing in the faint aroma of dope and fabric and oil that was as much a part of every hangar as the girders that held the roof. Then he bent and sidled between the wing tips of the clustered ships until he came to the new Pitcairn, sleek and glistening in the lights. But Keith was shocked at what he saw: the spark plugs were out of the engine, lying in a pan beneath it, and every rocker-box cover was removed. Eugene, one of Gafferty's four mechanics, was sitting astride the cowling just behind the engine, thoughtfully fingering a lead wire. Keith knew him as a glum, taciturn man, a former race-car driver—a sour man, but smooth and even in his actions like a well-oiled valve.

"Trouble, Eugene?"

"Don't know. Drops off two hundred revs on the left mag. Mebbe plugs, mebbe mags, mebbe a lead or two." With a downward glance he acknowledged Keith's presence, but his interest was inside the engine.

"Guess I won't be able to go, huh?"

"Why not?"

"Can you get it back together in time?"

"Don't mind if I do."

"How soon do you think?"

" 'Bout an hour."

"Okay. The mail will be here then."

"Dear Aunt Sadie . . . having a wonderful time . . . wish you were here. . . ." Eugene grumbled softly to himself.

Keith walked slowly around the ship, his eyes catching every flowing line from nose to tail. Gafferty's plan for every pilot to have his own ship had not materialized. His businessmen couldn't see it that way; it didn't make for utilization of the equipment, they said. But for this flight, this was Keith's plane, and he felt more than quasi-ownership in it. It was his charger for the time, and he believed that he could command it just a little better than any other pilot, even his

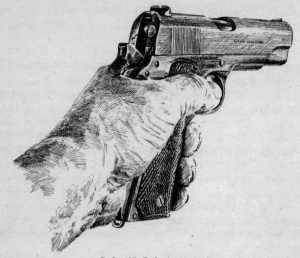

*Colt .45 Cal. Automatic*

own brothers. This was the kind of confidence that was so essential to his calling. It was never Keith who would fail. Never Keith who would be killed. It happened, of course—but always to the other fellow. Always. Entertaining any other thought was suicide. He walked back and stood beneath the engine again.

"You like these engines, Eugene?"

"It's a Wright, ain't it?"

That seemed to settle the matter as far as Eugene was concerned, so Keith glanced at his watch and walked away. It was almost three-fifteen.

He went into the little office below Gafferty's on the ground floor of the hangar. A young man of about Keith's age sat behind a counter working on an aircraft logbook. Keith had heard about him. He was Jewish and the brothers liked him. He worked interminable hours at tasks no one else wanted to do. What was more important, he never failed to have a good story, and since he told his stories with considerable talent, he was invaluable. He was never out of temper. He was thin and soft-eyed and his name was Sydney.

"You're Keith MacDonald, aren't you?"

Keith smiled and held out his hand.

"I just called the post office," the other said. "The mail's on the way over. Be sure to sign the mail form when they load your ship, and keep the original. Here's your gun." He shoved a forty-five automatic across the counter.

Keith examined it gingerly. "Who'm I supposed to shoot with this?"

"Post Office regulation. If you're forced down in the mountains, maybe you can get yourself a venison steak with it. Who knows why the government does anything? Sign for the gun here. That's your chute in the corner; sign for that here. Here's your ship's logbook; sign for that here. Here's the maps of your route. You don't have to sign for them. I don't know why—somebody must have forgotten."

When Keith had finished scribbling his name, Sydney asked him if he had ever been over the route before and Keith said that he had not.

"Who am I to tell you how to fly? Anyway, you go up the Hudson to Albany. The courses are all marked on the maps. Fellow by the name of Sweeney, a loafer if I ever saw one, will meet you if he's awake and take off what mail you have for him, and maybe put some more on. If he isn't awake, buzz hell out of the field and he may come to life. Tell him special for me, I said he was a loafer. Then you go to Utica, Syracuse, Rochester, and Buffalo. Behave yourself and get some sleep in Buffalo, because you'll probably start back here tomorrow night." He looked quickly at the wall clock. "What am I talking about? Tonight!"

"What about the weather?"

"A fair question. The United States Department of Agriculture says it will be good, which means it may be anything. Sweeney sends a wire down every night. He makes his observation from the hangar roof and before this clambake started he was an interior decorator, so you can take it for what it's worth. He said things looked good, whatever that means; he may have been talking about the colors of the sunset. Now, take this number and call it long distance on the 'phone: Kingston, New York, 47. You'll get a Mr. Baldwin. He's a farmer. Gafferty made arrangements with him to keep an eye on the weather, but be sure to apologize for getting him up. His farm is on a mountain and he can see a long way. Here." Sydney handed him the 'phone. "Already this is a crazy business."

Keith asked for the number and waited a long time. Finally a voice rasped faintly in the receiver.

"Yup!"

"Is this Mr. Baldwin?"

"Yup!"

"This is MacDonald, an air-mail pilot."

"Which one?"

"Keith."

"Don't know ye."

"I'm sorry to get you up."

"I was up anyway. Got a sick heifer. Up all night, as a matter of fact."

"How's the weather, Mr. Baldwin?"

"Good. Good. I can see clean over to Poughkeepsie. Plenty o' stars and no clouds 'cept for a few hangin' on the mountaintops. Bit cold though . . . temper'ture's forty even. Good weather fer this time o' year."

"Any wind?"

"How's that?"

"Any wind?"

"Yup. A little. North wind. Wanta know anything else?"

"No. Thanks, Mr. Baldwin. Hope the heifer's all right."

"She'll be all right come a day or so. It's the feed the mother gits these days."

"Good-bye, Mr. Baldwin."

"Good-bye."

Keith hung up when he heard the receiver click.

"Now you know everything," said Sydney.

Eugene had put the Pitcairn's engine back together again and the ship was standing in front of the hangar with the blocks under the wheels. It looked frailer now in the half-light from the hangar windows. The red and green riding lights on the wing tips and the small white light on the tail seemed very close together. The reflection of the airport beacon flashed periodically along the fuselage.

Keith put on a pair of white coveralls, leftovers from his barnstorming days. Then he slipped his arms into the shoulder straps of his parachute, leaving the leg straps undone; it was more comfortable to wait that way. He sat down on the chute, being careful to select a clean area in front of the hangar before he did so.

A car with the top down passed along the airport road, its body covered with names and bright sayings. In the flashing beacon, Keith caught a few: "Screaming Meemie"—"Bucket of Bolts"—"Queen Marie." The car was full of young people shouting and singing "Show Me the Way to Go Home," and because Keith was the same age—if anything, younger—he smiled, and caught up the tune from them. He hummed it softly to himself. He wondered for a moment what it would be like to go to college, like those young people, and have a car and girls and many things to talk about. It might be nice to be always around people his own age. Then he decided he wouldn't like it.

The mail truck came a few minutes before four. Two men climbed out and began loading the mail into the Pitcairn. They put it into the compartment just in front of the cockpit. Keith walked clumsily toward the ship, his parachute banging at the back of his legs.

One of the men handed him a mail form and a pencil. "Sign here, fella. One registered pouch."

Keith placed the form against the fuselage and wrote his name, feeling a new sense of importance.

"Nice night for flying, fella."

"Sure is."

The men climbed back into the truck and drove away. Keith was checking to make sure they had fastened the compartment door properly when Eugene came out of the hangar.

"Ready?"

"All set, I guess."

"Git, then. I want a cup of coffee."

Keith snapped his leg straps in place and climbed into the cockpit. He spent a few moments adjusting his safety belt, then slipped on his gloves. Eugene was standing in front of the propeller.

"Off?"

"Off."

Keith checked the magneto switch in the off position. Eugene stepped forward and pulled the propeller through a few turns. Then he stepped away from it to the wing tip.

"Contact!"

"Contact."

Keith worked the primer five pumps. He pressed the inertia starter switch and listened as a low whine came from the engine and climbed rapidly in pitch. When the whine reached its highest note and held there, he pulled the mesh lever. The gears squealed together with the surprised sound of a stuck pig. The propeller turned over very slowly and Keith switched the magneto to "both." Smoke shot out from the exhaust ports. The engine fired, then coughed, and finally settled to an even, flat blatting as Keith advanced the throttle.

He fastened the chin strap of his helmet as he waited for the oil pressure to fall to normal. He tried the controls, moving the stick and rudder pedals through the arcs of motion, then pulled his goggles down to make sure they fitted the way he liked them, and had a moment of impatient trouble adjusting the small light over the instrument panel. There was no place for his maps, so he slipped them between his leg and the seat. He did these things absently, for the Pitcairn was trembling now, vibrant and alive and tensing with energy. Keith knew and understood this mutual preparation, understood it better than he did the singing young people in the car.

He ran the stabilizer through its full travel and pulled the stick all the way back between his legs. The engine was ready now, so he advanced the throttle, calling forth its full power. He watched the tachometer wind round to 1950 revolutions per minute and, as it held there, the engine roaring and the ship shaking and eager, he checked both magnetos. Satisfied, he pulled back on the throttle until the engine was barely ticking over. He switched on the landing lights and saw Eugene blink against the glare.

"Chocks out!"

Eugene ducked beneath the wing and pulled out the wooden blocks in front of the wheels. He did not bother to wave as he turned away. Keith gave the engine a burst of power against full rudder and swung the ship around. The wheels rumbled slowly over the cinders toward the southeast corner of the field. The time was four A.M., April thirtieth, in the twenty-first year of Keith MacDonald's life.

At four-nineteen, he checked his position on the map—he was over Haverstraw, New York. Here the Hudson bent for the last time before it joined the sea. The street lights of the town made little puddles of yellow in the gloom below. As they slipped quickly beneath the wings, Keith fancied the town was moving while he sat still, suspended in night—a unit of the star scheme above him.

He breathed deeply of the night wind, laden now with the special, not unpleasant, smell of the engine's combustion. He watched the blue and purple exhaust flames licking back beneath the wing, then turned again to the stars, checking Polaris against the gently rocking compass. Polaris, the star that had guided men on all the seas in all the times. Arcturus, dangling brightly from the Dipper's handle. Saturn, retiring in dignity to the west. These were greater and more lasting things than the little river towns below, or even the river. They shone coldly, without favoritism, on villain and wretch and saint alike—and on young men like Keith, who at least was closer to them.

Bear Mountain grew and enlarged upon itself beyond the leading edge of the wing. Keith saw the first streak of day in the east. It pleased him to think that because of his altitude he was the first to see it. Those who slept below and even the few who might be awake would have to wait—if only a few moments longer than he did.

When Keith looked up from his map at four-forty-four, he was over Poughkeepsie. The propeller, turning at 1600 revolutions per minute, was now a distinguishable blur against the horizon. The stars were gone and the sun touched the cowling bright red. Every peak of the Catskills wore a scarlet cap.

He had made good time. Keith figured the wind had dropped almost completely—perhaps a bare five miles an hour on the nose. The air was perfectly smooth. He lightly touched the stick from time to time. He looked down at the earth, wet with morning dew, and wondered which of the neat little farms was Mr. Baldwin's. Then, as if his senses had awakened with the sun, he felt chilled and very hungry. It would be good to get to Albany.

At four-fifty-nine by the clock on the instrument panel, the sun was blazing full. At five-fifteen he was over Ravena. There was a smoke pall and a mottling of the landscape on the horizon ahead. That would be Albany. Keith nosed the Pitcairn down a trifle, beginning his descent. The air speed increased to a hundred and fifteen and the sound of the wind in the flying wires crescendoed.

Yes, there was Albany—according to time and space it had to be; but there was something before it in the area of rolling country to the south of town, where the airport should be. Keith forgot the sun and the blue river beneath him.

There were clouds hovering over the little hills near the airport. He could see now that they joined with others that lay low and flat to the west, along the valley of the Mohawk. If it were only ground fog, the companion of a still and early morning, he would feel better. In that case he would wait aloft until the sun's heat burned off the fog. It was an old trick. But these were heavier—real clouds—a leftover, perhaps, from a rain squall the night before, a leftover that no wind had bothered to blow away. And the annoying, the tempting, thing was that the clouds covered such a small area. The rest of the countryside was free.

Keith pressed the nose down farther and left the throttle alone. He put his head out against the slip stream, letting the wind tear at his cheeks. He was anxious now to discover the depth of those clouds.

And he had good reason to be anxious. The clouds were thick and settled-looking, gray-white like the backs of browsing sheep. The sun tinted their tops, setting off the slight rolls that separated them.

Keith knew that unless he was very lucky he had a problem on his hands—a problem the map makers hadn't foreseen. No one could help him, because his own skill alone guided his ship through space. The Pitcairn moved at destructive speed. It moved very smoothly in this morning air, in any direction, like a fish in a vast tank. Its direction and behavior could be controlled by the slightest touch of Keith's hands. But his hands were only party to the effort—they did not decide.

It was his senses, now perceiving and alert, that controlled his hands and feet. If those senses were blinded, the inadequacy of Keith or of any man in flight became at once apparent. The liquid in his ears, brushing against the millions of tiny hairs and through them telegraphing sensations to his brain, might send out the wrong signals and Keith's confused body would do the wrong thing. Or it might do something without his knowing it. If he were on the ground, he might fall off a chair, or turn without meaning to turn.

Now, in the air, he could cause his ship to move in any of the directions, without willing it. The birds knew this and so did Keith. The low clouds that hung over Albany airport could trick him into anything. The little turn-and-bank instrument on the panel was supposed to help protect him against this danger, but it demanded absolute faith, a trust that Keith could not bring himself to give.

So he swung the ship around in a wide bank over the hazy city and turned northwest along the Mohawk. It was ridiculous to think there might be betrayal in this morning's sunshine.

He turned back south toward the airport; he could see a corner of it now through a small hole in the clouds. He guessed there was perhaps a hundred feet of ceiling beneath the clouds. And the top of the water tank that Roland had warned him about was barely visible to the west of the airport.

It couldn't be so bad, then. Those clouds were hardly more than two hundred feet thick. If he could get a line on the airport itself—perhaps through that hole—he could turn away and come back again in a straight line, and so let down through the clouds. His senses would be blinded for only a few seconds; that he could manage. But he wished that the water tank were not so close to the airport. He must be very careful not to turn—even a little. He must keep his feet off the rudders. Then he wouldn't have the urge to push one, even if the seat of his pants told him to. If he got lined up just right, he couldn't miss. He mustn't miss. He circled the area again and laid his plans.

Of course he *could* go to another airport. Utica might be

open. He had plenty of gas. And to the north and south of Albany, on the other side of the river, there were plenty of open pastures. He could set down the Pitcairn in one of those and wait. And wait? On his first flight with the mail? One of the MacDonalds at his first destination, and the youngest one at that? Roland wouldn't say anything, nor would Colin or Tad, but they would think—because they weren't there at the time. They couldn't help thinking, when there wasn't another cloud in the sky except those few, exactly in the wrong place. By the time anyone got to looking around, those clouds would be gone and Keith would look like a proper young fool, sitting in some pasture, his wheels covered with cow dung.

Keith had been flying back and forth at three thousand feet. He smiled a little to himself when he thought of the questions and answers in his head, smiled and thought that he was getting to be a regular old woman. Too long on the ground— that was the trouble. If that hole would just stay put for five minutes longer, this thing was a setup.

He shoved the throttle forward and peeled off, straight down at the hole. The Pitcairn shook with speed. Just above the cloud tops, he hauled back on the stick. His cheeks sagged with the pressure. The Pitcairn zoomed back for the sun. Keith could hear little change in the sound of the engine, but he knew that on the ground it would sound like a thousand buzz saws. That would wake Sweeney up. That would roll him out of bed. Then he would get up and look out the window and see the ceiling and go back to bed. He would be a surprised man when Keith came rumbling in. Keith would be casual about it; just climb out on the ground and act as if there was nothing to it. Maybe ask for a cup of coffee or something like that. People would come to know about the MacDonalds. . . .

He was south of the airport at two thousand feet. He turned north on a compass course of ten degrees and held it. He pulled the throttle back and began descending. He crossed over the airport. The hole was still there, just big enough to show the end of the hangar.

He held his course for three minutes. Exactly three minutes. Then he turned back south on a course on one hundred and ninety degrees. He pushed the nose down again, descending slowly until his wheels were just brushing the cloud tops. There was not a ripple in the air, which made it easy to hold his course. Now, for two minutes—then shove her right down through to the ground.

He took his feet off the rudders and put his head out of the side, feeling the hard wind against his face. He'd have to watch it now. At a hundred miles an hour, things happened fast.

Two minutes. He shoved the nose down and was immediately enveloped in the clammy gray overcast. The Pitcairn tossed and heaved, not badly, but more than he had counted on. It made the compass swing round. Keith tried not to move a muscle. He had started out right. He would come out right if he could hold it. But the first thirty seconds seemed a very long time.

He could see the wing tips, but they were obscured and unfamiliar-looking. The dank clouds threw a mist at his goggles and for a moment he could see nothing. He quickly shoved the goggles up on his forehead. Now, with the wind tearing at his unprotected eyes, he retreated behind the windshield. That movement, slight though it was, made him dizzy.

He was going down—fast. He knew that. The altimeter was unwinding rapidly. When it reached three hundred feet, he pulled back a little on the stick. The altimeter stood still. He dared not go any lower. He glanced at the compass. Damn it! The compass was swinging dreamily. He touched his foot to the rudder and tried to stop it. The compass spun. He was in a bank, or turning—how much he could not tell. But the thirty seconds were up. The airport should be here—now—this second, beneath his wheels. But he was still in the clouds. Little patches of ground were slipping swiftly beneath him.

Keith was afraid now. There was that tight feeling in his stomach. His hand closed over the throttle. It was time to get out of this place—back up into the sunlight where he could breathe and live again and think things over.

Another patch of ground. Looked as if it would take only another fifty feet. He pressed his lips together and shoved the nose down. This would be it. Boy, would Sweeney be surprised! Yet still the clouds. The hanging tendrils, gray, and whipping past. Ten seconds. No longer. An age—get out! That water tank. Get out, fella! Get out fast! Two hundred and fifty feet—Jesus! Get out! He slammed the throttle full forward and hauled back on the stick.

Keith held his breath. In a murky flash he saw it—too late. The right wing tip hit the black thing with a sickening crunch. Keith was slammed against the instrument panel. The Pitcairn screamed as if in agony, and then began to shake wildly. Keith brought his bloody head back for an instant. Over half the right wing was bent back and crushed together. He knew it wasn't any use, but he reached for the controls that had been torn from him. Then everything exploded. He hit the ground viciously. Every part of his body felt it, but only for a moment. There was dirt in his mouth and in his eyes. The instrument panel was all crazy and broken. Packets of letters were everywhere. There was absolute silence. Then he smelled smoke, and somewhere the sly, beginning crackle of flames. That was the last sensation Keith MacDonald had. The time was five-forty-six A.M.

**10**

Mr. Gafferty?''

"Yes."

"This is Sydney."

"What's the trouble, Sydney?"

"The five-o'clock schedule. Roland MacDonald was sup-posed to take it out. He hasn't shown up and no one knows where he is. Time's wastin'!''

Gafferty turned from the 'phone and studied the wall clock. It was four-thirty. He looked out the window, appraising the weather. The late afternoon sun burned a hot red spot in the heavy haze, but there was not a cloud in the sky. Canceling the schedule was out of the question. The almighty Post Office Department, the feeding hand of the airlines, would never stand for that. There had already been cases where pilots, sometimes in collusion with their companies, deliber-ately took off in impossibly bad weather, only to circle the airport tightly and land at once again, thereby recording an "attempt." Thus the company kept its record and the pilot collected his pay for the flight. Such practice went along with officials' mailing registered letters to each other and enclos-ing an occasional telephone book for good measure. These were among the sometimes desperate and often ludicrous efforts to increase pay loads. Gafferty did not operate that way. The five-o'clock trip would leave on schedule if he had to fly it himself. Gafferty smiled thinly when he thought of that. Hmm—it had been a long time.

"I said time's wastin', Mr. Gafferty."

The 'phone receiver rattled in Gafferty's hand. Good

Sydney. He was going right ahead, as if nothing—"I know."

"Ten against five, Roland isn't going to show up either."

"I can hardly blame him. Who's next in line?"

"Colin MacDonald."

"Oh. . . ."

"There's no one but MacDonalds in town. You fixed it that way so they could all go to the funeral together. Juggled the schedules on me, remember?"

Yes, Gafferty remembered. And he had gone himself and wished he hadn't.

It wasn't that anyone said anything much. It might have been different if it had been one of the older brothers. But Keith—he was the one they had all looked after. To hear any mature man sob is a terrible thing, but somehow in a big, heavy, muscular man like Roland it was even worse. He had made no attempt to hide his sorrow; perhaps he knew it would be useless to try. The tears rolled down his big red jowls and his unshaven chin. His shoulders sagged. His breathing, so noticeable in the stillness, came in short, caught gasps. From time to time he would reach out and touch Lucille's hand, and that seemed to give him some comfort.

"It's my fault," he kept saying over and over again, and there was nothing they could do to stop him.

Tad had stood very rigid behind them all. His strong square hands, the hands that had held Keith's weight so many times, were clasped before him. He did not cry, at least not that anyone could see, but Gafferty noticed his dark eyes were dead as if staring through the casket and far beyond. His face was pale and Gafferty thought he looked very tired. He didn't even say thank you when Gafferty tried to offer to do anything more that he could.

Colin had sat on the edge of his chair, his face buried in his hands. Once he said, "Maybe somebody ought to sing 'Just a wee doch-an-dorris.' Keith would certainly like it"—but he did not finish. Lucille stood behind him, tall and lithe and starched-looking as always, with her hand on Colin's shoulder. Gafferty suspected that she had unconsciously eased some of her own grief through her concern for Colin.

When the dapper little undertaker came in and solicitously

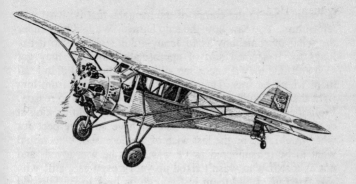

*Curtiss Robin*

explained the details of the funeral arrangements, Gafferty thought she was going to break. She wavered a little and worked her lips tightly against each other like a wounded creature holding back a cry of pain; but then she seemed to shake her head—though Gafferty could have sworn she made no actual movement—and she became composed again.

The casket was closed, of course, as practically all pilots' caskets had to be. By the time Gafferty reached Albany they had taken Keith away. Porkie Scott landed about an hour after the crash and helped Sweeney and the men who had found him. Porkie called Buffalo on the 'phone and at last reached Colin and Tad. They borrowed a Curtiss Robin from a man whose chief claim to flying knowledge was his managership of the Buffalo airport hamburger stand, and flew full throttle to Albany. They jumped from the Robin demanding to see Keith, and it was a long time before Porkie could dissuade them.

"I told them they hadn't any right to see him," Porkie said when Gafferty finally arrived. "They didn't know it and they never will know it, but we had him wrapped up in a piece of tarpaulin over in the corner of the hangar—that is, what was left of him. You saw how the ship burned. We laid him under the wing of somebody's old Jenny—don't know who it belongs to. It seemed sort of appropriate. Anyway, they got mad and said they'd knock me all over the field if I didn't tell them where he was. They were standing fifty feet from him right then. I finally got them to sit down and listen to reason. I told them nobody but strangers ever had any right looking at dead bodies, and for God's sake to have some respect for what would sure be the last wish of the deceased, who would want to be remembered as he was when he was loved, and not as a stiff who wasn't fixed up yet or even as a stiff who *was* fixed up. I told them just you go on back to Buffalo and take your regular schedule out and remember the way Keith turned up his nose and smiled and said 'Take it easy' to you the last time you saw him. That's how I put it, and I think I did right. That's the way I would have wanted to remember Keith. It was just my rotten luck that I had to land so soon after, and—well, I can't quite remember him the way I'd like to. Before Colin and Tad went away I told them he wasn't banged up bad at all, that just a little blow on the back of the head must've killed him—couldn't have suffered one second. They insisted on going up to see the wreck, and I guess they knew then I was lying. But they went back to Buffalo, and you know the rest. I didn't have so much trouble with Roland when he came. Roland's been at this game a long time. He didn't ask to see anything. He knows better.''

Roland and Colin and Tad, somehow even closer together now. Gafferty envied them, even in their grief. He sat with them as long as he could stand it, and then went away. He could not explain his real sorrow any more than he could explain with certainty the cause of Keith's death.

But why get so upset about it? After all, Keith was just another pilot. Gafferty was very much aware that they couldn't all die in bed. You did the best you could and kept the average down—that's all. It would have been a little easier, of course, if it had been one of the old-timers; Gafferty would have felt less responsible.

But someone had to fly the schedule tonight. His mind came back to Sydney.

"How about Tad MacDonald?" he said into the 'phone. Of the three, Tad had seemed the least affected, perhaps because his face was so hard and set to begin with.

"I'll try him."

"No. I'll do it. What's the number?"

Sydney read it off and Gafferty asked the operator for it.

Tad was lying face down on his bed. He had done everything he could think of and made out fairly well until he came to Keith's smaller possessions, kept in a battered suitcase in the corner of their room. Tad found among them things he had half-forgotten—things that meant as much to him as they must have to Keith. Things that were now of value beyond his belief. He had knelt by the suitcase a long time taking out the objects one by one, setting them carefully on the floor around him, and remembering.

There was the harmonica that Keith never quite mastered, except for one tune, "Just a wee doch-an-dorris," which he said was so simple anyone could play it. Tad remembered the afternoon Keith won the harmonica at the Minnesota State Fair. They had never been foolish enough to play the various carnival concessions, but there was one that had always fascinated Keith, where for a nickel you could swing a big mallet at a lever and send a piece of iron up a pillar to ring a bell. If you rang the bell, you won a prize. Keith, so deceptively strong for his age, grinned and spat on his hands and rang the bell three times. He chose the harmonica instead of a Kewpie doll, and for a long time afterward none of them had any peace.

Here was a knife that had once belonged to Tad himself. Keith's eighteenth birthday had come along just when they were flat broke that winter in Humboldt, Kansas. The sheriff had a lien on their planes. Roland would go to a little Greek restaurant and order one complete meal. Such an order included the bottle of ketchup on the table and an unlimited supply of bread. Then Colin and Tad and Keith would join him casually. They would spread the ketchup on the bread, which was filling, and divide the meal four ways. The scheme worked admirably until the proprietor refused them further service. Then they had to shift their operations to a Chinese restaurant where there was no free ketchup. They all lost weight, but Keith received a birthday present—Tad's knife, wrapped appropriately in a paper napkin.

Keith's logbook was here, with the hours and minutes of his life aloft carefully recorded and summed up to the day of his last flight. Here was part of a correspondence-school course in English composition. Colin had given him that; he always felt that Keith should have more schooling. They used to argue about it until far into the night—but Keith had never done much with the course, and none of them could blame him.

Here was an envelope full of snapshots. Their mother, whom even Tad hardly remembered. Their father, whom he could not remember at all. Two snaps of Keith and Poppy Samonetta standing by her diving tank. Another snap of Keith and a girl Tad did not recognize. Here was a tie pin shaped like an airplane propeller. A drawing of a plane Keith designed and swore would win every race if he could only get someone to build it. Keith should have done more drawing. He was very good at it. A box of twenty-gauge shells. A pair of gloves and an old white helmet. Not much—not much to leave behind, even if a life did extend over only twenty-one years.

Tad must have fallen asleep on the bed, for he did not hear Mrs. A come into the room. When he opened his eyes she was standing over him and he could see that she had been crying.

"You're wanted on the 'phone," she said. "I told them to wait. I didn't think you'd want to talk to anybody."

"Who is it?"

"The airport, I think."

"All right. I'll talk to them." He rose slowly from the bed and went down the stairs.

Mrs. A had never seen Tad walk so slowly, but when he reached the 'phone he straightened and somehow the metallic hardness came back to his voice.

"This is Gafferty. How are you feeling?"

"All right."

"Any idea where Roland is?"

"Wandered off somewhere. Said he wanted to help Keith into heaven. He said Keith would understand."

"Is Colin with Lucille?"

"Yeah."

"You're all alone?"

"Yeah . . . alone. What do you want?"

"We're in a jam, Tad." Gafferty hesitated. "Somebody's got to fly this five-o'clock schedule. I don't like to call you, but—"

"Why not?" Tad's voice was cold.

"Could you make it?"

"Sure."

"Hop in a cab, then. We'll have everything ready to go. And . . . and . . . thanks."

Tad hung up the 'phone and somehow felt happier. Keith would want him to go just like this . . . as if nothing much had happened. But when he turned back up the stairs, he took them only one at a time.

After Gafferty finished talking to Tad, he sat back and lit a new cigar and wondered that Tad had agreed to go. Still, Gafferty had known his kind before. Flying was full of them. They simply did not require the powerful elixir of companionship. They had few friends. They seemed content with valor and lived with it as with a mistress. While most men alone were naturally timid, there were always the Tads who went unerringly on their own. But even the Tads, since they were seldom men of pale imagination, took their valor diluted, in the sense that they had at least the company of inspiration. Sometimes it was love of country, or of faith, or even of a woman. But for Tad himself Gafferty was sure it was none of these things.

As he got up from his desk and put on his hat, he found himself wishing that he could be as hard as Tad. It was useless wishing, and Gafferty knew it. Not alone with valor. Not he, Gafferty. Like most men, he preferred valor to be a chance acquaintance, met in company if at all—a meeting to be politely avoided if possible.

Gafferty wanted to be with Roland now. He was sure he knew where to find him. He wanted to be with Roland because *he* would understand; of that, Gafferty felt certain. Although they had wrangled and disagreed, there was a bond now—a very strong and strange one that came from a complete understanding of the mistress they served. It would be the same with Colin or Porkie Scott or Shorty Baker.

How could they love a way of life that killed and sometimes maimed and forever tried them? Now Gafferty felt like spitting upon it. He reviled this faithless love that held them captive—that seduced clean, slow-smiling youths like Keith MacDonald and then dashed them violently against the earth they had fought so hard to leave. Gafferty had known twenty, thirty, fifty Keiths so fated. But he had never been able to harden himself against their passing. Each one, he had tried to tell himself, was part of the pattern—a sacrifice to a wonderful endeavor that would some day be justified. But what achievement could vindicate the loss of a single Keith?

When was the payoff coming, the compensation for the lives these Keiths might have led? Where was Keith's wife, for example, and his home, and his children? That girl on the street now, strolling in the May sun just ahead. She looked about the right age. She probably lived in Newark. It was conceivable that Keith might have met and married her. That very girl. Would they have had a brown house or a white house? Now, they would have no house. She—yes, that girl—would never come to flower under Keith. Perhaps under someone else, but not Keith. He was scratched. Out of the race. A dud, fired and forgotten. If it wasn't that girl, then it would be some other girl who would miss Keith forever, without ever having known him. And their children, whatever their number, were already slain within him.

It was a stinking business, thought Gafferty—a forlorn, impossible business. Why in Christ's name couldn't he have been a chief butcher, or a baker, or a candlestick maker? Or a banker with nice neat rows of young clerks to frown on in the mornings? Then if they died, it would be because of overwork, or overdrink, or overstale air, and be damned to them. Be damned is right. To be resolute alone, Gafferty found again, was an extremely unpleasant experience.

He found him at Romeo's. Roland was leaning against the bar like a buttress. There was a pile of money in front of him. He held his glass as if someone might snatch it from him. His bushy eyebrows were arched and he was studying the contents of the glass minutely. Drunk, thought Gafferty. Very drunk.

Except for Roland, the bartender, and a few people sitting at tables back in the shadows, the place was deserted. Gafferty moved along the bar until he stood beside Roland. He asked the bartender for a whisky and soda. Roland looked up when he heard his voice, though he gave no greeting.

Gafferty sipped his drink in silence. An energetic newborn May fly buzzed frantically up and down the bar. The people in the shadows seemed to have little to say. The bartender, with his fat, freckled arms folded across the top of his paunch, was thoughtfully sucking a toothpick. It was very quiet. Too quiet, except for that fly, thought Gafferty.

He watched Roland out of the corner of his eye until he had finished the contents of his glass. "Can I buy you a drink?"

"I'll buy my own." He pushed his glass forward.

Gafferty watched while the bartender poured Roland another drink. "I've shut up shop for the day. Felt a little drink would do me good, too."

"Can't you find anywhere else to have it but here?"

"Yes, but—"

"Well, stay the hell away from me. I know what you're thinking."

So that was it. No wonder he was drunk. "I wasn't thinking anything."

"I told the kid about that water tank. And I didn't lie about his hours. He had just what I said he did. Was a little short on night time, like I said."

"No one thinks it was your fault, Roland."

"We should've stayed with Madame Moselle. But, Jesus, he shouldn't have tried to shoot that low a ceiling. Sweeney said it was right down on the ground."

"It's one of those things. You'd have done the same thing yourself if you were Keith's age."

Gafferty knew that was not entirely the truth. Roland would have tried it regardless of his age. Age in flying was a very elastic matter. He had seen pilots supposedly of middle age do some of the damnedest things. In this breed, at least, recklessness was not allotted by age groups. And the older ones were just as cocky as the younger when they stuck their necks out without having them broken. Gafferty tossed off his drink and ordered another.

"I know why he got killed," said Roland. He was tipping the liquid in his glass slowly back and forth. "He almost made it. He must have been right in line with the field at one time—practically ready to roll his wheels. Then he turned toward that tank. . . ." Roland paused to wipe his hairy hand across his mouth. He spoke distinctly but very slowly, choosing each word with the care of a man whose mind was sodden. "But he didn't know he turned because it was so gradual. Just a little turn. Little . . . understand? It could have been the other way just as easy. He didn't know it, because he couldn't see."

"That's what we put those turn-and-bank instruments in there for." Gafferty wished he hadn't said that. Very few pilots trusted a turn-and-bank instrument completely. There were not enough additional aids to make their use practical. And the less said about what Keith should or could have done, the better—especially to Roland MacDonald. But to his surprise, Roland made no objection.

"Yeah, that's part right, maybe, but those things don't show a gradual turn good enough—the kind you'd be liable to make if you put a wing down just a little. You gotta have something that works like this drink. Look." He held the glass before Gafferty's face and tilted it slowly back and forth. "See the level of that top liquid? Well, suppose that was an airplane wing. It would do the same damn thing in relation to the earth's surface. Look. I tip it just a hair. Now, if you'd draw a line on the outside of the glass, level with the liquid, and watch that line carefully enough, you'd know right away when you had a wing down—no matter if you couldn't see a thing. Understand? You need something like that. Something that'll catch a guy's eye when his face is hanging out in the rain and the breeze and his eyes are busy somewhere else."

Roland tossed off his demonstrator and ordered another.

"A lot of people have worked on that idea. Why don't you do something about it?" said Gafferty.

"Me? I quit flying, Gafferty. Day before yesterday."

Oh, that ancient bluff! As well try to quit a bride at the altar, as well the hunter try to ignore the geese, the lush to deny fornication. Gafferty smiled within himself and ordered another drink. There was only one way he knew to handle Roland's hoary threat.

"When do you want to pick up your check?"

"Tomorrow. I'm busy today."

"Know of anyone we can get in your place? Someone good?" That should arouse his pride, anyway.

"Nope."

"What are you going to do?"

"Sell cars. Stutz cars. Good job. Big commission. Got the job this morning. Safe too." Roland looked at Gafferty and raised a menacing eyebrow. "What's wrong with that?"

"Nothing's wrong with it. Only you won't stick to it. Why, damn it, this thing is just beginning. We've got hold of a lion's tail and because we don't know it, half the time it swings us around. Look at that fellow Cobham in England. . . . Flew all the way to Cape Town in a DH. And how about the Army boys? . . . Around the world. How about Amundsen

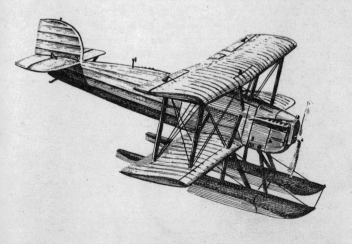

*Douglas DT-2*

up north tooling around in those Dornier-Wals? And this fellow Byrd? He and Floyd Bennett only a couple of weeks ago—over the North Pole! In a Fokker, at that. Don't you ever read the newspapers? This is the biggest thing since the invention of the wheel! I told you before, you aren't always going to fly these little ships. Some day you'll load 'em up with passengers and carry them all over the world—San Francisco, Canada, Los Angeles, Mexico . . . and it won't make a bit of difference how bad the weather is. Maybe even England and China and Africa. There'll be more airplanes and more pilots than you ever dreamed of. . . ."

"Gafferty!" Roland pronounced the name sharply. He tipped his head down and peered at him in open disgust. "Gafferty . . . you're drunk."

His look brought Gafferty back to Romeo's. Yes, the place *was* spinning a little. Maybe Roland was right. Sounded just like one of those crackpots.

"Mebbe," he admitted finally. "Mebbe . . . I *am* drunk."

## 11

Sunday evening, after Colin left for New York, Lucille had a long talk with Mrs. A, and finished by borrowing her sewing machine.

"Sure you can use it, dearie," Mrs. A said. She flashed her unreal white teeth and nodded knowingly. "Go ahead and fix up your place. It'll cheer things up for you. I know just how you feel, dearie, without a question of a doubt. Same as I felt when poor Nicholas went. Go right ahead any time you want."

So that was better. If she kept herself very busy, especially when Colin was away, then missing Keith would not hurt so much. She left Mrs. A sitting at the kitchen table, sipping contentedly on a bottle of her home-brew, and walked slowly up the stairs and sat down on the bed.

She would put up curtains in Roland and Tad's room first—very deep red material of some kind should do. They would probably kick like steers, but in time they would like them. Then there was so much she could do to their own room. Take down that picture of Daniel in the lions' den, for one thing, and that long framed series of Mrs. A's nephew when he was a baby—eight cute poses. The gold-framed poem "To Mother" hanging by the door was not exactly necessary, either—at least, not yet. She'd find some gay watercolors to replace these things. She'd have the photograph of the Flying Scots framed for Colin. He'd like that.

These little efforts at homemaking had to be carried through. She had to change this sense of being a transient—both in the rooms and in Colin's life. Colin wasn't going to wait around forever. *He* might, but his spirit would not—and Colin's spirit was not yet wed. It was a vital, handsome spirit, and unless she soon achieved some hold on it, the spirit would wander off elsewhere. Now it was, in a way, standing back and appraising her, willing but wary—and most of all, waiting. For what? She wondered about that. It was so evident that Colin was waiting, evident in the little things he did and the way he did them. She sensed this very definitely.

You could go through a wedding ceremony, but it did little more than legalize a few superficialities. It allowed a man and a woman to hang their clothes in the same closet and be seen sleepy-eyed at breakfast together, as a matter of course. People who were officially married could do with ease and assurance a number of things that were embarrassing and complicated for people who simply enjoyed being together. But the ceremony of the ring had nothing whatsoever to do with real marriage. Nothing. It did not guarantee that she would share Colin's life in any of its ramifications. She had a ticket of admission, and that was about all. She couldn't agree with Mrs. A, who was so fond of saying that she was a lucky girl because she had such a fine man. She couldn't agree because she knew that as yet she didn't have him.

Not that Colin ever found anything amiss—far from it; but he had not changed his way of life one iota since the day of their marriage. He had simply moved a girl into his rooms, making an honest woman of her while he was about it, and let things go at that. When he was away, Lucille could shift for herself. When Colin was home—and she smiled wryly when she thought of his "home"—she trotted around after him like a rather well-kept Pekinese. Since they always ate out, there was never any worrying about meals—except when Colin asked her where she would like to go. And no matter where they went, Colin always had steak and French fried potatoes. Most of the time they ate alone.

On the few occasions when Roland or Tad or Keith was in Newark at the same time, they had a sort of celebration, which Lucille enjoyed with all her heart . . . though her head invariably ached the next day. But even on these expeditions, which usually ranged from Porkie Scott's room to Harlem, she felt like a spectator rather than a participant. As simple as it should have been, she had never been able to harmonize with their heavy voices on "Just a wee doch-an-dorris"—at least, not to their satisfaction.

It would have been a little easier if she had met some other wives who enjoyed the same indeterminate status, but even this was denied her. Of the eight pilots based at Newark, only two were married, and one of them was Colin. The other she had never met—a Frank Sinnitch, whom she had heard about only vaguely. He lived on a chicken farm near Closter and was apparently noted for his silence. Roland said that he conducted most of his affairs in a personal sign language—a nod of his head meaning one thing and a wave of his hand something else. Lucille could only guess what his wife was like. They didn't sound very promising.

She stood up and walked over to the mirror, feeling the need to examine herself more carefully than usual. She wished there were some kind of mirror that would let her look inside, beyond her eyes that had not changed and her nose that had not changed, and her figure that was as embarrassingly tall as ever. So many things had happened in these few months—there had been so much ecstasy and sadness that there had to be some change. But the mirror, like all mirrors, was unrevealing. It ignored her problems altogether, showing her only as a gawky girl with a none-too-beautiful face.

This is what Colin married, she thought, and she honestly wondered why. The hair—confound her hair—looked no better than it ever had. The eyes perhaps had something, though now she seemed to detect in them a hint of fear and indecision. She skipped the nose with its freckles and came more happily to the mouth that Colin kissed so often and in so many ways. The mouth, said the mirror, was the best part of her face. It was large and warm and full, and sharply defined even without lipstick. Yet what that mouth would say, and what it had said, was not to be seen in a mirror. She tried to tell herself that it had said the right thing tonight—that for a bride, if she could still call herself that, the mouth had done fairly well. But like her eyes, it revealed some degree of uncertainty. At times a bride can feel very insecure; and this, Lucille said to the mirror, was one of those times.

Waiting to find out if she had said the right thing was the

worst of all. In a way it was a test of what she had accomplished in three months of marriage. It was a test she was by no means ready for, but it had been thrust upon her, and she had had to do something about it.

Colin had come to her that afternoon with the letter from Poppy. He handed it to her without saying anything.

Dearest Colin—

I read about Keith's death in the paper. It was a terrible shock to me, as I know it must have been to you. Please—I *must* know more about what happened.

I am rehearsing for a new show. They've been working us night and day and I just haven't had a minute to get to a telephone. So please, come to my apartment, at 114 Central Park West.

We have no rehearsal Sunday night, I'll be waiting for you about eight. I know I can depend on you, Colin.

Please come Sunday.

As ever,
Poppy

And this was Sunday night.

She had handed the letter back to him, trying very hard to look unconcerned.

"I suppose I ought to sit down and write it all out for her," he said. "She . . . used to be a pretty good friend of ours."

Lucille wanted to say that she couldn't see how a girl who passed out bad liquor could be considered a good friend, but she managed to hold her tongue.

"Don't you want to see her?"

"No . . . that's all gone now."

"Maybe you should. Maybe it would be better."

It would be better for *her* if this ghost of Poppy were buried forever. She was taking a chance if she sent him, but she would be taking more of a chance if he wanted to go and would not admit it.

"I'll write her a letter . . . when I get around to it."

"But you can't just let her sit there and wait for you."

"Why not?"

Well, that was it—she couldn't say why not. She could

explain for the next year and still not tell Colin why not. It was a sort of reasoning peculiar to women—unexplainable and hidden in her kind. It involved feelings that Colin could never follow. It went back a long time—a thousand years or so—and it was as necessary now as it was then.

"I think you should go see her," she said with finality.

So he left—reluctantly, but in time to keep the appointment. Lucille was alone with the brass rods that held the carpet to the staircase and the bronze statue of the discus thrower on the pedestal in the hall—and this time she was alone in a different way because of Poppy.

No matter how she fought it—the name alone disturbed her. Poppy. A brunette, of course—dark, luscious, probably small and full-bodied. The name created in her mind a person who was much too attractive. Probably Poppy could appear to know things she did not know and she would swing along with Colin's mind, whatever its direction. Yet that direction would be cleverly guided, and Colin would like it. Why shouldn't he like her? They had lived the same kind of life together. As a high diver she must have an understanding of physical danger unusual to a woman, and that would bring them together. Then there must be old times, old laughs, and old happenings to talk about.

Colin would not be home early. She might as well make up her mind to that. Undress and go to bed—and wait until his step sounded in the hall. Forget this Poppy. She had sent him to her, insisted when he said he didn't want to go—and now she could wait upon her rashness.

*Poppy had blue eyes. She was fatter than Colin had remembered her. She said she didn't get the exercise she had in the carnival, and she didn't seem to care. She even laughed about it and slipped into the infectious chuckle Colin had always liked. She said the chubbiness came from eating more regularly. Colin had almost forgotten her chuckle and the way she had of referring to herself in the third person— Poppy did this, and Poppy did that. But her hair was as red as ever, the golden red that had caused her father to name her Poppy.*

*Colin walked into the room, furtively using the back of his*

*hand to wipe off the welcome kiss she gave him at the door.
She took his hat and set it carefully between the two porcelain
guardsmen in the entranceway. Then she slipped her arm in
his and led him into the apartment. She said it would surprise
him, and it did, for the room was expensively furnished. One
wall consisted entirely of mirrors, and this was something
Colin had never seen before. The floor was heavily carpeted
in green, and he found it had a strange muffling effect upon
his voice. At first he sat very stiffly on the couch, exactly
where she told him to sit, and he said very little. She gave
him a cigarette and lit it for him, and asked him how he liked
the place.*

*"Fancy. You must have prospered. Not much like the old
days." He was thinking of the carnival wagon that once
housed Poppy and her acrobat father. Poppy—with the laundry hanging out of the rear of the wagon.*

*She chuckled and her deep blue eyes snapped with mis-
chief. "I'm a sinner, Colin," she said. "Poppy always was a
sinner. He's rich and old and awful lonesome—but he pays
the bills right on time."*

If Poppy was in some kind of show, she probably knew a
lot of interesting people. And show people ate late—Lucille
knew that. Maybe they would go out to dinner. But Colin
wouldn't care too much about the people unless they could
talk flying. Even so, he would be a curiosity to them—probably
not many of the interesting people had met an air-mail pilot.
For a time, at least, Colin might be the center of attention. He
would be asked to tell about his adventures, which he would
not do, but he would feel pleased just the same because he
was human and had been asked. Then sooner or later one of
the interesting people would ask him if he had ever crashed,
and Colin would say yes; and then one of the interesting
people was bound to ask finally whether he was married, so
that they could further ask whether his wife worried about
him, and where was she—and Lucille wondered what he
would say.

*They talked about Keith for a while. Colin didn't say
anything about the bad liquor.*

"Does Roland still dislike me?"

"Afraid he does."

"Tell the old bear to go to hell, then." But she said it without malice, in a merry way that made Colin laugh.

"What about your wife? What's she like? You never gave Poppy a chance, Colin. At least you could have warned a girl you were in a marrying mood. Tell me what she's like."

"It came on kind of sudden," he said, feeling embarrassed. He didn't want to discuss Lucille in this place. He hadn't come to talk of Lucille or of himself. "She's a grand girl."

"Plenty of 'it'—huh?"

He loathed the expression and it seemed everyone used "it" these days to describe everything. "That's not quite the description." No, it certainly wasn't. At least it would be well to get the right description. It seemed important, somehow.

"Do you love her?"

The sudden question astonished him. One thing about Poppy—she never pulled her punches. She thought as directly as any man, and thus certain men like Colin found it easy to admire her.

"Yes."

"Then say it. Come on, are you afraid to tell Poppy?"

"Say what?"

"Say you love her, if you do. In front of me. Then I'll know you do."

He looked at the mirrored wall and the image of his face reddened. He didn't know why it was so very hard to speak the words, yet it was. He felt ashamed that they were hard to say. He felt even more ashamed that Poppy seemed so attractive to him. The skirt she wore left almost nothing to his imagination and her hair was loosely dressed and exciting in its red-golden ringlets. There was something wrong. He had come to talk a little of Keith and leave—and now he found himself physically comfortable on the big couch. And ever since he had walked in the door, he had felt a strange sense of exhilaration at seeing Poppy again. There was something wrong, because he could not picture Lucille with him in this place. He could not picture her as anything more than an idea.

*"You get better looking every year. More distinguished, sort of,"* she said. *"Colin, your wife is a lucky girl."*

Well, now that was the first time anyone had ever said that to him. It was nonsense, but it pleased him momentarily. She followed immediately with a host of questions about his flying and these were exactly the kind of questions he found it comfortable to answer. Poppy understood his problems. He never had to say he loved Lucille.

All right, it *was* eleven o'clock. After a while it would be midnight too—naturally. Lucille slipped off her mules and turned into bed. You said yourself he would not be home early—you said it, but he didn't. You took the chance and thought it had to be taken. Now go to sleep and he will come, for this is his place beside you and he is that kind of man. Switch out the light and go to sleep, Lucille, and so make the waiting easier. And anyhow, what difference does it make, except that he is so impetuous and sometimes unthinking? Why couldn't she have met him in a hotel lobby—or even in a speakeasy? Those steps on the stairs—no, not Colin . . . too heavy. Roland, home in the night and snorting about his room now, angry because he also was alone. But she flicked out the light so that he would not ask for her.

*Conversation that was at first labored became easier with time and Poppy. Her chuckle and the drink she gave him warmed the room. Still, there was no invitation to put down. She arranged herself carefully at the opposite end of the couch—revealing, but not inviting. When he grew conscious of his own talk and asked about her career, she moved to the piano and sang for him.*

*"Poppy doesn't sing so well yet, but I'm going to, Colin. You just watch. A few shows like this one is going to be under my belt, and if I keep my ears open and learn to speak real-lady English, then your Poppy will go places."*

She sang *"When Day Is Done"* and *"Whispering."* He thought she sang very well. He didn't want to leave, but certain memories were flirting with his will, becoming too difficult to put aside. So he said it was time to go. She made *no protest, but laid her hand lightly on his. Her skin felt very soft and smooth and warm.*

*"Sure, I know. That gal's waitin' for you. All right, run along. But Poppy won't have you leavin' hungry. It's a long drive. There's something in the icebox."*

*And there was. A tempting cold roast chicken on a platter and some Canadian ale to wash it down. They passed an hour at the kitchen table.*

This was thinking Lucille had never done before. Bypass it. No—because sooner or later it had to be done, as she supposed every wife must some time do. She lay in the dark with her eyes open, wondering at how little she knew about Colin. Suppose her mother were alive and asked her to describe the man she had married. The husband. She could say he's a trifle shorter than tall, that his hair is an indeterminate shade of brown, he has a cleft chin, and his face is nicely chiseled, Mother. His voice—well, that was easy: deep and resonant; but what he might say was something else again. He sort of saves his words, Mother, so that when he speaks you listen to each word and value it—but it makes him hard to know in a moment, or an hour, or, I'm afraid, a year. I really couldn't tell you what he's like and it's unnecessary anyway, since I love him whatever he's like. Even if this night, or some future night, he were to share with someone else those private passions that are supposed to belong to me.

Yes, even if he did.

*At the door he said good night and stood fumbling with his hat. He looked down at the top of Poppy's head and decided he would like to kiss her. When he stooped to do so, she slipped easily into his arms. Her body felt soft against his— softer than Lucille's and therefore strange and exciting. He bent farther until his lips were almost with hers.*

*Then something mysterious and surprising occurred within him and the moment was lost. He began to laugh a little and eased his hold. He shook his head slowly. He laughed in a way that plainly disclosed that he was laughing only at himself.*

*"No, Poppy. No. Not tonight or any other night."* He dropped his hands and shoved them firmly into his pockets.

And Poppy had the wisdom and the courage to laugh with him. *"You Boy Scout! You damn big Eagle Scout! Poppy must be slipping. Come back and let me try again."*

*"Good night."*

It was something like hedgehopping, he thought, as he sauntered down the hall. You skimmed your wheels along the fences and the treetops, but if successful you never quite touched them.

Lucille did not hear him come up the stairs, but she heard him slip through the door. He groped in the darkness for a moment, searching for the light by the dresser. When he found it, he apparently changed his mind and did not turn it on. Then he fumbled in the closet until he found a place to hang his coat. She sensed him staggering in the darkness as he slipped off his pants and hung them on the tall foot post of the bed—as he always did. There was a jangling when the change in his pocket fell to the floor—as it always did. She heard him swear softly, and that made her feel good because then she knew he was not being furtive but merely considerate of her.

"Why don't you turn on the light," she wanted to ask, "before you break your beloved neck?" But she remained silent, because somehow speaking might break the spell.

He sat down on the bed gently, and removed his shoes and socks. Lucille was very wide-awake. She could not explain the excitement she felt as he turned back the covers, except that she was sure this moment was very important to her. Everything would depend on how close he came to her and how he took her in his arms—if he did.

If he merely lay beside her, unmoving, and so a thousand miles away, then she would have failed somewhere, once or many times, in their relations.

He slipped in beside her, breathing deeply, yet still away. So careful not to touch her. In that horrible short time before he moved and she could already feel the warmth of his body, she lay almost rigid with fear—wanting with all her being to reach out and touch him, to search for his eyes in the gloom and hear his voice, and most of all to be taken completely. But even if he so much as caressed her shoulder, she would be satisfied; she would know of his desire and be content.

He turned a little toward her. She held her breath and felt a warm thrill flow through her body. Then after she had almost despaired of his moving closer, his arm came slowly around her—tenderly at first and then with increasing pressure. She turned to him in absolute surrender and gave her lips to his. His mouth was hot and his beard hurt, but this peculiar pain became a fierce and intense pleasure.

## 12

Shorty Baker's figure bundled in a flying suit was almost equal in height and width, like a square block of cement. From the front, however, there was a suggestion of foreshortening about his barrel chest and ample shoulders, and there were the nicks in the cement that indicated his sharp, beady eyes. There was also a somewhat larger hole, irregular but efficient, which was his mouth. It was the outlet for his thoughts, which were strange and by some considered wonderful.

Shorty's background was hazy; certainly it included a minimum of formal education. He had once been a mechanic and was said to be one of the few men alive who could properly time a Hisso engine without losing his temper. The fact was that Shorty had no temper, and this lack may have had something to do with the way he dedicated himself to making other people lose theirs.

Not content with being a mechanic, he had made frequent parachute drops about the country, developing a technique of waiting until the last possible moment before he pulled the rip cord. As a result, he received considerable gloomy advice, to which he gave not the slightest piece of his fertile mind, and the title of "Bullet-Drop" Baker of which he was very proud.

By thumbing through a moldy book on flight written in the era of Blériot, and supplementing it with Octave Chanute's *Progress in Flying Machines* and Langley's *Experiments in Aerodynamics,* and further by surreptitiously watching the pilots who parachuted him to earth, he eventually taught himself to fly, as Shorty put it, "like a northbound pregnant goose.'' And like Roland and Colin and Tad, he had at last achieved the dizzy social stratum of pilots who ate as regularly as they flew.

It was not because of Shorty's past ambition or his aerial accomplishments that Gafferty had misgivings when he hired him. Gafferty knew that on just such a night as this, when the summer breeze was soft and not a cloud hung east of Buffalo, Shorty's restless mind might break under the strain of polite regularity. At such times, no one—not even perceptive Porkie Scott, who knew him best—dared forecast the result.

For the sake of his own nerves, Gafferty had arranged to base Shorty Baker in Buffalo. Thus he was obliged to notice only the major explosions of mischief and could more easily let the minor infractions take care of themselves. And so Shorty flew the mail from Buffalo to Cleveland, and more frequently from Buffalo to Albany.

The heat of the day had not yet departed when Shorty stepped from the operations shack deep in thought—so deep, in fact, that he almost forgot his "rations": half a dozen bananas, which he claimed were restful to peel and eat in flight. He went back into the office, retrieved his paper bag of bananas, and strolled pensively through the screen door again. He was waiting for his friend and collaborator in all things evil, Mr. Whispering Johnny Dycer, who would drop out of the evening stars with the mail from Cleveland. It would be up to Shorty to take the mail east from Buffalo.

Whispering Johnny was over an hour late, and Shorty hated to wait for anything. To pass the time, he had been rummaging through the drawers in the operations desk. At first, finding little of interest, he merely helped himself to three erasers, a fistful of envelopes bearing the Mercury Airlines trademark, and a box of pencils. These he regarded as perfectly legitimate though not very interesting loot.

He finally ran across a New York Central train schedule, sometimes used by the operations personnel when weather or mechanical difficulties obliged them to "train" the mail. Much as he despised the railroads, Shorty fell to studying the timetable. Slowly, without the slightest burden on his mind, an idea began to take shape.

While he stood waiting for his plane to come out of the last transparent slit of twilight in the west, he added a few final touches with the care of a perfectionist. He teetered back and forth on his small feet as he thought how annoyed some New York Central engineer was going to be. He considered it positively providential that Whispering Johnny was late.

Whispering Johnny was so called because of his bullfrog voice, which was a thing of wonder. It had often been heard on the ground while Johnny was still in the air, booming maledictions over the side of his cockpit. Wind and engine noise fought an ever-losing battle against its power.

Finally one of the western stars began to move among its fellows and took on a greenish hue. That would be Johnny's right running light. In a few moments the plane slipped soundlessly to earth and, though Shorty could not see Johnny through the glare of the landing lights, he heard him when he was still a good way off across the long grass.

"HULLO! HULLO! YOU LITTLE BASTARD!"

But Shorty, absorbed in his plans, held his counsel. He walked clumsily toward the plane, bending beneath the weight of his parachute.

He asked the usual question. "Is the ship all right?"

"YEAH. IT'S ALL RIGHT!"

"Git out, then. I'm in a hurry."

Whispering Johnny pushed his goggles up, revealing a jerked-venison face with a large red nose. He whipped off his helmet and shook his mane of white hair. Whispering Johnny was fifty; he had been flying a long time—some said since before the Wrights, which would be the beginning of time.

"It gives me hope whenever I see you. You're getting uglier every day. Uglier and uglier. Some day they will put you in a cage," said Shorty. "Now, c'mon, hurry up and git out before they do."

"HUMPH!" Johnny looked down at him with just the proper degree of condescension. "THIS IS A JOB FOR MEN, NOT FOR BOYS. COME BACK WHEN YOU GROW UP, SON. WORK HARD AND WE MAY HAVE SOME-THING FOR YOU."

"C'mon . . . git the hell out."

Whispering Johnny stretched and rubbed the back of his neck. He was very tired. The weather had been perfect from

Cleveland, and still he was tired. This was something he could not explain. He pushed himself out of the cockpit with a groan.

"I'M GETTING OLD, SHORTY . . ." He paused a moment on the edge of the cockpit with his legs dangling, and looked back toward the west, toward the bronze and cobalt evening sky out of which he had come. "VERY OLD, SHORTY." And though there was great strength in his voice, the fading light betrayed a weakness in his eyes that Shorty had never seen before.

"Sure you're gittin' old. You're dead from the neck up. Now git out. I'm in a hurry."

Shorty glanced anxiously at his watch, then looked up in surprise when Johnny put his hand on his shoulder and let himself down with a heavy sigh. Johnny leaned against the fuselage and rubbed the back of his neck again. Shorty started to climb past him, then paused with his foot on the wing. There was something wrong. This was not the old Whispering Johnny. This was not the man who had flown along with Locklear and Lincoln Beachy—not the indestructible Whispering Johnny who had survived nine blood-spattering crackups and sat up an hour later to take his pint of whisky. Those sagging shoulders did not belong to the man who had built his own airplane of sailcloth and bailing wire in 1910 and taught himself to fly it. Shorty went back to Johnny's side.

"What's eatin' you?"

For once, Johnny's voice was subdued. "I don't know, Shorty. . . . I been feeling a little funny sometimes, lately. Could be that old ticker of mine. Never gave it much mind before. If you aren't in too big a Goddamned rush, maybe you'd walk over to the operations office with me."

"I ain't in that much of a hurry."

"Okay. I'd sort of like to lie down for a while."

Shorty tried to hide his shock with a laugh. "With who? There's no dames in operations."

"This time I guess it better be alone, Shorty."

On the moth-eaten couch, Whispering Johnny unbuttoned his collar and lit a cigarette. His face was covered with perspiration, but the strength was coming back to his voice.

"AH! THAT'S BETTER. NOW GO ON, BEAT IT, YOU

LITTLE RUNT, AND GIVE WHOEVER IT IS IN AL-
BANY MY LOVE.''

Shorty turned for the door and then came back again.

''What's the matter with you, anyway? You look like
you're about to croak.''

''AND MEBBE I WILL! It'll be no loss. But just remember you didn't see this. Don't tell ANYBODY, see, Shorty?''

''Okay.''

''You didn't see anything . . . get it?''

''I got it.'' Shorty started for the door again, but Whispering Johnny caught the expression on his face.

''DON'T EVEN THINK ABOUT IT TO YOURSELF,
SHORTY. You know how news gets around . . . like Roland
MacDonald.''

''What about Roland?''

''Quit flying.''

''The hell you say!''

''Fellow flies for N.A.T. told me in Cleveland. Said he got
it from Tad in Newark early this morning.''

''What's he gonna do?''

''I don't know. . . . WHAT DOES ANYBODY DO? . . .
SO JUST REMEMBER . . . YOU DIDN'T SEE ANYTHING!''

''All right. But if you don't feel so good, watch your step,
Johnny.''

''Beat it.''

Shorty went out of the door and climbed into the Pitcairn.
The mechanics had finished refueling. He signed the mail
form and placed his bag of bananas carefully on the floor
beneath his seat. In a few minutes he was flying east, a part
of the upper night.

He would have to hurry if his calculations were correct. He
therefore speeded up his usually elaborate greetings to certain
earthly companions in the night below. These greetings were
of the greatest importance to Shorty, as they were to so many
pilots, because they gave him a sense of being still a member
of human society. They eased the loneliness, the sense of not
being exactly alive, of being suspended in space like a ghost
without portfolio.

At the railroad junction near Batavia a man named Sullivan whom Shorty had never met in person would be waiting

at the window of his switch tower for the sound of the Pitcairn's motor. When Shorty saw the lights of the tower blink three times against the black earth, he shoved the nose of the Pitcairn sharply down, blinked his own navigation lights, pulled up, and continued on his way. Old Sullivan would wonder what was the matter—not very low, no circling, no nothing. Give him the works next trip.

Then there was that good-looking widow who lived just north of Churchville. Shorty laid it down on the treetops for her, but he did not tarry. That would be the widow herself standing in the street waving a lantern, faithful as only a lonesome widow could be. Shorty made a mental note to get up to Churchville more often.

He swung around over the lights of Rochester, sprinkled like diamonds on velvet. He pushed on full throttle and dove southwest to the field. He cut back the engine when he passed over the canal that bordered the field, flicked on his landing lights, and sank down their beams to earth. Deliberately holding the Pitcairn's tail in the air, he half-taxied, half-flew, across the grass to the hangar lights.

When he rolled to a precise stop, the Mercury Airlines agent put his head down against the propeller blast and climbed quickly forward along the wing to the mail compartment. He was very young, full of eagerness and personal sacrifice, and so obsessed with the idea of flying that his eyes brightened at the very sound of an airplane.

"Shake a leg, Charlie!"

"What's the rush?"

"Got an appointment."

"Don't you ever get tired of that stuff, Shorty?"

"This is different!"

"Sure . . . sure."

"Hurry up."

The agent removed a very light mailbag from the compartment and tossed in another, equally light. He slid back off the wing, and held the mail form for Shorty to sign against the propeller blast.

"Gee, business is lousy. My kids are hungry and Gafferty says he can't raise me. Sometimes I wonder what I'm goin' to do."

Shorty reached for the bag at his feet. He fumbled in the cockpit darkness for several moments. "Have a banana."

"Thanks. Don't think I won't eat it." The agent walked away and Shorty called to him over his shoulder as the engine roared again:

"Don't eat it all at once!"

As the sound of the Pitcairn diminished, Charlie finished peeling the banana. But first he removed the twenty-dollar bill that had been neatly folded in the end.

As the lights of Marion slid beneath his wings, Shorty descended until he was just above the rolling hills. He followed their contours up and down for a while, like a buoyant chip on a wave. Then he pulled up again over Clyde, noted his time and air speed, and made a guess at the wind on his tail. He brought his knees together to hold the stick and sat back to eat a banana. He held the flapping tongues of skin in the slip stream a moment and then released them. He liked the way they disappeared instantly. It was said that Shorty Baker would never become totally lost, since if ever he had reason to doubt his course, he had only to turn about and follow a trail of banana skins back to his point of origin.

Then, just as his cheeks were comfortably filled, pouching like the chops of a squirrel preparing for winter, he saw the train. Mixed feelings of joy, triumph, and power rose within him.

So business wasn't so good, huh? If you looked at the matter in a certain light, the responsibility lay squarely on railroads. Of course. In a mighty conspiracy they took all the mail and thus starved the airlines in infancy. And here, thought Shorty, was the railroads' prime representative, soon to be at his mercy. Unless his calculations were awry, that beam of light in the distance trailed by a dimmer ribbon of lights was the Twentieth Century Limited. It was a monster begging for attack, and Shorty wheeled his mount to meet it. He knew that he could not kill it—indeed, he did not wish to; but he could humiliate the beast.

He switched off his navigation lights and made a diving turn back to the west. He picked up the railroad tracks at Weedsport, then turned back east again and followed the tracks curve for curve. He could no longer see the train, but it was rushing toward him somewhere beyond the little hills ahead. He was flying as low as he could without knocking off his wheels on the telegraph poles. He put one hand on the switch to his landing lights. He stopped munching on his banana and waited, his head just out in the slip stream. It was a good thing there was no moon. The engineer would never see him until he was ready to be discovered.

He throttled back a bit. He must judge the distance just right— not too close and not too far away. Then he saw the Century bending along a gentle curve. He eased his ship a trifle lower and made certain his wheels were directly over the tracks. He compelled himself to wait until the headlight was barely half a mile ahead. He could see sparks flying back from the engine stack and the boiler fires flickering beneath the wheels.

The two, the tiny challenger and the behemoth, came together head on in the night. Shorty snapped on one of his brilliant landing lights, kicked rudder just a hair, and stabbed the beam straight at the engine cab. Shorty saw a flash of the engineer's startled face. Even above the roar of his own engine he heard the frantic screaming of the train whistle. He switched off his landing light and at the same time zoomed almost straight up. He gave the Pitcairn full throttle and hung her on the prop. Then he eased off on the stick and throttle, turning back and down in a slow almost noiseless glide over the train to survey the results. What he saw provided him with immense satisfaction.

The Twentieth Century Limited was grinding to a stop. As he swung back to the east, he saw a red flare blossom near the observation car. The crew would be looking up and down the tracks now, puzzled and angry. Sooner or later they would look up and spot his exhaust flames against the stars. Shorty wished he could see the ruffled dignity of the engineer's face, but that was a desire best unfulfilled. There was no sense in letting them identify the plane. Then he would have to explain things to Gafferty, who just wouldn't understand why anybody should ever buzz a train.

So, reluctantly, Shorty pushed the throttle forward and set his course for Syracuse. He reached in the bag for a banana and was soon chewing thoughtfully.

The expression on Whispering Johnny's face came back to him suddenly and vividly, and he could not drive it away. He saw it plainly when he looked at the dim horizon and when he looked inside the cockpit at his instruments—that ugly, weatherbeaten mug, twisted with pain in spite of his will. He saw the face when he took off southwest at Syracuse and bent around the abandoned canal, cutting between the hills for altitude, and again when he zoomed down over the farm near the Fort Plain emergency field, where there was a crippled boy who wrote him letters. He had the latest one in his pocket now. He brought it out and leaned forward to read the cramped scrawl by the panel light.

Dear Shorty—

I sure am glad I know yur full name now. My uncle Martin Freeman was down to Albany last week. He asked at the Mercury Airlines office and they told him yur name.

I wait up sometimes to near midnight waiting for you. If the plane don't buzz here then I know it must be some other pilot because I know you won't let me down.

Like I told you in my first letter I guess the braces on my legs won't never let me be an airmail pilot but my Uncle Martin says never give up hope. I guess he's right, huh? Uncle Martin was the one who gave me the aseteline (spelling?) light so you could always find the place easy. I am building a model of your airplane and when it is done I will send it to you. I am pretty good at building things, if I do say so myself. Ha! Ha!

Now Shorty, I'll be waiting for you every night. Even when the weather is bad. Also I will pray for you just like if I had a big brother. So long Shorty.

Your Pal,<br>GERALD AMUNDSEN

P.S. I am learning the morse code so you can signal me.
P.P.S. Forgot to tell you. I am 12 years old.


Whispering Johnny's face disappeared for a little while as Shorty circled the acetylene light like a giant moth around a candle flame, and, though like most of his kind he was not a letter-writing man, he promised himself he would write to the tiny figure standing spellbound beside that light.

But when he turned away and hastened on toward Albany, he saw the face again and sickened as he realized he ought to do something about Johnny. Tell Gafferty? No, that was not the way. Whispering Johnny would never forgive him, though it might save his life. It would be better to get him to a doctor, one who could talk some sense to him before it was too late. Such a meeting would be almost impossible to bring about, but as he passed the last winking beacon at Schenectady and nosed down for Albany, Shorty put his mind to the problem.

By the time his wheels slithered through the grass at Albany, he had figured out a way. Colin MacDonald was waiting to take his ship and the mail on to Newark. That was a stroke of good luck. Colin was a man you could depend on to carry through a delicate matter.

"I got a job for you," he said to Colin. "Bein' married and all, I know you won't get sidetracked."

"That depends." Colin was thinking that the usual job stemming from Shorty Baker was full of complications known to all but the chief victim.

"This is on the level. Do you know a good doctor—a doc, now, not some vet?"

"That fellow Timothy who gave us our physicals seems all right."

"He'll do. Now, listen, tomorrow night Whispering Johnny will fly here from Buffalo."

"But it will be your turn again, won't it?"

"Yeah, but I'm goin' to be sick down in the hotel. Sicker'n hell. Johnny will fill in for me, and when he gets here to turn the ship over to you, you ain't gonna be here either."

"Tomorrow night is Tad's run."

"Then *he* ain't gonna be here. *Nobody,* see? Johnny will have to take the mail on to Newark."

"You certainly mix things up. Sydney will go into a flat spin trying to straighten the schedule out again."

"It has to be done. When Johnny gets to Newark you tip this doctor off he's got a special appointment. Find out where Johnny's staying and tell him somethin' new has come up with the Bureau of Commerce. They're issuin' new licenses or somethin' . . . make up anything you want, but get him to that doctor."

"What's he supposed to do?"

"Just pretend there's nothin' outa the way. Pretend everyone has to do it. You know how Johnny is. Take a physical yourself if you have to."

Colin shuddered at the prospect. "It's none of my business, Shorty, but I might do a better job if I knew what goes on. Maybe I'd better get Porkie and Roland to help me. Johnny's a hard man to convince."

"Do it alone, Colin . . . and stick by the guy. Tell the doc to look at his heart."

"Oh." Colin scrunched out his cigarette carefully. He looked over toward the lights of Albany, then studied the flashing of an August thunderstorm over the Catskills. He gave Shorty a gentle punch in the midriff as he walked out to his ship.

Whispering Johnny Dycer did not mind the unexpected run to Newark. No man ever loved flying more fervently. Some said he had been born with wings, but this was an exaggeration, for Johnny was twenty-four years old before he ever left the ground. That first time, he was perched on a Series B Wright, with his cap turned backwards and a high stiff collar streamlining his oxlike neck. Johnny grew misty-eyed when he thought about those early flying days—and nowadays this was much of the time. Tonight, with the Hudson curving and widening beneath him, he could almost smell the sick sweetness of the castor oil engine lubricant in that first ship.

The beacon lights that winked alternately red and white and swept knowing fingers along his course to the south stood like mileposts in his own career. That first beacon at Ravena (now far beneath the Pitcairn's tail) away in the past, like the unbleached muslin and linseed-oil period—yes, like the covering of his first ship. And the next beacon at Catskill, advancing dreamily toward him. That would be the Mexican campaign in 1916—Pershing, and just plain Johnny Dycer then, and a tractor biplane that miserably failed both Johnny and the bewildered Army. And beyond Catskill, still only a

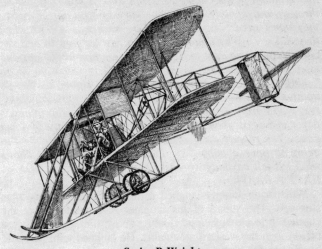

*Series B Wright*

flash on the horizon—1917. Johnny Dycer as an instructor then. An old man of forty-one. That's where the nickname of Whispering Johnny had come from. His perspiring, anxious students never had any trouble hearing Johnny.

But beyond Catskill there was only one more beacon. This was the one at Haverstraw and, as frequently happened on a summer night, if the tongue of an errant cloud brushed down from Bear Mountain, he would not see it. There would be only darkness beneath—fathomless and somehow, this night, very saddening.

Johnny pushed up his goggles and wiped a beefy hand across his brow—the hand that had delicately guided so many ships in so many skies. The dizziness had come again. That was twice now since his departure from Buffalo, and with it came a sudden pounding in his temples and wrists. He could not account for it. When he looked up and discovered he was in a slow bank to the east, he was frightened. He straightened the ship and began to talk to himself and to the wind as he had always done when he felt alone and afraid.

*"All right, you old bastard. . . . Spin in . . . fall asleep*

*like grandpa in his chair. . . . Spin in . . . you're about all through and nobody needs you, anyway . . . not anymore, they don't need you. . . . But there sure was a time when they did. . . . Why don't you take a rest . . . go in and see Gafferty when you get to Newark . . . see him in the morning after you've had some sleep. Tell Gafferty you want to go fishing for a couple of weeks. . . . That's right . . . there's nothing in the world wrong with you that a couple of weeks' rest won't fix . . . nothin' in the world. . . . Old Johnny's ticker is just as good as it ever was . . . and that was damn good. You're just dizzy on account—Hah! . . . Mebbe I'm going to have a baby. . . . That's it, by God! . . . That's what I'll tell anybody who asks fool questions. . . . GONNA HAVE A BABY!''*

Whispering Johnny laughed at the night and pounded his stomach. The sound of his laughter reverberated from the startled little nimbus cloud floating above him and ricocheted off through the western mountains. He laughed until he could hardly see for tears.

Bear Mountain passed beneath his wings and it reassured him that he could sense its outline in the murk. He was very tired, but he felt better now because Newark lay barely twenty minutes ahead. Johnny even began to think of the ham and eggs he would have. He would call Porkie Scott at the hotel and wake him up. Make him come down and eat with him. It would be good to see Porkie again, and Roland MacDonald, if the rascal could be found. They would chew the fat for an hour or so, or longer, retracing old flights, pleasantly swapping tales of loss and survival, arguing and agreeing in a language that only those completely absorbed in this new element could speak. Those were the good things, the savory trimmings.

After the ham and eggs and maybe a couple of stiff drinks, if Porkie had any, there would be a good night's sleep. Then he'd go to see Gafferty in the morning.

Suddenly it struck again. Quicker than ever before, it seemed to clutch his body and shake it violently. Someone was choking him. He gasped and reached for the cockpit's leather trim to stay the whirling. Then, almost as quickly as it had come, the seizure relaxed and passed away. But it left him grunting in relief and wet with sweat. When he was able to breathe a little more freely, he found the words for what was in his mind. Words that fell with unaccustomed pleading from his lips.

*"God . . . please. Don't take this from me . . . not yet. I sure never thought I'd talk this way, but . . . I can use some help now. . . . Don't make it this way. . . . Fellows wouldn't know me . . . not this way . . . not for a while yet . . . not for old Johnny . . . please, God."*

The Pitcairn bored into a heavy haze. As it neared the lights of Newark, the haze took on a soft, golden tint which gained intensity as he descended over Snake Hill, and grew each moment more brilliant and mellow until he was flying in a golden sphere within the encompassing walls of black night. And so for him it seemed the glorious golden portal to a magic city, opening wide for Whispering Johnny.

In the car Colin and Lucille waited for Johnny's ship to come out of the night, content for a while just to be alone with each other. Though the night was very warm, they sat close together, as if they had discovered something new and secret in their relation. They had come only to help Johnny, but the unexpected sensations that possessed them became increasingly stronger and more deliciously exciting. Something seemed to happen when Colin switched off the motor and leaned over to give Lucille a quick kiss. He had intended it simply as a familiar salute, the nice-to-have-you-with-me gesture that he frequently made, but he found such pleasure in her lips that he held the kiss and finally slipped his hand beneath her soft summer dress to feel her breasts. And that was their undoing. In his strength he broke the strap to her brassiere and they parted, laughing softly.

"Colin . . . now look what you've done!" But there was no annoyance in her voice; he could have broken a thousand straps and she would have been that much happier.

"I don't see why you wear those things in the first place."

"Sometimes I think if you had your way I'd be walking around naked."

"Fine idea. Save a lot of bother." He took her in his arms again, crushing her to him until she was almost breathless.

His strong hands pulled her legs across his own. When he finally eased his hold she twisted just a little away.

"Say! . . ." She waited to catch her breath. "Say . . . my love . . . don't you think there's a time and a place for these things?"

"No. Hell, no. Time and place has nothing to do with it. You can't plan passion."

She pulled a little farther from him so that she could study his face. She shook her head and laughed. "That statement from you, my love, is one I shall always remember."

He looked at her, bewildered. "What's the matter with it?"

She leaned toward him and brushed her lips against his mouth and his nose and his eyes, speaking softly. "Oh, nothing . . . nothing is wrong with it, Colin. Just nothing. You'll never understand if we're married for fifty years. But if you'll please go on saying things like that to me . . . ah, Colin . . ." She laid her head on his shoulder. "I didn't think married people were supposed to behave this way."

"Did you think it would be just a friendly get-together, with me earning the money and you running a house and maybe a quick peck on the forehead every night once the honeymoon was over? Then maybe once or twice a month a quick roll in the hay if nothing else more important happened to be going on? When people do that, they don't marry . . . they incorporate. Besides, I don't just love you—"

"How's that again?" She drew away in surprise.

"I'm *in* love with you. There's a big difference."

Lucille nodded, and in that moment concluded that however Colin wanted to put it his feeling was all right with her. And since Colin was in a mellow mood, there was one other thing she wanted to discover.

"You're in love with flying, too. Don't you sometimes wish you had your freedom back?"

He took her in his arms again and gently patted her thigh. "Sure I do. You're one hell of a nuisance, but you're something I've got to have."

They moved very close together again and remained so until they heard the soft rustle of Whispering Johnny's plane glide down for a landing. Colin gave her a last hard kiss and stepped out of the car.

"I'll go get him," he said. "Now remember. Be casual . . . don't act like we want him too much. Just invite him to stay the night in Roland's bed. Leave the rest to me. If he suspects anything, he won't go with us."

Gafferty hung up the 'phone, tightened his thin lips, and studied the notes on the pad before him:

Aortic insufficiency due to leaking,
Aortic valve, with hammer pulse.
Heart becomes greatly enlarged (oxheart).
May have mild to considerable shortness of breath and
vertigo at times.

So said Dr. Timothy—and he said a few other things that made Gafferty uneasy. He hadn't seen Johnny Dycer for some months—not since the line had first started. Johnny was an old dependable wheel horse, unofficially Gafferty's own delegate in airline matters between Buffalo and Cleveland. He did not want to see him now.

The day had started off wrong. Gafferty had been called over to New York by the businessmen. It was one of those hot sticky mornings when automobile smoke hung over the city and seemed to fill in the gaps between the buildings with a heavy yellow gas. Even the businessmen looked wilted. Their collars were wet and their questions short. They politely wanted to know a great many things, but they were frank enough to say that their own brains were outside the windows—on Long Island somewhere, anywhere away from the city.

"We've been going over the payroll figures, Gafferty," said the neatest, youngest one with the Harvard accent. "Frankly, we're astonished. Some of these pilots, for example. We don't want to be unreasonable, but their salaries seem quite out of line."

"How do you mean?" Gafferty was doing his best to like the young man, but diplomacy had always been difficult with him. "We're only paying what we agreed to pay."

"I know. But some of these men make seven hundred dollars a month. A few of them have made eight hundred. And one fellow made nine hundred in July!"

"Well?"

"Isn't that quite a lot for flying an airplane?" The young man arched his eyebrows and glanced about the room for agreement. One of the others poured himself a glass of water from a silver thermos and said he thought it seemed like an awful lot.

"It depends on how you look at it," said Gafferty. Yes, it was out of line for "flying an airplane"; seven or eight hundred a month was too much for the manipulation of a ship's controls, however skillful. But there were other things involved that the businessmen either could not or would not see. He looked out of the window at the boats in New York harbor and followed the river up to where it merged with the morning haze toward Albany. He wondered if Keith Mac-Donald had been overpaid.

"It seems incredible," the young man went on. "Why, a lot of my classmates—good men, too—aren't making that much."

Gafferty held his peace. There was, he thought, no answer to that statement.

"As a matter of fact," the young man went on, "I do a bit of flying myself. There's nothing so difficult about it."

"May I ask when you fly?"

"Weekends. I'm rather busy other times."

"That must be great fun. Do you fly straight through the winter?"

"No. I can't say I do."

"Don't. It's uncomfortable and likely to be—unhealthy."

"But don't these wages seem rather strange to you, Gafferty? Your own salary isn't that much."

No, Gafferty reflected rather bitterly, it wasn't. But he was still hoping there might come a day—in that flying future that never quite arrived. . . . Oh, the hell with it. The less said the better just now. This was one of the headaches involved in the infancy of any enterprise, and it was up to him to keep the peace between theory and practice. No one else in the company knew both sides of the operation. He was the buffer, the man in the middle, and hence unlikely to become popular with either side, or rich.

"They're fair wages," he said. "Lower than N.A.T. pays."

"But you're in charge of these men. Compare their salary with your own."

"Let's leave my pittance out of this." Gafferty managed a smile. "Actually, when they are flying—which is what we pay them for—they are in charge of themselves." There was no sense in trying to explain that there were right ways and wrong ways of slipping into Syracuse on a rainy night. The right way delivered the mail; the wrong way stopped the pilot's salary forever.

"Gafferty, how can I, without giving offense, make you see that . . . Well, these men are hardly of the caliber for that salary bracket. We should be able to hire them for much less. Now, I've figured out a basic rate. . . ."

"Oh, for the love of God!" The young man did give offense. Maybe it was the heat, maybe it was the young man's voice, but if he said another word Gafferty would tell him to come out and do his own flying. "Now you listen to me. You wanted a job done. You asked me to do it. I explained very carefully to you that, with their night time and all, these pilots would make good money. I got the best men available, considering all things. They're doing a fine job now, and when this winter hits, believe me, there'll be plenty of times when they'll earn a year's salary in five minutes . . . or thirty seconds."

"But, Gafferty, this is a *business*, and we've got to start looking at it in a business way. We have an obligation to the stockholders. We've got to cut somewhere. We're losing money."

"Then cut somewhere else. Leave my pilots alone or you won't have an airline!"

He didn't win and he didn't lose the argument. The businessmen said they would study the matter further. Just what they meant by that, Gafferty could not discover. In the meantime, he had to talk to Whispering Johnny.

Johnny was sitting in the outer office. Gafferty had kept him waiting because in these matters he was a complete coward. It was one thing to dress down a man for foolish flying—that was within Gafferty's sphere, and there had been times when he took a certain sadistic pleasure in doing so; but to tell a man like Johnny Dycer that he was through forever—that, as far as he and top-notch flying were concerned, he could fold up his wings and go nest in an armchair—Gafferty didn't know about that.

He had only enough courage to glance at Johnny's eyes when he came in at the door. But he saw that Johnny held his shoulders stiffly and his big chest unnaturally inflated, like any man trying to convince himself of his own virility.

"Good to see you, Johnny. Sit down."

"OKAY!" Johnny's voice was also trying to prove something. He took one of the yellow oak chairs and eased into it. He still wore his leather flying jacket and beneath it a rumpled tan shirt open at the collar. He turned a battered hat round and round with his big lumpy fingers.

"I've been wanting to talk to you anyway, Johnny. How're things in Buffalo?"

Johnny's eyes brightened. Maybe the whole thing was a false alarm. Maybe Gafferty didn't know about the—doctor. It could be worked out some way. Get a rest first, then go see some other doc and get fixed up with another license—somehow.

"ALL RIGHT. ALL RIGHT. I TALKED TO ED MULDOON THE OTHER DAY. HE SAID HE MAY BE ABLE TO GIVE US SOME HANGAR SPACE NEXT WINTER. N.A.T. KEEPS BEATING US OUT OF THE MAIL IN CLEVELAND. THEY'RE FLYING A LOT OF WEATHER BETWEEN CHICAGO AND CLEVELAND."

"Yes. I know about that. Got any particular beefs, Johnny?"

"NO . . . NO . . . not that I can think of. Course there's room for improvement. Always is. We could use another pilot based in Buffalo. Separate the schedules a little."

"I'll look into it."

There it was. Silence. Gafferty could hear the typewriter clicking outside the door and it sounded very loud, like hail on a cockpit windshield. Johnny looked at the floor and turned his hat.

"Have a cigar, Johnny?"

"No, thanks. I QUIT SMOKING A COUPLE OF MONTHS AGO."

Another silence, deeper this time—accentuated by the scrape of the match when Gafferty lit his cigar. It snapped like a firecracker. There was no use stalling any longer; he was only prolonging the agony.

"How've you been feeling, Johnny?"

"FINE! FINE! OF COURSE, I'M NOT QUITE AS YOUNG AS I USED TO WAS!" Johnny threw back his head and achieved a ringing laugh that for a moment shook the flimsy office walls, and then as suddenly faltered and diminished and floated out of the open window. But Johnny did not look at the floor again. His eyes challenged Gafferty's, and there was about them a desperate, fighting look that told him Johnny knew.

"I guess neither of us is as young as we'd like to be, Johnny." Gafferty picked up the pad with the doctor's report. He read it again. The reading gave him something to do—something to look at besides Johnny. "Johnny, you've been around a long time. You've got a lot of experience. I could use a man like you—to sort of help me out. Lot of little details I can't seem to reach."

Johnny looked at him steadily. "You mean on the ground?" He said it slowly and his voice faded.

"Well . . . yes."

Of course, there would be only one answer for a man like Johnny. Gafferty had no job for him and certainly Johnny would guess that he had none. Sometimes a pilot took to the ground by choice, as Gafferty himself had done; it usually worked out with only minor dissatisfaction. But to be *put* down was an ordeal very few pilots survived for long. Yet Whispering Johnny twisted out a smile from the brown-leather wrinkles around his mouth and his voice rose to something like its old volume as he talked.

"Mighty nice of you to think I'd do, but . . . I CAN'T JUST SEE OLD JOHNNY BEHIND A DESK. MATTER OF FACT, THE REASON I CAME DOWN TO SEE YOU WAS TO SAY THAT IT LOOKS LIKE YOU'LL HAVE TO GET ANOTHER BOY. Old friend of mine IS MAKIN' A FORTUNE flying up to them tin mines in BOLIVIA. Wrote me the other day to join him, and after thinking things over, I DECIDED I WOULD. . . . Giving you proper notice, of course."

"I appreciate that, Johnny. It sounds interesting but—"

"I'D LIKE TO HELP YOU OUT, but HELL'S BELLS, you ought to know. Why, it wouldn't be fair to you. You ought to know. I COULDN'T KEEP MY TAIL IN THE SAME SPOT FOR MORE THAN TWO DAYS AT A TIME IF MY LIFE DEPENDED ON IT!"

"Your life may depend on it, Johnny. That high altitude is tricky . . . the flying, of course." Gafferty spoke before he thought. It would have been a lot better if he hadn't said that—a lot better. But bless Johnny—he had the nerve to eye him narrowly and scratch his beef-red nose thoughtfully.

Johnny stood up and scraped back the chair. "You just leave the altitude to me. I been taking care of old Johnny for a long, long time. GUESS I CAN MANAGE FOR A FEW MORE YEARS." He walked over to the door a little too briskly. "You just relax about old Johnny, and keep your eye on the boys this winter. IT'S GOING TO BE A LULU!"

"We'll do the best we can."

Gafferty cursed himself because that was all he could think of to say. When the door closed behind Johnny he saw his shadow through the glass. It stood very straight, too straight for a man who had lost his life, for a man who didn't have a flying job in Bolivia or anywhere else—too straight for a man who would never fly again.

After a moment, the shadow melted away.

## 13

As Roland drove the shining new blue Stutz off the Cortlandt Street ferry and headed up West Street, he pulled the cutout on the exhaust and derived some satisfaction from the barrage of noise that followed. As he turned into Canal Street a policeman stopped him. Taking his time about his movements, the policeman looked over the long, flashy car from end to end and frowned at the yellow wire wheels and then at Roland.

"I suppose you think this thing makes a pretty racket, huh?" He tapped the spare tire gently with his billy. "Mighty fancy car you've got here."

"It isn't mine." Roland was in no mood to discuss his possessions with anyone, let alone the law.

"I s'pose ye borried it?"

"No. I'm about to sell it. Selling these things is my business." Roland found that this admission had lately become very distasteful.

The policeman stepped around to view the license tag. "Ye don't say? Make a good living? I mean do many people go for these circus wagons?"

Roland shrugged his shoulders. Since there was obviously not going to be a ticket involved, he lost interest in the conversation. He reached in his shirt pocket and fished out a card that gave the name of the man who would be awaiting his arrival at eleven—a Morgan Seibert Stallings, Park Avenue.

"All right. You look like a pretty good guy. But don't try it again, see?"

Roland nodded and assumed the expression of stoic martyr-

*Stutz Roadster*

dom that now came so easily to him. He brushed his mustache and mumbled his slightly derisive thanks, then drove off aimlessly across Canal Street.

Somewhere in the vicinity of Mulberry Street he became confused and eventually got lost, but he maintained the same air of monumental patience despite numerous false turns down crowded streets and the consequent oaths of truck drivers. Even that fool behind him who kept blowing his "How Dry I Am" horn failed to ruffle Roland's composure. And this was indicative of his spirits, since under normal conditions Roland would have stopped his car and quite cheerfully gone back to choke the man. But his vigor had begun to evaporate the day he ceased to fly, and the rate of evaporation had been markedly increased by dilution with alcohol.

Roland hated his new life. He hated Stutz cars and he hated the people who bought them. He found himself thinking more and more of Madame Moselle and of the days when he was what he liked to remember—a free man. The sunlight in the mornings was different now. The breezes meant little to him. His days were the same, regardless of rain or any other vagary of nature. There were no endless conversations under a sheltering wing, with nothing to disturb one's peace of mind but an occasional ant. Now, indeed, he considered that he was living among the ants. There were no mornings lying in insolent half-sleep while the rest of the world labored, and no nights of starlit speculation while the rest of the world slept.

It did Roland little good to tell himself that for once he was earning an honest living. He had not imagined that without his aid flying would come to a standstill, but he certainly expected at least some plea from those obliged to carry on without him. No word had come.

In fact, the few old friends he saw seemed to avoid the subject of flying in his presence. Porkie Scott had turned into an impossibly dull person. He was forever asking Roland what he thought of this car and that car. He even spoke of fishing, though he must have known that Roland was thirsting for news of the airport. Colin and Tad dropped a comment now and then, which Roland seized upon and mulled over as long as he could. But he seldom saw his brothers. They were always sleeping when he was awake or dressing for an early flight while he grappled with his morning hangover. They greeted him cordially enough but without interest. Lucille had suggested once that since he was drinking too much anyway, they might as well get together and have a "wee doch-and-dorris" party—but it had never come off. On the night they set for it, Newark had gone to fifty feet and a hundred yards of visibility and Colin had turned back to Albany.

This informal isolation made Roland beat his breast in the dark of his thoughts. Still, he was too proud to give up his present mode of life and go back to flying, so he satisfied his pride by selling cars in a way frequently astonishing to his customers.

"Here's your car, Mr. Stallings," he said, when he reached the apartment house.

Mr. Stallings had proved to be a fat, energetic little man with a very bald head and an air of sweeping authority.

"I ordered a red car," he said testily.

"You'll have to take a blue. We haven't got a red."

Mr. Stallings shot him an executive's searching look and pushed his little white fist into the leather seat.

"Well, I'm not buying it for myself, but you ought to furnish what's ordered when a deal amounts to this much money. This is an expensive automobile."

"Yeah. You're crazy to buy it."

"What's that?"

"I said you're crazy to buy it. But if you're a bootlegger it's probably just the thing."

Mr. Stallings gasped and said that he was certainly not a bootlegger and that he would be damned.

"Most people that buy these are cracked somewhere. . . ." Roland stared gloomily down Park Avenue. He hardly heard Mr. Stallings sputter and speak again.

"My man, how long have you been selling cars?"

"Two months . . . maybe three. I forget. And don't call me your man. The name is MacDonald."

"I can't say I see much of a future for you."

"Right you are, Mr. Stallings."

"If I should decide not to buy this car, you'd lose considerable commission, wouldn't you?"

Roland turned a cold stare on the top of the little man's shining pate. "Look, Mr. Stallings. Either buy the car now, or don't buy it. Never mind the personal questions. I have a lot on my mind this morning. Just write out the check so I can get going."

The little man plumped down on the blue leather cushions. The sun had made them scorching hot and the heat made him squirm. But he reached importantly for his checkbook and wrote out a check for seven thousand dollars.

"All right, my man—excuse me—Mr. MacDonald. I'll buy it, although I must say. . . . Humph." Apparently Mr. Stallings could not decide precisely what it was he must say. He handed Roland a card along with the check. "Now I want you to deliver it to this lady. I'll 'phone her you are on the way. She'll be waiting."

"I'll bet."

"Now, if there's any trouble with this car, whom do I get in touch with?"

"Any garage. The nearer the better. Just don't bother me, my man." Roland pulled away and completely drowned in a blast of open exhaust whatever it was that Mr. Stallings was saying.

He drove across Fifty-ninth Street toward Central Park West—the address indicated on the card. He slipped through Fifth Avenue and glanced up at the sky, and then his glance became a fascinated stare, for the sky was marked with mares' tails—white, searching fingers across the blue. They were still faint summer mares' tails, and these Roland knew would mean little more than a few days' bad weather beginning tomorrow or the next day. Low ceilings, perhaps, and rain—nothing to worry about.

But why should an automobile salesman worry about God's weather? Roland didn't know. Why should he give a damn what the sky looked like—why should he even look at it? He stopped for a drink at a little speakeasy he knew near Columbus Circle and finally pulled up in front of the correct address. There was a red-haired girl with a skirt almost above her silken knees waiting for him.

"Well—Roland!"

"Poppy Samonetta!" He read the card. "Miss Samone, huh? Charmed . . . and I'll be damned."

"Drivin' cars these days, Roland?" She pouted those full lips that Roland had always disliked. She said it again and it hurt worse than the first time. "Drivin' cars these days?"

"No. I'm a sales representative. If this chariot is yours, take it."

"I'll take it." Poppy slipped in beside him.

"Sure you will, and you didn't get it for being nice to his mother."

"No, I didn't, Roland." Her frankness hushed his answer. He handed her the papers and the registration.

"Won't you come up for a drink? I live in this building."

Roland's eyes went up its modern facade to the mottled sky—and there were the mares' tails again. He brushed his hand across his mustache and jerked his tie away from his collar.

"No, Poppy. Thanks. But it's something to see you're still the same little bitch."

"Same old Roland. Can I drive you somewhere?"

He seemed to consider the offer a moment and then made a quick decision—an important one.

"Yes, by God, you can." Roland got out of the car and

pulled her to the wheel. "Drive me to Newark airport. Make it snappy."

From the ferry they could see the sea gulls, and the mares' tails in the sky, and there was a gentle breeze from the west. On the Jersey side there was an annoying guy, probably out from Teterboro Field, who did lazy eights over and over again. His plane was soundless in the crystal air, easy to see, easy to follow for a man who understood and had only to lay his head back against the leather seat to follow every maneuver. The sight of this quiet spectacle so absorbed Roland that even Poppy looked up at the plane.

"I understand you quit flying," she said.

"Who, me? Whatever gave you that silly idea?"

"This car business, then, it's something you do on the side—sort of a hobby?"

"Yes . . . yes, sort of a hobby."

"Gives you a little rest from flying."

"Yes. Of course, you understand I'm one of those men who can take flying or leave it alone. You understand that, don't you, Poppy?"

She saw that he never took his eyes from the sky. He spoke more to the breeze than to her.

"I understand, Roland." She watched his hungry eyes, and was careful not to smile.

After a while he turned to her and examined her minutely, as if he had never seen her before and seemed pleased with what he discovered.

"You know, you're not such a bad gal, Poppy. Not such a bad gal at all."

There was a small room on the ground floor beneath Gafferty's office. Since it was off the hallway where the lockers stood and the operations office where Sydney worked, it had become an unofficial pilots' lounge. The room was furnished with two old chairs and a battered couch left by some tenant long before, and the floor was always littered with cigarette butts. But there were two fine windows overlooking the airport and it was pleasant to sit and smoke and see who could lie the most, and watch the ships land and take off and finally disappear in their appointed directions.

In this room there were always a few pilots either off duty or about to go on duty, and Roland was accordingly careful to have Poppy let him out of the car on the opposite side of the hangar. There was no use in making his return more embarrassing than it was going to be anyhow.

He walked through the open door and saw Frank Sinnitch buried behind a newspaper, and he felt relieved. Frank wouldn't say anything, no matter what the occasion. He might look, but he wouldn't speak, and that would help. Frank did look. A faint flicker of surprise came into his cold blue eyes. But he only nodded his head in recognition and went back to his newspaper.

"Hello, Frank," said Roland.

Another nod, and that was that. Then Roland heard a mocking chuckle behind him and he shuddered inwardly. Shorty Baker. He could think of no one he wanted to see less just now. Shorty stood up and stretched his clublike arms lazily.

"Well, well . . . well! Roland MacDonald. What you won't see when you ain't got your gun!" He put his hand to his mouth and shouted into the hall where the lockers stood: "HEY, PORKIE! COMERE 'N' SEE WHAT CREPT OUT OF THE WOODS! HURRY UP AND COMERE!"

"Hello, Shorty." Roland maintained as much dignity as he could.

Then Porkie came in, buckling his helmet under his chins. He stopped in his tracks when he saw Roland, and a look of understanding passed across his face.

"Hello, Roland," he said. "Long time no see."

"I s'pose you just dropped by for a little visit," said Shorty, sticking his thumbs in his belt. "Wanted to tell us about the automobile business, maybe. That should be very interesting indeed."

Roland knew from the twinkle in Shorty's eye that he would never hear the last of this. "Gafferty around?" he asked casually.

Shorty turned to Frank Sinnitch and then to Porkie as if for an explanation of the question.

"Gafferty? Now, isn't it strange?—a man is gone from this clambake a few months and he forgets right away how things operate. Completely forgets we don't keep track of the boss—he keeps track of us. Sit down, Roland. Sit down right here and tell us all about that there auto business.''

Shorty waved him to a chair, but Roland held his ground. Get this thing over with and let time take care of the rest.

"All right, Shorty. Have your fun, but where's Gafferty? You might as well know it . . . I . . . well, I came to get my job back.''

Shorty pretended to be stunned at the news. "No! . . . *No!* I don't believe it. After all these years aviation has come into its own. Wait till Orville Wright hears about this!''

Then Porkie walked over to Roland and put his hand on his arm—and for this gesture and for the quiet words that followed, Roland could have kissed his fat, round face.

"I'm glad you're coming back, Roland. The place hasn't been the same without you. Gafferty's over eating lunch and I think he'll have a job for you . . . pretty soon, anyway.''

Roland hastily lit a cigarette to hide his feelings.

"And maybe now,'' added Porkie, without a change in expression, "I'll get back the thirty bucks you still owe me for that double bed.''

## 14

Late in September the leaves began to change along the route. From the Hudson to the Mohawk and through the rolling hills where the Erie Canal turned, and from the Finger Lakes to Canada and along the flat shores of Lake Erie, the fields were deep yellow and light yellow and sepia spattered with gold. The earth was an endless Oriental carpet beneath a pair of wings. In the nights the valleys were soft with fog.

In October the winds swung to the northwest and held there. On most days the air sparkled and you could see from the Catskills to Lake Oneida if you climbed a ship high enough. As the air cooled a little more each day, there was a different feel to the ships. It was a delicate difference hardly noticeable on the ground, but whereas the ships had seemed to mush off the hot summer fields reluctantly, now they were eager to take the newly dense air, and would do a sideslip down without a bump to spoil their even grace. Now the men who flew found it more comfortable to wear their leather jackets during the day, and when they flew at night they wore heavy wool shirts and gloves and tied a piece of string around their pants bottoms to keep out the chill drafts that came through the cockpit floor.

Even November held fair for a while, but the winds increased and buffeted the sculptured summer cumulus until it was transformed into indifferent layers of thick stratus clouds that covered wide areas with increasing frequency. Sometimes the whole route was heavy with them. You could fly on top if you had the will, skimming along the swells of a gentle aerial ocean with hardly a change in altitude, and feel the still, warm sunlight on your shoulders. Or you could work up between layers and so become a minute particle between two torn gray decks with sometimes a portion of the earth visible through a lower hole. And it was well to have such a hole near destination. Both on top and between layers the vapor forms were ever-changing, and the winds, unseen like powerful tides, could bar or deflect a ship from its assigned course without the pilot's realizing it.

The winter was making up. Tightening its muscles. The enemy that so far had toyed with a few lonesome invaders and allowed their puny strength some measure of success was now prepared to return the overwhelming balance of power to its proper possessor. Those who had reason to observe such things could see it all over America. The northers were making up in Texas; already the gumbo mud was wrapping like sticky bandages around landing wheels. It rained oftener and the ceilings fell lower and lower. Snow squalls over the Sierras tossed the Western Air boys as they spiraled into Salt Lake City, reminding them to cinch their safety belts a little tighter. Chicago and St. Louis were dingy with rain and smoke. Cleveland and Dayton, and Louisville, Cincinnati, and Oklahoma City, and Columbus and Pittsburgh and Washington were surrounded by cold fronts that moved eastward, as must all the nation's weather—relentlessly, one after the other. The N.A.T. boys pushing across the Alleghenies checked more carefully on their parachutes, and sometimes looked with longing at Bellefonte's emergency field. Even those who flew in the still humid Louisiana air and through Georgia and Alabama and Florida were aware of the opening of the conflict to the north, for their connecting mails were likely to be very late, and sometimes they did not arrive at all. The coming of this antagonist affected men in ways as varied as their styles of flying.

Though the first snow barely whitened the Catskill tops and melted away the next morning, Porkie Scott saw it with alarm. Acutely aware that he was violating what he had come to consider the basic rights of nature by flying through a winter instead of limiting his exposure to a hotel room, he made careful preparations against what he frankly admitted would be an ordeal.

He began to eat with astounding gusto, concentrating on whatever fatty foods he could obtain—"increasing the blubber covering," he explained. "Look at the whales and seals. They know what they're doing."

Porkie bought the heaviest pair of long underwear he could find. He bought a leather face mask, too, only to discover that it would not even begin to cover the various folds of his chins; so before a flight he quite openly daubed his face with smears of cold cream. He wore two heavy wool sweaters beneath his flying coveralls and a heavy fleece-lined jacket outside. Once accoutered in his boots and enormous gloves and weighted down further with his heavy parachute, which he always examined meticulously, he found it almost impossible to climb into the cockpit and wedge himself into position without aid. With grunts of appreciation he accepted such help as he could get from the mechanics.

A pilot's style of flying was a direct reflection of his personality—as much so as the way a man walks or sits in a chair or gestures with his arms. Porkie Scott, for example, would taxi along the side of a field very slowly, using a minimum of propeller blast to turn him into the wind at the end of the field. He made quite a little ceremony of the engine run-up, checking the RPM and the oil pressure with great care. Then he would tap his altimeter, which was none too accurate to begin with, frown at it, and then flick a gloved finger at his compass. He would move his controls through their arcs of motion and actually *look* at them as they moved—such was his caution and concern.

It was not that Porkie was afraid of a crash, or even of death if it came; he simply abhorred the discomfort of disaster and was making very certain it would not happen. He would take off exactly into the wind and climb slowly in a perfectly straight line. When he reached a thousand feet, he would sniff the air and begin a slow gentle turn toward his destination. If there was something about the en-route weather that displeased him, if it looked as though skimming the hilltops was required—with even the faint possibility of not being able to turn around—Porkie would turn about before the situation reached an impasse and return to the field from which he had come. Once on the ground again, he was plainly indifferent to public opinion. He would only smile blandly and mumble something about not being interested in experimentation.

Shorty Baker took the coming of winter in his stride. At his instigation, the widow from Churchville had moved to Buffalo and was keeping him warm. He had hired a Santa Claus costume for his flight on Christmas Day and was rapidly accumulating nonbreakable gifts to drop to the switch-tower man, the crippled Gerald Amundsen, and the many others of his wide acquaintance along the way. The thought that weather might defer his flight did not occur to him, for Shorty ignored the weather, winter or summer. At all times he flew so low and was so well informed as to who lived on that farm or at the bend of the river just there—and who had just put a new roof on his barn, or had cut a road, or was digging a well, or sitting up late of nights—that his flying had become virtually an unobstructed form of surface transportation. Flying was almost a sideline to him, a means to an end whereby he avoided hard work and into the bargain managed to carry on an amazingly complicated network of personal affairs. He had not the slightest interest in life-expectancy curves.

Even among blood brothers the difference in flying habits was strongly marked. Colin flew his ship without show, although to the practiced eye his landings and maneuvers were movements of lovely precision. He would throttle back his engine a long way from the field, then slip evenly down and down without a change in his glide angle. He would land, whether over high-tension lines at Syracuse or over the trees at Rochester, exactly where he wanted to land, and then roll up within a few feet of the waiting agent without further power. In a way this was show-off, since it took considerable skill and application—and Colin knew it. But in Colin it was not an exhibition but an example of the work of a skilled artisan.

Tad was the virtuoso. For their own sake, he loved the bravuras, the cadenzas, and the fortissimos of flying. And he was as quickly bored with the routine. His whims were many and sometimes nerve-racking to the men on the ground. All too often when they stood watching the horizon, awaiting his arrival and almost abandoning hope, he would come slicing straight down on their heads from no one knew how high. One moment they would be upset because at last Tad Mac-Donald had succumbed to the law of averages; they would even begin to plan how to rescue his lost ship, discuss whom to call and not to call, estimate how much the search would cost. Then the next moment they would be cursing Tad MacDonald and ducking lest the Pitcairn's wheels part their hair. Sometimes they thought they could hear his mocking laughter mingled with the screeching whine of the flying wires. Gafferty had more than once talked to Tad about his flying, and it looked as though he could go on talking to him, for Tad's only answer was a cynical smile.

Roland flew according to his mood. Sometimes he would race across a field and whip his ship into position; at other times he would haul it up in a climb until it hung on the propeller. He was often heavy-handed with his ship, but always he was its master. He stood on equal footing with the weather. The winter's tricks were obvious and well known to him. He would fly parallel to a front that was dark and brooding, and watch it with a jaundiced eye. He knew that if a flatter shelf of clouds preceded the main cloud formations, like a massive rumpled bedroll, he was then on the advancing side of a front; and if he was flying west, the weather would unquestionably become worse. Yet if those same gray masses built abruptly to a ceiling, and merely trailed perhaps some rain and lower scud, then he was behind the front. His westward progress would improve then, and he could sit back and relax—at least until the next day or night, when, depending on the location of the front, he would have to fly through it eastbound again. Roland often passed the same front as many as four times in two days. Thus he came to know far more about its contours and speed and behavior than did the earthbound weather bureaus.

"It's these early winter fronts you can't half the time get under," he said to Porkie Scott, who had just landed at Buffalo in a mire of mud and wet snow. "Now what we need is some kind of half-decent set of instruments and something to tell where we're going. Then maybe we can go over the top of the things.''

Porkie's boots slobbered audibly. The seat of his pants was sopping wet, and his face was blue with misery. Whatever enthusiasm he had ever had for flying in general and the great outdoors in particular had congealed on this December afternoon.

''I am not interested in going over fronts, even if you could get over them. I am not interested in going under them, or through them—now or in the future, or forever more,'' he said with mournful determination. His pudgy hands shook as he searched through his voluminous flying suit for cigarettes. ''I have brought you an airplane, Roland. I also brought to the citizens of Buffalo and points west four sacks of mail—and I venture to say that their entire contents are not worth the puddle I sit in.''

''It wasn't so bad when I came through yesterday. Did you play the layers?''

''No. I crawled along underneath on my hands and knees, and I do not know why. You have your ideas and I have mine. One of mine is to get the hell off this clambake. I can't tell you where the front is, because it's everywhere—rain and snow from here to Newark, but mostly snow. If I had a foghorn I would have blown it. Just to keep me company.''

''If we just had the instruments . . . the right ones. And if we knew how . . .''

''Haven't you changed your ideas, or am I· hearing right?''

Roland looked at the floor. When he spoke again, the words came very slowly. ''Well . . . ever since Keith . . . I keep thinking something ought to be done.'' Roland thought a lot about Keith these days. Every time he circled Albany airport, the boy's face came back to him. He had studied and restudied the possible causes of his crash. He had questioned Sweeney again and again. He had reenacted Keith's last flight with his own plane as accurately as he could imagine it, trying to discover where the boy might have failed. The idea that it must never happen again became on obsession with him. He had come to think that preventing any repetition was something he owed to Keith.

"One thing for sure," said Porkie, shrugging his shoulders. "A man's future is rather limited around here."

Roland stood up. He towered over Porkie, working his heavy features and rubbing his mustache. To Roland, every thought and every act had to have its proper histrionic trimmings.

"I'm going to try something tonight, Porkie. I haven't tried it before. Could be it won't work out. If it doesn't, I'd like you to know why. Then maybe you could tell the others, especially Colin and Tad—and Lucille, too."

Porkie looked up suddenly. "You're breaking my heart. Listen, you're too old to be a hero."

But Roland had that faraway look in his eyes. He could already hear the trumpets blaring.

"Just the same, I'm going to try it. Porkie, I've been doing a lot of thinking. We're barking up the wrong tree, all of us. It's an old tree, and it's rotten inside—and if I'd done more thinking awhile back, maybe what happened to Keith wouldn't have happened. Maybe if I'd taught him to pay less attention to the seat of his pants and more to that little turn-and-bank instrument when he couldn't see—well, maybe Keith would still be around. Looking out over the side with your ugly face in the slip stream is fine for Sunday-afternoon flying, for hopping a bunch of farmers at ten bucks a head around some pasture, but it just won't work out in this kind of flying. You can't see fast enough, if you get what I mean. By the time you do see something, it's too late. Corn-pasture flying and this mail business won't mix . . . and it's my fault for not figuring that out sooner and telling Keith. I taught him everything he knew, and when I talked he listened. So in a way it's my fault, and no one can ever tell me different. Maybe I can sort of make it up to him, Porkie . . . just by proving I was wrong. So here's what I'm going to do tonight—and remember, the reason I'm telling you is that it may not work out. If it doesn't, the idea will still be the right one. It'll just be because I made a mistake somewhere along the line. Tonight, when I hit a cloud I'm not going to duck underneath it or around it. I'll stay in it on that silly turn-and-bank. I'll hold my altitude and course all the way to Newark if I have to . . . if it can be done."

"All right. I'll remember. I'll remember you thought you knew more than the birds, who have been at this thing long enough not to try any such foolishness." Porkie rose and stretched. He flicked some cigarette ashes to the floor and studied them. When he looked up to Roland again, there was understanding in his pale eyes. "All right, you old fool. But just be sure the turn-and-bank is working, which will be a miracle in itself, and don't pick a cloud that's stuffed with a mountain. Just be very sure. . . ."

Roland pulled his jacket sleeve back from his wrist watch. "I've got two hours to wait," he said. "Think I'll go eat a half-dozen hamburgers to sorta clear my brain. . . ."

Colin took off in a climbing left turn against a buffeting forty-miles-an-hour northwest wind that checked his forward progress so much he seemed to climb straight up. When he finally turned back over the Newark swamps, he swooped down out of the oatmeal-gray sky and held the nose of his ship directly on the open Ford roadster parked beside the hangar. A few feet above it, he jammed the throttle forward and pulled back on the stick. The Pitcairn shook and climbed again. Glancing quickly back over the tail, he saw Lucille wave to him. Then the white flash of her face became indistinguishable as the ground sank rapidly. He thought he saw the car begin to back away, and again he had the feeling that had recently come to plague him. It was intensified by Lucille's good-bye kiss, still strong upon his lips.

This feeling confused him and made him slightly angry because it was so persistent. He could offer no logical explanation for it—except that, as in so many men, the two loves of his life were clashing and hence he was unable to embrace either one completely. Whenever he left Lucille at the airport, as he had just done, he sensed that it was a considerably more complicated act than merely calling forth a certain amount of mechanical power that would separate them for a period. He was not just going off to work, though physically that was all he had done. The difference was that the moment he was in the air, a connection was broken; his very thinking seemed under a spell, and he seemed to join another love—not only physically, but spiritually. He looked into the distances and saw there, not Lucille, but beauties that were strangely personal, as if he alone possessed them.

Now there were snow squalls misting down a thousand feet like slanting gauze columns. How could Lucille be asked to comprehend their majesty? And later there would be the stratus racing on the December wind across the hills, and the deep, soft evening that would so quickly, as if ashamed, blot out towns and cities and villages and all the marks that man had made across the earth. How could Lucille share this ever-changing splendor aloft, when the column of a church sufficed her, or a brook, or twilight on a street, or any other earthly thing?

Colin felt guilty when he thought this way—uncomfortable, as he had felt the night he was at Poppy's. But he could not do anything about it; apparently there was no sharing this love except with others of his kind. His attempts to describe to Lucille how he felt, and why, had failed, even in their moments of deepest understanding—even though Lucille had listened and questioned and had even been wise enough to encourage him. Colin had finally come to regard Lucille as his earthly life in all its manifestations.

His flying was another life entirely. After he had left Lucille, spotted that last wave of her hand, she shrank to less than a memory. Thus, in a way, he had to start all over again once he returned to her. The gap in time was not filled as it might have been by some other man gone on a trip—filled with thinking about things to be done together, with plans for some future enterprise. Colin was completely enchanted by the life at hand.

He worked his way up the Hudson beneath a very low ceiling, banking around Bear Mountain far beneath its summit. Then night enclosed him. The visibility became very poor—less than a mile, he guessed. There was even in this entombment a wild beauty that sparkled when he flicked on his landing lights to watch the snow streaking through the wings in spitting horizontal streams. But he turned the lights off at once, lest they blind his vision. Only the dark and brooding bank of mountains on his left and his compass gently rocking in the soft glow of its tiny light rem' guide him. The red running light on his left wing tip green light on the right flared occasionally as he flew through a heavier snow squall, casting an eerie phosphorescent halo around the ship. Finally he turned off the lights completely; there would be no one else about, anyway.

At Poughkeepsie he had bare clearance between the cloud ceiling and the bridge. The town itself was nothing but a white crystalline glow on his right. Colin hoped that it would not be snowing so hard at Albany.

He had just checked his time past Poughkeepsie when he noticed that his engine oil pressure had dropped to twenty pounds. He had been so absorbed in following the river bank in the gloom that he had not watched it, and now he had no idea whether the drop had been fast or slow. And this was important—very important. If it had been slow, the engine would doubtless carry on to Albany; but if it had been fast, there was more than a leak or a faulty pump and he would never reach Albany.

He felt his parachute harness. The quick, hard feeling that had come to his stomach subsided a little. The sudden loneliness passed. If the pressure dropped much more, he would have to anticipate the engine's failure. Before it came, he would have to pull up into the overcast and jump, and he must be sure to pull away to the east at the same time so as to clear the river. At this low altitude he couldn't wait until the last moment.

So he divided his attention now, watching the snow, the still steady beating of his engine, the dark, winding bank, the compass, the ticking minutes on his watch, and the oil-pressure gauge. There were many things for him to watch with the greatest care, any one of which could defeat him. But the minutes passed with painful slowness.

When Roland came out of the little hamburger stand that huddled brightly in the snow next to the hangar, he stood breathing deeply of the cold night air and patting his stomach contentedly. Three hamburgers with onions had satisfied his hunger, but the side plate of fried potatoes with onions, the double portion of apple pie with cheese on the side, and the two mugs of coffee had put him in a mellow mood. He belched resoundingly against the wind and strode straight-backed through the snow to his waiting ship. He felt able and magnificent.

He began to croak his favorite song, but his words were
swept away in the snow and the wind, beyond the hamburger
stand, beyond the glow of Buffalo, and off into the darkness
where lay his future.

> Just a wee duck an door'es,
> Just a wee drap, thas aw,
> Just a wee duck an door'es,
> Before we gang awa.
>
> There's a wee wifie waitin'
> In a wee but-and-ben;
> If you can sa-a-a-a-a-ay
> 'It's a braw bricht moonlicht nicht,'
> You're all richt, ye ken!

Yes, this night Roland was very ready. He felt that the
signs and portents were right. In anticipation of his success he
had bought a bottle of Canadian whisky from the man who
ran the hamburger stand. It was good whisky and it would be
well used when he landed safely at Albany. He stowed it
carefully in the back pocket of his flying suit and patted it
now to reassure himself of its presence.

As he walked around the ship, giving the control wires his
customary inspection, it began to snow very hard. The agent,
a small, timid man who had been waiting patiently for him,
shivered, wiped his running nose, and looked around miserably at the snow. He plucked at Roland's arm.

"Aren't really going, are you?"

Roland snorted. He towered above the agent like a giant
breathing steam in the night.

"Why not? The night is as fair as a lover's wish. It's a
braw nicht. The stars are putting my eyes out."

The agent looked up. His mouth opened in a swirl of snow.
"I don't see no stars, MacDonald."

"You just don't know how to look for 'em. Is the ship full
of gas?"

"I did like you told me."

"Set with the mail?"

"Yeah. I hope it gets there."

"Back the prop and stand clear then. I'm late." Roland belched again, tightened his helmet strap, and swung up to the cockpit.

The agent put out a restraining hand and looked around unhappily. "Please wait until morning, MacDonald."

"I'm just climbing in here for a cozy night's sleep," snarled Roland. The man was beginning to annoy him.

"But you *can't* go! The weather reports are all rotten. Gafferty will have a conniption fit. He'll blame *me!*"

"Blame you?"

"Yeah. Come on—forget it! The weather's lousy everywhere. Please be sensible. Please. . . ."

"Blame you for what?" Roland insisted.

The agent hesitated. There were some things that were hard to say to another man, particularly if it was one of these confounded MacDonalds. Yet he felt it his duty to speak.

"Well, if anything should . . . happen."

"What the hell are you mumbling about? Nothing can happen." Roland swung into the cockpit. He wiped the snow spray off his mustache, which now had a walrus droop to it, and began priming the engine.

The agent stuck his head over the side of the cockpit, his face pinched with worry. "Suppose something did happen, MacDonald? Suppose . . . well . . . if you cracked up? Gafferty would fire me."

"That," said Roland, continuing his priming, "would be a *real* tragedy."

The agent looked up and around him desperately. The philosophy that urged Roland on was beyond his understanding. Why would a man *want* to risk his neck? And even if he saved his neck, he'd lose his job, beyond doubt. A job, like one's neck, was a thing to be treasured—almost equally. A job was a bank balance, however small, a house with a piece of new furniture added from time to time, and a wife to polish it—and to warm one at night. A job was two weeks' vacation every year. The respect of one's fellows. The Saturdays and Sundays, the membership in a lodge, the insurance premiums, the haircuts and shoeshines, the credit at the butcher's. It was very hard to explain to a man like Roland MacDonald about security.

"If you go, just remember I told you about the weather."

"I heard you the first time. Quit worrying. I'm flying this thing . . . or am I?"

"I still think you're crazy to go."

Roland turned his massive head. He closed his eyes momentarily and allowed a look of infinite patience to cross his face.

"Just go to bed," he said. "Just go to bed and dream about becoming a vice president some day. Unless you want to freeze your ass riding on that wing, get the hell away from this airplane."

Colin tapped the oil-pressure gauge. The needle had dropped to fifteen pounds. That would be enough to hold the engine to Albany if it did not drop any more—and for a few minutes, when it seemed to stand still, he tried to believe that it would go no lower. Then it fell again, very slowly but steadily, to twelve pounds. Still, the engine was running smoothly; if it had been daytime and he could have maintained a good altitude—one that would allow him to glide for a quick landing—he would not have been concerned. But he was still a bare two hundred feet above the river. He dared not climb any higher and lose sight of the occasional lights that appeared along the east bank like fireflies in the snow.

He took off his glove and reached over the side of the fuselage. He rubbed his palm along the fabric and then held it under the panel light. It was covered with congealing black oil. Now he had something else to think about: fire. If the engine oil, creeping inexorably along under the force of the slip stream, found its way to some spot on the fuselage where the engine exhaust flame came near enough—Colin had seen planes burn before and knew that there was no more willing mass of tinder. A few seconds, and the smallest flame would be nursed by the slip stream until the whole ship became a roaring torch. Then it would be a question of which could move the faster—Colin or the flame.

So he watched warily for a change in the color of the flickering purple exhaust. If it turned yellow, that would be oil flame. He must instantly pull up into the overcast, holding the climb for a good thousand feet. Then roll her over on her back, drop out, and don't bother to count. Colin unbuckled his safety belt and laid it carefully on each side of his seat. He rechecked his parachute harness. Every moment gained by these small movements might make the difference.

As the soft snow fell away beneath Roland's wheels at Buffalo and he swung gracefully into a climbing turn to the left, the compass turned contrarily to the right. This behavior brought home to him again the important fact that in an airplane this most simple and dependable of all instruments has a habit of going wild. In rough air the compass swings violently back and forth. As now, in a bank-and-turn, it backs around the opposite way, seemingly in defiance of all the laws that control it. Roland was prepared for this: he knew about "northerly turning error." But his foreknowledge did not make him like it any better. He knew that before the compass would make sense again, it would have to be treated to a period of calm and straightaway flight. And since these terms can seldom be met when the compass is most needed—as in turning about an airport in poor visibility, or even turning when one cannot see—the turn-and-bank instrument was contrived to supplement the compass. It worked with surprising delicacy, but it required the absolute faith of the user, since its testimony was frequently contrary to a man's natural sensory feelings. Flying solely by compass, altimeter, rate of climb, and turn-and-bank was a knack that very few men had acquired to any considerable degree. It meant that quite possibly the turn-and-bank would indicate Roland's left wing was down when the seat of his pants told him it was his right wing that was down. Or it might show that he was turning to the right when every sense shouted that he was turning to the left—or, indeed, not turning at all. And the turn-and-bank, if operating properly, would be correct.

It operated instantly and very simply, but the faith was hard to maintain and only complete obedience to its signals brought success. To rely partly on the instrument and partly on the seat of the pants resulted in indecision and frequently disaster. Roland knew this much, and so he had reason to be uneasy.

The turn-and-bank instrument was about the size of a small

alarm clock. Near the bottom of the face there was a short curved tube containing a ball that rolled freely from side to side and thus indicated the position of the wings. If the ball slid to the left, the left wing was down and the plane was skidding into the bargain. If it slid to the right, the right wing was down. Since the lowering of a wing initiated a turn in that direction, it was necessary to keep the ball in the center by judicious use of rudder and ailerons.

Above the ball was a pointer, a bar that leaned right or left like a metronome hand. If the bar leaned to the left, Roland was turning to the left, at a rate and degree corresponding to the angle of the bar. This bar was connected by a series of watchlike gears and levers to a gyroscope inside, which was turned by the action of a small Venturi tube fastened to the side of the ship. The strong slip stream, passing through the Venturi, turned small metal rotor blades, causing the gyroscope to whirl at tremendous speed. Thus it maintained its balance.

Roland's life hung on his ability to rely upon this mechanism. Normally the beacon lights along the course would guide him, and these were supplemented by Roland's personal knowledge of the route. At Rochester the canal turned *so,* at Batavia the railroads merged *so;* beyond Syracuse he should follow the shore of Lake Oneida just *so.* Then there would be the lights of Rome and Utica to the north, and perhaps the glow of an engine's boiler along the New York Central to reassure him. There was even Shorty Baker's little friend near Fort Plain, with his acetylene light so faithful in the night. And there were many additional signs and landmarks which were a part of each pilot's knowledge and equipment and which he shared with the others.

". . . There's a new sign on top the hotel at Rochester. You can see it for miles. It blinks one-two-three, like that, then goes out for about two seconds. Can't miss it!"

". . . If you go over a hot-dog stand—or I don't know, maybe it's a roadhouse with green and red lights hangin' all over it—you're south of the course about ten miles . . . about near Glenside, you are."

". . . They aren't working any more on that sand pit to the north of Woodward. Place is black as the inside of your hat

. . . like to got me lost the other night. . . . Know that bend in the railroad near Fort Plain? Well, you take a course of one hundred and twenty degrees and hang on to it . . . from Little Falls, that is. In about ten minutes you'll go right over the spur that runs north up to Gloversville. It's down in a ravine . . . hang on a little longer and you'll pick up the railroad again at Amsterdam. You can't miss, and it'll keep you north of them hills west of Schenectady.''

And there were many other things to look for in the daytime.

". . . Grab onto that single track with the high-tension wires running along the north side of it . . . right where it branches off from the main line near Churchville. It's the only one with single tracks and the wires, so you can't miss. Stick with it until it runs into a big switchyard . . . oh, several tracks . . . then do a sharp left bank, then follow the switch tracks till you pass over a big area of trees and then a high-tension line. Cut the throttle, count twenty . . . and you'll land right smack dab in the middle of Rochester airport. Won't make no difference if you can't see a quarter of a mile. You'll plunk right in the middle of it.''

These minutiae were supplemented by certain pooled observations on the weather.

". . . Watch a south wind at Buffalo in July and August. . . . The place socks in before you can circle the field. . . . Look for either southeast or northeast at Newark . . . especially in the early morning. One way brings in smoke from the factories, and the other way fog from the sea. It'll get you coming and going.''

It was knowing little things like these that kept a man out of trouble.

On this night, Roland proposed to abandon his usual methods and venture into a new world. He intended to leave hidden beneath him all the known landmarks. He would enter the overcast and stay in it until his calculations indicated that it was time to come down. Since most of these were based on incomplete information, he was well aware of the risk involved.

Some minutes before he reached Batavia, he took a last look at the farm lights below and satisfied himself that he was on course over a certain crossroads that he knew. He patted the pint of whisky and thought of Albany as he gritted his teeth and pulled up into the low overcast. Then he concentrated with all his will on the turn-and-bank instrument, relating it to his compass, which for a time held obligingly at eighty-five degrees. When he reached three thousand feet he leveled off—or assumed he did, since the altimeter and the air speed held steady. Now would come the test, not of the theory, but of himself. He would have to endure this new and strange flying sensation for exactly twenty-one minutes. Then, according to his figures, he could let down until he broke out of the overcast and Rochester would be just ahead. He had only to hold his course and believe the instruments before him.

Despite the cold night wind that swept into the cockpit, he perspired freely. His eyes moved quickly, anxiously, from instrument to instrument. Air speed. Altitude. Turn-and-bank. Compass course. It was like keeping track of a roomful of rambunctious children. Once he peered over the side, but the sight of the fragile-looking wings ghosting through the dark clouds disturbed him, and the blue flame from the exhaust flickered and lit his clammy world in a terrifying way. He quickly drew in his head and fastened his eyes on the instruments. The minutes ticked past. Suddenly he entered a region where the clouds took on an amber hue. He looked over the side quickly and saw an indeterminate blob of light in the depths. His spirits rose. That would be the lights of Batavia. Right on course.

He held longer and even kicked the rudder bar anxiously to see if the action would be transmitted on the turn-and-bank. The luminous pointer leaned sharply in the direction he had kicked. Good. He felt very confident until it occurred to him that those lights might have been Attica or Le Roy or even Akron Junction. Impossible. They couldn't be—not that far off the course in so little time. But what would the wind be doing—the wind that he could not see?

He tried to picture the countryside below: the gently rolling country, familiar, with the occasional farm light cutting a warming shaft through the snow. He found that he had developed a new affection for it. He repressed an almost irresistible urge to descend and look around; even if he could not see them, he would know that people were there, as human as Roland himself, living upon the earth in a way that he understood. But this world, in which he sat an all too temporary prisoner, was so boundless that it confused his mind. The altimeter read three thousand feet, but judging from all bearings that met his eye he might be at thirty thousand feet or thirty thousand miles. The altimeter could not measure his ultimate separation, or his degree of loneliness. This, too, was a new experience, for Roland had never been lonely in an airplane before.

When the time came, he pushed the nose down, though the only indications he had that the ship was descending were an increase in air speed and the quick erratic unwinding of the altimeter. Something was wrong with the rate-of-climb. It did not move. Stuck, probably. Roland gulped when he reached nine hundred feet and still flew in blackness. The time. There should be lights now. The lights of Rochester. But he was still in a black cavern. Rochester itself was five hundred feet above sea level. That would leave but four hundred between him and the hard earth. And still there were no lights. Well, now, that was peculiar—or was it?

Colin was scudding along just beneath the overcast. That glowing birthday cake now silhouetting the rocker boxes of his engine would be Albany. If one malicious snow squall did not select this time to blot out the city, he would make it. He told himself that no engine, however ornery, would choose to function with almost zero oil pressure for so long, and then quit in the last three or four minutes. To ease its labors, he had cut the engine back until it barely held the Pitcairn in the air. Thus it might last longer because it would run cooler, but the decision required Colin to be absolutely sure of the maneuvers to come. He must approach the airport in a straight line and be certain not to overshoot when he got there. Any turning or climbing would demand extra power, and he doubted very much if the engine had any to spare.

Although the airport itself was invisible, he was operating with familiar equipment now—the seat of his pants and his knowledge of the route. He eased his ship over toward the west bank of the Hudson and worked the rudder slightly left and right so that he might see everything before him. Despite the snow that stung his eyelids, he pushed up his goggles. This was where the niceties of pilotage came in. He must keep to the west, though not too far to the west. There would be hills there, just high enough to make him turn or climb for altitude. He slowed the Pitcairn to sixty miles an hour, barely hanging it on the propeller.

As the town slipped beneath him he looked away from its glowing comfort and waited until the sky began to darken again. The airport was not far off now—a mile, a mile and a half—but far enough away from the town itself to be still hidden in the murk. He looked along the earth for a high-tension line. If he could cut across it at just the proper angle, he would be headed directly for the airport. It took a special kind of observation, a feeling for how things looked from aloft, to discover a frail net of wires in the half-darkness and the driving snow within the few seconds allotted to him. But Colin saw it—as Tad or Roland, or Porkie or Shorty Baker, or Whispering Johnny would have seen it—and immediately he felt relieved. Now keep to the east; along the road (his reason for turning slightly made him think of Keith) that water tower still stood to the west. Then he saw the field with the wind sock on the hangar roof looking like a long Japanese lantern. The wind was north, but Colin would not have tried to circle no matter what the wind.

"Just thirty more seconds," he murmured to the engine. Then he cut it back and said, "You can quit now," and glided down to the snow.

There were no mechanics at Albany, so Sweeney and Colin had to remove the cowling behind the engine and search for the fault themselves.

"Same as I thought," said Sweeney. He wiped his cold fingers free of oil and pointed to the pipe joint between the oil pump and the engine. "A wonder you made it. The fluting must've cracked after somebody tightened this here nut. Then the crack spread with vibration and you've been pumping oil overboard at a fancy rate. But that's all right. I've got some more pipe inside, close enough to this size. We can cut a new piece and fit her up good enough. You're lucky that thing didn't let go altogether—specially on a night like this."

They took off the pipe and went inside to warm their fingers. Sweeney was a thin, self-important man. His eyes were very small and difficult to see beneath his pronounced overhanging brows. His only concession to vanity was the neatly trimmed mustache that stood stiffly along his upper lip—and even more stiffly when he habitually pursed his lips with an air of giving a matter great thought.

After they had stood before the potbellied stove a few minutes, he looked carefully at Colin. "Did you want to go on tonight?" he asked.

"Sure. Why not?"

Sweeney looked unhappily around the bleak hangar and shuddered as a gust of wind shook the big doors.

"I just thought—well, no one could exactly blame you if you decided to stay the night. This weather . . . and with that oil line and all. . . ." He pursed his lips, opened them again, and made small mewing noises as he sucked air through his teeth. "It's going to be cold work out there. We could fix it easier in the daylight . . . and I could set you up with a nice warm room in town."

Colin looked at the man and smiled. It *would* be pleasant in a warm room—much pleasanter than in an open cockpit, bucking the freezing wind all the way to Buffalo. And Sweeney was right! no one would blame him. Personally, he stood to gain nothing by continuing, except an inevitable case of shivers and possibly a broken neck. And like all the others, he was cynical about the actual urgency of the mail waiting in the Pitcairn's cockpit. The more he thought about it, the more sensible and attractive the idea of the warm room became. Sweeney was clever enough to hold his silence. He stood motionless, puckering and unpuckering his lips, letting the stove and the wind speak for him.

"Sounds like a good idea," Colin said finally. Sweeney's face brightened. "Only thing is . . . I might have trouble sleeping. We'll fix the pipe now."

"Guess you know what you're doing." Sweeney shrugged his shoulders and went out to the ship.

The Buffalo agent could stand it no longer. At least he would do all the right things. Then if any trouble came of this madness, he would still be in the clear. His job would be safe. His house would be safe. His warm wife would be safe. Roland had been gone two hours and forty minutes when the agent went to the 'phone and put a call through to Albany. The company didn't like to have him making long-distance calls. He would have to account for the call no matter what happened and he dreaded this, but he could not sleep until it was done.

"Hello? Albany? Sweeney?"

It was Colin who answered the 'phone on the hangar wall. "No. Sweeney's outside working on a ship. Anything I can do for you?"

"This is Buffalo. Who's talking?"

"Colin MacDonald."

"Oh. . . . Well, can you get Sweeney? No, wait a minute—that will take too much time. Did your brother arrive?"

"No. Why?"

"I just thought . . . well, he left here over two hours ago."

"For here?"

"Where else?"

"Isn't he landing at Rochester and Syracuse?"

"You know your brother."

Yes, Colin did know Roland. And he knew this night's Albany weather, too. "Stay on the job," he said. "I'll have Sweeney call you if he has any news. Now hang up." When he heard the final click he jiggled the receiver and put through a call to Rochester, fuming over the delay.

"Hello . . . Rochester?"

"Yeah?"

"Did Roland MacDonald land there?"

"No. I heard a ship about an hour and a half ago somewheres off to the south, but then he went on. . . ."

"How's your weather?"

"Stinking. Can't see a thing."

Colin hung up abruptly and called Syracuse. "Has Roland MacDonald landed there yet?"

"No. Haven't even seen him. Been waitin', though."

"How's your weather?"

"Not good. It's blowin' pretty hard and my car's stuck in the snow."

"Can you see the lights of the town?"

"Sometimes."

"All right. Stand by and listen. If you hear a plane, light every flare you've got in the place."

"I haven't got any flares. They said I was supposed to get some, but—"

"Goddamnit, burn down the hangar then!" Colin slammed the receiver on the hook and ran out to his ship. He pulled Sweeney from the wing.

"Have you got any flares, Sweeney?" He looked toward the western darkness where the water tower would be standing hidden in the snow.

"Yeah. Five or six."

"Get 'em out, then. All of them. Get going. I'll fix that pipe."

"Whatsamatter, Colin? You been drinkin' in there?"

"Get those flares out! My brother is coming in!"

## 15

Roland was deeply troubled. He had let down as close to the earth as he dared—even a little more, until the perspiration stood out on his forehead and his hands felt clammy. But still he could not break out of the overcast. And when the altimeter read six hundred and fifty feet, which meant that he was barely a hundred feet above Rochester, he began to recall the number of things that could stick up that high. He gave the Pitcairn full throttle and pulled up to think things over. No Rochester. No lights where there should have been lights. A brilliant city vanished in the gloom. Now this would take some thinking. And what confounded him was that he had finally come to trust the instruments. They had supported him well in the overcast, though they would not do so forever. And getting down through the overcast until his senses could take over their function was proving a very difficult matter.

All right, then. The hell with Rochester. The city was just being obstinate—hiding itself in a squall, perhaps. He could not be far from it; no manner of reasoning could put it over five miles away. Very well. Hide, Rochester. He would carry on to Syracuse, only fifty-three minutes away.

Except for two small breaks through which he briefly saw the lights of a farmhouse, and once a section of a small town in the swirling snow, there was nothing to interrupt his dreamlike passage through the atmosphere. Then, almost exactly as he had planned it, after he had nervously smoked two cigarettes, the overcast again took on luminescence. He was sure that this welcome light came from Syracuse. Though the town and its environs were still invisible to him, he could picture it exactly in his pilot's mind. So he waited, holding his eastern course, until the most brilliant light lay beneath his tail and the overcast began to fade again. He would be over Lake Onondaga now.

He cut the throttle and pushed the nose down sharply. He applied a little left rudder and was pleased to see that the pointer on the turn-and-bank instantly agreed with what his eyes could now tell him: that he was turning left and back toward the west, back toward the town.

The Pitcairn shuddered as he dove rapidly. The engine coughed and backfired several times. Roland cleared it with a quick burst of throttle. Every moment the overcast grew brighter. He turned away from the lightest area again. For all he knew, the buildings of Syracuse were hidden in the bottom of the overcast. It would be a shame to hit one of them now. Turning away, he would break out over the lake, or even to the east of it—and there was no high ground in that direction. Then he turned back again, toward the light, shuttling down and down.

"God bless the Syracuse Light and Power Company!" he muttered.

Then he caught a glimpse of a lighted city through a break in the lower clouds. He pushed up his goggles and shoved the Pitcairn's nose down hard. The flying wires began to moan. There were two main streets, then nothing, then the streets, some houses, a building in the snow, some chimneys, then nothing again but clouds, then—Jesus, Jesus, *this was not Syracuse!* A sharp hill came swiftly toward him, looming out of the snow. Not Syracuse! Cortland, maybe, or Auburn? His face felt hot. Something twisted in his stomach. That hill—it shouldn't be there! Turn. Get the hell out! You don't know *where* you are. He jammed full throttle again to the engine and hauled back on the stick. At once the lights became a mere glow within the clouds and quickly melted to infinity. And now Roland knew that something was very wrong.

He was shrewd enough to realize that he had now been under a strain for a long time and that as a result any little thing that went wrong would become magnified in his thinking, for it was common airman's knowledge that tension led to fatigue and fatigue to anxiety—and the latter emotion in an airplane set up some very peculiar reactions. It could make you go down when you should stay up. It could make you turn when you should continue in a straight line. Looked back upon, in cool analysis on the ground when the mind and body were rested, the causes of the anxiety and the resulting action frequently appeared both needless and silly.

The heat in his face subsided and he felt cold: cold physically, as if some great and invisible force were laying a wet blanket over him, by degrees, a little bit at a time, cunningly, so that he would not notice it. The compass began to swing dreamily, just a little at first—and it should not have swung. When he saw what was happening he was puzzled; he had not moved the controls and the air was perfectly smooth again. Then the compass swung almost around to the north and hung there, dead-eyed, accusing, and motionless. Roland shook his head. He reached forward and gently tapped the compass. It was free, rocking in the liquid, yet it still pointed just east of north.

Then the seat of his pants told him the ship had taken on a new and uneven vibration, still very little, but enough to be felt through his boots on the rudder bar and his gloved hand on the stick. He sat motionless for a moment trying to think the thing out. That compass. It was turning slowly again. Around to the north—slowly.

He pushed the rudder bar tentatively, almost as if too much pressure might break it. As he did so, he watched the turn-and-bank instrument. The ball went slightly to one side in its tube, but the bar did not move. And it should have moved. He kicked the opposite rudder. Nothing happened. It was uncanny. The turn bar held perfectly steady.

It was then that Roland began to fear. He sat very still. He could feel his face growing hot again. He reached up and loosened his collar, and his neck felt very warm. He swallowed a few times, with difficulty. Then, though he did not want to do so—for any man hates to confirm his worse suspicions—he reached forward for the landing-light switch. As he flipped it on, the lights stabbed the dirty, dismal white that surrounded him. His eyes went reluctantly to the Pitcairn's flying wires that stretched between the wings. Then he knew that his suspicions were correct. The wires were thrumming in the slip stream, and along their leading edge there was a thin white encrustation. Ice.

Roland swore. There was not enough ice to make the ship heavy or even to make it vibrate very much. That would come later, unless he did something about it. But already there had been enough ice to clog the Venturi to the turn-and-bank instrument and so render it useless. He could go up or down to escape the icing stratum in which he flew—this certain layer of the air mass that had become saturated to just the right degree and held a temperature close to thirty above zero. But he would be only complicating matters by going up, if indeed he could ever get high enough to escape the ice. It would be better to go down. The question was: how far down? He would have to do something before the seat of his pants and what he saw on the instrument panel began to conflict and eventually get him into a spin. Or he could jump.

Jumping, however, involved a great many considerations that Roland disliked. He didn't like to leave a ship until every last hope was gone. Standing in a hangar the Pitcairn was not a living thing; it was simply a machine. But in the air a ship became a friend and companion, capable of understanding and feeling and reacting to sympathetic treatment. And when a ship crashed, it was always as if something had died painfully. The twisted, broken longerons and spars inevitably seemed to point accusing, burned fingers at the pilot who was responsible. To a professional, leaving a ship while it still lived within its element was a sorry escape—an admission that the man had failed while the ship had not.

Jumping might mean a night or even several days and nights in the snow before he could walk to some farm. Then there was Gafferty. The failure of Roland's experiment was not going to be easy to explain. And if he lost a ship into the bargain? Roland would not do it. He pushed the Pitcairn down.

He was lost and he knew it. As a wise pilot, he admitted it. If there had been a mountain ten feet in front of his nose, he could not have seen it. And he knew enough of his position to realize that there were many mountains around. But he held the nose down again, watching the air speed build and build, and feeling the ship begin to vibrate more and more violently.

He would stay with the Pitcairn until three thousand feet. If he saw nothing then, he could leave gracefully. Anything lower would be stretching his luck. In his anxiety, he began smacking his lips. His mouth felt very dry. Then suddenly the idea struck him.

"Hello!" he said aloud.

He reached into his back pocket and fished out the bottle of whisky. He removed the cork with his teeth and took a long draw at the bottle—to get the liquid down from the top, he reasoned. There was no sense in spewing good whisky into the night. He immediately felt better all over. He even found time to sigh with appreciation. Then he held the whisky bottle before his eyes so that the light from the instrument panel reflected through it. Taking care to make sure the bottom of the bottle was parallel to the cockpit floor, he watched the top level of the liquid very carefully, just as he had done at Romeo's bar when he was talking to Gafferty. And he was immensely pleased with the result. The liquid was forward in the bottle, which confirmed the fact that he was going down, and it was tipped at a slight angle to the left, which meant that he was banked in that direction.

"Crude, but worthy. Very worthy," Roland breathed with satisfaction. "Now . . . so long as I don't drink my instrument, I can fly on forever. Very worthy. . . ."

He pulled on the stick until the liquid was level fore and aft and then eased the stick over to the right to correct the bank. He even ventured to climb a little, cautiously watching the whisky and noting with warm pleasure that the level of the liquor responded accordingly. After several minutes he reached the conclusion that the level was too near the top of the bottle. It would be easier to see, he decided, if the level were lowered a trifle. So he took a judicious swig and sat back in his seat more relaxed than he had been since his take-off from Buffalo.

He continued to fly by whisky level for the better part of an hour without undue difficulty. Eventually he got the compass to settle down to the south of east, where it should be. His arm ached badly from holding the bottle before his eyes and he thought how much easier it would be if the amount of liquid were reduced, but he resisted the temptation and concentrated instead upon the very real problem of his gasoline.

Although his blind-flying problems were temporarily solved, he was completely lost. At the very first break in the clouds, he must land—near a town or a farm if possible. He was very glad the ice had grown no worse; indeed, it had altogether stopped accumulating. The Wright engine was using just slightly more gasoline than normal to keep the ship in the air. Even so, the fuel supply could hardly sustain him more than another thirty minutes.

As Roland began again to review the possibilities of jumping, he ran into the break he wanted. There was a lone light on the ground, barely a thousand feet below him. He dove for it without hesitation. He cut back the engine, recorked the whisky bottle, and stuffed it hastily into his rear pocket. He flipped on his landing lights and instantly flipped them off again, for the rays against the driving snow blinded him completely. It would be better to feel his way down without lights. He cut the ignition switch and glided hopefully into the first white field he saw that was free of trees. The Pitcairn plumped softly into the deep snow and came to a stop with such sudden force that Roland was thrown hard against his safety belt; he felt the wind go out of him. Then the ship lurched up and forward. The nose went down steeply. The propeller thumped into the snow, plunged against something hard, bent wildly askew, and finally stopped. So Roland came home to earth.

When his wind came back, he braced himself against the Pitcairn's forward tilt and looked about him. The light that he had seen from aloft was gone. The wind shivered the ship and purred softly through the flying wires. The snow was making delicate little tapping noises against the fabric and on the top of his leather helmet. He was in an open field and the snow was up to the Pitcairn's lower wing. Beyond these observations, he could be sure of nothing except that he was suddenly cold again and very lonely.

"H-U-L-L-L-O-O-O-W!" he shouted.

There was no answer. He unfastened his safety belt, wriggled out of his parachute, and clambered out of the cockpit. The Pitcairn stood at a grotesque angle, on its nose in the snow, as if in obeisance. Roland stepped to the wing and sought for the familiar step place with his feet, but in the dark he missed and slipped. His feet went out from under him. His chin came around at an odd angle and hit the hard trailing edge of the wing with a force that sent his brains stinging down the back of his neck. He landed finally on one shoulder in the snow. He lay there on his back, looking up at white nothing, positive that he had broken his neck.

"Oh, my God, what a life!" he said, and spat out a mouthful of snow.

Then he took off his glove and felt his chin and found that he was bleeding to death. When he stood up at last, the wrench in his shoulder convinced him he had broken his back. But he looked sheepishly at the Pitcairn and even patted the engine cowling.

"Thanks," he said. "I'm sorry."

He opened the mail compartment, took out the three heavy sacks, blessed the writing public that they were not any heavier, swung them over his good shoulder, and turned clumsily away. Since it was impossible to see anything, he walked away from the wind.

After what seemed miles of falling down in the snow and picking himself up, he came upon a barn and found that it was attached to a small house. The house was dark. Roland worked his way around to what he presumed to be the front door. He pounded upon it for some time before there was any movement inside. Then at last he heard a scuffling, and a lamp came weaving slowly toward the glass-paned door.

"Open up in the name of the United States Mail," Roland commanded, for want of anything better to say. "Also, I'm freezing to death."

The door swung open and a man in long winter underwear stood looking at him. He wore thick gold-rimmed glasses badly in need of polishing, and his face was leathery and deeply lined. It was a strong face except around the mouth, where his lips collapsed in a hundred wrinkles, like the twisted end of a toy balloon.

"I'm an air-mail pilot," Roland continued. "I just cracked up in your field." The man merely stared at him without making any move of welcome. "My name's MacDonald. How about my coming in? I'm freezing."

"That so?" He motioned Roland into the house and led him through a long hallway until they came to the stove in the kitchen.

"The weather got kind of bad on me," said Roland, warming his hands over the stove. "I had to land. Just let me warm up a bit . . . and, say, have you got a 'phone?"

"Yup."

"I'd like to call Albany and tell 'em where I am."

"Ain't connected." The man's face expanded in a sudden toothless grin and then snapped back. He plainly felt that no further explanation was necessary.

"Hum. . . ." Roland considered his isolation a moment. "How far west of Albany are we?"

"Ain't west. Sixty-nine miles northeast."

Roland groaned. Oh, this was going to be a daisy to explain. He could hear Gafferty already.

"Oh, well . . . how about some transportation? That mail on your porch will have to keep moving."

"Ain't none. This snow will close the road."

"When will they open it?"

"By-and-by." The man's mouth clamped shut again as if he were ashamed to have said so much. He sat down in one of the kitchen chairs.

By now Roland realized that this reticence was not a sign of hostility; in this part of upper New York state, words were at a premium. But the realization did not make him any happier about staying until the sweet by-and-by. Hoping to ward off the depressing thought, he reached in his pocket for the bottle of whisky and offered it to his host.

"Have a drink, Mister. I don't believe I caught your name?"

The man took the bottle without further urging. "Phipps," he announced, and put the bottle to his mouth.

Roland shuddered to see the liquid disappear down Mr. Phipps's scrawny neck as if it were the purest rain water. When the man had finished, he wiped his mouth with the back of his hand, and then cleared his throat thoughtfully. Roland thought he was going to say something, but he should have known better. He regarded the whisky bottle with new affection. Obviously it alone would have to provide him with strength and companionship during the coming ordeal.

"Have you got any neighbors, Mr. Phipps?"

"Yup."

"Close by?" Ah, there was an angle. Go to the neighbors in the morning. Maybe they—

"Nine miles."

Roland took a stiff drink and passed the bottle in resignation. Then a soft step sounded in the doorway and Roland turned to see a girl standing there in a heavy bathrobe. He immediately reconsidered spending the winter with Mr. Phipps. Although her eyelids were pouched a little with sleep, the girl's eyes were wide and very blue and her face had a sparkling country beauty that reminded Roland of his barnstorming days.

"Stella," explained Mr. Phipps, pointing toward her with the mouth of the bottle. "Daughter."

The girl came toward Roland questioningly. "Are you hurt very badly, Mister?"

For a moment Roland wondered what she was talking about, then he quickly raised his hand to his chin and felt the clot of blood. It had practically stopped bleeding, but this, Roland considered, was no time to admit it.

"Oh, it's nothing . . . nothing at all," he said bravely, and shrugged his shoulders. The gesture shot a bolt of pain through his left shoulder, just bad enough to cause an effective wince. "I have probably broken my shoulder too." He looked ruefully at the frosted window. If there was sympathy to be had, he intended to get his full share. "I am very thankful to be alive. . . ." He allowed his voice to drop until it struck just the right note of piety.

Stella responded suitably. "I'll clean you up a bit and then get you something to eat," she said. She dampened a towel in a bucket of water that stood in the sink and came back to Roland. "That is, if you don't mind. . . ."

"Mighty kind of you." He raised his chin and, while she gently patted off the blood, he watched her with the look of a gravely wounded and grateful Saint Bernard.

"If your shoulder isn't better in the morning I'll put some liniment on it for you."

"It will probably be much worse in the morning," said Roland.

"Yup," said Mr. Phipps.

Roland could not tell whether the man was laughing at him or not. Against this possibility, he made a sign to Mr. Phipps that another go at the bottle would not be considered amiss. Mr. Phipps caught the signal and obliged him instantly.

Roland's disappearance was greeted with varied emotions in the cities of Newark and New York. Two of the New York afternoon papers found space for a paragraph saying that one Roland MacDonald, air-mail pilot, was missing and presumably lost in the early winter blizzard that had swept the upper part of the state. The night and morning tabloids told a more elaborate story, possibly because they were supplied not only with a photograph of the pilot, but also with some eye-catching eight by ten pictures of a good-looking redhead, one Poppy Samone, of Central Park West. Miss Samone was reported so stricken by the loss of her sweetheart that she found it impossible to continue her nightly performance at the Chimney Club. The editors were pleased over the choice of photographs submitted by the press agent of the Chimney Club; the single one of Roland was somewhat faded and certainly was not very recent, but those of Miss Samone—head, head-shoulders, head-shoulders-bust, full figure with crossed legs—were very satisfactory, having been taken that very morning, presumably at the height of the young woman's grief. The fallen hero and the pining songstress combined such irresistible story elements that the editors found it easy to give it the full measure of their talent—and take the rest of the afternoon off. Through their efforts and the cooperation of Miss Samone's representatives, Roland was well on his way to glory.

Gafferty was in early communication with the Syracuse agent and with Sweeney at Albany, instructing the latter to tell Colin MacDonald to begin an air search at once—an order that was superfluous since Colin of his own accord had departed with the early dawn. Gafferty further directed Shorty Baker in Buffalo and Tad MacDonald in Newark to proceed at once to the area between Syracuse and Albany and institute a search. He called the state police, the businessmen, and the insurance agent, and told several reporters who called for further details to go to hell. He called National Air Transport and asked them to have their pilots keep a sharp lookout in case Roland had worked down along their route. He waited impatiently, hoping, lighting cigar after cigar and jumping at each ring of the telephone. He held off as long as he dared before calling Lucille.

"I've got some rough news for you," he said. "You've just got to be a good girl and promise not to get excited."

"Colin is down?" Her voice was flat and empty, as if she had been waiting for the news.

"No. It's Roland. He hasn't been heard from since he left Buffalo last night. But it's much too early to worry yet. He could be down safely in a thousand places."

"Oh . . . Roland!" He could hear her catch her breath.

"Now, don't worry. I just wanted to call you before you heard any rumors. If I know Roland MacDonald, nothing has happened to him. He's sitting somewhere in a bed of roses, probably. He'll call us up when he gets around to it."

"Do you honestly think so?"

"Absolutely." And for once Gafferty spoke his full conviction.

"Then please, Mr. Gafferty . . . when he calls, tell him . . . oh . . . tell him to hurry home. I . . . I love him."

"I'll tell him." But Gafferty said it to a dead wire. Lucille had hung up. He wished he had time to go to see her. There would be time for that later, however, if things didn't take a turn for the better.

Roland slept like a child in a down bed befitting his size. Mr. Phipps had given him the room just above his own and, though the room was extremely cold, Stella had so piled his bed with comforters that he could have slept in the front yard and kept warm. And in the morning she arrived smiling at his bedside with a pot of coffee and a bowl of hot cereal.

"I let you sleep," she said. "Papa wanted to wake you up, but I said no, let you sleep."

Roland opened the other eye and was again delighted with

the girl's freshness. In fact, he was pleased with his whole situation.

"What time is it?"

"Eight o'clock. Papa has been at the chores for two hours."

Roland winced and slid farther down in the warm bed. According to his memory, the three of them had not gone to bed until three o'clock. Mr. Phipps was obviously an iron man in more ways than one.

"It's still snowing. Papa says it will be two or three days before the roads will be open." She sat down on the edge of his bed and pushed the inviting tray toward him. "That means you will have to stay here until someone comes through."

"By-and-by? I don't see how I'm going to stand it." Roland rose and reached for the coffeepot. He shook his head and scratched the red hair on his chest and tried to convince himself he was not dreaming. "Tell me, Stella—how old are you?" As long as he was going to be in residence, it would be just as well to get things straight, he thought.

"Twenty, next month."

"Ah. . . ." Roland modestly covered his chest and smiled into his coffee cup.

Despite its grayness on this morning, the world was very beautiful. He allowed himself further leisurely examination of Stella's strong neck and full bouncing figure. Her legs and arms were somewhat on the thick and muscular side, but this Roland accepted as part of the picture. They matched to perfection her full, rounded breasts. Very agreeable. His only regret was that the picture of Stella sitting so on his bed could not somehow be recorded for such miserable unbelievers as Tad and Shorty Baker. Even Colin, he mused, might appreciate his position.

"Do you have any boy friends, Stella?" he inquired searchingly.

"Just Tony."

"Tony?" Well, there was a fly in every ointment.

"Yes. He works in the garage down to Hoosick Falls. We don't see each other most of the winter. Tony don't like to get stuck in the snow."

"A-a-a-ah. I can understand that. Tony is very smart. So most of the time you're sort of alone, eh?"

"Just me and Papa. When you get to know Papa you'll like him. Of course, he don't say much. But then, when you really mean something, words are just so much noise, anyway. Don't you think so?"

"I do indeed," Roland agreed.

They laughed at his solemnity and she poked him none too gently in the stomach.

"You get dressed now. I've got some eggs and flapjacks downstairs for you. I hope you'll like my cooking."

"I think I will. I'm sure I will." Roland was convinced Stella's cooking would be to his taste even if she made the flapjacks out of concrete. "This," he muttered as he crept out of bed when she had left the room, "is where all good pilots go when they die. . . ."

In the afternoon all three of them went out to the Pitcairn and looked at it gloomily. They pulled the tail down from its unnatural position in the air. Then they got some rope and staked it firmly into the hard earth.

As far as Roland could see, there was no other damage than the twisted propeller. Once it was replaced and the ship filled with gas, he could take off again. He had picked a good field to land in, with plenty of room ahead. In a way, Roland was glad about the propeller; no amount of effort could straighten it. The very thought of leaving Mr. Phipps and his blessings was unpleasant—especially now that Stella followed his every move with open admiration. Her face was constantly alight with smiles at whatever he said, and just now it was flushed to a healthy pinkness by the wind and the snow.

He and Stella stamped through the snow back toward the house, arm in arm, laughing and pushing each other into the deeper drifts. Mr. Phipps walked ahead, apparently not caring how much fun his daughter had.

Then at night Mr. Phipps brought out a gallon jug of applejack. "Made it myself," was his only comment.

"He's been savin' it a long time," added Stella.

She rubbed Roland's shoulder with liniment, and afterwards he and Mr. Phipps dragged the old organ from the living room into the kitchen where it was warm, and Stella played for them. She didn't play very well and her repertoire consisted mostly of hymns, but they sat close to the coal stove and drank the applejack, and were very, very happy.

It was Stella who brought Roland the momentous news some three days later. It was a sparkling morning, with the sun blinding upon the snow and the icicles drip-dripping from the window ledges. She came running to him while he sat in the kitchen contentedly putting away his third batch of flapjacks. She threw her arms around his neck and rubbed her soft cheek against his ear.

"There's someone coming up the road. It must be open down below the bend. You'll have to hurry if you want to go."

The sweet syrup soured in Roland's mouth. He put down his knife and fork with an angry gesture and went quickly to the kitchen window. What he saw spoiled his breakfast entirely. A sleigh was slowly working its way between the drifts. Then he felt Stella standing close beside him and he put his arm around her, squeezing her firm waist for what he was forced to believe would be the last time.

"Now, who *could* that be?" he said unhappily.

"Looks like the mailman."

"It would be." He looked down at Stella and examined her shining face very carefully so he would not soon forget it. "I guess you'll be glad to get rid of me."

"I wish you could stay till next summer."

"Till Tony comes back?"

"Well, he *is* supposed to marry me."

Roland took this as a thrust at his own intentions. He rallied manfully. "If he doesn't, just you let Roland know."

"Are you sure you're well enough to go? It'll be a long ride."

Roland looked down at her and winked. From the beginning he had not been able to determine just how seriously Stella took his injuries, and even now the expression on her face was a puzzling mixture of concern and mischief.

"I'll never be well enough to leave this place, Stella. But there is a man in Newark, New Jersey—a man whose heart was chipped off a cylinder block. He is going to want to know a few things. Still . . . I might be back. Somebody has to come for that airplane, right away. I *will* be back. Just you wait for me. . . . I'm like that fellow out there in the snow, see? I'm a sort of mailman, too."

Gafferty did want to know a lot of things, and it made the interview no easier for Roland to realize that for once he must hold his tongue and handle the matter with the greatest diplomacy in order to attain his final objective.

"I suppose you know you've made a damn fool of yourself," said Gafferty, enjoying Roland's discomfiture. "In a way, I'm sorry you didn't break your neck. You lost an airplane. . . ."

"I did not. All it needs is a new prop. The landing was perfect. Snow was a trifle on the deep side, that's all."

"A trifle. Just what the hell were you doing flying around in weather like that? I hired you—and rehired you, which was my second mistake—because I thought you had some sense. I was wrong."

"I was sort of . . . experimenting. It worked, too. I flew all the way from Buffalo to where I landed on instruments. Then my turn-and-bank froze up and I had to do something. There was a hole and my good sense told me to take advantage of it."

"Sixty-odd miles northeast of Albany. I wasn't aware that we had inaugurated mail service to Mr. Phipps's farm. How is that going to look on our report to the Post Office Department?"

"I'm sorry about that. I must've picked up one hell of a tail wind."

"Wonderful. And you sat there, fat, dumb, and happy, while it blew you halfway to Boston. It seems the tail wind stopped blowing when you landed. You disappeared for three days . . . completely. The least you could have done was to turn in the mail. Roland, listen, the government is funny about that. They don't like to have you keeping the mail under some dame's bed for three days and nights.

"I told you about that, and besides, there wasn't any bed—I mean any dame. The snow was just too deep to get away from that awful place. You can't imagine what I've been through, Mike."

"I can imagine, but you'd better make a good story of it before you see Lucille. She may be married to your brother, but she worries about you, too. God knows why she bothers. Colin and Tad are going to have a few questions, too. While you sit with your feet up, taking life easy, they fly all over hell and gone in all kinds of weather, trying to save your skin. And this doesn't help either the airline or you."

Gafferty had been waiting for this moment ever since he had heard that Roland was safe. He opened his desk drawer and brought out several tabloids. He carefully pressed them out across his desk and invited Roland to examine them. There was no question about the enterprise of Poppy's press agents: they had done a thorough job. Roland blinked as he read the captions below the pictures. He blinked and reddened, he chewed on the ends of his mustache, he opened and closed his fists.

"*Now* aren't you proud of yourself?" Gafferty demanded.

But Roland held his temper—until a better time, he thought bitterly. Enough was enough. Gafferty mustn't have every last sweet morsel of the day. It took him a moment to retrieve his dignity. Then he scratched his head.

"I just can't figure out where she dug up that lousy old picture of me," he said calmly.

Gafferty bit into his new cigar and secretly saluted the rascal's outward calm; but he struck out once again, lest Roland emerge the victor.

"All right, Mister Hero. This is positively your last chance. Go make your peace with Lucille, then get Eugene and a new propeller, and take the next train up to your ship. Get back here in a hurry. No detours and no delays, understand? I don't care if you have to dig a runway through ten-foot drifts with your fingers!"

Roland looked at him from beneath his bushy eyebrows, and across his face spread the look of a man consigned to a living death.

"Ah, no, Mike! Please! *Please* don't send me back to that God-forgotten place. I couldn't stand another look at it. And it isn't fair to send Eugene. Let some local boys at Albany do the job . . . please, Mike."

"You heard me the first time. Get going."

Roland shook his head sadly as if he had agreed to an enormous sacrifice. The corners of his mouth drooped. If Gafferty had not been so angry, he might have felt sorry for him.

"Okay, Mike. I made a mistake . . . but there's no reason why anyone else should suffer for it. I won't need Eugene. I'll do the job on my own if I have to freeze doing it." There was, after all, no need to bring Eugene and Stella together.

"Just get the ship back here by day after tomorrow, or don't come back."

"Have it your way, Mike. I know how to take orders." Roland picked up his helmet and strode sadly from the office.

## 16

The snow had melted along the route before Roland heard the last of Stella and Poppy. When the earth began to look green beneath the wings again, when the first big warm-weather cumulus began to build upon the horizons, a new energy and sense of enterprise pushed such trivial matters into the background. Roland was grateful for the change. He was tired of Shorty's innuendoes, and the mere mention of his blind flying escapade made him look absently at the ceiling and change the subject.

Roland was conscious of his seniority in the MacDonald clan; he wanted to be the revered patron, the venerable chieftain—as now, when he sat in quiet dignity and watched the foibles of what might have been his court.

The occasion was important and the guest list was distinguished. Colin had been working over the details for some time. It was May and it was Lucille's birthday, an event she still considered suitable for celebration. Even so, she was somewhat uneasy when she found that the only other women invited were Mrs. A and Madame Moselle.

Mrs. A was a splendid sight. She had resurrected the yellow dress covered with barely tarnished sequins that poor Nicholas had bought her for New Year's Eve in 1919. It was much too long, but she cut off the skirt just at her knees, cleaned and pressed it herself, and invested in a pair of orange silk stockings. The afternoon before the party she spent three hours and twenty-seven minutes at the hairdresser's. She instructed him to renew the glory of her hair with peroxide and then arrange it in very tight ringlets and wave it ack behind her ears. She labored over her face with the concentration of an artist, applying a suggestion of robust health to her cheeks. She outlined her still sensuous lips with Louis Philippe's "Angelus," guaranteed not to dry the lips. She attached a pair of long brass-and-lacquer earrings that poor Nicholas had brought her from Alexandria, and snapped exactly six bracelets of various designs around her chubby forearm. She reluctantly decided to wear only three rings and one chaste imitation-pearl necklace, lest she prove too great a temptation to wandering thugs. For reasons he found it hard to identify, Porkie Scott could not take his eyes from her.

Madame Moselle had given her apparel an equal amount of thought, although the result was considerably more subdued. Her black hair was encased in a deep green turban, which, as it happened, was both appropriate and fashionable. She confined her makeup to a softening with powder, which unfortunately did not match her skin very well. She wore a black dress of very conservative cut, relying upon a tin scarab clipped to her neckline to give it an air of festivity. Lucille told her she looked very nice—and so pleased Madame Moselle immensely.

Colin unwillingly sat the full length of the table from Lucille. Porkie Scott was on her left and Roland on her right. Mrs. A sat next to Porkie, then Tad, and then Sydney, who by the utmost diligence had managed to juggle the mail schedules so that they could all be present. Dr. Timothy was there, too, smiling quietly and looking like a Billiken next to Shorty Baker.

Owing to his vast acquaintance in all walks of life, Shorty had made all the arrangements for the party. Their host was Mr. Sal Delphino, who at one time had shared a cell with him in East Rochester, New York. Shorty had been incarcerated there overnight for buzzing the inmates of the Auburn prison, thinking only to provide them with an evening's diversion. Mr. Delphino was booked as trafficking in liquor. He had since progressed from such menial work to the proprietorship of the Club Sphinx, which featured a small orchestra, a pink bar, and delicious food. Mr. Delphino had promised Shorty the most careful attention and had thus far been as good as his word. The flower-covered table was a perfect setting for Lucille's still beauty. She wore a black satin dress and a corsage of gardenias that Colin had bought for her, and the combination blended perfectly with her amber skin.

The band played "Happy Birthday to You" at her entrance, and three times afterward. Mr. Delphino hovered appropriately, and in a moment of enthusiasm even announced that all drinks consumed after the stroke of twelve, which marked the official beginning of Lucille's birthday, would be on the house. Even Porkie Scott could see that the affair held promise.

Lucille loved Porkie because he was Colin's friend, and because of his pale blue eyes and his gentle manner. She loved him particularly when he held forth on any subject, as he was now doing on the subject of birthdays.

". . . . Birthdays are always an accident," he rumbled into his glass of gin and ginger ale. "And they are very seldom accurate. If people had any sense they would select a birthday for themselves and base their selection on the time when they begin to live, which certainly does not happen at birth, or for several years afterward. Only a mother and a father should celebrate a child's actual birthday . . . the mother because at last she is relieved of pain, and the father because at last he can go home and get some sleep, or go out and brag, as the case may be. Now, you take the birds. They have things figured out right. When the eggs first break and all the chirping begins, they see to it that the little ones are fed, and let it go at that. But some time later, when the little ones first fly, there is great rejoicing. . . ."

"How the hell do *you* know there is rejoicing?" asked Roland across the table.

"Because, my thickheaded friend, I lived with a family of ravens one winter!" And the way Porkie made the statement, it was easy to believe that he had done so. "Now, humans should select a day, preferably with the advice and counsel of those who know them best—a day when they were *really* born, when they really became citizens of the world. That would, if they honestly loved living, give them something to celebrate."

"Like the day I met Colin?" asked Lucille. She blew a kiss to her husband down the length of the table, and Colin wondered what the devil was holding those two in such deep conversation at the other end.

"Yes, if you honestly feel that way," continued Porkie with undiminished gravity. "Although some people might select a day of tragedy, which in the end made them really human. Or a day of some considerable sacrifice, or accomplishment . . . any day on which some event occurred that made them grow up, so to speak. For instance, certain native tribes in Africa celebrate the day when a boy reaches puberty. . . ."

"What's this puberty?" asked Shorty Baker with a gleam in his eye.

"Something *you* were born with, so don't worry about it," Porkie flashed back.

Mrs. A, already slightly tipsy, reached across the table and patted Shorty's hand. "Don' you let 'em pick on you, short and handsome!"

Shorty responded by quickly moving his eyebrows up and down several times and making a small clucking sound with his mouth.

Lucille looked down the table and laughed. She wondered if other wives of two years' standing felt the same. Her marriage was still neither certain nor uncertain, but—whereas she had at first been suspicious of any flying marriage—now she believed in it completely. The frequent separations, the goings and comings, were hard to get used to, but she grudgingly gave them some credit for the fact that she and Colin had never had a quarrel. Each of his homecomings was an exciting event to her, and he was gone again before the excitement had a chance to wear off. And he seemed to feel the same way. When he was delayed, she worried and missed him terribly, but romance had survived in their marriage, and she knew that this was even more important to a man like Colin than to herself.

And now he would never again leave her completely. When she first went to Dr. Timothy, he nodded his head and told her not to get excited, and to wait just a little while longer before she told Colin. He explained that the prospect of becoming a father was often a shock to a man like Colin. He might even resent it as a step toward domestication. It would be better to wait until she was absolutely sure, and then break the news at just the proper time. By now she was sure, and that increased her happiness; but when she looked down the table at Colin, so carefree among his fellows, she wondered whether it was the right time to tell him.

Madame Moselle was already daintily in her cups, to Colin's pleased astonishment—though if he had known that it was the first time she had seen real whisky since "Beaver Boy" won the Preakness, he would not have been surprised. She was happily engaged in reading Dr. Timothy's fat little palm and forecasting the usual dire weather ahead.

It was ten minutes to twelve—ten minutes before another "Happy Birthday" was likely to be sung—so Colin slipped from his chair and worked his way through the smoke and the banging and yelling from the next table until he stood behind Lucille. He tapped her on the shoulder.

"Pardon me, young lady. Do you dance?"

When she turned to look up at him, he was absolutely certain she had never looked more radiant.

"Never with strangers, and I have a husband down there who will teach you to keep a civil—" She pretended to be shocked by Colin's absence from his chair. "Well! The old boy has flown the coop. What he doesn't know won't hurt him. Why not, Mister?"

Colin bowed and led her to the small floor. The band was playing "Sleepy Time Gal." He held her very close to him, feeling her warm breath against his cheek. They moved slowly, not in time to the music, since Colin was as poor a dancer as any pilot. Like most others, he had more interesting things to do with his nights.

"What kind of fellow is this husband of yours?" he asked.

"He's a terrible dancer."

"Ah? That's too bad. Old boy?"

"Not too old."

"Is he rich?"

"Very rich."

"Well, well. What does he deal in?"

"The wind . . . and the stars."

"Sounds like a rotten investment. Do you love him?"

"Not in the least."

"A marriage of convenience? Then maybe we can get together."

"No . . . this . . . is, you see. . . . Well, Mister . . . please don't think too badly of me. I don't tell everybody, of course, but it's a marriage . . . of necessity!" There it was out, and she hadn't even considered whether it was the right moment. Now that he was looking at her, holding her at arm's length, she was terrified. He dropped her hands and took them up again.

"You mean . . . ?"

She thought she was going to faint, but she managed to nod her head and look matter-of-fact about it.

He stood motionless. He started to speak and then paused.

"Well . . . *well* . . . WELL!" Then he was kissing her as if there were no one else in the room. He broke away a moment and took a deep breath. "HAPPY BIRTHDAY!" he said, and kissed her again.

Lucille wished she could swoon like a Victorian lady, but she was much too happy in his arms. That was one of the nicer things about being a pilot's wife, she thought. Pilots didn't care who was looking, and the time of day meant nothing to them. They did what they wanted to when they wanted to. Once you got the swing of the thing, she thought, you loved it. Especially when he kissed her again and then walked back to the table in a benign daze.

They all stood up and began singing "Happy Birthday," while Mr. Delphino ushered in two waiters bearing a very large cake. Shorty Baker took his air-mail gun out of his pocket, which with unaccustomed caution he had filled with blank cartridges, and shot several times at the ceiling.

Lucille laughed and blushed because everyone in the Club Sphinx was looking at her. Then she made her wish, which was that this life would go on forever and ever, and blew out the candles—all but six, which Porkie maintained was not a bad average, considering she had had so few years to practice in; she would doubtless become more proficient as life went along. Then just before she cut the cake, Roland held up his hand for silence and gave a sign to Tad and Colin. They locked hands all around and began to sing "Just a wee doch-an-dorris" in their very best voices. And as they sang, Porkie and Dr. Timothy joined in, and Shorty and Mrs. A and Sydney, and Roland in his deep bass, Tad and Colin in good harmony, and Madame Moselle barely audible with her faltering little soprano—their eyes moist with the joy of being together.

Only Tad left the party early, for—despite Sydney's efforts—somebody had to fly the two o'clock in the morning schedule. He kissed Mrs. A and Madame Moselle, took a huge chunk of the birthday cake, wrapped it in a napkin, and stuffed it into his pocket. Then he kissed Lucille on the lips and gave her a resounding spank before she could protest.

When he reached the street, it was raining lightly. But since he had characteristically allowed himself a bare minimum of time to reach the airport, he drove at fifty miles an hour all the way. And he hummed "Just a wee doch-an-dorris" as he drove.

He leaped out of the car, bolted through the hangar door, called "Hi-ya" to Eugene, who was readying his ship, and banged into the little operations office where Sydney's substitute was trying in mild confusion to check over a mail form. Tad said "Hi-ya" again and went swinging quickly to his locker. He whipped off his business suit and, though he had bought it especially for the party, he hung it carelessly beside a pair of dirty coveralls. In less than four minutes he slammed the locker door shut, completely changed into whipcord breeches, boots, and leather jacket. He stuffed the slice of birthday cake into the pocket of the jacket, grabbed his parachute, swung it easily over his shoulder, and fairly ran back to the office.

Gafferty was leaning against the wooden counter.

"Hi-ya!"

"Hello, Tad."

"You should have been at the party."

Gafferty reflected ruefully that the only thing that had kept him away was the lack of an invitation. "I wish I could have been there, but I'm sleeping in the office these days and nights." He watched Tad sign the mail forms and the maintenance form and put in a call to Mr. Palmer for the weather. He envied Tad the simplicity of his job.

"Why sleep here? Not much fun in that."

"No, there isn't. But it seems like Congress doesn't believe in the air mail. Same old story. . . . They don't want to appropriate the money again. They just won't see it has any permanent value. We try to tell them what's going on in other countries, and maybe some day it would mean a lot to national defense if we had some kind of an experienced airline system, but they don't care. It's the same thing every year.'' Gafferty sighed. ''Anyway, we're keeping them up nights with long-distance calls.''

Tad shrugged his wide shoulders. He didn't give a hoot about Congress or the air mail or any other thing save the actual business of flying. Such things were the business of men like Gafferty. For himself, he would be quite content at any time to return to the sunlight and the green fields and hanging by his knees from the landing gear. Just so long as he didn't become bored, so long as there was some physical challenge in every day.

He jiggled the receiver impatiently and demanded to know how the call to Mr. Palmer was coming.

''By the way,'' said Gafferty, ''did you hear the radio this afternoon?''

''Never listen to it.''

''That fellow Lindbergh from Robertson Airlines made it.''

''Made what?''

''Flew from Roosevelt to Paris, nonstop.''

''The hell he did. What kind of ship?''

''A Ryan.''

''Good airplane.'' Tad went back to his telephone and thought no more about it. Mr. Palmer told him it was raining and there had been some thunder. He said there were still flashes of lightning to the east. Tad thanked him and hung up.

''How's your weather going to be?'' asked Gafferty.

He wished Tad would talk to him. He wished that the man wasn't so obviously busy and confident about his business—so confident because he knew exactly what had to be done and how to do it. He had only to climb into a machine designed for a certain purpose and handle this machine in a certain way, thereby moving it and its cargo and himself from point A to point B. It was true that there were complications, but they did not pursue one to bed or cling tenaciously to the mind throughout every waking hour. When the ship had been

*The Spirit of St. Louis*

moved to point B, Tad was free to stretch out and sleep wherever he willed—free to do things that held no associations with what he had been doing. Tad and all the others, thought Gafferty, would never know what lucky men they were.

"Looks like there may be a few thunderstorms," he said, hoping for at least some reaction. Tad still had a few minutes to talk if he wanted to. Just a little conversation, very little, about the things that Gafferty loved, too—about ships and the weather, and the fields, and the winds. Tad wouldn't talk about appropriations and rates and debentures, or mortgages on equipment. Just a few words.

"Could be. It's hot for this time of year."

And Gafferty could see that though his strong body was still on earth, the man Tad had already left him. "Well . . . have a good trip. . . ."

Tad looked up and smiled quickly, almost in a comradely way, and Gafferty thought this was a very unusual thing for Tad to do.

"Thanks, Mike."

Then he was gone and the door banged behind him before Gafferty could express his pleasure at being called Mike.

It has been calculated that vertical air velocities of one hundred and sixteen miles per hour are required to sustain a hailstone three inches in diameter. But Mr. Palmer did not know this, and he did not care. He therefore reported to Tad only that there was lightning to the east and that there had been some rain. Then he went back to bed, where a man belonged at two o'clock in the morning. Whatever he said made little difference. Tad would have flown if Mr. Palmer had reported the millennium in progress on his farm. Nor would it have made any difference to either of them if they had known that there was an extremely unstable air mass brooding and surging over the Catskills—an air mass spawning thunderstorms and mixing and churning them together.

Tad was content. The light rain, which for a while had caused curious little globules of water to spin and dance with fairylike agility across his windscreen, had stopped. He passed over Haverstraw at two-twenty-one and saw that the streets were still wet and glistening black in the lights. He made a mental note of the time he had achieved since his departure from Newark and considered it good. He was flying at seven thousand feet, considerably higher than most men flew, but such an altitude, or even higher, suited his taste. It accomplished his complete removal from earthly attachments and allowed him to challenge this upper world with a feeling of fitness and independence. If Tad had been born to the ground, he would probably have been the kind of man who fights against society, or individual men, or anything at all, so long as he is fighting. Combat was as vital to him as breathing. Because he was clever and strong, and because he never doubted the outcome of his contests, Tad never lost.

Over Kingston he glanced aloft and saw the stars through a shredded hole in the overcast. It was the chance he had been waiting for, the invitation to enter the higher elements—though later, perhaps, he would be left to find his own way out. He accepted the invitation. He jammed full throttle to the engine, eased back on the stick, and held the Pitcairn in a steady eighty-miles-an-hour upward spiral. The stars spun slowly round and round.

At eleven thousand feet the Pitcairn was beginning to labor. At twelve Tad felt the first hint of mushiness in the controls. He eased the nose down barely a touch, but still continued to climb. He began to breathe deeply to get as much oxygen as he could, and swallowed to adjust his ears to the lessening pressure. At fourteen thousand he broke out into the glory. And the winds shut the gateway behind him.

Tad was exalted. Here was majesty. Above him the stars shone with such splendor that even the Pitcairn's wings reflected their intensity. As far as he could see in every direction, there were soft valleys and sharp black ravines, domes and minarets, towers and casements, arches and buttresses, walls and bridges, festoons and garlands—beginnings and ends of clouds. Here the wind played in silence with towns and villages and moved them about and changed their populations, or even banished them altogether. Then from the blue-white cumulo-nimbus blossoming above all, rearing gigantic anvil heads against the horizon, came quick white flashes of fire, repeated intermittently like frenzied artillery in action. Tad turned north, toward the flashing, for there lay his course.

Cumulo-nimbus clouds are the result of a quarrel between the more stable elements aloft. They are frequently formed when a mass of saturated air breaks from its surroundings and ascends, as it must do over mountains. Colin made wide detours around cumulo-nimbus clouds. Roland and Shorty Baker crept under them if they could, and cursed the dousing they invariably received. Porkie Scott would not even look at a cumulo-nimbus. But although this was his first meeting with them at night, Tad welcomed the encounter.

There are three ways to handle a cumulo-nimbus. One is to return to the point of departure without further argument and wait until time and the wind remove them. Pilots who consistently take such action often live to be very old men. Another way is to creep along on one's belly beneath them, bowing and scraping and asking for mercy, taking their insults of vomited rain and cringing before their manifestations of power. There is a third way, seldom attempted, and it is full of beauty and ugly hazard. It was the way for a man like Tad.

Cumulo-nimbus clouds frequently tower to twenty thousand feet, and sometimes their crowning anvils reach to twenty-five thousand and spread fan-shaped for three or four miles. These are the giants of the pack. They surround themselves with lesser counterparts, and even these find it easy to raise their haughty heads to fifteen and eighteen thousand. But there are always breaks between the heads, at the places where their broad shoulders meet, and there are even little caverns, narrow and tortuous, where one cloud stands just a little behind the other. Sometimes these lead to other even narrower channels at the same or different levels, and sometimes if a man can see and remain alert to every bulbous projection and hanging tendril, these cavernous passages can be negotiated as one might snake between the stalactites in a long, winding cave. By such procedure it is possible to emerge unscathed on the other side of a cumulo-nimbus line. But, since the clouds are in a constant state of motion and ferment, it is also possible to become trapped in these channels. They may beckon invitingly, and still prove to be blind alleys with the entrances closed behind.

At fourteen thousand feet, Tad knew he must rely upon his luck and his skill with the channels. If he could climb higher, the channels would be wider and more evident, but he was hindered by the Pitcairn's inadequacies and his own need of oxygen to keep his mind alert. He was certain he could find a way to slip between them and yet remain, taunting, just beyond their reach. He would dart in and out, twist and turn and dive at every weak spot, always keeping track of his varying compass course lest he become lost. It was a task he faced with heady anticipation.

As he approached the now brilliantly flashing wall, he snapped out the light over the instrument panel so that in the rare intervals of darkness the starlight might guide him. Then he reached in his pocket and brought out the slice of Lucille's birthday cake. He broke off a piece, returned the remainder to his pocket, and munched happily, flaunting his unconcern.

Soon he had but a little way to go. The first heads seemed to lean over to meet him. He brushed the cake crumbs from his breeches, hummed "Just a wee doch-an-dorris" to the fast-vanishing stars, and licked his fingers with studied casualness. For a few moments, while the clouds lay deceptively dormant, he could discover no entrance, then a flash of lightning on his left revealed a yawning chasm that cut down almost ten thousand feet. He banked the Pitcairn steeply for it. Then again, only the blue flame from his exhaust lit the night. He entered the maw of the chasm in a tight vertical to the right. He was at once enveloped in heavy cloud. An updraft shook him viciously. False entrance. A cunning trap. But Tad was not so easily taken in. He held the turn for the few seconds required, and burst out almost immediately in the clear.

"Ho!" he said, slapping his helmet in chagrin. "Ho! and hello, stupid!"

He was angered only at his own naïveté. He would approach the next hole more cautiously, giving it a better piece of his respect. He flew alongside the flashing bank, tense with eagerness, wary and watchful, like a swordsman waiting to thrust. This was living. This was a thing to be doing at three o'clock in the morning. He was so close that he could hear the thunder now, even above the roar of the wind and his engine—flat thunder, sharp and harsh, short-lived and without echo, as it always is in the sky. Then a flash, more brilliant than the preceding flashes, offered a possibility to his right. He swung off for it.

This was better. He had to dive down five hundred feet to seek the largest entrance, but it even expanded once he reached the opening. He had at least a mile of air space to turn and dodge in at will. Easy. A spatial highway fringed with palisades. One star, then three, a planet for good measure broke out above, straight up. Such a rent in the clouds' armor, such a tear, such negligence! Enough room for a squadron of Pitcairns. Tad smiled at their weakness and said "Ho!" and "Ho!" softly, yet just audibly above the thunder. He swung left, then right, and left again, weaving gracefully with the configurations of the channel. And the clouds, as if both frantic and furious at his success and audacity, writhed and boiled and spat fire at this puny buzzing thing among them.

He had no trouble seeing now. The lightning was almost continuous, one flash superseding and meshing into the other. The Pitcairn's nose and wings were etched in sharp, hard lines against the massive white formations. Tad could even see a small patch here and there where Eugene had glued the fabric. Everything he looked at—the veins in his hands, the screws along the cockpit coaming, the turnbuckles on the flying wires, the nuts on the engine rocker boxes—stood out with amazing clarity. Tad even fancied he could smell the hot fusing of the lightning and he breathed deeply of it.

He had flown so for perhaps five minutes when he rounded what he believed might be the last belching monster in his path. As he banked steeply about it to his right, the channel suddenly became narrower. In less than a minute he barely had clearance from wing tip to wing tip. A few seconds later he was heaving and yawing the Pitcairn, standing the ship in vertical banks to the right and left as he tried to escape the clutching cumulus—since the one thing he must not do if he hoped for an easy victory was to enter these maelstroms, for then the advantage would pass to them. Even if he could succeed in flying through them on instruments, a task he had little taste for, he would be obliged to hold one steady course, and that would be almost impossible. He would be blinded, helpless to seek a weak spot, entirely at the mercy of whatever violence the clouds held in store for him.

He rounded a last churning dome that looked as if it might be the exposed bubbling brain of a giant. Then he knew he would have to face it. Dead end. He looked quickly behind him over the Pitcairn's tail. The bubbling brain had closed and joined another. He looked up—not that he had the power to ascend, but for comfort. No stars. Blackness. Down? Only blackness. And to each side, to the quarters, ahead—staccato, blinding white cascades of darkness. A prisoner.

"Ho!" He doubled his fist and shook it in defiance.

He reached for his safety belt and cinched it as tightly as he could. He leveled the Pitcairn and put one hand on the throttle. He switched on the panel light and made a final check of the instruments. Oil pressure, sixty pounds. Revolutions, sixteen hundred per minute. Rate of climb, level. Turn-and-bank, straight. Altimeter, thirteen thousand five hundred. Air speed, which he mentally corrected for altitude, approximately one hundred and five. Gas—at least he had plenty. Then he was instantly swallowed in cloud.

The first jolt was a gentle one, quick and ineffectual; it

hardly jarred the compass. For a moment there was only choking darkness, then gradually everything about him took on an iridescent glow. St. Elmo's fire. Spectacular, but harmless in itself. It touched everything with a magic sparkling spray of greenish light. The propeller spun in a whirling wreath of incandescence. The wings and the very air racing over them glowed in a misty phosphorescent halo that bloomed and blossomed around the whole ship. He looked back quickly over the tail and saw that he trailed a column of pale green fire, like a weakling comet. The air was perfectly smooth.

Then it hit him—with the incalculable force of the heavens. It struck like the blow of a sledge hammer on a tiny nail. It pressed Tad against his safety belt until he thought the blood to his legs would stop. It pressed him, mashed him into the blackness below, plummeting him straight down. The flying wires screeched in agony. The altimeter unwound like a clock gone mad. The air speed jumped to one hundred and eighty, passed it, and stood foolishly at zero. The rate of climb sank to two thousand feet per minute, its maximum marking. Tad cut back the throttle and pulled on the stick— gently, lest the wings come off.

Then, as suddenly, the force hit him again, striking upward— sent him rocketing straight up, reversing everything. He slammed on full throttle and shoved the nose down hard, but he could as well have stayed a torrent with his little finger. The altimeter jerked and rewound. Back to thirteen thousand, fourteen thousand, fifteen, sixteen, seventeen thousand, pressing him tightly against the seat, draining the blood from his head, making every movement a weighted, straining effort.

Things were purple now—the instruments, the exhaust flame, the very flashes of lightning about him. Tad rubbed his eyes and hardly cared. He recognized only a feeling of well-being, almost of peace. He wanted to lie back and smile and dream. With casual interest he watched the altimeter go on past eighteen thousand. Who cared? Ho! Such pleasant stupor. To think was such a bore—to think or care any longer when he felt so sleepy. To dream was better, and eat a piece of cake and forget about this uneven struggle. Better, far easier, to ignore this insolent, pricking sensation in his brain that bade him over and over again to get down—down at once, where he could have some oxygen. What could be sweeter than oxygen? Down—down where the "Just a wee doch-an-dorris" and the fishes play. . . .

The Pitcairn shuddered sullenly. There was a jolt and a twist, a shove against the cockpit side—and he was on his back. He knew it only because his feet insisted on floating off the rudder pedals and up beneath the instrument panel. His rump left the seat and he hung on his safety belt, bent loosely in the middle like the leaves of a book spread across a chair. Upside down. Flying upside down and there was nothing, nothing to see . . . alackaday, who cared? The engine, which had never been designed for inverted flight, sputtered and quit.

Tad pushed lazily at the throttle and went to sleep.

Within every cumulo-nimbus cloud there are continuous currents of wind that travel vertically up and down like contrary waterfalls. The speed of these currents and their strength remain the secret business of the heavens. They are mighty enough to take the tons of water falling within one portion of the cloud and heave the droplets up until they pass the freezing level. There they become encrusted with a thin layer of ice. The now heavier droplets fall again until they are once more seized and thrust upward to the freezing level, where they acquire another coating of ice. Heavier still, they fall, only to be tossed up again and again and again, until they become sizable hailstones, perfectly rounded and capable of inflicting great damage.

The biting sting of water against his face brought Tad back to consciousness. He found that he was slumped back against the headrest, his hands drooping loosely in his lap. It was raining so hard that he thought for a moment that he must somehow be flying beneath the sea. The engine was running again in fits and starts, as if it too were awakening. Struggling to regain his senses, he looked first at the altimeter. Nine thousand feet. His feet were on the floor. He must be right side up. He shook his head to rally his spirits and moaned a weak "Ho. . . ."

Nine thousand. The highest Catskill was still four thousand feet below. He studied the air speed. It was swinging wildly from forty to eighty, to a hundred and fifty. He was either in a spin, a wild spiral, or some eccentric gyration he could not even picture. And he was sopping wet.

He pushed up his goggles, wiped his eyes, and reached weakly for the stick and throttle. Nine thousand? A good altitude to leave. Just unsnap his safety belt and wait until she rolled over on her back again. Gravity would take care of the rest. Then say very slowly, "Now I lay me down to sleep, I pray the Lord my soul to keep . . ." and wait for the blessed earth. An explosion of lightning that forked across his engine so close that he fancied he could have seized it changed his mind.

"Ho! . . . NO!" Too soon, for Tad. Too soon to crawl away whimpering, a beaten groundling who must some time explain to other groundlings that this went wrong, and that went wrong, and so . . . well-it-just-came-time-to-leave-you-know.

By pumping the throttle, he got the engine going again. He worked the stick and rudder against the gusts and began to watch the turn-and-bank, trying to hold a course. For a few moments he met with fair success, then a gust almost jerked the stick from his hands. At the same time a pandemonium of sound broke over him like a hurricane comber smashing a sea wall. R-r-r-r-r-r-r-r-r-a-a-a-a-k-k-k-k-a-a-a-a-a-k-k-k-k-a-a-a-a-a-k-k-k-a-a-a-a-k-k-k-k. Hail! The pounding of a million tiny devils. The instruments went insane again. The Pitcairn began to vibrate unevenly. When the pyralin windscreen broke and flew in his face, Tad clenched his teeth and wiped the blood away. He ducked as far forward as he could, now fighting with all his strength even to hold the stick. In surges, he could feel the pellets drubbing on his back.

Something was very wrong. This vibration. No ship in good strength should shudder so. He looked quickly at the wings, and ducked back at once, a half-decision on his bleeding lips. The wings were ghastly in the white flashes, pitiful in their pain. The hail had pounded and stabbed and torn tiny holes in the hard-stretched fabric. And each succeeding pellet, aided by the force of the slip stream, had made the holes a trifle larger, until now there were great rents and jagged cuts, shearing and ripping off in all directions. In places, he could see the main spar. There was no use looking at the stabilizer or the elevators, or the fin. They would be in as bad condition—probably worse. And the metal propeller would be chewing itself to bits. No wonder the Pitcairn shuddered. No wonder, with her bones laid bare. In a few moments he would be flying a skeleton. Now he could leave—with honor.

He took his feet off the rudder pedals and checked the leg straps on his parachute harness for tightness. He felt of the ring and made sure of the draw through the cable covering. He snapped the breast tackle with slow resolve, for even now he was sorry to leave the Pitcairn. He cut off the ignition switch, hoping the ship would not burn, and took a final look around the cockpit floor, for perhaps ten seconds—he never knew exactly why. He reached to unsnap his safety belt, and then the thing hit him.

There was a cruel jolt, heavier than any before, and a shrieking sound that pierced the noise around him. The right wing collapsed at the center section and crunched back, thudding against the fuselage and cutting him a stunning blow on the side of his head. The flying wires snapped viciously. The outer struts broke and the trailing edge of the wing slipped half over the cockpit. Tad shook off his dizziness. He put his hands on the side of the seat to push himself out of the cockpit—and found he was trapped.

He beat upon the wing angrily. He pushed up and shoved with all his might. He glanced at the altimeter. Six thousand. He would have to hurry. The Pitcairn was spinning wildly now. He braced his feet against the longerons that ran along the floor and heaved again at the wing. He tried to shake it. He cursed and clawed at it, trying to break off a piece of the aileron. Five thousand. Four thousand. He hunched himself with his feet in the seat and his back against the wing. He gathered all his tawny strength and called upon God to help him. He pushed upward with every last concentration of his will. The wing did not move.

Three thousand. Still fighting savagely, he braced himself for the ground. It came swiftly and mercifully.

## 17

Tad was glad when they finally laid him in the white bed and said that he would stay in one place for a while. It seemed as though he had been moved and moved again ever since he could remember. First they carried him from the plowed field to a farmhouse. There they laid him on the floor because he complained angrily when they tried to fit his long frame onto a Victorian couch. They took him in a truck to the general store in a village. Tad did not remember much about it, except that the doctor who arrived after many hours said he would take care of everything if Tad thought he could afford to have an ambulance come all the way from Poughkeepsie. Tad did not remember his answer, but the ambulance finally came anyway. It was a very painful ride to Poughkeepsie.

They washed away the blood and took off his clothes, which were drenched with oil. He remembered asking them to save the piece of cake that was mashed flat in his jacket pocket. They put him in a ward and he could have sworn he fell asleep instantly, but the other patients said later that he screamed until noon. Lucille and Colin came, but were not allowed to see him. They waited in a hotel in Poughkeepsie until Dr. Timothy arrived, and they waited longer while he went to the hospital.

Dr. Timothy said "tum-tum-dee-dum" and whistled quietly as his fat little hands probed among the bandages. There was a long conference with the hospital people—part of it Tad could vaguely recall as taking place near his bed. Finally Dr. Timothy said it would not make things any worse if they moved Tad to Newark. And now he lay in another hospital with a nice room of his own—though he could not move a single muscle. From the way he was bound, he knew that he was seriously injured, but he did not know just how seriously.

When Tad asked him about that, Dr. Timothy only said that time would tell.

Before the others went in to see him, the doctor said: "Just be sure you don't show it on your faces—that's very important now. He's not going to die; by some miracle, only his bones and certain nerves have been affected. But he may die for another reason if he learns the truth too soon. Then there will be nothing I can do to help him."

He rocked back and forth on his feet and looked into their anxious faces. They were seated in a line around the little waiting room. Colin and Lucille with their hands clasped together, and Roland, somehow shrunken, beside them. Porkie Scott and Shorty Baker, nervously fingering their caps. And Gafferty.

"I think it is probably best for you to know the truth, as far as I know it. Then later—much later, when he leaves this place—you can give him the help he will need so badly. I repeat: I don't know why he is alive . . . except that he is Tad MacDonald. His skull is fractured—not too seriously, however. His nose is broken. Most of his teeth are gone. His legs and arms are broken . . . his left leg in two places. His right shoulder is broken and there is compound fracture of the right clavicle. All of his lower ribs are broken, and the lower four of his upper ribs. This all sounds bad, but these things will heal eventually. He will have the use of his arms in a few months. Much more serious is the fact that his back is broken and in such a way that I'm afraid it will affect his locomotion. This man will recover, and should be able to lead a more or less normal life . . . in time. But he will never be the same man you have known for so long. Now it is too early to be absolutely positive about this . . . but it is something you as his friends should realize and start thinking about." Dr. Timothy cleared his throat unhappily and looked at his big gold watch. "I doubt very much if this man will ever walk again."

Lucille and Colin were the first to go in, as the doctor had advised. Tad peered at them between the bandages and, though his dark eyes still held their peculiar fire, they seemed more like isolated medical specimens than the eyes of a living man.

"Hi-ya. . . ." His voice was muffled and distorted, but Lucille thought it still rang with strength. "Hi-ya, Lucille," he said again.

She wanted to cry out when she saw him, but she stooped to kiss the swollen lips between the bandages. He closed his eyes a moment and then stared up at her. It was uncanny, looking at this man she knew so well and not being able to know whether he was smiling—Tad, whose smile had always been so much a part of him.

"That tasted good," he said.

She leaned forward a little to catch his voice which had faded. "Want another?"

"Ho! Sure."

"You're a fine-looking mess," said Colin behind her. She blessed his heart that he had overcome his shock enough to speak so lightly. "What ran into you?" Colin hated this false cheerfulness, but he remembered the doctor's admonition. "How many times did I used to tell you not to jump so low, wise guy? You're supposed to pull that rip cord, . . ."

The eyes beckoned him closer. He leaned to the voice, smiling—but feeling sick.

"Colin . . . what's this I hear . . . the Doc tells me . . . ?" The eyes moved up to Lucille. "About you and our girl . . . ?" The voice fell away and then came back again. "By God, I didn't think you had the nerve!"

"Listen, you," said Lucille, pointing her finger in mock seriousness. "I'm depending on you to carry off a very important job while you're lying around here. If time gets heavy on your hands, just start thinking. *We* don't seem to get anywhere."

"What's that?" asked the voice.

"Think of a name. I lie awake nights reciting the alphabet and don't get anywhere at all. Anna, Betty, Carl, Donald . . . Evelyn. . . . It's making me lose weight."

The eyes seemed to smile and beckoned again. "Ho! I've already thought of a name. Keith . . . it's got to be Keith."

Colin and Lucille looked at each other and tried to pretend that the idea had never occurred to them.

"Wonderful!" she said. "Only I just hope it fits!"

They stayed as long as they dared, and then, remembering the others waiting in the hall, they left saying they would be back the next day.

Roland eased past them at the door, his face set in a fixed smile. They heard his voice booming as the door wooshed shut.

"After all I taught you! Trying to ruin my reputation. I guess I'll have to start teaching you to fly all over again."

"Maybe you will. . . . I've got a hunch it will be a long time."

"You'll be up and around in no time. . . ."

"No time is right."

"Don't look to me for sympathy," said Roland, as harshly as he could manage. If he could only give some of his own strength to this rigid mountain of bandages. "I hear you broke every bone but the one in your head."

There was silence from the eyes and the mouth. When the voice came again, it sent a shiver through Roland's frame—it sounded so far away.

"Cut the acting, Roland. You're worse than the Doc. Just answer my question and tell me the truth. I won't tell anyone you told me. Am I going to die?"

"Hell, no!"

"I believe you. It's funny . . . I don't feel like dying."

"You were born to be hanged, same as me."

There was silence again. Someone was banging trays around down the corridor. Roland was about to remark sarcastically on how quiet the place was, when the question that he feared came.

"Will I fly again?"

"Sure. . . . Why not?" He wished he hadn't added the "why not"—it might lead to further questioning.

But there was only silence for a long time as if Tad had not heard him. The eyes were closed. For a moment, Roland thought he had fallen asleep.

Then the voice came again, almost a groan. "You're a liar, Roland."

As if in answer to Roland's prayer, Porkie Scott stuck his head through the door. And over his shoulder appeared the square-cut jaw of Shorty Baker.

"Time's up. Our turn," said Shorty.

They shambled shyly into the room as if they might not be wanted. But the eyes, deep-sunk in the bandages, gleamed with pleasure. Porkie stood over the bed and looked down at the eyes without flinching. He surveyed the bundled figure from end to end and scratched one of his chins.

"What a monstrosity!" he rumbled. "Now, I had a friend used to fly Chinamen across the border from Mexico in a Jenny. He got two hundred dollars a head and he earned every nickel of it. One night he had three Chinamen jammed into the front cockpit . . . don't ask me how he ever got the Jenny off the ground with the load he had, but he did. Now, this friend . . . name of Stinkie Eldebrand . . . wasn't off the ground twenty minutes and the OX broke some plumbing and began to spray hot water all over the sky. The Chinamen didn't have room to duck down out of the slip stream, so they were getting most of the water, and they didn't care for the temperature. They yelled bloody murder and kept trying to jump out. In the scramble one of them threw his bag away, which went back and hit Stinkie and knocked him cold. Well, the OX kept on running until it froze tight. Then, with that load in the nose, the Jenny headed almost straight for the ground, with the Chinamen yelling louder than ever. It hit somebody's windmill, which was turning up pretty good all by itself, and bounced off that, strewing a few parts of the Jenny around the countryside. But it kept on flying for a mile or so, bouncing up and down off the big bunches of cactus they have down in that part of the world. Finally the Jenny stuck its nose in a mine and knocked down some scaffolding around the place. The scaffolding set off a lot of dynamite percussion caps somebody had no business leaving around. Would you believe it, those Chinamen were hardly scratched, and Stinkie didn't look any worse than you do. . . ."

"No—I don't believe it," said the voice, and the three of them hoped the eyes were laughing.

They stayed only a little while, promising to return as soon as they were off schedule. Then Gafferty came in and pulled up a chair without saying anything. Remembering the number of times he had called Tad on the carpet for reckless flying, he thought that any heartiness on his part would immediately make Tad suspicious.

"I'm sorry about the Pitcairn," said the voice. And Gafferty knew he meant it. "Get the mail all right?"

"Yes. It was in good shape."

It wasn't. The pouches had broken open and whatever mail was not soaked in oil was scattered all over the plowed field, but the mail meant nothing now. Gafferty couldn't put down the memory of the last time he had seen Tad—so hard and strong and self-possessed. He realized that for Tad to lose a battle hurt even more than his injuries.

"Doesn't look like I'll be able to fly for a while . . . or have you fired me anyway?"

Gafferty managed a short laugh. "No, you're not fired. We'll keep your base pay going. Sorry about the flying pay. I just can't do anything about it for a while."

"Thanks . . . Mike."

"When you get out of here, you'll probably be a little weak on your pins for a time. About then, I'm going to need some help."

The voice came back evenly. "Help? Like you had for Johnny Dycer? Thanks again . . . but go to hell."

Gafferty stood up and leaned over the eyes. He looked straight into them so he would be believed.

"This is on the level. The Bell Telephone Laboratories have been after me to install radios in the ships. Of course, it's only experimental and there are a lot of problems to be worked out. But if we can get them to work, they'll make a lot of difference. We can keep track of the ships, give them weather from the ground, and maybe even help them sometimes. It will be a much more efficient operation, and as soon as we start carrying passengers, we've got to have something like radio."

"You still think passengers will pay to ride with us?"

"Sure. T.A.T. is doing it already, and the same goes for Pacific Air Transport. We may lose money in the beginning, but I'm sure it will work out."

"Where do I come in?"

"I need someone like yourself who knows flying and also knows the route and the weather and what it's like to be sitting in a cockpit when everything goes wrong. I need someone to get together with Bell and make this radio thing work out in actual practice. It's a lot more important than it looks right now. If you aren't interested, I'll just have to get somebody else."

Then Gafferty thought of the angle he hoped would convince Tad. "It isn't going to be an easy job. It won't be just playing around with a lot of wires . . . the Bell people will do most of that. It's getting the idea over and making it work instead of just being another nuisance. A lot of people, even some of our own pilots, don't like the idea. They say it will cramp their style. If you believe in it, you'll have to fight for it. You're likely to make some enemies on both sides before you're through. You don't have to say yes or no right now, but I would like to know if you're interested."

There was a long silence and the eyes closed again. Gafferty was afraid he had failed. He waited, trying to cover up his embarrassment.

"Sure, Mike. . . . I . . . I think you've got something. Maybe I *could* help on a deal like that."

Gafferty sighed in relief. "Swell. We'll get together on it as soon as they take off your bandages. I'll keep after Dr. Timothy."

Gafferty smiled and looked at the eyes and shook his own hands together to say good-bye. Then he left the room a much happier man.

Colin did not speak a word from the time they left the hospital until they reached their room at Mrs. A's. Even then he only suggested that Tad might like them to bring him the phonograph and play some records. He slumped in a chair and sat staring at the photograph of the Flying Scots that Lucille had had framed for him.

She knew what he was thinking, or hoped she did. She was almost afraid to break the silence, even when the afternoon light in the room had faded completely and he still sat in the gloom without moving. Finally she slipped quietly beside him and passed her hand across his hair. He seemed not to notice her.

"Don't you think we'd better go get something to eat?" she ventured at last.

"I guess so."

"Want to go to Romeo's?"

"No. Let's go somewhere we've never been before." He looked up at her and took her hand. Then he began to speak very slowly. He sounded as if he had chosen each word with care and pieced them together in his thoughts like a mosaic. "Lucille, I've made my last flight. I'm sure of that now. First it was Keith, and now . . . Tad. Next, it will be either me or someone I love. For what? For nothing that I can see. Tad would be better off dead. Someone will always have to take care of him, and you know what that will do to him. You're going to have a baby. Now, don't think I feel tied down, or that I don't want the baby. I do, very much . . . but that means someone will have to take care of the baby and Tad too. If anything happened to me, you wouldn't even have insurance. It just isn't fair to you or anyone else. So I'm going to see Gafferty tomorrow and tell him. I think he'll understand, and it won't make any difference if he doesn't. I want to get as far away from airplanes as I possibly can. I don't know what I'll do. I've been thinking a lot about it since the other night. There isn't much I can do except fly. But I'll get work somehow, and you can stop worrying nights. . . ."

So that was it. She had been waiting and staging her own little war inside, and the reasoning sounded familiar, but it was wrong and she knew it was wrong. She had felt the need of security ever since she learned that the child was coming. She couldn't help it, and the thought that something might happen to Colin was far more vivid and terrifying than ever before. She felt they were a unit now, and Colin was the keystone of their unity. It was a new and wonderful and exciting feeling as long as she knew he was safe.

But there was another persistent voice that was forever present, contradicting her feminine fears—or was it, instead, simply stronger? It told her she had married a certain kind of man. Her whole capacity for love had been concentrated on him and she had found it an easy, joyous state. What she had considered faults in the beginning had become his special qualities. His work and his skill had become matters of pride to her. Perhaps he would be just as good at something else, and perhaps another sort of life would not change him; but there was a risk—a risk she had finally decided was even more dangerous than his flying. She was sure of only one thing: she did not want Colin to change.

"What would you do?" she asked, to gain time—to choose her words so they would fall with effect and not, above all things, make him think she was just being noble.

"I'll have to look around for a while. Maybe I could sell, but I don't think so. If I could work into some office, maybe . . . an office that had to do with engines. I'm pretty good with engines. . . ."

"And what time would you go to work?" She slipped her hand down along his neck.

"Oh, eight or nine o'clock, I guess. It depends."

"Then you'd be home every day about six, wouldn't you, and have Saturday afternoons and Sundays with me, and Keith . . . ?"

"Yeah. Something like that. Sounds pretty good, doesn't it? Of course, we couldn't make as much. . . ."

"It sounds terrible!" She had to make herself say it. "It wouldn't work. In two weeks I'd be either married to a crazy man or without a husband. I can just *see* you! Now, you just listen to me, Colin. Stop worrying about *us*. We'll get along and be the happiest people in the world if you just stay the way you are. We'll get a house somewhere, somehow, and move Tad in with us."

"You know that won't work."

"Of course it will work. We'll get a place near some park where the baby can play. Roland and Porkie and Shorty and the whole batch of them can move in if you want. Only just stay the way you are."

Colin stood up and went over to the framed photograph of the Flying Scots on the wall beside his dresser. He stared at it for a long time, then gently passed his hand across the glass.

"I'm going to give it up, Lucille. There's no use arguing about it. I feel sort of dead . . . inside."

She knew that he was crying without tears. "Colin . . . listen. I love you more than I can ever say and there are many reasons why I love you so. When you feel this way about someone, you watch him and all the things in every day that influence him. Whatever makes him happy, you approve. Whatever makes him unhappy, you hate. And most of all you don't want him to change because that's what made you fall in love with him in the first place. Any happy woman will fight with everything she knows to keep her happiness exactly the way it is."

"I don't see how it could affect us."

"Oh, but it would! I don't know much about flying, but I can see enough to feel sure it's not all for nothing. It's making progress, and a man like you has to make progress . . . not just for yourself . . . it's got to be something bigger than that. Look how much flying has changed since we were married, and it seems to me it will change a lot more. If you leave it now, you'll miss all that, and deep inside you'll never forgive the things that made you leave it."

"I'm leaving of my own free will."

"No, you're not, and if you really were, there are two men who would never forgive you—Tad . . . and Keith."

He turned and looked at her angrily. Lucille knew he had never come closer to striking her.

"I wish you hadn't said that!"

"Darling, I know I sound all mixed up, but when I married you I married all your brothers. You even said it yourself. And I've come to know how much your flying life means to you. I won't have anything destroy it. Maybe flying has growing pains, just like Keith will have some day—that is, if it's a boy. Tad didn't quit, and *you* won't quit. Flying will be a big thing some day . . . bigger than you or Roland or even Gafferty ever dreamed . . . and it's men like you who will make it so!"

Then she knew she was winning. He took her hand and a slow smile spread across his face. He looked at her quizzically.

"That's some speech. I think you're jealous."

"I'm jealous as hell! But flying is as much a part of you as I am. It wouldn't make any difference how much it took you from me—I've got to cooperate with it. You keep on flying, my love . . . no matter what happens!'' She kissed him hard on the lips. ''Now keep that smile on your face. I'm starving. Take me to dinner and buy me some wine and come on back here to bed with me. Then fly your schedule tomorrow . . . and don't ever let me hear you mention your responsibilities again!''

She kissed him once more and rushed off to the bathroom, closing the door behind her. And there she could hardly make up her lips—they quivered so as she cried.

## 18

Roland strode into the store with the air of a man bent on completing a difficult mission. He had brought Porkie Scott along for general support, and it was not until the girl elevator operator looked at them suspiciously and asked their destination that they lost their bravado.

"Baby things," gulped Roland. Porkie nodded solemnly.

The girl looked them up and down, shrugged her shoulders and said, "Fifth floor."

They stepped gingerly out of the elevator and worked their way unhappily over the carpeted floors and through mazes of women's pink underthings lying on counters and pinker bathrobes hanging on racks. There were several women with hats on, turning and twisting and holding up more pink things, and devouring them with covetous eyes as they shook them out. There were other women without hats, standing behind the counters and looking at Roland and Porkie with the frank inspection possible only in their own domain. After the two men had been allowed to stand for a sufficiently humiliating period, one of the women conceded from behind the counter that she might help them. Roland pulled up his pants—a gesture that Porkie copied as he might a yawn—and said he wished to see some baby things. The woman smiled in an understanding way that made Roland even more uncomfortable.

"Over here," she said. "Boy or girl?"

"Boy . . . boy! Name's Keith."

"Congratulations."

Porkie looked at Roland's reddening face and began to whistle softly.

"Oh, it's not me . . . I mean not mine . . . though it is too, sort of. . . ." Roland quickly drew a crumpled piece of paper from his pocket. "I want a bassinet!" he said sternly.

"We have them at various prices," she said, "starting at seven ninety-eight."

"We want the best in the house!"

"Eighteen dollars. . . ."

"Then we want a lot of towels."

"How many towels?"

Roland consulted the list. "Six of the best. Then we want soap, baby powder, oil, sterilizer, bottles, and nipples."

"Maybe you'd just better give me the list."

Roland parted with it reluctantly.

"Don't forget the didies," said Porkie.

"Yeah, that's right. She didn't write it down. Three dozen didies! Best in the house."

"You sure you got that right?" said Porkie. "Seems like a lot of didies."

"I added a dozen. You gotta have plenty," said Roland, in the manner of a man who knows about such things.

Thus Keith's elementary needs in the new home were supplied. Lucille could give them no more than cursory attention, since December of 1927 proved to be what she remembered as the busiest month of her life. On the third of that month, an eight-pound boy had arrived three weeks ahead of time, thereby astonishing his mother and throwing into utter confusion the scheduling efforts of both herself and Sydney in the airline office. The boy had hardly been spanked into life when Roland arrived breathless, still in his flying clothes. He promptly named the baby Keith and, since Colin was grounded for two days by weather in Buffalo, it never became entirely clear to the nurses just who the father was—Roland, who took domineering charge of everything, or Colin, who eventually arrived and wandered about in a semiconscious daze, or the thin man who came in a wheelchair one afternoon and sat looking at the baby for a long time without saying anything. Such were the absorption and excitement that over in the office Sydney put his shaking head on his forearm and said that he didn't suppose any of the MacDonalds would fly for months.

Lucille had expected to spend Christmas in the hospital. Instead, on the fifteenth she found herself not only taking the baby home, but getting settled in a new house at the same time. Roland took this occasion to move in on Porkie, who accepted the change in his tranquil life with ill-concealed distaste.

The house, which was small and built of brick—"solid," Colin said—stood beside a small lake in Morristown. It belonged entirely to Lucille and Colin, except for the three-fourths the bank owned. It was only half furnished and it looked tremendous after Mrs. A's. There was a living room dropped one step from the polished flagstone entranceway, and a bedroom for Colin and Lucille into which their wedding bed fitted nicely. There was a guest room containing no furniture whatsoever except what Roland and Porkie had purchased two days before little Keith's homecoming.

Then there was a room for Tad, with a bed and a desk that Colin had built especially so that his wheelchair would fit under it. There was a kitchen with a view over the lake and a small breakfast nook painted red and white. The kitchen gave promise of being comfortable and efficient, but it was woefully lacking in pots and pans.

"What this place needs," said Porkie Scott, following the empty echo of his deep voice from room to room, "is a bang-up housewarming! I'll take steps to see that one occurs almost immediately. Now, let me see . . . it's ten days to Christmas. Christmas Eve will be a good time."

Lucille, still weak and dizzy from her ordeal at the hospital, sat on the bed because there was no place else to sit. She willingly agreed when Colin and Roland said they would take care of everything. That first night in her new home stayed long in her memory. Roland bathing and oiling the baby with gusto that kept her heart in her mouth. Colin running back and forth between kitchen and bedroom asking her to feel the bottles of formula to see if they were hot enough. All of them together preparing a dinner of Mulligan stew plentifully seasoned with advice. In that half-empty house, with the bare floors and the shadeless lights glaring, and with little Keith squalling for something—no one could imagine what—the homecoming was far from quiet. It was Tad who discovered that by holding Keith in his lap and taking him for a fast circuit of the house in the wheelchair he could give Lucille a chance to get some sleep.

The next day when Lucille felt a little stronger, the man came to put in the 'phone and rang and rang before he was satisfied. Other arrivals included the garbage man, the laundry man, the coal man, the newspaper man, the grocery man, the plumber who came to fix the toilet that wouldn't work, the vegetable man, the cleaning man, two boys with Christmas seals, the mailman, the woman next door, who was full of advice on how to handle babies (though she confessed to having none of her own), then came the expressman with a wrong address, the drugstore man, a man selling vacuum cleaners, a man selling brooms, a bootlegger who left his card, and a very persistent man who thought her husband ought to have more life insurance until she told him he was a pilot.

It was Tad, with his spirit still unbroken, with his almost pathetic cheerfulness and twisted smile—Tad and little Keith—who gave her strength and sanity those first few days of settled life. And before she knew what had happened to time, Christmas Eve arrived.

One year—it seemed a very long time ago now—Gafferty, in the spirit of Christmas, had gone to a foundling home with a view to adopting a son. He had convinced his wife, at least momentarily, that the idea had merit. The people at the home agreed—until they met her. Then they immediately became vague and overpolite. They suggested that he wait until he had been married a little longer and his plans were more definite. At least, that was the way their refusal was put to him.

And so Christmas was a lonely time for Gafferty. In the past he had been successful in ignoring it. There was always work to be done and he told himself that the ridiculous sentimentality aroused by the holiday was not suited to a man of his temperament. He made it a practice to refuse Christmas invitations, on the basis of a cold or the press of work. As the years went on, the invitations became more infrequent and finally ceased altogether. Gafferty derived a certain grim satisfaction from this: now people understood him, realized what kind of man he was. He was therefore caught off guard this Christmas Eve—long after there was any likelihood of an invitation.

It was eight o'clock and except for Gafferty the place was deserted. A cold front had moved in from the Lakes area and brought with it a mixture of wet snow and rain that had canceled all flights since early morning. It was dribbling audibly on the windows of his office, and they took on a kind of enchanted splendor when the airport beacon flashed across them.

He sat in the dark for a while, looking out the window and smoking a cigar as he reviewed what he had accomplished since he first came to Newark. He had built an operating airline from nothing, virtually on a shoestring. He now had seven airplanes, including one spare, a respectable inventory of spare parts, five first-class mechanics, eleven pilots, and seven station agents. They were all reasonably conscientious and efficient. The accident record was as good as that of the other lines, and better than most. The mail survey pleased the Post Office Department as much as they could be pleased. In recognition of his efforts Gafferty's own salary had been increased one hundred dollars a month. These things were on the credit side.

On the debit side, he thought, were the maneuverings of the higher-ups, who quite openly looked upon aviation as a stock venture, or at the very most a new avenue to political prestige and the public treasury. Mercury Airlines, for example, had already been headed by three presidents and three vice presidents, all of whom declined with open dread any invitation to leave the earth in an airplane. Each of the past presidents had made a brief obligatory visit to the airport and stood staring nervously at the Pitcairns, and said they looked to be in fine condition. Each had shaken hands with whatever mechanic happened to be on duty and, as soon as he reached Gafferty's office, had wiped an imperceptible film of oil from his hands and thrown the handkerchief into Gafferty's wastebasket.

One of them wanted to meet a pilot, so Gafferty called Sydney and asked if there were any around at the time.

Unfortunately, the only one present was Shorty Baker, who had just arrived with the morning mail from the West. When the president asked Shorty how he liked flying—a question comparable to asking the president how he liked being president—Shorty looked at the man in amazement and said it was a terrible way to make a living even if you were sober—and how the hell would he, the president, like crawling out of bed at two o'clock in the morning just when a beautiful blonde had decided to surrender? But Shorty didn't tell the president that such a life was life to him.

The newest president had so far not bothered to come to the airport. A conference in Washington with the operations officials of other airlines, however, had convinced Gafferty that this was not a unique circumstance. Aviation was still a plaything of Congress, which showed no signs of recognizing its worth. Gafferty was thankful that at least he was left in nominal charge and was not forced, as were some of the other airline managers, to put up with the sincere but fumbling efforts of rich young amateur aviators who had decided this was a fascinating way to lose their money.

*Tri-Motored Ford*

When he had finished his review of the past two years, Gafferty found himself remembering that it was Christmas Eve. He wondered what people like Colin and Tad and Lucille and Roland were doing in their new house, which he had not seen, and with their new baby, whom he had not seen. Then he quickly decided there was a great deal of work to be done.

He switched on the light over his desk and restudied his plans for passenger travel in the future. Fords were the thing. Trimotored Fords. T.A.T. were already carrying passengers on their coast-to-coast route. True, they transferred their passengers to a train at night and picked them up again the next morning; but they were still doing business, which was something.

He had hardly dug into the prospective-load factors when he heard slow but even steps coming up the stairs to his office. He waited, puzzled, unable to think of anyone who had legitimate business in the hangar at this hour. Then the steps hesitated and stopped. The door opened. Gafferty blinked, trying to identify the man who stood in shadow beyond his desk light.

"HULLO, MIKE!"

Gafferty rose quickly. There was no mistaking that voice.

"MERRY CHRISTMAS, YOU OLD SONOFABITCH!"

"Johnny Dycer!" Gafferty took his big hand and gripped it firmly. He didn't know why, but it flashed across his mind that he had never been so glad to see anyone in his life. He led Johnny quickly to his own chair behind the desk and pushed him into it. He wanted to see Johnny's face. He wanted to talk and talk to the man for hours. All reserve had fled from him.

"Sit down, Johnny! Damn, I'm glad to see you! Here, have a cigar."

He offered the box eagerly, like a small boy making up to an estranged playmate. Johnny sighed and took one, and Gafferty held a match for him. Now in the bright light he saw that Johnny's face was no longer red, but more of a sickly yellow color, and mottled like poorly tanned chamois. He wore a raincoat that was dirty and torn at the shoulder. His cap was soggy and the peak was shining with grease. When

Johnny threw open his raincoat, Gafferty saw that he wore an old sweater, a black tie, and a clean blue denim shirt. His trousers were wet and wrinkled.

"AIN'T MUCH TO LOOK AT, AM I, MIKE?"

Johnny had noticed his inspection, and Gafferty felt ashamed. Something about Johnny's eyes made him feel as though he were intruding.

"You look swell to me, Johnny. I've been wondering whatever happened to you. Somebody said you'd gone to South America."

"I did. Flew for Slim Fawcett a while out of Lima. Chickens and cows and pigs and natives up to Arequipa, and mining equipment up to Quito. SOME AIRLINE HE'S GOT DOWN THERE. THEM ANDES ARE HIGH."

"Like it?"

Johnny hesitated and looked at the end of his cigar. Gafferty noticed that his hand shook a little

"Well . . . WELL, NO. . . . Can't say as I did."

"When did you get back?"

" 'Bout six months ago."

"I wish you had come around to see me sooner, Johnny." Gafferty didn't have to be told. He knew that Johnny's South American adventure had been a failure, for his eyes and his manner spoke plainly enough.

"I didn't feel like coming to see you . . . or anybody else." Johnny looked at the floor. "I guess you were right, Mike . . . about the altitude. I couldn't take it. Same old thing. And the longer I stayed at it, the worse my old pumping works got. Slim had to let me go finally."

"I'm sorry to hear that."

"I come in on a boat to Galveston. Hell of a boat. Then I got a job in a garage for a while. Fellow liked to fool around with racing cars and I helped him some. Then I got sick again . . . good and sick. . . . Seemed like I couldn' do nothin' without I got dizzy. So I quit that job."

Johnny's voice fell lower than Gafferty had ever heard it before. He mumbled rather than spoke, and seemed to have forgotten that Gafferty was listening. He folded his big wrinkled hands across his surprisingly thin waist and Gafferty saw that they were callused and creased with dirt.

"I decided that maybe it was the heat down in Galveston was gittin' me. It weren't no use goin' to the doctors any more. They just took my money and give me a bunch of instructions and pills that never done a bit of good. So I come up North. Worked along sort of slow-like, up through Memphis and spent some time with Terry Muldoon in St. Louis. He was cookin' up an endurance flight and wanted me to fly the refueling ship. But when the backers found out about my license they got someone else."

"Sounds like you'd had a run of bad luck, Johnny."

"I did for a while. BUT THINGS ARE GOING TO BE ALL RIGHT NEXT WEEK! I'M FEELING A LOT BETTER NOW. . . . GOT CHANCES AT TWO THINGS RIGHT AFTER THE FIRST OF THE YEAR! I'M EITHER GONNA SELL SKY-WRITING TO THE COCA-COLA PEOPLE, OR GO DO SOME BUSH FLYING UP IN CANADA."

"Sounds fine . . . especially the sky-writing job." If Johnny wanted his opinion, he'd have it. The old Gafferty rushed back in spite of himself. "Anything I can do for you, Johnny?"

There was a long silence. Johnny rose heavily from the chair and went to the window. He put his hands in his pockets and studied the globules of water dribbling down the panes. His back was toward Gafferty. When he spoke again, he kept his face turned.

"Yeah, Mike . . . there is. Only thing I really ever liked about you was the way you kept your mouth shut. I need a little help till I can get on my feet. I need a place to sleep tonight and . . . mebbe a couple of nights after. I knew you wouldn't tell anybody. . . ."

Gafferty wanted to walk over and put his arms around the man, but he realized that that would be exactly the wrong thing to do.

"Sure thing. Plenty of room at my place. Stay as long as you can. Keep me company."

"Thanks."

"By the way, I hope you haven't eaten dinner? I was just about to leave."

"I'll go along with you, but I'm not hungry."

Gafferty knew Johnny was lying because he kept his face toward the window. He slipped quickly into his coat and hat and successfully banished the old Gafferty by confining himself to small talk. "Did you hear that Colin and Lucille MacDonald had a baby?"

That turned Johnny around with a smile. "No! Boy or girl?"

"Boy. They say he looks like Keith."

"NO! WELL, I'D LIKE TO SEE THE LITTLE . . . some time."

Gafferty was about to tell Johnny other news that he suspected he must be thirsting for, when the idea struck him. It would be taking a chance, but if it worked—he had heard them planning and talking to Sydney. . . . Maybe. He went back to his desk and searched through the top drawer anxiously. He found the notebook he wanted, ran his finger down a page, and asked the operator for the number he found.

"If you're too busy, Mike, maybe I could meet you—" Johnny started to speak, but Gafferty began to talk into the 'phone.

"Lucille? This is Gafferty." He was grateful that she was the one who answered; it would have been much harder to begin with any of the others. "Listen, I. . . . What? . . . Merry Christmas yourself. . . . What's all the racket? I can hardly hear you. . . . Oh. Well, listen, I was just thinking. . . . Yes. . . . Why, yes, I could . . . and would it be all right if I brought somebody with me? Sort of a surprise for the boys. . . . Fine . . . in about half an hour."

Gafferty hung up the 'phone and tossed his cigar into the wastebasket. He had the exciting notion that it would be a pleasure if the place caught fire and burned to the ground. He felt reckless and warm and happy.

"Come on, Johnny! We haven't got much time. The goose is on!"

"The goose?"

"Yeah. We'll stop by my place a minute, have a drink, and get into some more . . . comfortable clothes. Then you and I are going to have a proper Christmas!"

The little house rang with shouts, the shuffling of feet on the bare floors, the clink of glasses, and the screech of packing boxes being torn open. Porkie Scott, dressed in a Santa Claus outfit, said over and over again that only the wet roof prevented him from coming down the chimney and into the fireplace, although obviously the chimney would not accommodate his girth.

Everyone was exceedingly busy. Shorty Baker, who had brought the fresh-cut tree down from Albany tied to the fuselage of his Pitcairn, was lost in a maze of lights that would not work. He received considerable advice on the subject.

Roland had brought a new phonograph to the house, complete with the latest recordings of "My Blue Heaven" and "Sometimes I'm Happy." He divided his attention among the phonograph, the improvised bar in the kitchen, and the mixing of a powerful punch. He received many suggestions from Porkie's bootlegger, who had dropped by in the interests of his product.

Tad sat by the stove in his wheelchair. He had dedicated himself to basting the goose, which task he carried out with mathematical precision. He received helpful hints from everyone present, including Sydney and the girl he had brought with him from the office. Neither of them had ever browned a piece of toast, but like all people at Christmas they knew exactly how a goose should be handled.

Colin arranged and rearranged the new chair for the living room, the end table, the mirror, the one small throw rug, the two new lamps, and the small writing desk which he himself had bought. Lucille moved distractedly from the salad to the Christmas tree, from the goose to the telephone—to the punch—to the phonograph—to the baby, who clamored at once to be fed.

On the way in to Keith's room with the bottle, she passed the new mirror and paused to look at herself. There was a wisp of hair hanging down and she brushed it back, but what caught her attention was the harried expression on her face. It was a look she had never seen before—at least, on herself; but, instead of letting it disturb her, she laughed straight into the mirror and said to herself that she guessed this was married life at last—and she loved it. As if to confirm her thought, Colin appeared in the mirror behind her. He put one arm about her waist and swung her around.

"Listen, this is the first Christmas I've been home since we've been married. It means a lot to me."

"It means a lot to me, too."

"Then stop by and say hello once in a while, otherwise I'll give your present to some blonde."

"Present? Colin, I told you *not* to! What is it?"

He brought out the small package he had been holding behind him, and held the feeding bottle while she opened it.

"If you've gone and spent any money on me after all the expense we've . . . but anyway I love to open packages. . . ."

She found a small wooden box inside the wrappings. When she opened the lid, it tinkled out "Just a wee doch-an-dorris," the tune that had become so much a part of her life.

"Oh, Colin! *Oh!*" was all she could say. Then, while the music box was still tinkling, she turned and kissed him in a way she hoped he would never forget.

"Well, I'm glad you liked it!" He frowned at the milk bottle. "Maybe this is a good time to tell you that I'm tired of playing second fiddle to that short, bald-headed guy in the other room."

"I'll let him starve, then."

"Good, only he starves so noisily. Wait till next week some time, when I'm gone."

"OR JUST LET ME HANDLE THE WHOLE SHOOTIN' MATCH!" boomed a voice behind them.

They turned quickly and for a moment were unable to say anything. And their silence brought a sudden hush upon everyone in the room—for there stood Whispering Johnny, still with his hat on and looking like a great pillar holding up the ceiling. He shot a nervous glance at Gafferty beside him. Then a half-smile crept across his mouth. His eyes moved swiftly from Lucille and Colin to Shorty, who seemed hypnotized beside the tree, to Roland and Porkie at the fireplace, to Sydney and his girl, and to Tad beyond the kitchen doorway. Then he put his fists to his sides and pushed out his stomach.

"WELL! Ain't nobody going to say hello to Johnny?"

It was Lucille who broke the spell. She rushed to him and threw her arms around his thick neck. She pulled his head down and kissed his heavy jowls. "Oh, Johnny, Johnny! Merry Christmas and welcome . . . welcome *home*!"

Then they were upon him, all of them, shouting and laughing and shaking his hands and pounding his shoulders and tearing off his coat and throwing his hat across the room, until Johnny begged them to let up. Gafferty found that their warmth included him. His pleasure was equaled only by his embarrassment when Colin pulled him aside and said, "Thanks for coming . . . thanks for bringing Johnny."

"When do I see this mite . . . this Keith?" demanded Johnny.

"After you've warmed your hands," said Lucille.

"And the cockles of your heart," said Porkie.

They led him off to the kitchen, and Lucille slipped into the bedroom. She guessed correctly that she and the baby would not be alone very long; they never were when Roland was around. His devotion to Keith was something she had still not found time to analyze. She only knew that somehow, if he was in town, Roland always managed to be present when Keith was bathed, and as often as he could when Keith was fed. She was not surprised when Roland slipped in and closed the door softly behind him, oblivious to the fact that Keith was howling his head off and no noise created by humans could compete with him. Roland set his drink down on the floor and tiptoed ponderously across the room to them. He watched her place the nipple between Keith's lips, and when the squalling became a gurgle, Roland grunted sympathetically.

"Here. Let me do that."

"You'd better stick by the others. They need a sort of general superintendent out there."

"Then you go. I can do this just as well as you."

Roland looked so earnest that she gave in without further argument.

"Be sure he takes it all."

"We never miss. Say, don't you think we ought to set a place for him at the table? He might enjoy some of the goose."

"Oh, sure, we'll do just that. Maybe you'd like to take him flying with you tomorrow . . . a sort of Christmas present."

Roland looked up at her and his face was perfectly serious. "Why not? He's got to start some day."

They exchanged a smile and a look of understanding—and so it came to them that they were both very happy on this Christmas Eve.

# 1929

## 19

There were some men who claimed they could point out the exact date when the change came to flying—or at least they were quick to say it was this event or that event or most certainly some particular invention. There were those who credited the change to adjustable-pitch propellers, to air-mass analysis, to Henry Ford—or to themselves. There were those who blamed the change on Lindbergh, Martin's selling out, or Boeing's selling out. And there were those who said there had been no change at all. They were the unbelievers who feared change because they mistrusted their own progress. They were very few.

Now for the first time almost everyone could see that something remarkable was happening to aviation. But the actuality had been so long heralded that it emerged an anticlimax. Men like Gafferty, who had been going around for years insisting that airplane rides could be sold to the general public as a means of transportation instead of an afternoon thrill, could not suddenly burst forth and say, "It is here! Just as I said it would be!"

The change came in ways that no one ever foresaw and was accompanied by so many technical complications that when it finally arrived no one had time to stand back and look at it, and even the most astute and voluble prophets were lost in the confusion.

Porkie Scott, who could always be relied upon for a considered observation, allowed that he didn't know what flying was coming to when men contrived an airplane so large that it required two pilots. He was referring to the trimotored Ford, which he and many others considered a threat to their fierce independence. But the big Fords which had begun to drum their way over the country on some of the other airlines were not the only signs of change. Airmen were talking quite glibly of flaps and spoilers, lapse rates, super-chargers, and high-wing loadings. The Post Office Department paid the airlines over twelve million dollars, and that was certainly a change. Everyone concerned was very busy contributing to this change, yet no one could quite put his finger on what was happening. There was a general air of wary expectation and uneasiness among the men who knew flying best, as if an old friend noted for debauchery had suddenly taken up religion.

And so Roland felt uncomfortable the first time he flipped the shining new switch on the instrument panel during the run from Albany to Newark. He did so with an air of experimentation, as if it were a rather foolish and embarrassing thing to do. For one so accustomed to being alone in the air, the whole idea of radio communication gave him something of a shock. It was like having a perfect stranger guess the exact course of his thoughts.

The Pitcairn was the same, though worn by the wind and the men who had flown it for three years. The luminous dials on most of the instruments had turned slightly yellow with age. The metal hatch over the mail pit was dented and in need of paint around the buckles that held it fast. The fabric inside the cockpit where it had never been painted was spotted with oil. And the cockpit floor was coated with the fine grime of a thousand landings. And lately, ever since Gafferty had made the announcement that they would soon be flying a new type of plane, all the Pitcairns had taken on a frowzy, slightly down-at-the-heels look. Roland was sorry about this because he recognized that his art was entering another of its periodic transition spells. There would be changes in the way he practiced that art, and he was not sure he was going to like them.

This radio thing was an indication. Even though his own brother had been largely responsible for its installation, Roland regarded it with suspicion. He guessed he was getting old and set in his ways, like the Hudson that he knew was now flowing rigidly beneath the overcast. Old at thirty-four.

He laughed at the thought, but he knew it was not altogether ridiculous. He could see it not only in himself, but in his friends, Colin, and Porkie and Shorty—and he could see the reasons for it.

You didn't fly day after day in winter without having to land in order to beat the ice off the wings with a stick carried for the purpose. You didn't fly in spring without sooner or later finding yourself almost helpless over a fogged-in airport and short of gas. You didn't fly in summer without some day having it out with a thunderstorm or at best a good line squall. And in the fall there were the gusty winds to watch, lest the finish of a perfectly normal flight end with yourself the proprietor of your junk heap. It was a seasoning with the seasons that wore a man—like an old steak long hung and slightly touched with mold.

This aging also went on in the nights, when the engine sputtered and a woosh of silence made you think and remember your sins with startling clarity, or when the moon broke through a cumulus hole and mocked your dark, conjured fears. It was accelerated in snow squalls that began as innocent, lovely flurries to be easily avoided, and ended as two-day blizzards frothing on the horizon.

It was hastened in other ways, with brooding ideas such as that you'd better have a good time now because there's quite some chance there may not be any tomorrow. And the mildew came from the interrupted nights when you went to bed and got right up again, when you ate breakfast at three in the afternoon, when you did nothing at all for five days. It came when the Bureau of Air Commerce listened to your heart, when the wind and the rain felt of your skin.

This wasn't like making one big, spectacular flight that broke an endurance record—something you took months to key up to, that gave you a chance to settle back in at least momentary glory when it was finished. This kind of flying went on and on. It put wrinkles in your face ahead of time. It made the wrong men querulous and jumpy. And, most of all, it frequently made you mistrust new ideas in flying because the old ones molded by past alarms had always preserved your beloved neck in one functional unit. Yet you were absolutely sure of only one thing: that tomorrow, or the next day, or the following night, something would come that you had never met before, something that would demand your immediate and most concentrated attention.

After Roland had flipped the new switch, he bent down in the cockpit and turned a radio dial at his side until it read 42. Then he took a heavy black box from where it hung on a hook at the side of the cockpit. These were all new to the Pitcairn and new to Roland. He handled them as if they might break in his large hand. He glanced up at the aerial wire whipping above his head in the slip stream. It stretched from a short pole set in the middle of the upper wing to the top of the vertical stabilizer on the tail. Roland had the compelling feeling that he must look at it before he did anything further. He carefully reviewed the instructions on speaking which Tad had given him, and then put the black box to his lips. He cleared his throat and again felt embarrassed. He almost abandoned the idea of going any further before he finally pressed the button on top of the box and spoke haltingly into it.

"MacDonald one, calling Newark. . . ."

He pressed the headphones inside his helmet tight against his ears. Nothing. He moved the radio dial a trifle and heard only a faint crackling. He put the box to his lips again.

"MacDonald one . . . MacDonald one . . . calling Newark." No sound. No answer. Roland shook the box in annoyance.

He reviewed his instructions again. That was right. They had decided, for purposes of easy identification, that Roland would be called MacDonald one, and Colin, MacDonald two. What the hell was the matter with the silly thing? He looked down at the heavy white February overcast a thousand feet beneath him. He blinked thoughtfully at its brilliance. Then he looked up at the sun, a blaze at noon. It was foolish to be talking to himself in the midst of such pleasurable isolation. He did not like it. Whether it answered or not, there was an intruder present, ill-mannered and inefficient. Roland could see no logical reason to invite the intruder again, but he knew how hard Tad had been working and how much this meant to him. He tried again.

"MacDonald one . . . calling Newark. If you're ever going to say anything, say it now . . . or forever hold your peace. . . ."

MacDonald one calling Newark. . . . Hey! . . . Anybody hear me?'' He hung up the black box in disgust. Nothing.

In one way Roland was gratified; the radio's delinquency was simply silent testimony that flying could never be run from the ground, and that hanging an airplane full of gadgets, as everyone who ever brushed with aviation wanted to do, would not necessarily help matters any. In another way he was sorry. He knew Tad would be sitting by the receiver in Newark, leaning forward in his wheel chair—watching with anxious, thoughtful eyes every move the operator made. He had worked very hard for over a year, so hard and so stubbornly that sometimes he almost seemed to forget his handicap entirely.

But Roland knew that, in spite of Tad's surface cheerfulness, those times when he was left alone on the ground must be hard to bear. No amount of spirit had been able to hide his despair when he finally realized he would never walk again. Roland remembered that he had changed almost overnight. He was softer now. There was none of the old derision in his smile. He was humble, and seemed ashamed of the deep scars on his face. It was a dangerous tendency in a man like Tad, and they had all been thankful for this radio thing. Tad had worked slowly at first, and then almost frantically, as if its immediate trial meant life to him. Roland was sorry Tad would be sitting and waiting—and would hear nothing.

Then a voice touched his ears, faint and rasping, but a true trespass on his solitude.

"Newark calling MacDonald one. Go ahead, MacDonald one.''

Roland grabbed the black box. The thing worked! It worked—or he was dreaming.

"MacDonald one to Newark. . . . Go ahead . . . go ahead . . . I hear you . . . only talk louder!'' Roland felt unfamiliar goose pimples of excitement running up and down his arms. He wished he could see Tad's face. He listened carefully.

"MacDonald one from Newark. . . . What time were you off Albany?''

They were asking him a question! This was intelligence. This was wonderful. He would give them answer.

"Eleven thirty-two.''

There was a moment's silence.

"MacDonald one from Newark. Our weather is about two hundred feet with scud and blowing snow. Visibility one to one half mile. Suggest you turn around and return to Albany."

Ah! There it was. Roland forgot his pleasure. Not because of the weather, since he had hardly heard the report, but far worse—because they were telling him what to do! Who the hell was flying this airplane? Gafferty, sitting in his warm office? Tad, even? That radio operator so recently off a ship that there was still salt in his ears? Give those guys on the ground an inch and they took a mile. He hunched up his shoulders and gripped the black box firmly. He talked into it violently, earnestly, as if he held a small impertinent person in his hand—because for the first time in his career someone had tried to tell him how to fly.

"Listen . . . I'm headed for Newark. I'm coming to Newark. I've been away for three days and my shirt is dirty. Now don't give me any more argument, because I'm gonna turn this damn thing off and I won't hear you anyway!"

"That's tellin' them, MacDonald one!"

What was that? A new voice rang in his ears, close and clear.

"Who's that?" he asked the black box, though he recognized Colin's unmistakable quiet drawl.

"MacDonald two."

The thing worked too well. A regular party line, thought Roland. "Where are you?"

"Seven thousand over Elmira."

Well, now, *that* was a thing to know! Roland sat back in astonishment. His own brother talking to him through the tumbled waste of space, hundreds of miles away. Of course— Colin was flying the new direct route that noon from Buffalo nonstop to Newark. He had left Buffalo three hours after Roland. Roland held the black box tentatively and tried to think of something to say into it. He had about come to the conclusion that this was certainly the strangest flight he had ever made in an airplane. Then an idea occurred to him and he thought—why not?

"What's your weather, MacDonald two?"

"In and out. Between layers mostly . . . sometimes on top at seven . . . plenty of holes below."

"Any ice?"

"No ice today."

"Did you hear the Newark weather?"

"Yeah. I heard it. If it doesn't improve I'm going to turn back to Elmira. I've got a passenger!"

"A passenger?" What next?

"Yeah. He's gradually freezing to death in the mail pit. Nice guy, too, by the name of Harris."

"Tell Mr. Harris I think he is a very brave man to fly with you."

"Okay, MacDonald one."

"Okay, MacDonald two."

Roland hung up the black box and smiled. This invisible companionship had a peculiar value. To some extent it robbed him of his private camaraderie with the elements, but somehow he had the feeling that he was safer—attended in his efforts, able at last to ask for help. For the next hour, he thought frequently of this feeling, but he could not explain why it was so comforting.

He was much too busy trying to get into Newark. He was about to swallow his pride and turn back to Albany when he found a small hole in the overcast. He dove down at once from out of the sun, kicked the Pitcairn around in a tight vertical, and emerged a few moments later in the gloom beneath the overcast. He was over Long Island. Flushing Bay slipped by, black and cold-looking, barely a hundred feet below his wheels. There were heavy snow squalls in every direction. The Pitcairn tossed in the gusty northwest wind. He flattened out over the Brooklyn housetops and muttered to himself that this was not good, and that he would kiss each cylinder of the Wright individually if it would just keep running another ten minutes.

He turned west and almost ran straight into the Brooklyn Bridge. By standing the Pitcairn on its left wing, he just managed to miss its eastern approaches. He swept along the docks, pressed down farther and farther by the lowering overcast. He swung out over the river itself, lest the stacks and masts of a tied-up liner finish off what the Brooklyn

Bridge had almost started. Tugs hooted at him. He could see their bursts of white steam against the black water. In two minutes, he was at the Battery. The gray, half-visible wall of buildings fell off into nothing. He cut off southwest for the Statue of Liberty. It should loom up in a minute or even less. But he never saw the statue. The driving snow had spirited it away. He pulled up just over the promenade deck of a startled liner making port, turned a little to the west, and held his course.

Three minutes later—very long minutes—the docks of Newark slipped beneath. He saw a familiar crane poking a finger into the driving snow, then a dirty black line of hangars. Newark. His pride returned instantly. Now just who the hell was telling him how to fly? He made a tight circle over the field so he would not lose it, turned back into the wind, and glided swiftly to a soft landing in the snow. He held left rudder against the force of the wind and taxied at half throttle to the hangar.

He left the ship at once, walking stiffly through the fast-deepening drifts. He wanted to see Tad.

They were huddled about the new radio receiver that had been placed in a little room next to Gafferty's office. Tad and the new operator—a tall, thin, hawklike man whose name was Ole—and Gafferty. They looked up when Roland appeared in the doorway.

"How was it up there?" asked Gafferty.

"Not too good." What did they expect him to say? Roland himself would have looked askance at any pilot who said the weather was terrible.

"How did you get in?"

"Oh, I meandered here and there. . . ." Roland pulled off his helmet and sat down on the radiator. He lit a cigarette and smiled at Tad. "Your gadget works fine, son." The expression on Tad's face was worth everything he had just been through. "Is it still working?"

"Sure. We were talking to Colin a little while ago."

"Hmmm." Roland looked at the end of his cigarette and then turned for a look out the window. Now here he was, safe on the ground, and already thinking he knew all the answers. Still—

"I was thinking . . . maybe you might be able to get hold of him again."

"If he's listening—which is more than you did."

"Better try it, then. There's a couple of things he might like to know."

Receiving a nod of approval from Tad and Gafferty, Ole threw the switch on the radio panel. When the dynamotor reached a high whine, he began talking into the microphone.

"MacDonald two from Newark. Newark calling MacDonald two. Go ahead if you read, MacDonald two."

There was no answer. Roland looked out the window watching the snow.

"Try him again," said Tad.

"Newark calling MacDonald two. Go ahead, MacDonald two. . . ."

"Go ahead yourself. It's your nickel!" Obviously Colin. The drawl. The unruffled calm in his voice. Roland moved over slowly until he stood just behind Ole. He moved slowly because it would never do to show his concern, with this stranger in their midst and Gafferty looking on.

"Ask him what time he estimates here."

"Newark to MacDonald two: What is your Newark estimate?"

"Hold the line." They knew that Colin would be figuring his time from the last check point he had seen on the ground. "Twenty-two . . . maybe twenty-five minutes. I just passed over Scranton valley. How's the Newark weather?"

"Tell him it's spotty. Snow and about two hundred feet with a mile visibility except in the squalls."

"MacDonald one says it's spotty. Two hundred and one mile except in the squalls. . . ."

"So the old boy made it! The sun must be shining. If he can make it, I can! Tell him to wait for me."

"Will do."

They waited in silence. Roland consumed a second cigarette. He tried not to look at Tad. Instead he alternately studied the weather outside the window and glanced at the clock on the wall. It certainly didn't look any better out of the window; maybe he should have told Colin to turn back to Buffalo. But he probably wouldn't have the gas now. Still, there were Scranton and Elmira. He could make them if he turned around now. He tried to picture what he himself would do, and that was why he asked Ole to call again.

"Now what?" The answer was prompt and a little annoyed. His voice was much louder. Ole said that he couldn't be far from Newark.

"Let me talk to him," said Roland.

Ole handed him the microphone.

"MacDonald two, this is MacDonald one. It's getting a bit sticky around here. I found some holes over Long Island. You might have the same luck if you wanted to go over that way. Then you can work back over Brooklyn and across the harbor."

"Listen, Grandma, put on your carpet slippers and wait by the fire for me. I'm still between layers and will be on the ground before you know it. Now, stop bothering me."

"Okay, MacDonald two."

Roland handed the microphone back to Ole. His face was a mixture of pride and anxiety. If Colin was independent, whose fault was it? Who had taught him, not only to fly, but to do his own thinking in the air? He managed a short, nervous laugh.

"Feeling frisky, isn't he?" he said to Tad.

But Tad didn't seem to hear him. He was fumbling in his pockets for a cigarette and when he finally found it, his hands which were once so sure and strong shook until he laid down the cigarette without lighting it. So Roland looked at the clock and out the window again and tried to tell himself that Colin was as good a pilot as himself, if not better.

Colin had considered the possibility of ice, as he had every other deterrent to a successful flight. It was a matter of habit with him, as it was with any pilot who flew day in and day out. Since his take-off from Buffalo he had considered separately the wind direction at take-off, how best to taxi through the Buffalo snowdrifts without catching a wing tip or getting stuck, the freedom of his controls, the tightness of his safety belt, the amount of gas in his ship, the oil pressure, the way the engine sounded when he ran it up, and exactly which open field he would head for if the engine quit immediately after take-off.

The presence of Mr. Harris in the mail pit added an additional consideration and a small ceremony. Parachutes were not provided for passengers, yet a pilot had to sit on one since it was the only thing designed to fit the curved metal seat in the rear cockpit. It had therefore become customary—in fact, an unwritten law—for the pilot to remove the parachute straps from his shoulders, preferably while the passenger was looking on. This action indicated that the pilot intended to use the parachute only as something to sit on, and would not under any provocation abandon the passenger to his separate fate. Colin had done this with what he hoped was the proper degree of solemnity and had been rewarded by a wan smile of appreciation from Mr. Harris.

After the take-off he had variously considered the trim of the ship and just how much to move the stabilizer to accommodate Mr. Harris's weight forward. He calculated the amount of crab necessary against the northwest wind to bring his course over Elmira, the amount of speed the wind would add to his progress over the earth's surface, the choice of flying at three thousand feet where he would be required to work his way in and out among the hills, or at five thousand where a layer of cloud indicated he would spend most of the journey flying on instruments, or at seven thousand feet where there seemed to be broken layers.

His choice of seven thousand had proved a happy one. Even before he reached Elmira, the upper layers parted and shredded into thin wisps. Finally they dissolved altogether until he was flying just above a glaring white overcast. The sky above him was of the peculiar blinding, cold, cobalt blue that it always seems to be when the winter sun rides very high and alone at noon. Colin was cheered by its warmth upon his shoulders. Mr. Harris had turned around a few times to smile uncertainly and squint at the sun. He shouted a few questions over the engine noise, to find out where they were and when they would arrive in Newark. Colin answered to the best of his knowledge, but Mr. Harris seemed more interested in making some noise himself than in learning the facts. At last he abandoned the effort to communicate and sat motionless for a long time on top of the mail bags. Colin thought he had probably gone to sleep.

There were even a few breaks in the overcast beneath—one just east of Elmira where Colin spotted a railroad junction he knew, and a very convenient one over the Scranton valley which gave him an exact speed and course check. Thus when Newark called and asked his estimated time of arrival, he was able to give an answer that he knew would be accurate within a few minutes.

The Newark weather gave him some concern, though he was fairly confident he could work his way between the squalls by using a certain amount of aerial skulduggery. He smiled to himself when he reflected that Mr. Harris was in for quite a little airplane ride—one that he would not soon forget. He had paid some three times the price of the train trip from Buffalo for the privilege of freezing on the hard mail sacks. He would get his money's worth.

It was the overcast now beneath him that worried Colin. To get down through it without losing too much time and thus running the risk of getting lost, without hitting the last of the hills that sprawled out from the Appalachians, to get down and out quickly and emerge reasonably near Newark was a problem requiring great precision. Colin was aware that luck would play a very important part. A hole here or a hole there would make all the difference. Even so, he would not have attempted the task without carefully studying the character of the overcast from his comfortable vantage in the sun. He found that it was not the stratus type, which would unquestionably extend as a solid mass to whatever ceiling had been reported, and so remain for many hours. This overcast would be rough inside. That was good; the buffeting of the strong winds would cause it to break occasionally. It was a great congealed mess of snow squalls in loose formation. Through the breaks he had already seen the fat cumulus writhing together and trailing their gray veils of snow. Such a winter overcast was full of caprice. One moment it might blot out the ground in swirls of snow and scud. Five minutes later it might allow the sun to break through. Then again, it would close everything—as it must have done with Roland. It all depended, but Colin thought it worth a try. He called Newark again.

"MacDonald two from Newark. Go ahead."

"What's your weather now?"

There was a pause. Then the voice came back, a little more cheerful.

"About five hundred now and maybe four miles. We can see Staten Island. Clearing, but looks like another squall to the northwest."

Good. Good. Maybe Mr. Harris lived right. Colin was pleased with his decision. He was also hungry. He glanced at his wrist watch. Twelve-thirty. He hoped Lucille would save him some lunch.

"Tell that squall to wait till I'm on the ground. It will be another ten minutes."

He hung up the microphone and began looking for a yellowish blur in the overcast—the sign of a possible hole.

**20**

Roland lit another cigarette from the butt of his last one. He took off his flying boots and shook the melted snow off them, to give himself something to do. He looked at the clock again. Twelve thirty-two. He went to the window. Better—but damn, that squall was coming in fast. He had waited on the ground for other pilots. Many times, in worse weather. What was he so nervous about? It was this damn radio thing—that was it! In the past, what he didn't know didn't bother him. Waiting in ignorance was a comparative pleasure. Now he felt as if he were half on the ground and half in the air.

He looked at Tad. The guy had thrown the blanket off his legs again. He was always doing that, and the doctor had told him—Roland was about to say something on the subject and then decided against it. Tad was not in this room anyway. His thin, waxen face was expressionless, but his eyes showed that he was aloft—seven thousand feet up, wherever Colin was. His bony, tight-skinned hands twisted slowly, round and round until Roland wanted to tell him for God's sake to stop doing that and sit still.

Twelve thirty-five. That confounded clock must have stopped, or it must be stuck, or anyway something must be wrong with it. There was a crackle from the radio like bacon frying. He looked at Ole.

"What was that?"

"Snow static. Surprised there isn't more of it."

Why didn't Colin call? Was he going to sit up there all day? Why the hell didn't Gafferty go back to his office where

**254**

e belonged? Twelve thirty-eight. Well, the clock moved
nyway. Then, for some reason, the picture of Madame
Moselle passed across his mind and he had a hard time
etting rid of it. Looking at Tad made him think of Madame
Moselle and of long, clean grass brushing against his cheek
s he lay indolently beneath a wing. The grass of Minnesota
nd Wisconsin and Iowa and Ohio—the grass that always
eemed to be there to lie upon, in those days when things
ere sweeter and easier. Then Colin's voice broke into his
leasant dreaming.

"Hey, Newark. . . . Is MacDonald one still there?"
Roland stepped quickly to the radio panel.

"He's still here, MacDonald two," said Ole into the
icrophone.

"Well. . . ." Colin's voice dragged thoughtfully. "Ask
im . . . ask him if he picked up any ice on his descent."
Roland shook his head vigorously.

"MacDonald one says no."

"Well. . . ." There was a long pause. For a moment they
ought Colin had finished his transmission. ". . . I got
ome."

Then there was silence again.

Colin was down to five thousand feet. In one minute he
ould safely assume that he was over or at least very near
Newark. There had been holes aplenty at first, but most of
em perversely led off in the wrong direction—to the north
r south. Thus he had been obliged to fly through two
qualls. Neither had lasted more than a few minutes, but he
was astonished at the amount of ice that now clung to the
eading edges of the wings, the flying wires, and the tail
ssembly. And of the three types of ice, he had encountered
he worst: clear ice, rough and pitted.

Mr. Harris thought the ice was pretty. Colin thought it was
ile because he knew what it could do. The rate of accumula-
ion, on which hinges the real power of any ice, was much
aster than any he had experienced before. It blobbed on, as if
omeone had splashed the leading parts of the Pitcairn with a
reezing paintbrush. He could actually watch the growth of
he little mounds and crenulations that began as a transparent

film and in a moment took on a whiteness and ugly solidity And the Pitcairn was protesting—still mildly, but Colin coul feel it in the seat of his pants and even more markedly in the pit of his stomach. The crust of ice weighed perhaps fifty o sixty pounds, but the weight itself was unimportant. With a increase of power to the engine, the Pitcairn could handl several hundred pounds of additional weight. It was what th clinging ice did to the delicate conformations of the wing that concerned Colin.

The wings were built according to a precise mathematica formula. Even the slightest variation in the formula resulte in making the wings at first unclean, and finally incapable o supporting flight. And the propeller, which in a sense wa merely another whirling wing, was subject to the same weak ness. It had been fashioned to a more exact balance than an Damascus blade. It was turning at sixteen hundred revolu tions per minute. Anything that upset its balance, howeve small, caused it to vibrate and mush; it would no longer bit cleanly through the air.

Colin was worried about the way the propeller was vibrat ing now. It sent unpleasant shudders through the Pitcairn' lean fuselage. The instrument panel was beginning to shak unevenly. Yet these were but beginning complications. Coli knew that they would compound themselves with viciou momentum, interlock in subtle combinations until they forme an impenetrable net about him and his ship. There were stil certain things he could do—but every moment in the ice cu down their number.

Roland pushed up the window. It made him angry becaus it stuck halfway and he had to pound at it. He was angry wit the window and with himself because he was in such haste.

"We should be able to hear him now," he said. He pushe his head and shoulders out of the window and turned his fac to the sky. The ticking of a typewriter distracted him. H ducked back into the room. "Tell that damn girl to stop th damn typewriter!"

Gafferty left to do his bidding and Roland leaned out th window again. A tugboat whistled in the channel. A bu ground into gear on the road beside the airport. Off in th distance someone was shoveling snow. And in the soft inter

als of quiet, when only the wind brushed his cheek, Roland
stened intently for the one sound he wanted so much to
ear.

It began hardly as a sound itself, but rather as a minute
ifference in the silence. At first Roland was not sure he
eard anything but his own hopes. Then slowly the sound
ook on assurance, surged rhythmically against the atmo-
phere. At last it became solid and grew evenly in volume.
hen the single sound divided into several sounds, each
nique and intelligible to a knowing listener. That was the
ngine. *That* was the propeller slicing the air. *That* was the
ubdued whistle of the wings and flying wires like a light
tring background in a symphony.

"Tell him to hold his course. He's almost over the field!"

"MacDonald two from Newark. We can hear your engine.
MacDonald one says hold your course. Almost over the
ield."

"Let me know when I've passed it. I'll turn back."

"Okay, MacDonald two."

There was something about Colin's voice, even in its
nfamiliar radio distortion, that Roland did not like. The
uiet confidence was gone.

"He's worried," said Tad, and his voice was almost a
whisper. "I can tell."

Colin pushed the throttle all the way forward. He wanted
nd needed all the power he could get. But now the factors
ad combined in such a way that they blocked him on every
ide. He worked and thought as fast as he could to find a last
orner of escape.

The Pitcairn was heavy with ice. The elements had first
een to this. The ship shuddered miserably and began to sink
lowly—a hundred feet, another two hundred feet, another
undred feet. It mushed sluggishly when Colin tried to turn
ven a very little. It threatened to fall off in a spin at any
moment. Colin knew that, with its flying ability already
alf-ruined by the ice, he would never get it out of a spin.
Even so, he could hold his own if he could rally more power
rom the engine. But the elements had taken care of that. The
ngine power came from the explosion of air and gasoline in

the cylinders. Ice had formed a neat rim around the air scoop that led to the carburetor. The rim became an iris that closed gradually until now the cylinders were starving for air and Colin was desperate for power.

The only way he could keep his speed was by diving slightly, but this expedient had its limitations bounded absolutely by how much altitude he could expend. The altimeter now read two thousand feet. Diving could only subtract from this figure.

Colin unbuckled his safety belt and reached forward to tap Mr. Harris on the shoulder. Mr. Harris was fortunate: he still thought the ice was pretty.

"Mr. Harris! You'll have to do something for me!"

"Yeah? Sure!"

"Reach under you and get hold of those mail sacks. Throw them overboard!"

Mr. Harris looked bewildered. "Now?"

"Yes. Now. Quick! All of them!"

For the first time, Mr. Harris looked worried. His head disappeared into the mail pit. Then one by one he pushed out the sacks. When he had finished, he looked back at Colin. He didn't ask if anything was wrong, and Colin liked him for it. He only sat woodenly and looked at the gray, dank world around him. He turned to Colin again with the helpless look of a man who knows his life depends upon another. Colin managed to smile and wave his hand. He pointed straight down.

"Newark! They just heard us!"

Even with the mail gone, the Pitcairn was beginning to yaw and wallow. Colin reached instinctively for his parachute straps, then he remembered Mr. Harris and put them down again.

Roland swung quickly from the window.

"Tell him he's— Here, let me talk to him!" He took the microphone from Ole and went back to the window. "Mac-Donald two from MacDonald one. You just passed over the field. Hold your course for one minute, turn back . . . and I'll pick you up again. Visibility is better to the south . . . about a mile. We'll bring you in that way."

There was no hesitancy in Roland's manner now. If Colin objected he could have it out with him when he reached the ground. But his orders met only with silence. He shook the microphone.

"Is this thing working?"

"Yeah," said Ole.

"Did you hear me, MacDonald two?"

"Yeah . . . I heard you. I got trouble. Plenty!"

"Turn now . . . before you get too far away!"

"I can't. . . . Losing power fast. Ice."

"Backfire your engine then. . . . That will clean the scoop."

They waited at the window. Then faintly, to the east, they heard the flat pop-popping of an engine. Roland repressed his desire to call again; he knew how busy Colin would be. He kept his face to the sky. He did not have to look back into the room. He could feel the arm of Tad's wheel chair now beside his leg.

Then Colin's voice came through again. "MacDonald two to Newark. . . . That helped some. But she still won't hold. . . ." There was a crash of static and they missed some words. Roland beat his fist on the windowsill. ". . . fifteen hundred and will try a turn. . . ." The voice was drowned in crackling static again.

"Tell him to jump," said Gafferty. "Tell him I said so."

"He—" Roland started to explain about the passenger.

But this was his own brother. He looked at Tad and wondered if he knew. Of course, he must have heard them talking together in the air. Tad's face was expressionless, but Roland knew what he was thinking. A brother and a stranger—and Gafferty wouldn't know until it was too late to do anything about it. This was Colin's life and he deserved to live. They were sure of that—and the passenger was an unknown quantity.

"MacDonald two from Newark. Gafferty orders you to jump."

Let him make up his own mind—at least the suggestion had been placed. Colin's voice came back instantly.

"Uh-uh! No dice. Mr. Harris wouldn't like that one bit!"

His voice was firm and cheerful. For the first time some of the gaiety returned—and it brought so much warmth and pride to Roland and Tad that they smiled at each other and shook their heads. And Gafferty, watching them, understood.

"Here goes the turn. . . . Hang on, you guys!"

The altimeter read eleven hundred feet. Colin could keep the engine surging with fair power by backfiring it regularly. But in order to do so he had to cut the ignition switch momentarily, and he lost another hundred feet every time. He had very little left to expend. Any steep turn with ice on the wings is dangerous—an invitation to a spin. He would have to turn gently, diving slightly at the same time to increase his speed. Then straight for the field and push her down.

"MacDonald two to Newark. How's your weather coming?"

"Breaking a little . . . three hundred, maybe . . . thick blowing snow. . . ."

Three hundred. That didn't leave much room. There was a smokestack higher than that just northeast of the field. He hit a break and flew in the open just long enough to make the turn, but it cost him four hundred feet. Four hundred from eleven hundred, minus another hundred just now backfiring the engine, left six hundred—with this wallowing, shaking, protesting, unmanageable craft.

"Listen carefully, boys! . . . I'm headed your way . . . from the southeast. Sing out when I'm over! . . ."

Five hundred. Four hundred. More ice again.

They waited, hardly breathing. The telephone rang and Gafferty reached quickly to take it off the hook. They waited forever—and still no sound. Gafferty bit off the end of a cigar and then put it back into his pocket. A loose piece of tin on the hangar roof clanged in the wind. Someone slammed a door. They waited two minutes, and then an endless third. Roland closed his eyes that he might hear better, but his ears caught no sound save the soft sigh of the wind and the brush of snow against the building. When four minutes had passed, they ached with fear.

Tad's eyes began to fill with tears. He rocked in his chair. Then he could hold back his terror no longer.

"Ask him!" he cried. "FOR CHRIST'S SAKE ASK HIM!"

Roland put the microphone to his lips and spoke slowly.

"MacDonald two from MacDonald one. You must have missed. We haven't heard you. . . ."

His answer was a crash of static. Roland handed the microphone back to Ole.

"Here. Take this. Keep calling. . . . I'm going outside where I can hear better." On the way out, he patted Tad on the shoulder without knowing that he did it.

He stood bareheaded in the snow for a long time, looking and listening in all directions. His hands hung limply at his sides and he had no feeling of the cold wind or the snow ticking against his face. And while he listened, he prayed. But there was no sound from aloft.

He stood there looking up, until Gafferty came and took his arm.

"We just had a 'phone call, Roland. You don't have to listen any longer. . . ."

"No. He might—"

"It was the Staten Island Police. He never got this far. He hit the hills. They've just found him, Roland. The passenger . . . may live. We'd better go up there now."

Roland looked at him without saying anything, until Gafferty wondered whether he had heard him at all. He looked at the sky and at the place to the southwest where the sun had broken through and sent down a shaft of cold gold. He felt of the wind before he turned away.

"Someone . . . Mike, somebody should . . . oh, God, Mike—I've got to tell Lucille."

There were so many things to think about that he drove very slowly from the field in the early starlight. There was the grass to think about, and the summer sun blazing on a hot, laughing crowd. There was the smell of fabric dope that blended so ludicrously with the smell of cow manure. And the price of gasoline to think about when you hit a stretch of bad weather and couldn't take any farmers flying for their five dollars. And the music of a band, and a wagon to sleep in, and coffee with Madame Moselle. There was the leisure of following the slow seasons. The girls. The never getting out of boots and breeches, the pleasant shudder of an old Standard when it fell reluctantly into a spin—and snapped out before a crowd just when you wanted it to. There were the arguments on the timing of a Hisso, the best way to hang by your knees from a landing gear, and the rig that So-and-so fixed so that he could pick up a handkerchief with his wing tip. There were the section lines stretching to infinity in the sunlight, and the time when Keith and Colin and Tad watched him curse and sweat for an hour while he turned the propeller on an OX; they had hidden the distributor finger in a hay-stack. There were these and many other things to think about.

Still there was no reason, save for the sweetness of the memory, to hold these thoughts any longer. Like the morning haze after the sun, they had melted into nothing. He knew there could never be a return to the old ways, any more than he could bring back his own youth—or Keith—or Colin. Neither they nor the life existed any longer. That old and merry world and his brothers, Porkie and Shorty and Johnny Dycer and—yes, even Gafferty and himself, were a part of each other. None of them had been forced into the life. They chose it, and who could say that either Colin or Keith had felt cheated? In this, Roland found some comfort: at least they had served their life well. The "some day" that they had scarcely dared to dream about was already in view. No one could ever deny that they had made an important contribution to it.

A man could leave now, with dignity, and seek protection and tranquillity on earth. But it would be like leaving a finally consenting bride at the altar. He would be alone now in many ways, but always in illustrious company when he flew—and this thought pleased him.

When he reached the house, the porch light was on. He stopped the car and looked at his watch. He had an hour before Gafferty would bring Tad along. He clumped up the steps through the snow, decided against ringing, and opened the door.

Lucille was playing on the floor with the baby. Her back was toward him, but he could hear her laughter. It was warm in the room and there was the smell of supper cooking in the kitchen. Roland saw things in the room he had never noticed before. Colin's chair by the lamp, and the small pile of books beside it. The music box that played "Just a wee doch-an-dorris.'' Along the mantel, the line of snapshots of everyone and everything they had loved together. Together—that was the word he had been seeking in his mind. They had been so together, and this place in which he stood was their temple of delight.

She must have heard him shut the door because she turned suddenly, her face alight with pleasure. This was Colin's house. This was Colin's woman—and his welcome home. She half-rose from her knees, but when she saw it was Roland, her face altered in a mysterious way: it was smiling still, but without anticipation. That would be for Colin—special joy to be taken only by him. This was life of plenty. Roland yielded to it. Perhaps some day he could save some of it for her and for Keith . . . bring back the together-MacDonalds.

''Roland! Stay to dinner . . . Colin's so late. . . .''

She put out her hand and he took it gently. He looked away when her face began to change—when he saw that she began to fear his very silence. He went to Keith and stood over him a moment, and that was the hardest test of all. The child became blurry through his tears, but Roland answered his smile. He bent down and took Keith in his strong arms and lifted him slowly toward the ceiling, because he knew that Keith loved to go so high. Then he brought him down to his chest and held him very tightly.

''Come on, son . . . it's time we went to bed.''

# A Note About the Author

ERNEST K. GANN spent 19 years as a commercial airlines pilot, flying a million and a half miles. In his twenties he was a barnstorming stunt flier and became an airline flier in the early years of commercial aviation. During World War II he attained the rank of captain, flying missions for the Air Transport Command, and was decorated with the Distinguished Flying Award. After helping to chart aerial trails around the world, he left flying to devote his full time to writing. Among his best-selling books are *The High and the Mighty, Blaze of Noon, Benjamin Lawless, Soldier of Fortune, Trouble with Lazy Ethel, Fate is the Hunter*, and *In the Company of Eagles*.

# A Note About the Bantam Air & Space Series

This is the era of flight—the century which has seen man soar, not only into the skies of Earth but beyond the gravity of his home planet and out into the blank void of space. An incredible accomplishment achieved in an incredibly short time.

How did it happen?

The AIR & SPACE series is dedicated to the men and women who brought this fantastic accomplishment about, often at the cost of their lives—a library of books which will tell the grand story of man's indomitable determination to seek the new, to explore the farthest frontier.

The driving theme of the series is the skill of *piloting,* for without this, not even the first step would have been possible. Like the Wright Brothers and those who, for some 35 years, followed in their erratic flight path, the early flyers had to be designer, engineer, and inventor. Of necessity, they were the pilots of the crazy machines they dreamt up and strung together.

Even when the technology became slightly more sophisticated, and piloting became a separate skill, the quality of a flyer's ability remained rooted in a sound working knowledge of his machine. World War I, with its spurt of development in aircraft, made little change in the role of the flyer who remained, basically, pilot-navigator-engineer.

Various individuals, like Charles Lindbergh, risked their lives and made high drama of the new dimension they were carving in the air. But still, until 1939, flying was a romantic, devil-may-care wonder, confined to a relative handful of hardy individuals. Commercial flight on a large scale was a mere gleam in the eye of men like Howard Hughes.

It took a second major conflict, World War II, from 1939 to 1945, to provoke the imperative that required new concepts from the designers—and created the arena where hundreds of young men and women would learn the expertise demanded by high-speed, high-tech aircraft.

From the start of flight, death has taken its toll. Flying has always been a high-risk adventure. Never, since men first launched themselves into the air, has the new element given up its sacrifice of stolen lives, just as men have never given up the driving urge to go farther, higher, faster. Despite only a fifty-fifty chance of any mission succeeding, *still* the dream draws many more men and women to spaceflight than any program can accommodate. And still, in 1969, when Michael Collins, Buzz Aldrin, and Neil Armstrong first took man to the Moon, the skill of piloting, sheer flying ability, was what actually landed the "Eagle" on the Moon's surface. And still, despite technological sophistication undreamed of 30 or 40 years earlier, despite demands on any flyer for levels of performance and competence and the new understanding of computer science not necessary in early aircraft, it is piloting, *human* control of the aircraft—sometimes, indeed, inspired control—that remains the major factor in getting there and back safely. From this rugged breed of individualists came the bush pilots and the astronauts of today.

After America first landed men on the Moon, the Russian space program pushed ahead with plans for eventually creating a permanent space station where men could live. And in 1982 they sent up two men—Valentin Lebedev and Anatoly Berezovoy—to live on Solyut-7 for seven months. This extraordinary feat has been recorded in the diaries of pilot Lebedev, DIARY OF A COSMONAUT: 211 DAYS IN SPACE.

The Bantam AIR & SPACE series will include several titles by or about flyers from all over the world—and about the planes they flew, including World War II, the postwar era of barnstorming and into the jet age, plus the personal histories of many of the world's greatest pilots. Man is still the most important element in flying.

**Here is a preview of the next volume
in the Air & Space Series,**

**FLYING FOR THE FATHERLAND
by Judy Lomax**

$$(1)$$

# A Patriotic Childhood

Hanna Reitsch was a child in one world war, and a heroine of
Nazi Germany in the next. During her childhood in the
eastern German province of Silesia, she absorbed the patriotic
and religious beliefs of her parents. To these she added as a
young woman an obsession with flying which, with her love
for her Fatherland, became her lifelong inspiration and placed
her on a public pedestal as a test pilot in the Third Reich.

She was born on a wet, windy night at the end of March
1912. Her character, even as a small child, showed all the
contrasts of stormy weather: she was at the same time a
compulsive extrovert and a self-conscious introvert. Her infectious laugh and sudden tears came equally readily, and she
seemed to have inherited both her father's puritanical Prussian
thoroughness, and her mother's Tyrolean exuberance.

Her mother, the eldest daughter of a widowed Austrian
aristocrat, had convinced herself that she would die during the
birth. It was always accepted in the family that this created an
unusually and perhaps an unnaturally strong bond between
herself and Hanna. Emy Reitsch was not normally a worrier;
she talked effusively, with a basic common sense which drew
family and friends alike to her for comfort and encourage-
ment. Small and delicately built, she dressed simply, almost
puritanically. Hanna adored her.

Neither Kurt, who was two years older than Hanna, nor
Heidi, who was four years younger, caused Emy any serious
concern: it was Hanna whom she considered the most sensi-
tive of her three children, and whom she felt she had constantly to protect against real or imagined dangers, and Hanna
who needed to be calmed and guided.

Hanna also loved her father, but from a respectful distance. Doctor Willy Reitsch, an eye specialist, spoke only when he had something to say. He was thought to resemble Beethoven, with heavy eyebrows and a dark brooding expression, until he smiled: then he seemed more approachable. His outlook on life was serious, based on traditional Prussian concepts of honour and duty, and his appearance was always immaculate. Strict and expecting high standards of behaviour, he found it easier to deal with his son's misdemeanours than with the naughtiness and high spirits of his daughters. Kurt could be beaten, a ritual in which, while he was still small enough, his father would lay him across his knee and apply the full force of his hand.

On the one occasion when her father raised his hand to Hanna in anger, she ran away from home. She was seven years old, and had belched loudly and proudly, an accomplishment which she had just been taught by Kurt. It was long after dark when she returned home, frightened out of the woods by trees which seemed in the gloaming to have turned into menacing villains.

Both her parents were deeply religious and intensely patriotic, making no distinction between their respective Prussian and Austrian origins; their shared German-speaking background was more important than artificial territorial boundaries, and both felt themselves to be Germans in the broader cultural sense. Hanna learnt from an early age to believe in God and Germany, and to love her home in Silesia.

Doctor Reitsch and his wife had settled soon after their marriage in Hirschberg, a picturesque old Silesian town in a peaceful valley of fields, farms, and sun-dappled villages surrounded by wooded hills and snow-capped mountains. To the south lay Austria, to the east Russia; in 1918 Czechoslovakia became the southern neighbour and Poland the eastern. Although Silesia had for a short time, more than six centuries earlier, fallen under Polish rule, it had for several hundred years been under Austrian or German domination. In the nineteenth century it was firmly and patriotically a part of Germany, with strong Austrian traditions. The mountains reminded Emy, who never lost her soft Austrian accent, of the Tyrol.

One or other of the children often accompanied their father, a respected member of the community and of the local Masonic lodge, on home visits to his patients, or went with their mother on Lady Bountiful tours to distribute presents of food to those considered to be in need.

Hanna joined happily in the rough-and-tumble of her brother and his friends, dressed as often as not in practical lederhosen. After Heidi was born, she was fiercely protective, but still preferred the company of boys. Heidi, who was quieter, more even-tempered, and less physically adventurous, was considered the prettier of the two girls. Both were blue-eyed and blonde, but Hanna's features were sharper, her expression more intense, and the set of her jaw more determined.

When she was four, according to a much-told family story, Hanna made her first attempt to fly, and had to be restrained from leaping with arms spread as wings from the first-floor balcony. Later she took to climbing trees, and when she was eleven fractured her skull after falling from her perch on a high branch.

Their life was frugal and peaceful. The girls' dresses were lengthened and passed down until they could no longer be made to fit. Pleasures were made rather than bought, and among the most eagerly anticipated were family walks on fine summer weekends: then the children were sent to bed early on Saturday evening and woken at half past one in the morning to dress in the dark, before taking a tram through the valley to the foot of the nearby mountain range.

The sense of adventure made the three-hour uphill walk as dawn gradually broke over the mountains seem easy, although Heidi occasionally flagged. Then Hanna kept her going by telling her stories, old familiar tales and new ones drawn from her endlessly fertile imagination—her cousin Gertrud, who was nearer Heidi's age, never forgot sitting under a tree while Hanna kept a group of children enthralled with her story-telling ability.

Even after such an early and strenuous start to the day, there was always a family service at home before Sunday lunch. Grace was said before every meal. The existence and presence of God was accepted unquestioningly by the children. Willy Reitsch was a Protestant, but hated to parade his feelings in public and so rarely went to church. Emy, a devout Catholic, had agreed to bring the children up in her husband's faith, but made secret early morning visits to her church, often taking Hanna with her. The grandeur and solemnity, and the pervasive smell of incense and burning candles, made a deep impression on the child.

Music was as natural a part of their life as religion. Indeed, it was through their mutual love of music that Willy and Emy Reitsch had met. Willy was an accomplished amateur cellist. Although he was not otherwise a sociable man, he liked to invite other music-lovers to his home to play and to listen to string trios and quartets. The connecting doors between his consulting-room and the living-room were then thrown open to make more space, and Emy acted as hostess to both listeners and performers. Her parents' musical gatherings were among Hanna's earliest and happiest memories.

Almost before she could talk, Hanna could sing in tune, in a clear, high voice. One of her mother's favourite three-part Austrian yodelling songs was a prelude to every meal. Kurt played the violin, and Hanna and Heidi the piano, although they often found their father's perfectionism discouraging when they were practising.

Hanna was six when the First World War ended, leaving the family unharmed and life in Hirschberg outwardly as quiet and uneventful as before. Although Willy Reitsch explained to his children that patriotism was equally valid and important to people of every nation, it was felt particularly strongly in Silesia. By the Treaty of Versailles the eastern territory of Upper Silesia became part of Poland, and in the rest of the province the terms imposed on Germany by the Allies were bitterly resented.

Emy and Willy Reitsch shared the general feeling of injustice, and the fear that Communism might spread. Militant Communist uprisings in their own country following the Russian Revolution, and the experiences related by refugees from Baltic areas previously partly occupied by Germans, as well as by returning prisoners of war, strengthened the conviction that Communism was an evil which must at all costs be resisted.

Hanna absorbed her parents' patriotic outlook. She loved the town and surrounding countryside of Hirschberg as much as the spacious first-floor flat which had always been her home. In pride of place in her bedroom was a framed photograph of Emy Reitsch; posters and pastel drawings of the mountains partially covered one wall.

Heavy, dark wooden furniture, art books, pictures, and piles of music gave the flat an atmosphere of genteel and cultured solidity. It had a distinctive smell, neither pleasant nor unpleasant—a combination of aromas drifting from the kitchen, where simple but plentiful food was prepared on a huge range, from the consulting-room, where ether and other substances were stored in a row of carefully labelled jars, from the polish used on the parquet floors, and from a heating stove which stood in one corner of the living-room.

The dining-table was the family focal point. Mealtimes were cheerfully prolonged gatherings at which each member of the family related the experiences of the previous few hours. Hanna and Emy talked most. It was over the dinner-table that Hanna shared her enthusiasms, and voiced her grievances when she felt that she had been unfairly treated at school. This was usually when her 'honour' was at stake: then she would plunge from her normal exuberance into a depth of depression in which she sometimes convinced herself that she could no longer bear to live. She had inherited her sense of honour from her father; but it was sometimes difficult to tell exactly what she meant by it. Emy, who was protectively aware of her daughter's sensitivity to criticism, was usually ready to rush into school to sort out any difficulties; her husband was less sympathetic.

Hanna was, as a friend at the girls' school she attended in Hirschberg put it, 'difficult to overlook'. Outwardly she had such an air of self-confidence that few people outside her family were aware of how unhappy she sometimes felt. She could rarely stop talking for long, and laughed loudly, suddenly, and—or so it seemed to those who found her laugh irritating rather than infectious—unnecessarily often. The school class reports frequently commented that 'Hanna Reitsch laughs without reason.' She enjoyed being the center of attention. If she considered a lesson to be boring it was often because she had not had enough opportunities to speak—'and that', she admitted, 'is terrible for me.'

Hanna was aware that she talked too much and was inclined to exaggerate, a tendency which she made strenuous but unsuccessful attempts to curb. 'Hanna always talked in superlatives,' one of her schoolfriends told me. 'Everything was larger than life when she talked—but that was just her way of expressing herself. There was no malice in her, although she could sometimes seem bossy or overpowering.' Her natural ability to talk was useful when she was required to give a class lecture, but the rest of her school work was rarely better than average.

When there was a disruption in the class, Hanna could usually be found at the bottom of it, well aware of the weaknesses of individual teachers and of how to play on them. She saw nothing wrong in minor deceptions, provided they hurt no one, such as using her excellent sight to catch a glimpse of some other girl's work, or copying a crib for a Latin translation. In spite of her highly developed sense of honour, Hanna never considered such subterfuges to be cheating. It was rather an expression of friendship both to give and to accept whatever help was available.

Although she was friendly and sociable, Hanna also enjoyed solitary walks and bicycle rides. Her destination during her last few years at school was often to some vantage point from which she could watch the activities of a gliding club on the Galgenberg: her parents never knew how often she cycled the few miles from Hirschberg to lie on the grass gazing enviously at the easy soaring flight of the birds and the attempts of the gliders to emulate them.

Walking, cycling, tree-climbing, and shooting with an airgun, as well as skiing and skating, were a natural part of life in Hirschberg, though Emy Reitsch discouraged other sports in case they caused injury or unfeminine muscles. Running in the streets, as many of the other girls did, was forbidden because it was unladylike.

It was in music, rather than in sport or study, that Hanna excelled. Her clear, high, soprano voice, and her ability and willingness to show off, made her a favourite of the music teacher, her father's friend Otto Johl. Among the sopranos in his 'Little Choir' Hanna's was the dominant voice, and on school open evenings she was often called upon to sing a solo, or a duet with the star of the contraltos.

Her social life was unsophisticated. Although many of her classmates had boyfriends, and Kurt's friend Gustav-Adolf admired her adoringly from a distance, she showed no romantic interest in the opposite sex. She was not allowed out alone in the evenings, and could only go to the local cinema if the film was considered suitable. Visits to her schoolfriends, who came from socially acceptable families in the area, took much the same form as the tea parties of their mothers.

From time to time there were receptions and dances, usually given by army officers and their wives: open sandwiches and wine were served and everyone, young and old, fat and thin, joined enthusiastically in old-fashioned waltzes and olonaises. Cavalry officers, many of them sporting Iron Crosses from the First World War, provided occasional daytime entertainment on horseback at steeplechases and mock hunts.

Sometimes a military band played in Hirschberg, stirring the patriotic feelings which Hanna and her friends shared with their parents. But the schoolgirls of Hirschberg were not interested in politics. Their school study of history stopped with the 1848 revolutions in Germany, Austria, and France, and discussions on current affairs were not part of the curriculum. According to two British students, who stayed with the Reitsch family, Frau Reitsch would occasionally launch into a tirade against the government, in which she indiscriminately blamed other nations for anything she thought was wrong in Germany: sometimes the culprits were the French, sometimes the Russians, sometimes the British, occasionally the Jews, but most often the Italians—as a Tyrolean, Emy Reitsch was aware of problems and tensions with Italy in the southern Tyrol. The message from Willy and Emy Reitsch was however more often one of international tolerance.

Frau Reitsch extended a warm welcome to the two British students, who spent Christmas 1928 as guests of the family in Hirschberg. James Tucker, who bore his inevitable nickname of 'Tommy' with fortitude, was struck by the depth of the Reitsch family's religious fervour; but Nora Campbell, a puritanical Scottish Presbyterian, considered the dolls dressed in Tyrolean costumes which represented the holy family in a crib under the Christmas tree to be little better than pagan idols.

It was a Christmas to be remembered, a Christmas of clear skies and crisp snow, skiing and skating, concerts in the town and musical evenings at home, visits and visitors, church in both the Protestant and the Catholic churches, and ceremonial present-opening round a candle-lit tree on Christmas Eve. In the evening of Christmas Day, they were joined by the von Bibersteins and the von Müllenheims, family friends whose aristocratic names Nora and Tommy found secretly amusing.

At nine o'clock, Frau Reitsch clapped her hands and made an announcement: 'You will all take the last tram to Himmelreich and climb to Spindler-Baude and spend the night on the mountain.' They felt and looked like polar explorers as they climbed in the clear, cold light of a full moon. The snow was frozen on the trees so that it did not fall off however hard the branches were shaken. Hanna enthused inexhaustibly, de-

manding agreement from the others that the light on the
snow, and the snow on the trees, were beautiful, glorious,
heavenly; that a particular tree looked like a king with a
crown; that it was like being in fairyland.

For Willy and Emy Reitsch it was a Christmas tinged with
sadness, the last one for which it could be guaranteed that the
family would be together. Kurt left home to join the navy in
the New Year. Hanna was already working for lier school
leaving examination, the Abitur. It was the door to the future
enabling her to start studying towards becoming a doctor.
When she passed it in 1931, her parents were delighted, and
presented her with a gold watch. She refused the gift: it was
not at all what she had been waiting for.

Instead she was determined to keep her father to a bargain
which had been her chief motivation during her last few years
at school: he had promised that she could have a course of
lessons at the gliding school at Grunau, a few miles from
Hirschberg, provided she did well in the Abitur and did not
mention flying again until she had had her results. Dr Reitsch
had imagined that her strange wish was merely a passing
childish whim, particularly when she kept her side of the
deal: Hanna was normally so little given to reticence that he
had taken her silence to mean that she had forgotten about
wanting to fly.

Hanna's obsession with the idea of flying was, however, so
great that she had exercised a self-control of which no one
had considered her capable. Keeping quiet about something
which she longed to talk about was the most difficult thing
she had ever done. She had been helped by a book which she
had come across in the school library, a slim volume trans-
lated from sixteenth-century Spanish with the unexciting title
*The Spiritual Exercises of Saint Ingnatius Loyola*. The pre-
scribed prayers and meditations, which involved considerable
soul-searching and depended on a firm belief in the tenets of
Christianity, were to be repeated three times a day. Hanna
found no difficulty in thinking about herself and God first
thing in the morning and last thing at night, although remembering to do so at midday was not always so easy.

Quite why she wanted to fly, she could never explain: she
talked vaguely about the love she shared with her mother for
the mountains, about birds, about physical and psychological
freedom, and about being nearer to God. After seeing a film
about the start of the flying doctor service in Australia, she

decided that she would combine flying with medicine by becoming a flying medical missionary.

Although Dr Reitsch was reluctant, his sense of honour gave him no option but to keep his promise. He had encouraged his daughter's interest in medicine by describing the intricate mechanism of the eye, and had demonstrated operations on pigs' and sheep's eyes which he had brought home from the local butcher. Hanna's mother assumed that both medicine and flying would be interludes before marriage, but stoically accepted Hanna's right to make her own decisions.

When Hanna left the girls' school in Hirschberg, with the intention of studying medicine, she was an idealistic and ambitious nineteen-year-old. Her promised flying lessons would, or so she persuaded herself and her parents, eventually enable her to take her skill as a qualified doctor to those most in need of her care in some dimly imagined and vaguely exotic, but deprived, part of the world. Once the cloud of secrecy was lifted, she could chatter gaily about her intention of becoming a flying doctor in Africa. The ambitions of her schoolfriends were more mundane: marriage, domesticity, and motherhood, or, for the more emancipated, teaching.

Before allowing her either to learn to fly or to embark on her medical studies, Hanna's parents insisted that she should make up for her lack of interest in domestic matters: cooking, washing, ironing, and cleaning had always been entrusted to a maid, or rather a series of maids. She was enrolled for a year's course as a boarder in Rendsburg at the Koloniale Frauenschule (Koloschule), an establishment where young ladies were prepared for life and work in the colonies. Although by 1931 there had been no German colonies for well over a decade, there were still strong ties with African territories which had been removed by the Treaty of Versailles.

The Koloschule, which overlooked the Kiel Canal, was opened in 1926. It served as a reasonably priced all-round finishing school, although the emphasis was on team-work and on practical rather than decorative and social skills. It was all supposed to be good character training, with the bonus that there was a plentiful supply of young men not far away at the naval training school.

Only the Koloschule girls were allowed to swim in the canal, a privilege which was however less appreciated than were the frequent opportunities to wave at the German navy. Whenever a naval ship approached, it hooted an advance warning and slowed down as it passed under the windows of the imposing purpose-built schoolhouse. By then, the girls had all run from the kitchen, the laundry, the fruit and vegetable garden, the hen run, and the pigsty, and were lining the bank. Hanna gained considerable kudos among her fellow pupils from having a brother in the navy, although on the one occasion when she and some of her friends were invited to spend a few hours at sea on his ship it was cold and rough.

For the first time in her life, Hanna was separated for more than a few days from her mother, on whom she was still unusually emotionally dependent: she later claimed that she would, she was sure, have died if anything had happened to Emy before she was nineteen. She shared a bedroom with a girl who became her closest friend and confidante in a tower overlooking the canal. In the evenings, Hanna and Gisela sat together at a window on the spiral stairs of the tower: they called it their Orion window, and considered it their private and secret place. They were there at Halloween, and made a pact that wherever they were and whatever they were doing, at eight o'clock every All Souls' Eve for the rest of their lives they would think about each other. Neither of them ever forgot the tryst.

The girls were divided into four groups. Hanna's and Gisela's group was always the noisiest: they sang while they were polishing, they sang when it was their turn to work in the garden or to make cheese, and they sang when work had stopped in the evenings. When they were not singing, they were usually talking and laughing. Almost the only time when they did not sing was during pig duty. The pigs were no problem when they were still small enough to be endearing; but the bigger they grew, the fiercer and the more frightening they became. Unfortunately for Hanna, her pig duty was the week before they were to be slaughtered, and so they were at their biggest and most ferocious.

Meals were prepared by the pupils, using as far as was possible home produce. Work outside, to which few of the girls had previously been accustomed, started early, and gave them all hearty appetites. The highlight of the day was the second breakfast, at which all the previous day's left-overs were set out. It was a free-for-all scramble for the best bits, and it was not long before Hanna had put on a considerable amount of weight. As she was so short, this did little for her appearance, and the bows with which her clothing was adorned gradually flattened as she became fatter.

The skills that Hanna was supposed to have acquired at the Koloschule were rarely used later. She never again mended her own shoes, made another pair of boy's trousers, baked her own bread, or bottled and made wine from freshly picked fruit. On her one attempt to demonstrate her culinary expertise at home, she cooked more than enough to feed the entire school, and her family were so sick of rice by the end of the week that any further half-hearted offers to cook were refused.

There were tears when the time came to leave Rendsburg. First Hanna cried, and then Gisela, and then Hanna again, and soon everyone was vowing eternal friendship. Hanna had by then had her first taste of flying, during the school holidays, but still expected to become a doctor.

# Winged Student

It was during her first holiday from the Koloschule that Hanna's ambition to enroll in a course at Grunau was at last realised. Gliding was a peculiarly German sport, developed in the years after the First World War as a way of circumventing the ban on powered flying imposed by the Treaty of Versailles. It was predominantly a male activity, although women were not barred, and Hanna was the only girl on the course.

'This looks easy,' she thought on the first day when it was her turn to climb into the pilot's seat and fasten her harness. The other pupils were the ground team, and were ordered first to walk and then to run forwards, keeping the bungee attached to a ring in the nose of the glider taut. As it started to move forwards, Hanna concentrated on what the instructor had said about using the ailerons and foot pedals to hold it steady. Then it was released: ignoring the order to stay on the ground, she gave way to the temptation to see what would happen if she pulled the stick back a little.

After a series of kangaroo jumps the glider came to an ungainly halt. Hanna's attempt to laugh as if nothing had happened was interrupted by the anger of the instructor, Pit van Husen. As a punishment for her disobedience and lack of discipline, she was grounded for three days: she was not even to sit in a glider.

It was not a good beginning, but she put a brave face on her humiliation and frustration while the others progressed to their first free flight. She told herself over and over again that in gliding the one unbreakable law was strict discipline, and that disobeying an order could involve both the pilot and others in unjustifiable danger.

When she arrived home every evening, she avoided her parents, explaining that she was tired and locking herself in her room. During the daytime she joined in the team-work on the ground and concentrated even harder than before, watching what the others did and listening to the instructor's comments so that she could learn from their mistakes. In her determination to keep up with their progress, she pretended that her bed was a glider, using a walking-stick as a rudder.

Her nocturnal exercises paid off: when her three-day punishment was over, she had not after all dropped behind, and was the first to complete the thirty-second A test successfully. To prove that it was not a fluke, she did it again. A gratifying roar of approval went up from the onlookers. She no longer minded that as the only girl on the course she came in for considerable teasing from the men about her size—she was only just over five foot, and weighed only a little over six stone.

The director of the school, Wolf Hirth, who was almost a god to the younger pilots, was intrigued: first he had been told that this chit of a girl was a positive menace to flying, then that less than a week later, when she had missed much of the practical experience, she had passed her first test with apparent ease. He decided it was time to make a personal assessment, and was impressed. Hanna was given his particular attention throughout the remaining days of the course, during which she successfully completed her B test. It was the start of a lifelong friendship with Wolf Hirth and his wife Lala, as well as with a fellow pupil called Wernher von Braun. While they sat together on the grass between lessons, von Braun told her about his dream of a rocket that would fly to the moon.

During her last few months at the Koloschule, Hanna told Gisela again and again every detail of her introduction to flying. She stood on a table so that she could be seen while she re-enacted her experiences for the entire school. If her parents had hoped that she would be satisfied with one gliding course, they were to be disappointed: she was obsessed, and extracted a promise of another before she started her medical studies so that she could take her C test.

Again she was the only girl on the course, although this time she was treated with greater respect as the protégée of Wolf Hirth. Her enthusiasm was however once again to get the better of her self-discipline: on her test flight she was revelling so much in the sensation that she was at last flying as freely as a bird that she forgot that she was supposed to be in the air for only ten minutes. When she at last looked at her watch, she realised to her dismay that she was already several minutes overdue. So that the glider would not have to be hauled back before the next flight, she decided to land on the starting-place. It was a maneuver requiring a skill and control which Wolf Hirth, who was watching anxiously as she made a perfect approach and landing, did not expect from someone so inexperienced. 'From the flying point of view,' he told her, 'the performance was perfect.' Hanna glowed with pride, although she had also again been reprimanded for disobedience.

As a mark of his trust in her ability, Wolf Hirth allowed Hanna to fly a new glider which normally only he and the instructors were allowed to touch. She had permission to stay in the air for as long as she liked. A strong west wind over the ridge ensured perfect gliding conditions, and she sang as she made full use of the weather conditions to soar to her heart's content. Every now and then, the less privileged pupils, among them a young journalist called Wolfgang Späte, looked up to see if she was still in sight.

When she landed, after five and a half hours, Hanna was astonished to find that she had broken a world record. Records were constantly being made and broken in the early days of gliding: it was only ten years since it had been considered an achievement to stay in the air for nearly a quarter of an hour.

For the first time, the name of Hanna Reitsch was heard on the radio. Wolf Hirth and the Grunau school also received considerable publicity. Since the first post-war gliding camp in 1920, Hirth had been working hard to catch up with his elder brother's pre-war reputation as a pilot. In spite of the disadvantages of needing glasses and of having lost a leg in a motorcycling accident, he had achieved his childhood ambition of becoming as famous as his brother. By the time Hanna became his protégée, he was one of Germany's leading glider pilots and designers.

Hanna set off for Berlin for her first term as a medical student with only one thought: she must continue to fly. Her studies took a poor second place. She spent much of her time at a flying school at Staaken on the outskirts of the city, working towards a license to fly powered sports aircraft and hanging round the workshops. Powered flight presented her with no problems, but she found it neither as challenging nor as stimulating as gliding: it lacked the poetic appeal and closeness to God and the elements of flying without an engine.

'Powered flying is certainly an unforgettable experience, but gliding is incomparable,' she explained. 'Powered flight is a magnificent triumph over nature—but gliding is a victory of the soul in which one gradually becomes one with nature.'

Several other women flew from Staaken, but it was only with one, Elly Beinhorn, that she struck up more than a passing acquaintance. Elly, who was five years older, had just returned from flying round the world: she had had a pilot's licence for three years and had already become a household name for her solo long-distance flights. Her pleasure in flying was, however, different from Hanna's: for Elly, it was principally a way of enjoying new experiences, and she made it pay by writing about her travels.

Hanna also struck up a friendship with a fellow pupil, the actor and broadcaster Matthias Wiemann, and a brief acquaintance with a gang of workmen who allowed her to drive their tractor. When they started arguing among themselves about politics, the divisions she discovered upset her. Her political interests were limited, and there had never been any dissension on the subject in her family. She felt that it was enough to be patriotic: it did not occur to her that this could be expressed in a variety of ways, nor that politicians could be devious. Because she was open and honest, she assumed that other people were equally honourable, and could not in any case imagine that politics could have anything to do with flying, or have any direct bearing on her own life.

Hanna wrote to her mother, with whom she exchanged frequent letters, that unless she could bring herself to go about Berlin without continually thinking of flying, she would never again be able to learn how to stand with both feet on the ground. At the same time, when she was in the air she felt somehow closer to God. Her mother wrote her homilies about humility whenever a flying success threatened to go to her head. Hanna often resented these at the time, confident that she had deserved any praise which came her way; but then she would search earnestly for any sign that her mother might be right, and be grateful for Emy's determination to keep her feet, metaphorically at least, on the ground.

Wolf Hirth, whom Hanna called her 'flying father', also urged her to keep her flying in perspective. The career opportunities for male pilots were limited enough; for women, there were, in his opinion, none. At home in the holidays, Hanna nevertheless spent most of her time either at Grunau, or at the

Hirths' home. In the evenings, she spent hours going through the typescript of a book Hirth was writing about the art of soaring flight.

It was a mutually beneficial exercise: through Hanna, Wolf could assess the clarity of his explanations, and she in turn absorbed the theory of soaring in thermals and air waves. Hirth had discovered the technique of soaring in cloudless thermals; he had deliberately flown in search of thunderstorms and into a strange elliptical cloud with an even stranger name, the Moazagotl. This appeared in southerly winds above Hirschberg, a phenomenon first noted by and so called after a farmer, Gottlieb Moetz. After Wolf Hirth and the son of a local teacher, Hans Deutschmann, had flown simultaneously into the Moazagotl in March 1933, Hirth's report on their experiences was greeted with excitement. Gliding had until then relied chiefly on the air currents created by hill slopes.

Hanna longed to put her new theoretical knowledge to the test. The opportunity presented itself, out of a clear sky, in May 1933. She had returned to Hirschberg from Kiel, where after her first term in Berlin she was continuing her medical studies with increased dedication—there were no opportunities for gliding on the flat north German plains, where there were neither ridges to give lift nor airfields from which a glider could be towed. Wearing a light summer dress and sandals, she was invited by Wolf Hirth to join him and Lala, who were on their way to do some filming at Grunau. She could fly a new training glider, a Grunau Baby: it would, Hirth suggested, be useful practice if she were to fly blind, using only her instruments.

There was no indication as he towed her to 1200 ft. that she would find herself for the first time really 'flying blind', although the prospect would not have alarmed her: she was confident that in any situation she would be able to react immediately and correctly to the readings on her instruments. Knowing that one day she would have to rely on them, she had trained herself to take whatever action would be necessary to keep control: using a set of nine flash cards showing every combination of readings she had tested herself until she was sure that she would instinctively have the right reaction in any emergency.